crutches

JeVon E. Thompson

DANDELION PRESS • OLYMPIA, WASHINGTON

Dandelion Press
P O Box 11633
Olympia, Washington 98508

Revised Edition 1996, softcover
10 9 8 7 6 5 4 3

Library of Congress Card Catalog Number 96-83777

ISBN 0-9651568-0-X

Printed by Gorham Printing, Rochester, Washington, USA

Dedicated with the highest love

To Vivian and Robin

And to my children, Deva, Micah and Courtney.
That another generation will not have to
experience the insanity.

ACKNOWLEDGMENTS

With deepest sincerity I would like to thank the following:

God, The eternal divine source of all creativity.

To Renee Klosterman, my steadfast best friend through thick and thin.

My parents, Bel and Jim Thompson, for all their love and support. My sister and guardian angel, Jackie Davis (Lillian), whose love, support and memory kept me on track. Dr. Beverly Jennings for her caring, love and unconditional friendship during the first of many drafts. Mirrilla Senterfit who helped me to be at peace with myself after I dug up memories that I had previously buried very purposely. Marion and Vernon Rowe who lovingly opened their home on two separate occasions. God Bless.

I would also like to thank author Charles Johnson for his example, Trent Angers (Acadian House Publishing) and his wife, Cindy, for encouraging me to complete the manuscript. Dick Hamby for his initial analysis and wonderful encouragement. Robin Gregg for her great suggestions and years of friendship, Joan Henry for always being there.

Patricia Baker for her long-lasting inspiration.

Connie Lovelady, Emily and the gang down at Graphic Concepts. Kurt Gorham, Kathy Campbell and the staff at Gorham Printing. Tracy Smith for editing and Val Dumond for her Copy editing and wonderful spirit.

I would also like to thank all those who painstakingly read through uncorrected drafts and shared their ideas and inspiring insights; Twila you're at the top of the list.

Thank you all so very much.

I AM A CHILD

I am a child.
Quietly come I,
Come to move a world
With just a little smile.

I am a child.
Like changing winds come I,
A warrior raising mountains
With pail and sand I try.

I am a child
Born of eagles' wings.
Tell me of my choices
Then a future I will sing.

1

MAY 1957

It WAS SPRING, BUT THAT HAD NOT HELPED. The final fight between Jessie Rose and her daughter, Vivian, had occurred on one of the first warm days in May. Jessie Rose sat at the dining room table feeling old and weary, hypnotically snapping string beans. One of the beans fell from her lap and grazed Savannah across the whiskers. The plump cat shook briskly, stretched and walked to a place between her dinner bowl and Jessie Rose.

With a bean in each hand, Jessie leaned toward the cat. "Why did Elder go and give that girl a car when he knowed how she drink and do?" She snapped another bean and tossed it into a bowl of water. "She been gone for two days without a word!" Savannah sat with her tail curled tight. "She ona binge. I just know it. Surely as Jesus is my witness, I just know it." Jessie's hands lay motionless on the pile of beans as she sat by the window and watched.

Vivian turned the Chevy onto Wooden Street at a speed too cautious to be normal. Still wearing the clothes she had worn to work two days before, she was calm and peacefully anesthetized. Her breath was laden with bourbon, her thoughts muddled and inseparable.

In her attempt to park, she hung onto the wheel with two hands. The car ran over the edge of the curb and fell back onto the street. The engine stalled, leaving a wake of silence behind it like a radio with its plug suddenly pulled.

The railing that lined the brick stairs leading to the porch was strong and for this Vivian was grateful as she pulled herself up the stairs. On the porch she stooped to the level of the doorknob, breathing heavily, and fumbled through the keys on her keyring. The house key was next to the lucky rabbit's foot with smooth pink fur. She thumbed it wondering why people had thought the rabbit's foot so lucky when it had done so little for the rabbit. She bumped the key next to the hole several times, missing the slot and then was overwhelmed with another thought.

7

"Thank God Momma's not home." The thought of facing her mother drunk enveloped her with guilt, but mostly fear. "Thank God for Tuesdays and garden clubs."

Jessie Rose rushed through her normal ritual of lifting the curtain on the door window. She knew who was outside. She jerked the door open so fast it was all Vivian could do to keep from falling forward into her mother's arms. "Momma!"

Jessie Rose was whipped into a fury borne of worry and anxiety. With her fist on her hips, she cocked her head to one side and glared at her daughter. "And, just what do you mean by stayin' out for two nights in a row without callin' me to let me know if you dead or 'live? Don't you think I got nothin' better to do but sit 'round here worryin' 'bout you?"

Vivian tried to gain some composure. "But Momma, I haven't been gone for two…."

"Vivian, don't you 'But Momma' me. You think I cain't count? You left here Monday morning for work and we ain't seen hide nor hair of you since. Today is Wednesday. You got some way of countin' I don't know nothin' 'bout?"

"Wednesday?" Vivian's eyes darted from side to side. "But Momma…."

"But nothin'," Jessie Rose snapped. "You stay out all night like a drunk. You won't keep a job or do anything you suppose to do…."

"But Momma, I wasn't drunk. I…."

"Vivian!" Jessie exploded. "You drunk now. Don't tell me you wasn't drinkin'. You don't even know what day it is. Look at you. You smell like a bar room skunk. You don't take care of your kids or yourself. You becomin' a bum, Viv, a regular street tramp. And, I'll tell you somethin' right now; if that's what you plan on doin' with yo' life, you gonna have to do it some place else 'cause I ain't gonna sit here and watch it, no, sir! No sir! No sir!"

"Momma, please don't call me a bum! I haven't done anything wrong," Vivian whined.

"You ain't been doin' nothin' wrong? Then where you been?" Jessie Rose shouted. "You been uptown in front of Kresge's Five and Dime? You been some place you ain't ashamed to tell me 'bout? Well?" Jessie pressed the question right up to her daughter's face. Vivian fell back against the wall at the foot of the stairway. "Where have I been? It's...it's none of your business!" she screamed back. "I'm a grown woman. I don't have to ...."

Jessie's open hand caught the cheek of her daughter's face with a jolt that sent Vivian reeling to the floor. "Them people you call friends is common as pig tracks, Viv. And you becomin' just lik'em. Just lik'em!" Jessie Rose could count on one hand the number of times she had struck her daughter. She didn't believe in sparing the rod, but that had only been necessary for the boys. Vivian had been a near-perfect child, seldom needing more than a stern look or a few sharp words.

Jessie looked down on her daughter, her gut pulled tight by hurt and disgust. "Vivian. Never in all my days! How could you let this happen to yo' self?" she queried in a low, intense voice filled with gravel. "Surely as Jesus died on the cross, this is gonna be the death of both of us, Viv." I never, never, thought I'd be bringin' no tramp into this world." Tears rolled over Jessie's cheeks. She shook her head from side to side in disbelief.

Vivian crawled to the bottom of the stairs on her hands and knees. Trembling, she pulled herself up on the bannister. She desperately fought to hold back the terror building within her, but it lapped over the sides like a bucket overflowing. In her mind the words "tramp...bum...bar room..." echoed again and again. She climbed the stairs pulling herself more than stepping, whimpering more than crying. She climbed upward to the safety of the small attic bedroom and yelled over the bannister, "I'm not a tramp! I'm not a tramp!"

Jessie held onto the bannister shaking, looking up as far as she could. "It's time you pack yo' things," she said, "We too old to be puttin' up with this. You hear me, Viv? It's gonna be the death of all of us!"

Little Von loved the scent of pine trees and the feel of their needles against his skin. Seldom a day would pass when he and his best friend, Lawrence, wouldn't climb to their secret lookout places among the limbs of the pines. The two boys sat with their legs straddling branches, dropping pine cones on targets below, whistling, pretending they were like the bombs falling in the war movies.

"Direct hit! I got five, Von. You got two."

"Lawrence, you got more 'cause you're older. I'm six and you nine."

"All right. I'll give ya a bigger target. Okay?"

"How about my bicycle seat?"

"Okay. Let's climb up higher."

With Lawrence ahead of him, Little Von started upward. He had just reached the third limb when a sharp pain in his leg stopped him motionless. His eyes slammed shut and he was breathless as he waited for it to pass.

Lawrence looked down on him wondering what had happened. "Hey!" he said watching the face below him, "You get stung by a bee?"

The pain left as suddenly as it had come. Taking deep breaths Little Von put his hand over the spot where he had felt the pain. He looked to see if his pants were ripped or if there was blood. He realized with some confusion that the pain had come from inside.

Looking up at Lawrence, he started his climb again. "I just got a big 'ol pain in my hip like somethin' stuck me or somethin'."

"You alright?"

"Yup. I guess."

"Come on, then."

He looked across the field from Hazel Street to Wooden Street and saw his mother's two-toned Chevy pass between houses. "Lawrence! My mom's back! Gotta go!"

"Okay. I'll see ya later."

His descent was slow and flawless. As he reached the lower branches, gooey sap froze several fingers fast together. He hung from the lowest branch, excited, his toes stretched out searching for the bicycle seat from which his climb had begun. "See ya!" Lawrence yelled, as he tried to spot the boy and bike through the pine branches.

Little Von sped through the tall weeds in the field. He sailed between the hedges that separated the field from the Walkers' yard. This was a breach of promise on his part, but it was the only time this week, and surely he had a good reason; Mommy was home. The thought was as chilling as it was comforting. He had worried about her for two days and now he was unable to hold back his excitement to see her.

As Little Von emerged on the far side of the yard, he saw Mr. Bush's hunting hounds. Barking wildly as they jumped, they frantically tried to scale the wire pen when they saw him. It was frightening. It was almost as bad as running into Old Man Bush himself. Old Man Bush was built low to the ground and bowlegged like a bull dog. Little Von had never heard him utter a mean word to anyone, but he had six fingers on each hand. His eyes were dark yellow where most people's were white.

Little Von reached the back of his grandparents' house. He dropped his bike, leaving the tires spinning, and climbed the stairs that led through the pantry to the kitchen door. He stood panting, taking in the familiar and comforting smells of salt pork, dried herbs and Virginia hams. But that's where he stopped, frozen by the vicious fighting between his mother and grandmother.

Vivian finally reached the top of the stairs. Crying and trembling, she tried to slam the door to the little third floor room, but it was swollen from the humidity and only banged against the jamb. She pounded it frantically with her hands until the metal tongue found its place. She ran and fell across her bed. The bedsprings sang out as the springs screeched across the faces of empty bottles she had hidden there over the weeks. Burying her head in her arms and tucking her knees to her chest, Vivian tried to blot out the noises of the bottles and her mother shouting at the bottom of the stairs, but the horror came from within as well as without. She was caught deep within herself. She didn't hear Little Von's footsteps climbing the stairs or his whimpering as he curled up on the bed and lay beside her. She didn't feel him place his small arm around her own. She didn't feel the spring sun across her face. She turned her back to the window and slept.

Downstairs Jessie Rose returned to her beans feeling older than her seventy-plus years. Drained and exhausted, she took up a handful of beans and snapped a few, but in time she stopped and stared into nothingness.

2

"VIVIAN, YOU CAN DO BETTER." Jessie Rose had said it count-
less times over the three days of Vivian's recovery as she sat on
the side of her bed caring for her daughter. The fight had been
horrible. The words had been sharp and painful to both of them.
The bent and twisted feelings that had been evoked would rest
for a time, but not undo themselves.

Jessie Rose grew more tired and depleted with each episode. The fight was only one aspect. The period of recovery with
its puking, shivers, sweats and hand squeezing etched new lines
in Jessie's face and left fissures in her heart. On the other hand,
her husband Elderiah became reclusive, staying out of the house
as much as possible. He suffered quietly, being a man of few
words, and having said all that he could to his daughter to no
avail.

Jessie prayed silently as she crossed from sink to stove, and
as she pulled herself up the three flights of stairs to Vivian's room.
Little Von had played with one toy or another for three days, re-
fusing to play outside or eat decent meals. Often, he turned his
face out of sight and sobbed.

Robin, Vivian's second born, was fifteen and suffered the
most. He was tall and strong looking with rounded shoulders,
but, like his mother, he failed to recognize his own strength. His
light complexion was speckled with freckles like his mother's,
but, like his father, his hair was silky black and thick. Jessie
Rose said he had "good" hair. The other grandchildren, she had
shaken her head and said, had Brillo-tight and nappy hair.

During his mother's bouts with alcohol, Robin grew more
quiet and more lost than normal. He sat in his room and played
Johnny Mathis albums, staring at the ceiling, or slept. His tor-
ment was the helplessness, not knowing what to say or do. He
agonized about his feelings. "After all..." he thought, "I'm nearly
a man. I should be able to deal with this." He couldn't. No matter how he tried, the pain was too much.

Lillian, eighteen and the oldest of the three, was away at
nursing school. When she came home she changed sheets, fed,
and helped her mother to bathe. The neighbors spoke of Lillian's

strength. Jessie Rose, however, saw what they didn't. She saw the pain and hurt neatly bundled up and placed away behind the face of the nurse and caretaker. Lillian was the first born, three years older than Robin. She had grown up watching her mother's drinking and periods of illness grow worse. She had grappled with pain, anger, and embarrassment for many years, and now she knew how to dispose of these feelings quickly. One day Jessie Rose had called to her husband and said, "Elder, It's no wonder that girl want to be a nurse, 'cause that's what she always been." Lillian spoke of her mother's drinking matter-of-factly, saying that it was "...very unfortunate and bad for her liver."

Everyone at the dinner table froze with their mouths full of food, and forks poised above their plates, when they heard Vivian descending the stairs from her room. She stood at the door of the living room smiling, using the wall for support. "I'm really starved. Is there enough for one more?"

The storm, for now, was over. She had lost weight. Her face was gaunt and pale, but she had survived. She ate carefully the first night and throughout the next day. Her meals consisted of soup, crackers, and her favorite, cherry Jell-O because it was easy to keep down.

For a week Vivian's appetite grew steadily and everyone's mood elevated from the doldrums of the past days. Vivian's boss had called every day angrily threatening to fire her, but Jessie had talked him into waiting a day or two more. Things were slowly returning to normal. Little Von was complaining about the vegetables on his plate. Robin complained about Little Von and talked about parties and girlfriends. Elder filled vases with cut flowers instead of just pulling weeds. No one left the table while he and Jessie swapped funny stories for an hour after dinner. It was after this that Vivian made her announcement.

Vivian took Jessie Rose's hand and gave it a gentle squeeze. She took a deep breath and began by looking around the table. "I was really sick this time. I was so sick that I wanted to die. I know everybody was worried and..." She sniffed and fought back tears and turned to Jessie. "...Momma I'm really, really sorry."

There was a chorus of support led by Jessie. Vivian shook her head. "I love all of you and I just want you to know that I'm finished with it. I say this every time after I get sick, but I've had enough of the gettin' sick and gettin' well, gettin' sick and gettin' well. It's tearin' me up inside. Guess I'm just sick of being guilty and sick of being sick." She smiled. "I really wanted to die. It felt so bad." She said, as her smile turned to sobs. "I hated what I was doing to everybody. It hurt so bad all I wanted to do was drink and make it go away. I can see what it's doing to everybody. We all know what it's doing to me. I don't want to hate myself anymore. I want to live and make a good life for you guys. I know I can do it. But..." She turned to Jessie squeezing her hand tighter. "I can't do it here. We're gonna move out, Momma. It's the only way."

Elderiah frowned as his pain went deeper. Jessie was shocked. "What you talkin' 'bout girl? Where you gonna go? You don't have to leave."

"I do, Momma." Vivian was resolved. The bonds of love were deep. She could see it in Jessie's face. Vivian knew, however, that she could not depend on Elderiah and Jessie Rose forever. Nor did she want to be the continual source of their hurt and embarrassment. "As long as I have you and Daddy taken care of all my responsibilities, I'll never do any better. I have to do this. I know I do."

"Mommy?" Little Von said, wiping his nose on his sleeve.

"Where we gonna go? I don't want to leave Wooden Street. I won't get to play with Lawrence and I won't know anybody if we leave."

"We're not going too far, Von. Just down to the Fredrick Douglass projects. Lawrence can come and visit." Little Von could count the number of times that he had been away from the white house on Wooden Street. Even when his mother and father lived together, the family was in another house on Wooden Street just down from Elderiah and Jessie Rose. He didn't know what to say or how afraid to be.

When Robin heard the name Fredrick Douglass he groaned. Most of his friends lived in the Fredrick Douglass projects. It was down the hill, situated around the Pocahontas River. He knew that life there would be more difficult than he was used to. "Mom, isn't there anywhere else?"

"Maybe later, Rob. But that's the best that I can do right now. Actually things will work out good. It has a daycare center for Von, it's close to my job and even closer to the high school. I can afford two bedrooms there and I'm really gonna need you to help.

You're gonna have to be my man around the house."

Jessie Rose wanted this foolish talk to stop. "Elder!" She said sternly.

Elderiah sat back in his chair, sullen. Vivian had been his little girl. She had been the brightest in school. She had grasped her Sunday school lesson so fast it had amazed even the minister, who quoted the cute things she said during the main service. That had all been a long time ago in Culpeper, Virginia. Then they migrated North looking for better opportunities. With each move, Washington D. C., Newark and finally Morristown, life seemed more promising. In her last year of high school Vivian had begun to drink with her friends. From that time on, Elder watched his little girl slowly become someone that he could not understand. What Vivian was saying was true. She would have to do it on her own to prove it to herself. "Honey, you tell us what we can do to help ya and we'll do everything we can."

Vivian turned to Jessie Rose who had buried her face in a napkin to catch her tears. It was rare to see Jessie cry; until now, it was something she simply didn't do. "Momma, you said that I could do better. Anybody could do better than what I've done so far. I have to see what I can do on my own. I know now it's the only way." Jessie didn't uncover her face. She reached out with one hand and groped for Vivian's hand, finding it on the second try.

3

THE MOVE FROM THE TALL WHITE HOUSE on Wooden Street to the projects had not been a difficult one. It happened on a Tuesday. With Jessie Rose at her garden club there was only the silence to hinder one's progress. Toys and a bag of clothes for Little Von, a few odds and ends, along with her work clothes draped over the backseat, and a tape-bound photo album, completed the list of "most important things for now."

Vivian stood behind the brown-and-tan Chevy and slammed its trunk. She waited a few moments and gently lifted her hands to see if it would stay. When it didn't, she slammed it again, harder. It had been her father's first new car when he purchased it four years ago. He had made it a gift to Vivian who had stayed sober for a considerable time and had finally found a steady job.

She walked to the front of the car and surveyed the blue speckled dents in its chrome bumper and grill. Turning around, she stared at the matching dents and broken tail light on Old Man Bush's blue shark-finned Cadillac. It had been a week since that drunken attempt to slip home quietly, a hellish week of puking and feeling near death that she never wanted to repeat again—never. She had not set the brake properly and the car had rolled forward sometime during the night. Her father had come upstairs quietly, found the keys and backed his old pride and joy to their side of the driveway without waking her.

Sitting in the driver's seat with Little Von beside her, Vivian sighed heavily. She was all out of tears. She turned the car out of Wooden Street and headed toward the valley floor.

The first thing Little Von saw in the Hollow was the condemned stilted houses. Stores and bars lined one side of the street while dilapidated shanties on stilts lined the other. The old houses were raised to avoid the waters of the Pocahontas River that rose during violent storms. Some of them still contained transient residents. Unlike the later brick dwellings, they were built at the turn of the century and never repaired. The brown rotted wood and slumped stairs looked as if they would collapse with the gentlest of winds. It wasn't long before Little Von began to grimace.

"Oh Mommy, look at those old houses over there. They look

like they about to fall down. People don't live there, do they?"

Vivian saw things new through her son's eyes. "Yes, honey, people do. Not everybody is as fortunate as Grandma and Grandpa."

"But Mommy, they so old and brown. Is that where we gonna live?"

"No. We'll live in the newer brick apartments."

"But Mommy, look at them stairs. They look like if you step on 'em you just fall right through."

"Honey, these were really nice houses when I was a little girl, but they are just old now and some people don't have enough money to live anywhere else."

"And how come they so high up like that?"

"This area floods a lot from the river, so people..."

"What river?" Little Von said, with excitement.

"You'll see it. So the people built up off the ground to keep dry."

The brown-and-tan Chevy moved along Flag Street, past the tangle of four-story brick buildings on the left and single-story dwellings on the right. A swarm of kids played in a small field separated from the busy streets by a hurricane fence.

Little Von had never seen so many kids together at one time. Between the buildings Little Von could see flashes of a brook and young boys standing about with fishing poles. Further along he saw that the brook had come from beneath a dam with a wide lake behind it.

"Look, Mom, a lake. I saw some boys fishin' back there."

"That's Poke, Von," Vivian said, happy that some aspect of the move appealed to her son.

"Poke, Mom? What's Poke mean?"

"Well, that's not the real name. That's just what people down here call it. The real name came from a beautiful Indian girl named Pocahontas. People just call it Poke, though."

Vivian found a parking place in front of the building that was to be their new home. Little Von jumped out to see if he could still see the lake. In the process, he banged the car in the next stall. On Wooden Street people parked their cars in front of their houses along the curb. Here the cars were angled into the sidewalk like sardines in a can with their noses pushed over the curbs. He slammed the car door and strained to see between the buildings that lined the street on the other side. His eyes were caught up in the business of what he saw before him. From his grandparents' quiet porch on Wooden Street, a dead-end street, he had only been able to see up and down, or across the street. Now he saw buildings, people and cars rushing one after another. Kids were everywhere, running and shouting in large crowds. Mothers hung from windows, watching and periodically yelling.

Across the street, he could barely make out the big fence and the riverbank on the other side of the lake. His eyes followed the flow of the scenery from the far bank of Pocahontas to the tall trees stretched one behind the other higher and higher. He looked up the hillside until he saw a clearing. There he saw three small white houses, the last one larger by almost a third than the other two. He was about to look away when he saw white window frames on red bricks peeking from behind a group of tall pine trees. Little Von stood still as his mind raced to identify the distant scene poised so small that he could cover it with his hand before his face.

"Mommy!" he called, squinting to get a clearer view. "Look up there! Is that...."

Vivian pulled an armful of dresses from the rear seat of her car. "Yes sweetheart, that's Lafayette School," she said, hoping he would let it go at that. Vivian didn't want to think of Wooden Street. "Grab some of your toys from the back, Von."

Little Von pictured the distance between the school and Jessie Rose's house, slowly moving his eyes across the tree tops. This time he recognized the two smaller white houses, but more so the third and tallest one. "Mommy, look! That must be Grandma and Grandpa's."

"Hey! You did that pretty good, " she said.

The foyer door opened with a loud whine. Robin came toward the car in long, slow strides. He had left school early to meet them. "Mom, I can't get the key to work in the lock."

Little Von smiled at the sight of his brother. "Ey Rob, we gotta go see what the river is like."

Robin smiled as he strained under the awkward load he had taken from the car. "Better find some boots, bean head. Lotta mud around Poke, snakes too." With his arms full, he turned sideways at the door and vanished into the darkness of the hall.

With the passing of two weeks, the apartment began to take shape. Each floor of the apartment building had four green doors badly in need of paint to cover names and partial phrases etched into the metallic surfaces. Behind the doors were small, identical living spaces, each beginning with a long hallway that gave entrance to rooms to the left.

First was the kitchen. It harbored a miniature gas burner, a one-basin sink, a short narrow 'fridge with a latch handle and a table pushed against the wall. Sharing the space was a host of quickly scurrying bugs that Vivian called "goddamned roaches." Little Von had heard Vivian say it so often that he had actually thought that was the name of the bug. For fun, Robin would turn off the light coaxing the roaches from their hiding places. Then suddenly he'd pop on the light and catch several in a jar. Little Von dabbed them with fingernail polish and named them Red Racer, Brown Bullet, and the Pink Flash. The two boys would sit with the jar turned upside down. Little Von yelled with excitement as Robin played the part of the announcer. The jar was lifted and the roaches would race toward the wall. The roach reaching the edge of the kitchen floor first became the winner.

The living room was down the hall. The bare wood floor made it seem bigger than it actually was. After the couch, the chair with the scratchy blue cover, the table with its vase and single-stemmed vine beneath the picture window, and the television with a "rabbit ear" antenna on its top, there was still room for a circle of old Lionel model trains in the center of the room.

Vivian's room, the first along the hallway with a door, was nothing special. It was a square room, large enough to hold a square queen-size bed with a wooden headboard, and a square dresser topped with a mirror. Little Von and Robin shared the room at the end of the hall, next to the bathroom. Two slender beds touched the walls on opposite sides of the room, leaving barely enough room for one person to walk between. At the foot of the beds stood a short dresser, its finish darkened with age. The boys divided it, two drawers each. On its top sat Robin's prized possession, a Sears monophone record player with a Johnny Mathis recording of "Misty" on the turntable.

In the kitchen, Vivian stood with the stillness of a manne-quin holding the lighted match and listening to the hissing of the antique oven. She wondered if it would one day blow up and consume her as it had much of the food she had attempted to cook in it. After two weeks she no longer noticed the missing number plate. She rotated the greasy dial back and forth, approximating the 350-degree position and waited for the oven to heat itself.

She sat at the window, elbows on the sill, fingers locked beneath her chin and reflected on the move. "My God," she whispered, "I'm happy." The first decisions she had made were fraught with fear and insecurity. Now she enjoyed the freedom to fail or succeed on her own.

Vivian's eyes darted from the fly that had died in the dust of the window track to Little Von kicking a ball on the asphalt court two stories below. Her mind wondered over the events of the last two months, overwhelming her with the pain of the move and joy of being on her own.

Little Von came in quietly and stood next to her. "Momma," he said, startling her. He crawled up on her lap with some effort. His first thought, "You ain't been drinkin'," went unspoken. Instead, he started, "Can't we go back and live with Grandma now?"

Vivian looked for a way to avoid answering the question directly. "Do you miss living with Grandma and Grandpa?"

"Yeah, and I wanna go back. Robin don't, but he gots lots of friends."

"Has, Von," she corrected. "Robin has lots of friends. You have friends too, don't you?"

"No."

"You could play downstairs."

"But Mom, that ain't no playground like Lafayette."

Vivian looked through the window again, but this time with Little Von's eyes. Their building had a fenced-in concrete square. It was originally intended as a children's play area. Instead, winos drank and smashed their empty bottles there in the middle of the night. Compared to Wooden Street, she thought, it must seem like a jungle.

"Mom. The big kids always tell everybody what to do. If you don't, you get beat up."

Little Von's mouth turned down at the corners. He thought about Lawrence and climbing the pine trees.

Vivian's mind raced for solutions. "Von. Did you meet the

boy downstairs. You know the one who looks a little different. He has a funny name too...what is it?"

"Jing-Wei." Little Von's voice was just above a mumble. Jing-Wei, like his mother, had light skin, almond-shaped eyes, and big teeth. But, like his father, he had black nappy hair and was bigger than most kids his age. Jing-Wei was mean. He seemed to thrive on anger and loved to bully the younger kids.

Robin had said, "Jing-Wei ain't really all that crazy, man."

"Yes, he is, too!" Little Von had answered quickly without having to think. "Ask anybody."

"No, not really, man. He just acts that way because he looks so weird. If the other kids didn't think he was nuts, he'd be gettin' his butt kicked every day."

Little Von had stood, testing the new idea. "Robin! He beats me up every mornin' when I come out. I don't even know why he does it. I ask him, but he just laughs with all the other kids that be standin' around."

The sound of Vivian's voice stopped the vision. "Do you guys ever play together? He could introduce you to some of his friends."

"Mommy, he's mean. His friends are too."

Vivian felt drained. "Von" She hesitated, giving herself time to look for the right words. "Things can't always stay the same. They change. They change like people change."

Little Von lifted his head and looked into his mother's eyes. No one knew better than he that people changed. He knew that his "real" mother changed into what he called the "Other Self" when she drank.

"Why, Mommy? I hate it here, and I want to go back to Wooden Street." He slumped. Vivian pressed his head into her breast and rocked him gently as her own tears came. "Things change, baby. Things just change."

Liberty Curtis came in. Respectfully flipping the knocker, she pushed past the door left ajar by Little Von, carrying a bag of groceries.

In her late forties, Liberty was beautiful with no reason to hide her small, delicate body. Nevertheless, she wore an out-of-season woollen coat that buried all of her short frame, leaving only the black, silky hair and high cheek bones to be seen. Her New York accent, still retained its night-life lustre. The throaty sound brought the small kitchen back to life.

"Hey, baby! I was just coming from the store when I saw your door open. Baby, this ain't no safe place to leave no door open." She laughed at the pictures forming in her mind of what Vivian's old neighborhood must have looked like. "You ain't up on the hill now or out in the country some place, you know."

Liberty stopped when she saw Vivian quickly wiping the tears from her face. "Ey Viv, you all right?" Liberty put her grocery bag on the table and took a closer look at Little Von on his mother's lap. His eyes were red and puffy. "Ey little man, what you doin' sittin' in here on your momma's lap cryin' when you could be outside playin' wit yo' friends?" she asked, in a low raspy voice.

Little Von stole a look at Liberty. "Ain't got no friends." He pushed his face deeper into his mother's dress.

"Ain't got no friends, huh?" Liberty smiled at his choice of words. She eyed Vivian now understanding the problem.

Vivian glanced up at the ceiling and back to Liberty. "I asked him about Nate and Yoshi's kid downstairs. Von said that he was mean."

"He is Mom!"

"He is," Liberty said, knowing something of the boy's reputation. She waved the thought off, and continued to work on her own plan. "Ey little man," she said after a time, "Is your brother home?"

Unsure of himself, Little Von looked around the kitchen and listened to the emptiness of the house. "No," he answered, realizing nothing had changed.

Playing the part of a general reprimanding her troops, Liberty set her worn shoulder bag down on the table beside her groceries and threw her shoulders back. "Then what you cryin' for?"

Little Von rotated his head from his mother's chest and looked at the short, fiery woman.

"Do you see any other men in this house?" she pressed.

Little Von was puzzled by her stern tone. Taken aback, and intrigued all at the same time, he watched her cautiously. He had never seen her eyes more than "cracked-lid" as his Grandmother would say. But now she glared at him, allowing him to see two coal-black pools that demanded an answer. "Nope," he said, turning his head to avoid the hypnotic gaze.

"Then what does that make you?" she insisted.

Little Von furrowed his brow in contemplation, but then shrugged his shoulders.

"Then tell me. What does that make you?"

He furrowed his brow a second time, searching deeper. He shrugged again.

"You don't? You don't know? No other man in this house—you the only one—and you don't know what that makes you?" Liberty forcefully exhaled, shaking her head from side to side. She looked over Little Von's head to Vivian and spoke in a whisper. "He the only man here and he don't know what that makes him. Well, I-will-just-be-damned."

Little Von was very excited now. "What, Libby! What does that make me?"

Vivian had hoped he wouldn't ask since she, too, was caught by Liberty's mystery.

"Well, if you the only man in the house...well, then, that makes you 'Man of the House,' don't it?"

Little Von's eyes popped wide open. This certainly sounded official. He quickly turned to his mother. She was already nodding a slow, solemn affirmation.

Still intense, Liberty finished the job. "Stop that cryin' and wipe that snot from yo' face, boy."

Vivian frowned as Little Von ran two quick strokes across his nose with his shirt sleeve. A sly, motherly grin formed on Liberty's face and her eyes returned to their inherent "cracked-lid" position. She went to the grocery bag and began fumbling with its contents. "And since you the man of the house—that is true, isn't it?"

"Yeah," Little Von replied eagerly, sensing a treat near at hand.

"Good," she continued, pulling a popsicle to the top of the bag. "Then you deserve a little something extra." Liberty placed the popsicle on the table when suddenly the apartment door opened and closed.

Robin's heavy footsteps approached the corner of the little kitchen making it feel crowded. "Mom, there's something wrong with the lock. Hi, Liberty. Hi bean head, what you guys doin'?" he queried, surprised at the gathering.

Little Von became fearful in his brother's presence knowing that he was no longer the "Man of the House." According to

Liberty's reasoning, he no longer deserved the treat. Liberty also recognized the problem and instantly began to glare in Robin's direction. "Good-bye, Robin," she said pointedly. Robin looked to his mother for an explanation. Instead of giving an explanation, she, too, said simply, "Good-bye, Robin!"

Robin had also never seen Liberty's eyes open. Now that he had, he didn't think she was in any more of a mood to argue than was his mother. Raising an eyebrow, he retreated, closing the door behind him. Vivian leaned toward the window when she heard the foyer door bang shut two floors below. She waited for her son to look up to the apartment window. Outside, Robin leaned against the fence and held his hands up questioning. She held up one finger, signaling him to wait.

Feeling reassured that his position was secure once again, Little Von looked to Liberty. "Libby? Can Robin have a popsicle, too?"

Liberty smiled and pulled another popsicle from the grocery bag. "Here, Baby. Go tell Robin to take you down by Poke and see if you see anybody fishin' so you can watch 'em." She trailed him to the door and watched him descend step by step, each time leading with his right foot while concentrating on not dropping the treats. Liberty shut and locked the door and returned to the kitchen.

"Viv, you blessed to have two beautiful boys like them two," Liberty said as she comfortably moved around the kitchen that was a replica of her own and two hundred others in the projects. "We both blessed. My Charlene's a beauty. She smart, too," she mused, opening the refrigerator and sliding the ice tray from the freezer. She ran it under the tap before pulling its rack handle back shattering the block of ice into cubes.

"Now, my boys…," she paused and sighed and clicked her tongue and teeth at the side of her mouth, "…well, you know, they boys. What can I say?" All three of 'em. On her toes, she stretched as far as she could, opened the cupboard with one hand and pinched two clean glasses with the other. With one smooth motion, she brought the tall bourbon bottle from the shopping bag and deftly cracked its seal. She let the cap spin free in her hand and partially filled both glasses before spinning the cap in the reverse direction.

"One thing about living in the projects, Viv…" she continued, pushing one glass across the table toward Vivian and taking hers to the window, "…we struggle like a bitch to survive, but we got each other." She let out a short, derisive laugh. "Huh! Sometimes I think that's all we got. So, we gotta stick together, right, babe? Havin' real friends, ones you know gotcha covered when you need it, is like havin' a good pair of crutches 'round when you got a broke leg or somethin'. When you need them, they there to lean on."

Liberty turned briefly toward the window, her face stiffening as she reflected on the discordant elements of her own life. She glanced below to see Little Von steal a bite from his brother's popsicle. "Yeah…," she sighed, "We got each other." She turned to hold her glass up to Vivian, waiting for her to complete the toast to survival.

Vivian stared at the glass, inwardly weakening to its magnetic pull. The weight of all that had been leading up to the move rushed in upon her. She picked the glass up and touched it to Liberty's telling herself, "just this one." The two women drank deeply and quietly.

Liberty leaned against the window frame and watched the two boys below as they walked toward the river and disappeared from sight.

4

CLOVIS LAMB, LIVED DOWNSTAIRS behind another of the green doors. His face was a series of small circles within a mass of wrinkles. His eyes had the orange glow that accompanies seventy years of bourbon and Lucky Strikes. It was because of his wife Matty that he was forced to give up smoking. On her death bed he swore off one of what Matty called the "Devil's twins." She never pushed about his drinking. Perhaps she knew the reality of it.

Bones and joints that no longer fit smoothly together caused a hop that punctuated an otherwise quick shuffling step. Often he wore a blue three-piece suit with large pin stripes, circa 1930, that appeared to be three sizes too big. He wore it with a boldly-flowered tie, broad and improperly tied. This had been his uniform since Matty's death. Today he wore his fishing hat made of a tightly-woven straw, blocked in the style of the riverboat gamblers of his native Missouri.

"Hey, you boys!" Clovis shouted upstream at the two figures just beyond his focus. "Wha-the-helllll you doin' up there?" He squinted, trying to get a better idea of who he was yelling at. "Well, well, well, ain't this somethin'?" he mumbled, standing as tall as his calcified spine would allow; "I'm fishin' and you pissin'. And you pissin' upstream down on me!"

Clovis wasn't ready to turn his attention away from Robin and Little Von, but his pole suddenly jumped off the twig fork and was making its way in small jumps toward the waters of Pocahontas. He hobbled over the rocks and wet spots as fast as his chimp-like bowlegs would carry him. He grabbed the pole just as it skirted the muddy edge of the water.

"Got damnit, Kitty, I knowed it was you!" he said, jerking the pole up into the air. He leaned back putting tension on the line, now zigzagging back and forth across the deep stream. "Only your ornery ass would pull a brand new pole through the mud. That's right! I knowed it was you the first time you...HEY! HEY, get away from there!" Clovis yelled at the water watching the line take a sharp turn up river to the left. "I know what you up to. You tryin' to get my line around that old rusty shoppin' cart under there. Yes, sir! I know what's under there. I didn't come down with yesterday's rain, ya know!" Suddenly Clovis looked upstream. "HEY, YOU BOYS! QUIT PISSIN' IN THAT GOT DAMN WATER!"

After a struggle, Little Von had managed to get the stiff zipper of his pants down. Imitating his brother, he pushed hard to make his little arc of pee reach the water's edge. Then he heard the old man yelling. Startled, he twisted around sending his miniature stream up Robin's leg.

"Von!" Robin cried, busy with his own flow. "You peed on me!" He tried to jump out of the way, but Little Von drew closer, absorbed in the picture of a man shouting and fishing and wearing a suit.

"Hey Von, that's Clovis the Lamb. He lives downstairs in 5503. Looks like he has a fish on; wanna go check it out?"

Little Von stood silently, watching, still holding himself outside his zipper.

"Come on man, zip it up and let's go." Little Von looked up at his brother, unsure if he liked the idea.

"I got you this time, you old son-of-a-bitch." Clovis watched the line cut through the green surface scum as the fish took a new tack. He let his false teeth slide forward in his mouth as a means of sharpening his concentration.

Robin and Little Von stopped a little distance from Clovis excitedly watching him and the line slicing through the water. Clovis skillfully guided his ancient foe around old tires, protruding tree limbs, and the other debris he knew existed beneath the surface of the Pocahontas. At one time or another he had snagged all of them.

The line cut one way and Clovis gave his laugh which was little more than hissing air. Then the line darted in another direction. Clovis's face showed that the move was less to his advantage as the mass of wrinkles and grey stubble sagged and became motionless and more focused.

Without warning, the fat catfish boiled to the surface of the water, its large, broad tail flopping green droplets in every direction.

Little Von unconsciously reached up and grabbed Robin's hand. He had never actually seen anyone catch a big fish before, and after seeing the contrast between the skinny line and what appeared to him as an explosion in the water, he wasn't sure he wanted to.

Seeing the fish's tail, the only glimpse of the actual fish he had ever had, Clovis's eyes widened with new life. Over the years he had guessed the fish's size by the pull of the line and the skill with which it had always managed to stay out of his frying pan. "Good God Almighty! Thirty pounds if it's one!"

The fish made a sudden turn churning the water. *SSSnaaappp!* The naked line whipped straight back into Clovis's face, and with it came the stench of Pocahontas.

Both the boys turned sharply to Clovis the Lamb waiting for the eruption of swear words and foot stomping that was sure to come. Instead, he stood statuesque, eyes fixed upon the spot where the line had left the water. A wry smile and the shaking of his curved finger were the only affirmation of the battle's end and Clovis's defeat. He pulled a white handkerchief from his back pocket to wipe the river off his face and left out his hissing chuckle.

"Well, well, well," he said in a soft and calm tone.

The old man turned his attention back to the boys, searching for traits that would give away their identities.

"Robin?" he asked, squinting and leaning closer. "That you, boy? Well, I'll be. Look atcha. Whoowee! Boy, I knowed you when you was knee high to a grasshopper's ass," he said, laughing to himself. "Well, now," he said again, stooping over, both hands on his knees. Admiration filled his voice as he studied the small figure. "And you must be Vivy's baby." Clovis smiled at the sight of the small child with smooth bronze skin and eyes still full of expectation.

"How old you, boy?" Clovis fumbled in his pocket without looking away from Little Von. He smiled with anticipation as he waited for the sound of the small voice.

Little Von released his big brother's hand. "Six, but I'll be six and a half pretty soon my momma said, didn't she, Rob?" Clovis's faced bounced up and down, his eyes jammed shut with silent laughter.

Robin had heard his mother talk about Clovis Lamb on more than one occasion. He had thought the words she had used to describe him were strange words, like *original*. Another time, she had said, "Without question, he is a very *different* kind of person." He was a little bent-over man with bowlegs. Most of the time he was fussing and swearing; still she found a way to love him.

Clovis Lamb handed Little Von the man-size fishing pole. "Boy, yo' momma and I used to have a lot of laughs, yes sir, big time fun." Clovis spoke quietly as he put another worm on the hook. "Okay boy, put yo' hands next to mine and let me show ya how to make a cast."

Little Von held the pole awkwardly, feeling sorry for the writhing worm stabbed and looped around the sharp hook several times. Clovis placed one arm around Little Von and eyed the water carefully, his own childhood anticipation coming to the fore. He drew the pole back over both of their shoulders and with a little grunt sent the line sailing in an arc over the croaking bull frogs and drifting leaves of the Pocahontas. "Boy," Clovis mumbled, more to himself than to anyone else, "There's a big ass ornery fish under there somewhere; maybe you can catch 'im for me."

5

With Little Von and Clovis engrossed in fishing, Robin struck out on his own. He followed the narrow path that ran along the water's edge under the green canopy of giant oak and birch trees. He was astonished at the cool solitude that enveloped him. Just a short distance away people lived crammed together in the projects, one on top of another without enough space to dream.

He walked, unaware of time, watching the darting and hovering flight of majestic dragonflies. A school of minnows scattered as his shadow crossed the water. After a while he noticed that the sun had passed its crest in the sky, and Robin tried to guess the time. As he looked up, he stepped on a rock that sank steadily in the mud. He jumped forward onto another, but it too, started to sink. Ahead the path was solid and dry. Gathering his strength he lunged forward in one final flailing attempt to remain free of the muddy stench of the Pocahontas. As his foot hit the path, it slipped off one side and into the muck. The school shoes disappeared in the mud. He felt the cold water seep in and soak his foot from heel to toes. He tugged his foot free and stood examining the result. The mood for adventure was lost.

Through the trees at the edge of the wooded area, he caught a glimpse of Jimmy Lee's Best Fill station. The round headed pumps that lit up at night with "Gas" written in large red letters, marked the beginning of the Hollow.

Nearly twenty minutes passed as Robin carefully picked his way through the overgrown path. Suddenly it came to an end at the foot of a steep, rocky precipice that rose abruptly from the natural slope of the bank and jutted across the path into the water. The slope was covered with a heavy growth of thorny blackberry brambles; their long spike-covered tendrils made the trail impassable.

Robin grimaced. None of the choices were appealing. Behind him, a half-hour's walk and the mud. Before him, a gauntlet of thorns, hungry for his skin and the rest of his school clothes, but beyond this, the Stone Bridge, Jimmy Lee's and freedom from a walk-turned-nightmare.

Robin stood, mentally weighing the pluses and minuses of

the situation. He spotted a thin path between the water's edge and the thick stand of blackberry bushes. He took off his shoes and socks.

Looking around, he found three baseball size rocks and threw them as hard as he could along the area he would be walking. He had heard many stories over school lunches about the water moccasins and copperheads that thrived around Poke, showing themselves at the most unexpected moments. The thought made his toes curl. He found three more rocks, slightly larger than the first three, and sent them bouncing across the trail as well. When nothing moved he started forward.

Robin moved cautiously. The bank curled in to form a small cove. At the center of the cove a gigantic oak hung over the water with a large thick rope hanging from its lowest limb.

Three figures appeared from a gully beneath the big oak, shouting, waving their arms and pointing. Startled, having thought himself alone, Robin stumbled off the strip of land and into the water. He sank deeper with every step.

"Ey man, it's Robin Thompson!" one of the figures shouted. "What you doin' wadin' around in Poke, man? You practicin' for the beach at Atlantic City or somethin'?"

"Where's your b-b-b-b-beach b-b-ball?" another yelled louder. And then there was a wild burst of laughter from all three.

Robin finally recognized Lester Jackson, Matt and Scootch Williams. He laughed with the others as he waded to the dry grassy area where they lay laughing.

Scootch, the larger of the three boys, leaned back on his elbow. "Hey man, you looked more scared than Matt that time the old man came to school and kicked his ass in front of everybody! Remember that?" Scootch and Lester laughed hysterically. Matt had always been in a specialized class in school because he was emotionally less stable than other kids. In private, most thought Matt was quietly crazy. At times he was shy and painfully insecure. Other times he overreacted with an explosive temper. Robin had not been close to Matt like the others. He watched to see what Matt would do.

"Well, what about the time Daddy caught you in the laundry room with Shirl Tibbs?" Matt returned, hoping to one-better his brother. Lester howled. "Gi..g.g.give me s.s.ssome skin on that!" Matt slowly dragged his open hand across Lester's. Robin watched while feigning a small laugh.

"Yeah, okay, okay, but he only punched me a couple of times. And besides, it was worth it." Everybody nodded in agreement. Scootch let the laughter die down.

"Least he didn't catch me in the bathroom doin' it to my hand like you," said Scotch, proud of his come-back.

Laughter came in a burst. This time Robin was unable to hold back and was soon rolling on the hillside with the other two boys, laughing and having a good time.

Matt's embarrassment was deep. He bobbed his head up and down. With one eyebrow held slightly higher than the other, his lips pulled tight, Matt fell silent.

Scott "Scootch" Williams lived in the projects all his life. He was tall, aggressive and muscular, with a deep voice. Despite the fact he had been kept back twice in school, he was intelligent, but had chosen to master street wisdom as opposed to memorizing facts about the Revolutionary War. He cared little about who signed a piece of paper written with quill and fountain ink that guaranteed a freedom that "Colored" people were never allowed to have. He was angry, but savvy. Scootch Williams was strong of heart and will, had carameled skin, large brown eyes, and po-made-brushed wavy hair, and he was liked by most men and all women.

Robin was sitting on the side of the bank, laughing and wiping mud off his shoes. Scootch smiled, "Say man, what you doin' down here? You hawkin' on some spots to bring the ladies, huh?"

Robin looked up, "Naa. I saw Clovis the Lamb over there fishin', so I came down with my little brother to check it out. He was fishin' in a suit."

"Yeah, man, that d-d-d-ddude is cr-cr-crcrazy!" added Lester.

"No he's retarded," Matt said, pointing up the river.

Scootch grinned, "Matt, both y'all retarded."

The flood of negativity toward Clovis caught Robin off guard. He was glad he stopped when he did, he *was* on the verge of saying what a cool dude he thought Clovis was. He began to listen more cautiously to the conversation adding only carefully selected words as if each one might betray his naivety. "I never seen anybody fish in a three-piece suit," he said in a factual tone, "He's definitely different," he added, remembering his mother's words.

"He do-do-do-do every th-th-th-thing dressed like dat," Lester managed, misjudging his ability to complete the phrase smoothly.

Scootch's head snapped around toward the bushy hilltop which hid the entrance to the bay and he held his hand up for immediate silence.

The tension on Scootch's face eased when he recognized Cootie. Cootie was a wino, no more, no less. Everyone knew Cootie. He had lived in the delapidated stilt houses of the Hollow all of his life until the great outdoors had become his home. Cootie seldom spoke. His needs were obvious, and people accommodated and used him when it suited them. Life had passed him by long ago, taking with it the pride that makes even mediocre men bathe and seek a change of clothes. Cootie staggered through the opening at the top of the hill with a shopping bag held tight before him. He neither spoke nor changed the enigmatic gaze that had become a permanent part of his face.

At the bottom of the hill, the boys crowded around Cootie, slapping his back and congratulating him for making it back. Through it all he stood silent, hand outstretched and palm up, waiting for what was promised for a job well done. Robin watched Cootie take the two dollars and stuff them deep in his pocket. He used his other hand like a swinging balance as he climbed back up the slope to the top of the hill.

Sitting on a stump, Scootch took a six-pack from the bag and began to peel a can from its side. "Beer or wine?" he asked, turning to Robin.

Robin's pulse surged. He had never drunk before and didn't want to now. In fact, he hated liquor because of the way it changed his mother, but he couldn't turn back now. "Beer's cool," Robin said, making it sound as uneventful as he could manage.

Scootch tossed the can without making it spin or tumble and followed it with a can opener. Likewise, he passed cans to Matt and Lester, keeping the wine for himself.

Robin tried to open the can with the opener, waiting for the beer to spew when he noticed he had the bottle end of the opener forward. He quickly reversed it, hoping no one had noticed. Turning the can up, he took four long draws and exaggerated a burp hoping the show would be convincing. "All right, Rob, you cool, man!" Matt affirmed, smiling and nodding approvingly. Robin smiled as he watched Cootie make his way back up the hill. He saw little more than a crooked trail with a beaten man at its end. He pulled his eyes away and picked up his can again. He hated his mother's drinking and now he was doing the same. No matter how convincing the show, it was wrong.

God A'mighty, boy! Whooo!" Clovis laughed and shook his head. "Ain't no fish up there. What you gonna tell yo' momma, you caught a tree fish? Good God! He put his hand over his face chuckling and hissing. Little Von looked back over his shoulder smiling as Clovis untangled the line from the branch. "Okay boy, go 'head, giv'em hell again."

Casting had not come as easily as Little Von thought it might. He had released the spool on the backswing, throwing hook, sinker, worm, and several yards of Clovis's new line into a tree directly behind them. He tried an underhand cast, but forgot to lift his thumb up to release the spool. The worm and line made three perfect circles at the end of the pole before returning to snag Clovis's hat and swing it into the water.

"You's a hellll of a fisherman!" Clovis had shouted, laughing while retrieving his hat from the stream with a stick. And then it happened, the perfect cast. Both jumped about yelling and shaking hands, Clovis using little more than his thumb and index finger.

They cast and laughed for several hours. Clovis stood several yards away, relieving himself on a bush with his back to Little Von, talking over his shoulder and trying not to splatter his shoes.

"Boy, I'll tell you why I don't piss in the watta. When I was little my daddy tolt me, 'Clo' —that's what my old man called me—Clo. He said, 'Clo, never piss on anything that you might eat later.'" He frowned as his urine came in spurts. "Ferse of all, when you a old man, you lucky if you can piss at all!" He dangled, tucked, and ran the zipper. "Now...a, some peoples likes to go to cherch every Sunday and they prays, but me, I do my prayin' with a hook, line, and sinker, yessir. This here is as spiritual as you can get." Clovis lay down on the grassy bank resting his head on a small log. He chewed on the end of a long weed and let his hat drift over his eyes.

"That's right, watta is spiritual. Every fisherman know'd

that. Why you think they baptizes peoples in rivers? Well, they don't anymore, but they use to. Now they got big fancy cherches and, and, tubs behind curtains, and not enough peoples to fill 'em."

Little Von listened, but he never took his eyes off the skinny line in the water that began to do funny things from time to time.

"That's right. Ain't like it use to be. Seems to me the bigger the cherches gets, the smaller God gets." The line moved slowly to the right and stopped. Little Von sat as still as a marble statue.

"You know, I remember one time when a preacher in my hometown, not like these here jackleg preachers runnin' 'round here now, a real preacher, anyway he was baptizin' my friend, Ezra Tomlin, uh huh, 1937 it was. Hard times back then. They said the Great Depression was over, but colored peoples was still hungry. Well, sir, the whole town was out to the river in they Sunday best. The preacher took 'em out in the middle of the river and come dis a preachin'. He preached and he preached. After a little bit he grabbed old Ezra up around his head, 'Aaand in the naaame of the Faaather!'" Clovis laughed at his own imitation of the oldtime minister.

Little Von was standing straight up, nearly petrified as he watched the line run silently to the right and then to the left, making the pole jump up and down on the twig fork like a jittery seesaw.

"'Aaaand the Son!'…then he pulled Ezra's skinny little ass under that water. 'Round 'bout that time a great big o' water moccasin come slitherin' down behind them. Oh Lordy! Nobody seen 'em but me and Johnny-boy Row, and we knowed how scared Ezra was o' snakes! Didn't make no difference how big or little it was neither, that boy didn't like no snakes. Well, sir, Ezra seen that snake from under the watta, but the preacher had hold of his head. You should have seen that boy come up out of that watta!" Clovis was nearly in tears. "Whoooosh!"

Little Von was silently and steadily backing away from the pole, which now danced like crazy.

"Them old ladies in the choir come dis a shoutin' 'Ezra got the spirt! Ezra been touched!' Well, they was almost right 'bout that, but Ezra wasn't 'bout to let that snake get close enough to touch him! No-sir-reee, buddy! He towed that preacher all over that river tryin' to get away from that water mocassin."

Little Von had backed away from the dancing pole until he was standing right next to Clovis's head.

"Me and Johnny-boy Row was 'bout to roll in the water, we was laughin' so hard. We woulda, too, but we knew that big ass snake was in there." Clovis was laughing so hard he rolled over on his side and then his hat bumped Little Von's leg. Startled, Clovis looked up and saw the pole which seemed now to have a life of its own.

"Got damn, boy! Grab the pole! Grab the pole!" Clovis roared, wrenching the pole from its wooden cradle and shoving it into Little Von's hands. "Crank 'em in, boy! Crank 'em in! Bring that son-bitch home!" Clovis brought a pint bottle from the inner pocket of his jacket and took a long swig. He hopped and shouted, determined to make Little Von's first catch an unforgettable moment. "You got 'em! Yessir! Keep 'em comin'! Keep 'em comin'!"

Two fish later and in near darkness, Clovis the Lamb and Little Von made their way through the brush bordering the banks of the Pocahontas. Little Von's first fish was barely more than a minnow, but his chest stuck out with pride as he walked beside Clovis carrying the stringer and listening happily to stories of Clovis's battles with Kitty, the elusive giant catfish. "Clovis. Do you always drink when you be fishin'?"

"No sir. I never drink and fish at the same time. But this time you was fishin'. I keeps my business and my fishin' and my drinkin' separate much as possible. That way it don't come to be a crutch.

Little Von stopped, suddenly remembering his brother. He looked up and down the the river's edge.

"Who you looking for? Robin? Don't worry 'bout him. He's a big boy now; he knows how to find his way home."

6

IT WAS DARK. THE FOUR BOYS staggered drunkenly through the opening at the top of the hill, Robin in the lead. Firmly established as one of the boys, he now laughed freely, and, unlike himself, without regard of whose feelings were at stake.

Matt aimed at Lester, "Studderbug, your momma ain't changed her draws in so long, scientist follow her 'round to make penicillin from the chairs she sit on!" The boys howled. Matt relaxed, sure that Lester, breathing through his open mouth and tripping as he walked, was too drunk to retaliate. Robin, really into the swing of things, had been the first to laugh. He swayed over to Matt and slapped his hand, the laughing and giggling from the others ebbed. All except Robin, who slowly realized that Matt had taken an awful chance involving someone's mother in the game.

Les stood as still as any drunken person can manage, lips drooping, eyes fixed, glaring in Matt's direction. Robin, once again scrambling to fit the mold, began to take mental notes, although this time on an inebriated state. He waited to see what action Lester would take.

"Wel-wel-well least dey don't m-m-m-make it from what grows on her teeth, l-l-l-like yo's."

Lester had no idea what penicillin was made from, but even in his drunkenness he knew it was necessary to make a good comeback. As the laughter escalated relieving the tension, he fell to his knees laughing and slapped the ground hoping the quip was as good as he thought.

Robin's roar was the first to be heard. He stumbled into Lester's path howling, both hands extended for a double five. Like the rest, Scootch was drunk, but, unlike the rest, he was adept at always keeping a sober place inside.

He had been watching Robin getting into the fun of the game, but he also noticed that it had been cautious participation. "Hey Rob, I was talking to Joleena the other day. She said she really dug you."

At the mere mention of her name the other boys stopped and looked around, thinking the game had come to a hasty end to make way for more serious discussion. Joleena had been every boy's secret love at one time or another. More than anyone,

she had been Matt's greatest fantasy for as long as he could remember. His love for her made him crazy, yet he never said a
word. Fear and rejection had been constant companions in Matt's
life. He lived in Scootch's shadow, nearly invisible to everyone. His
love for Joleena was private, sacred, not to be laughed about or
mocked. It was one of his few joys in life and with his silence he
held it inviolate, even from her. More than a little drunk, Matt's
response was loud and unchecked. "What! Joleena with Robin?
She said that?"

"Jo..Joleena, Joleena. Jest jest jest once before I die, Lord,"
Lester chanted.

Completely taken by surprise, Robin came unglued, "Oh,
man, you kiddin' me? Joleena said that?" Robin's mind jumped
into high gear. He gave a long whistle as mental images of him and
Joleena flashed through his mind. "Man! Oh man! Joleena
Cleary. You shhure man? Joleena Cleary with the watermelon...."
He extended his hands in front of his chest and waited for ac-
knowledgment. Scootch nodded and held his hands out, fingers
spread to the straining point. "Scootch, you serious or drunk?"

"Hey man, swear to God and seven other white dudes I don't
know nothing about," Scootch crossed his heart.

Wobbling as he stood, Robin whistled again and shook his
head slowly in hopeful disbelief.

Scootch nodded and replied, "I swear! She told Charlene
she would love to you-know-what with you, but..!"

The others screamed, "What!" and "She w-w-wwould!" and
"Joleena would with Rob!" mingling with Robin's excited, slurry
"Wi' meeee? B' what? B' what!" he repeated, his emotions the
most unguarded they had been all night.

"But!" Scootch said, raising one finger, his pinky finger. "She
heard from one of her friends yo' pee-pee was ssoooo small you
had to use a magnifying glass and a string to find it!"

For a moment there was silence as everybody's mind groped
for reality. One by one they began to realize that the game was still
on.

Matt broke the silence with a sigh. It was soon followed by
hoots of derisive laughter and straight fingers all directed at
Robin.

Realizing he had been stung, Robin stopped dead in his
tracks, pursed his lips, and looked straight ahead. The combined

din of the other boys reached a peak, died down, and rose again. Lester lurched forward catching Matt's arm and both fell to the ground. Scootch waited beneath the laughter, observing and analyzing Robin's response. Robin's silence persisted, and the tension stemmed the flow of laughter. Lester's breath came in small gulps. Matt was finally silent, getting up slowly, brushing weeds from his clothes. Dead serious, Robin turned to Scootch. "Maybe so..." he cooed, leaving a Scootch-style dramatic pause, "but my pee-pee was big enough to bring you into the world!" His giggling trailed off into a snort behind a protective hand.

Lester's eyes expanded twice their normal size, and darted back and forth from Scootch to Matt who shared the implicated mother.

Quite satisfied that his test had been passed in a decisive manner, Scootch allowed his low rumble of a laugh to relieve the final tension. He extended his open hand to Robin. "Man, I knew there was a cold dude underneath that Mr. Nice Guy routine. You cool! Gimme skin on that!"

Two hours later, Scootch, Matt and Lester stood in a tight circle beneath a street lamp, harmonizing and snapping their fingers. They belonged to a second generation quartet named the "Swan Tones." Robin sang with them, replacing Benny Tillerman whom no one had seen that day.

Later, Benny came down the dark street—short, squat, looking like a gangster, strutting like a peacock in sunglasses, with a "do-rag" for his hair hanging from his back pocket.

"Hey brothers, everything cool?" Benny said, walking up and sticking out his hand that nobody slapped. He looked around curiously, not surprised, since rejection was an everyday occurrence for Benny by his own choice. But he wondered what was the cause of this unplanned rejection. He was too high to analyze it. Looking for some way to diffuse the tension, he saw Robin. "Ey, Robin Thompson, what you doin' hangin' out down here?"

"Just moved in 5509," Robin stated in a neutral voice, sensing trouble but too inexperienced to know the depth of it.

Scootch spoke up, making no attempt to hide his irritation. "Say man, you gettin' to be a problem child."

"What you talkin' about, man—problem child?" Benny came back.

"Where you been, man? We suppose' to been havin' a rehearsal this afternoon. I guess you overlooked that on your calendar."

"Calendar? Man, what you talkin' about? We suppose' to be rehearsin' t'morrow, ain't we?"

"Ey man, tomorrow is today. Look man, if you don't want to be a Swan Tone anymore, why don't you just split?" Scootch said, becoming more angry with each return.

"Split? Ey, man, what you talkin' about—split? My brother was a Swan Tone. This is a family tra-di-tion, you dig? If I missed a practice it was just a little misunderstandin'. Ain't nothin' to it, man. If you want to rehearse, than let's get to it." As he said this he tipped his head forward, gingerly removed his hat being careful not to mess up his process hairdo. He carefully tied the rag from his back pocket around his head to hold his hair, which had been straightened and waved with a mixture of lye and hair cream. He took off his glasses and placed them in his shirt pocket, exposing his red and puffy eyes.

Scootch watched him with a scowl. "Man, you been smokin' reefer. That's what you been gettin' to and that's why you forgot practice."

"Ey man, I told you, I thought it was t'morrow. And big deal, I been smokin' a little weed. You smoke it, too. So what, big deal."

"But, I don't be missin' no practice. And by the way, neither did yo' brother."

"Come on man, what we gonna do? We gonna jaw, croon, or what?"

In his mind Scootch chose the "or what." But he held his temper. Even in defeat Benny would walk away with sympathy for having challenged someone twice as big and twice as cool as he was. Scootch would look bad having stomped on someone half his size, deserving or not. Even Benny's mother had said Benny was the Devil's son, a nuisance whose only purpose in life was to make everybody around him just as miserable as he was. Still, Scootch held back.

Finally, Benny cocked his head slightly to the side and said, "Do it." With a smirk, Scootch turned and said, "Hit it, Les."

Robin was so engrossed in trying to sing his part separate from the others, he never heard the uptown clock strike his midnight curfew hour. He marveled at Lester, who normally couldn't say three words in a row without stammering, as he gave everyone a very specific pitch and cadence to sing. Here Lester was king. When he spoke or read, he easily appeared to be a bumpkin. But, when he sang, he was smooth as a woman's silk blouse.

"N-n-n-no, Rob, you hit dis—'*Doooo, doooo, do do do waaa'*. Li-li-li-like dat. Den while you b-b-b-bbe doin' dat wit Matt a-a-a-and Scootch, I be sayin', '*Oh, my dar-ling, hold me close-ly.*' D-d-dig it?" Robin had no overwhelming quality in his voice, but his pitch was nearly perfect. Rather than deep and rich, his tone was thin, but it had a smoothness that was reflective of his style.

The boys sang on. They followed each other and stacked their voices with dazzling precision. One moment the voices made the loose chrome on nearby cars buzz with vibration, and in another, all would be down to an intense rhythmic whisper.

Three floors up a window slid on its track, and a flower pot, thrown from its sill, exploded on the sidewalk with the pop of a small shotgun blast. It sent the boys in every direction.

"You boys shut that noise up and take yo' black asses home! Don't yawl know what timeitiz?" Henrietta Leaman was a working woman in a cotton gown and a hairnet. Her armor against life was her attitude which she had brought north from somewhere between Mississippi and Arkansas. It was obvious that she was tired and pissed. She had to get up early to catch a crosstown bus to fix breakfast for someone else's children before they went off to private school, a school as far away as another country for her own kids. "I'm gonna be callin' the po-lice to hepya find yo' way, if you be needin' some hep!"

Scootch came out of his hiding place behind a parked car where he had ducked after hearing the crash directly behind him. Taking his cue from Henrietta's warning, he sang the lead and the others followed:

"Hep de do de ah
Goodnight sweet-heart
it's time-to-go..."

Another pot crashed to the ground. Henrietta Leaman left the window still shouting.

At the mention of the police, Robin was ready to run, but he saw that the others were undaunted. Instead he turned away from the spot beneath the street lamp at no more than a stroll, one arm swinging and fingers snapping in perfect unison with the others.

Matt sang alto and watched. He loved the fact that Robin had been given Benny's tenor part. Benny sang the lines with Robin, seemingly uncaring, but it was obvious that Benny was singing better than he ever had. Matt stepped out of the choir march the others had taken up and took a flower from one of the mounds of soil and broken pottery. Still singing, he sniffed its fragrance and visualized his secret love, Joleena Cleary.

At the corner of the next building, just before the courtyard, the song came to an end. They congratulated themselves with a final slapping of hands and each moved off toward his own apartment building. Benny returned the way he had come, back to the streets.

Standing alone, Robin felt the terrible sickness in his stomach that resulted from mixing too much beer and too much cheap wine. Now, alone with no one to judge his words or actions, he quickly made his way around the side of Building Five, past the Bendix laundromat, and began to heave. Vomit splattered the ground and his feet. His shoes were a mess.

He leaned against the building and tried, with no success, to slow the violent muscle contractions that strained his face and racked his torso repeatedly. He had never been sick in this way before, and he vowed never to be sick in this way again.

Robin held on to the side of the building flat-palmed, trembling and praying. "Oh God," he begged with his eyes closed, and spitting between the words, "Please stop this. Please." He heaved again and again. And even though his stomach was completely empty, he heaved, tasting the acrid bile in his mouth. Disoriented, his body weight buckled his knees as if they had been made up of toothpicks and rubber bands. He fell backward, hitting the ground with a thud. He was quite content to lie there for awhile. The ground was solid and secure. Eventually he sensed he could stand and probably even walk.

Eyes opening slowly, he was relieved to see each star hanging motionless in its own place. He stumbled to the corner of the brick building, listening to the unusual silence of the streets. It was late. No cars sped through. Mrs. Talbot wasn't calling her husband a dirty son-of-a-so-and-so at the top of her voice because he had ransacked her handbag. There were no smells of collard or mustard greens, black-eyed peas or navy beans, chicken, lamb or every part of a pig imaginable. Only the hissing of Pocahontas tumbling over the dam, falling to a rocky bottom, and a light coming from the kitchen window of his apartment disturbed the night air.

Robin swore aloud as he strained his neck upward trying to catch a glimpse of his mother. She was no doubt sitting there waiting. He turned his attention to the foyer door when he heard the uptown clock begin its opening melody. "Oh God," he pleaded. "I know a few minutes ago I said I would never bug you again if you would stop me from being sick, but I need this one last favor. Please don't let it be any more than eleven o'clock. I'm probably already in deep for leaving Little Von down by the river. If you'll just help me this once...again."

On the town square, across from Kresge's five and dime store, there was a cathedral with a clock and bell tower. Robin held his breath as the clock gonged the hour. He desperately wanted to count to eleven or twelve, but quickly told himself that he would settle for six gongs that would indicate the half hour of either.

It struck once and Robin extended one finger with his thumb cocked ready to go. He waited, but the first gong was followed only by silence. "One! Oh, man! I'm dead! I'm dead!" He said, running his hand over his face. He ran toward the foyer door with one hand around his stomach to minimize its jostling. "God, why did I do this?" He knew why and understood the consequences if he hadn't.

He flung the foyer door back and looked up the stairs, holding his stomach tightly. As the bang of the door echoed up the stairwell, he fully expected the door of apartment 5509 to fly open and his mother to march out to meet him.

No sooner than he had the thought, one of the upper doors opened. Robin hissed through his teeth, "I'm definitely dead now."

Looking up through the lattice work of stairs and handrails, Robin tried to catch sight of his mother's auburn hair, but he stopped suddenly when he noticed that the footsteps were coming down two stairs at a time, gliding off the edges, and moving much too quickly to be his or anybody else's mother. Then he saw her.

It was Charlene Curtis. Big Mouth Charlene who did and always would delight in telling the whole world anything and everything she knew. What Scootch saw in her he didn't know, but then again as he saw her perfect legs rounding each landing, and her breasts bobbing up and down in short strokes, he knew. Charlene, although he had never seen her in this way before, had somehow become beautiful.

As she rounded the last landing before the foyer, Robin spun around and headed for the door, but as he grabbed the handle, terror struck him as he saw Benny through the side glass coming up the walk. For a long moment he stood like a book caught between two ends. Then, at the last second before she came into full view, just as the spring of the foyer door began its cry, he grabbed the handrail and swung under the stairwell. It was a cramped corner space with the sloping stairs as its ceiling. It was a space where winos slept and urinated.

Knees aching from his squatting position, Robin held his breath not wanting to be heard nor wanting to smell the fetid air that stung his eyes. A faint thread of perfume found its way beneath the stairwell as Charlene jumped the last two stairs and into Benny's arms.

Benny gave a small smile as he examined his catch. "Ay baby, your momma know you out?"

"What do you think?"

"I think she probably told you it was a good idea to sneak out and meet me for a little moonlight." He used the words as an excuse to get his mouth close to her face and neck. "Don't you think it's a good idea?" He kissed her mouth and she kissed him back. The heatwave sensation slowly pulsed through her body in the dim light of the paint-chipped foyer. At first she put her hands up to hold him back, but now, as Robin watched, that idea seemed suspended. She moaned and clutched his neck as he balanced her on the end of the last step.

The door banged shut as Benny and Charlene disappeared into the outer darkness, and Robin backed away blinking, having watched the entire scene through a crack in the foundation wall. He never thought of Charlene in this way before. She had always antagonized him with her gruffness and he saw her as a big mouth and a problem to be avoided. Now his thoughts turned to Scootch and he shuddered as his mind ran pictures of the violent clash between him and Benny that now seemed inevitable.

He stumbled from beneath the stairwell sanctuary, his legs buckling from the numbness in his knees and the proximity to sex. It was as close as he had ever been. What he had heard and seen through the crack in the wall excited him. He had been squatting when his penis began to make a hard ridge along the side of his zipper. It made standing all the more difficult. All this was dampened by the sound of the uptown clock playing only half its melody.

Robin slowly pulled himself up the stairway feeling like he weighed a thousand pounds. Rounding the stairs that led to the second floor he heard one of the metal doors open. Sound flooded the halls with laughter and loud talking. He stopped for a minute leaning over the rail trying to detect from which of the green barriers it had come. His heaviness returned.

Allowing his mind to drift, he remembered a conversation that he had with his mother when he was ten years old. She had caught him stealing cherries from a neighbor's tree, but she had replaced punishment with understanding and a kiss on the forehead. "But Mom!" he had begun in frustration. "Sometimes I can't tell what's right and what's wrong," he had sobbed and looked down at the floor. The stern look on Vivian's face had given way to compassion. Taking him firmly by both shoulders and looking him straight in the eyes she said, "Robin, listen to me, honey." She paused, waiting for his breath to become more regular and he more focused. "I know it's hard to understand everything when you're young. It's still hard for me most of the time, but remember this…" Robin looked up, wiping his eyes with the palms of both hands somewhat reassured by his mother's soothing tone. "Never forget this!" she implored, tightening her grip to impress the moment on her son's mind. "Anything you can't do right up in the middle of town, right up in front of Kresge's five and dime store, in front of God and everybody, then you shouldn't be doin' it at all!" The insight had been so simple and clear that Robin had laughed. They laughed out loud together.

The memory faded and Robin laughed sarcastically at the thought of standing uptown in front of Kresge's, downing four beers, slugging out of a wine bottle, and talking about the prospects of "doin' it" with Joleena Cleary in front of God and everybody. He laughed again and shook his head from side to side. "I'm dead!" he said, facing 5509.

For a moment he stood fumbling for the key, but then he began to match the party sounds he had heard before with the muffled din he now heard on the other side of the metal door. He never liked it when his mother was angry at him, but the idea of bearing his mother's wrath in front of an audience added a new dimension to the rumbling hollowness in the pit of his stomach.

"Excuse me," a voice said as the door suddenly opened and an unrecognized face pushed by. Robin caught the door before it could close. Once inside he paused to assess the tone of twenty or thirty conversations all going on at the same time in two different rooms. A party was in full swing.

No one had to be told about parties in the projects. They were sensed like old bones predict rain, like a lucky feeling about the day's number whose payoff would satisfy the demands of unpaid bills long overdue. A party was an excuse to breathe, a reason to forget jobs lost and jobs never found. When parties magically evolved out of visits or grocery favors, people would come from all directions—upstairs, across the hall, the next building and the building across the street.

People filled the tiny living room and kitchen. An indistinguishable drone of voices was periodically broken by temporary bursts of laughter. To Robin it looked like mime. No particular person made the great cacophony that filled the room, yet all seemed animated by it.

For the first time Robin didn't feel totally out of place in a room full of adults. Now he had something in common with them. They were at least as drunk as he had been and were well on the way to being as sick as he was now.

It was a struggle for Robin to make the adjustment of seeing the tiny apartment crammed from one end to the other with so many people. At first he had barely noticed the sound of his Sears Monotone record player. Robin felt a flash of anger. His one prized possession had been taken from his room without his permission, its volume turned up beyond its ability to play. It was clear that it had been set up hastily. The wobbly antique table had been placed there for looks, it had never been trusted to support anything of value—but there it was, his Sears Monotone.

He stepped sideways through the torrent of faces, some familiar, and some not, looking for his mother. The kitchen table was pulled out from the wall allowing it to seat four instead of the usual three. Clovis the Lamb, very drunk, head down, and still in his fishing suit, sat in the rarely used space against the wall.

Clovis locked eyes with Robin. His words were mushy having no beginnings or endings, only middles. "Ay, Ay, Ay, Robby look, look what yo' lil' brotha' pull from d'ocean. Go head! Look ova-dare in d'sink see wha, wha I'm talkin' bout!"

Liberty, who sat at one end of the table, raised her head from a semi-conscious stupor and snarled at Clovis. "Oh Clovis!" she snarled, her eyes straining to open, her permanent straightened hair pointing in several directions. "Why don't you shut up about dem God damn fish. That's allll you been been talkin' about..." She burped. "...since you come in here!" A roar of laughter went up in the kitchen as her head bumped on the table and disappeared behind a mountain of empty glasses and bottles.

The different sizes of the bottles and glasses reminded Robin of the Manhattan skyline he had seen on postcards. He saw Vivian. Passed out, her head hanging over Little Von asleep on her lap. She looked as drunk as Liberty. Robin moved between two men holding tall-neck beer bottles, arguing about the Brooklyn Dodgers. Standing before his mother and brother, he first felt anger, but that was quickly replaced by heartache and disgust. Carefully he took the partially empty glass out of Vivian's hand. Then, moving her arm, he took Little Von. He carried his brother back through the two men now arguing another baseball point and continued through the crowd to the bedroom. He placed his little brother on the bed before lying on his own, fully dressed. Nauseated, and with tears swelling in his eyes, he had seen what Little Von had often seen and feared, the "Other Self," and it had begun to frighten him too.

The party had gone into the wee hours of the morning. Those still able returned to their own green doors. With the exception of Clovis who was passed out, it ended as it had started, with Vivian and Liberty. "Viv! Viv!," Liberty said, in a low but intense voice while shaking Vivian by the shoulder. "Viv, wake up, the baby's crying."

"Viv!" she barked.

"What what!" Vivian wrenched her eyes open and turned from left to right several times before recognizing Liberty.

"Viv, the baby's in the back cryin'. I'm goin' upstairs now, you okay?" Liberty felt like she was leaving the scene of an accident. She waited a few moments while Vivian became more familiar with her surroundings and repeated herself. "Honey, the baby's cryin' in the back."

Although it was dark, Vivian knew that she had awakened in the early hours of the morning by the coolness that crept through the open kitchen window at her back. With a deep breath she sat up straight on the padded chair and tried to clear her throat. She smoothed the strands of hair that had escaped the bobbypins, "Yeah yeah a…, I'm I'm okay. What time is it?"

Liberty had been saving her strength in an effort to survive the smell in the hallway and the two flights of stairs that separated her from her apartment. She scanned the counter where the clock with the lighted face normally sat. Instead of a clock she found another congregation of dirty glasses and empty bottles. She retrieved the clock from the dusty space between the counter and the refrigerator by following the cord from the plug on the wall. "Four, Viv. I'll help you clean this mess later."

Little Von burst into several short, loud shouts and Vivian recognized that the child would be fully awake in a moment and difficult. Closing the door behind Liberty, Vivian welcomed the support of the walls as she made her way to Little Von now sitting up in his bed half asleep. She picked up the child and went to her own bed where she put him down and lay beside him stroking his hair until they both found sleep once more.

The early morning sunlight was less intense than normal. It limped across a wide portion of Pocahontas's water and entered the apartment window, casting a weak shadow of the vase and its single trailing vine against the hardwood floor. In the bathroom at the end of the hall, Robin let the cold water run while he opened a bottle of aspirin. After tossing two of the tablets to the back of his throat, he drank from a reservoir he made by cupping his hands under the faucet. Although he knew the pounding in his head would stop soon enough, he also knew the pills would have no effect on the overwhelming guilt of having disappointed his mother.

Following the hall from his room, he felt the ghostly silence that hung in the aftermath of the party and walked quietly, shoes in hand. Stopping by his mother's room, he eased the door open and watched her and Little Von sleeping side-by-side. He felt empty. Nothing seemed right. And beneath it all, he felt a hollow sense that things would be worse before they were better.

He sought other thoughts. He thought about Joleena. It was comforting—like a wind buoying a falling leaf. She was so different from the rest. She was unlike any girl he had ever known. Joleena. He closed his mother's door letting the knob turn soundlessly in his hand.

Pulling the living room chair across the floor to its normal place, Robin lowered himself slowly in an effort to keep the throbbing in his head to a tolerable level. The Johnny Mathis album cover stood on end between the arm and the seat cushion. He looked at his watch and compared it with unusual darkness outside the picture window. Dark clouds had begun to gather. There would be a storm today, he thought. He retrieved the album cover and found the album sitting on top of a glass on the floor. He tried to visualize himself darting between cars collecting grocery carts in the parking lot of the Safeway supermarket until five that afternoon, in the rain. The thought quickened the pulse in his temples and made him wince.

There was a crash in the kitchen. Hurrying the bow on his last shoe, Robin entered the small room to find Clovis Lamb changing positions and trying to get comfortable on the cluttered table. Robin searched through Clovis's pockets until he found his keys. With the door keys dangling from his mouth, he placed the small man's arm over his shoulder, held him firmly around his waist, and guided him to his own green door two floors below.

Vivian had meant to speak when she heard her son wrestling Clovis through the door, but she could not. She eased herself to the side of the bed and waited for her head and stomach to settle before moving again. When she heard the door latch, she made her way to the end of the hall pushing off the wall at short intervals. She placed the chain across the door, while the smell of warm fish floating in the sink stung her nose unsettling her even more.

7

ELDER BOWMAN CAME IN FROM THE GARDEN and placed a variety of fresh vegetables on the kitchen counter. As he moved, he looked across the room at his wife Jessie Rose. He first thought that she was putting away the silverware from breakfast. Then he realized that she stood staring vacantly into the drawer, repeatedly drying the same fork. Her mind was filled with the grim pictures of Vivian and the children that accompanied her intuitive feelings.

"Jessie," he said, in a low tone to bring her back.

She started and looked around, realizing for the first time that she was not alone in the sunny Victorian kitchen. She resumed putting the utensils in their proper place in the drawer. Elder walked to a place beside her and pulled his special carving knife from a slotted oak block. Leaving the kitchen momentarily, he returned from the pantry with one of the smoked hams they had brought back from Virginia. "Thick or thin?" he said hoisting the ham to the counter.

Jessie Rose was caught off guard again. "What's that you say?"

"Jessie, this is a ham, and I'm planning on cutting some bacon, but I'd be much obliged if you would tell me how you want it cut, thick-or-thin?"

She was angered at having hid her worrying so poorly twice. "Elderiah Bowman, I know what that is. I was there when you bought it. Don't you 'member me standing next to ya?"

Elderiah stood holding the ham up on its side with the knife poised resting on its skin. "Well?"

"Well what?"

"Thick or…"

"Elder! I don't care how you carve that bacon. Right now I'm worried about Vivian down there with Robin and that baby. I declare, Elder. Why wouldn't you let me call them to see if they all right?" She dropped her drying towel in the drawer with the last of the utensils and unsuccessfully tried to close it. Seeing what she'd done, she snatched it out, slammed the drawer, and threw the towel in the sink. "She called me and said to call her back, didn't she?"

"Yeah, that's what I said, but I talked to 'er and it won't nothin' important. Girl just sounded like she wanted to talk. She didn't sound like she'd been drinkin' so we should leave her alone for a while and let her work it out for herself."

Jessie Rose balled her hand into a fist and held it to her chest and peered at her husband through tightened lids. "Elder, I got me a feelin' about this and I don't like it. I been tryin' to call her back since yesterday and I don't get nothin' but a busy signal. I tried callin' late last night and all I got was some more of the same. This mornin' she supposed to come and take me to Helen's to get my hair done and she ain't showed up. You tell me you ain't worried?"

"Jessie..." Elderiah said, still poised over the ham, "When she moved out you said you wasn't gonna interfere. Her phone probably off the hook or somethin'."

"Elder this ain't no interferin'. This here is worryin', and for a good reason too! If there ain't somethin' wrong, then how come the phone ain't on the hook. What if she...Elder, she ain't missed picking me up for my hair appointment because her telephone is off the hook."

Elderiah Bowman, strong and dark-skinned, was a deacon in the church and well known among his friends. He was a wise man and knew his wife had hit upon a point he couldn't argue. He nodded his head and went back to cutting the bacon.

"Elder! Don't cut that bacon so thick!" She snapped, anxiously waiting for his answer.

Elderiah stopped his cut midway through the ham and lay the knife on the cutting board. Examining his thoughts one last time, he turned to Jessie, who was close to exploding. "All right Jess, get yo' coat."

Jessie pulled herself up the high stepboard of the big dump truck with "BOWMAN DISPOSAL" written on the side of its door as if she were thirty years younger than her seventy. She sat straight-backed, arm out-stretched holding the dash, with her right foot pressing the imaginary brake peddle. She had never learned to drive and was very uncomfortable in cars. This was only the second time in ten years she had actually ridden in the truck.

The old red truck ground to a full stop at the corner of Evergreen Avenue. As was his habit, Elderiah let the smaller and faster vehicles go first, not wanting them to be held up in a line that always formed behind the slower work truck.

Jessie breathed a sigh and shouted over the noise of the straining gears. "Elder, can't you make this thing go no faster just this once?" He looked back at her, raised his shoulders and motioned to the cars behind him. Jessie grunted and turned her head.

Heavy on the road, the truck rumbled down the steep hill, past Jimmy Lee's Best Fill, over the stone bridge and into the Hollow.

When they had arrived in front of the correct building, Elderiah parked the truck in an empty space next to the brown '53 Chevy he had given his daughter. He scrambled around to the other side just in time to help his wife jump down from her perch on the step-board. Her hand was visibly trembling, her eyes clouded and teary.

At the top of the second flight of stairs and out of breath, Jessie released her husband's arm and made her way to the green door that read 5509. She knocked hard three times, waited, and when there was no response she knocked three more times harder than the first.

"Vivian!"

She paused with her ear to the door, but there were no sounds on the other side of the green metal. "Vivian, can you hear me?" She pressed close to the door with her head turned to the side. But still she heard nothing. "Elder, we got to do somethin'. I know she's in there. Vivian!" The sound of Jessie hammering the plated door echoed through the stairwell. "I know she's in there with the baby. I can feel it. Elderiah Bowman! Where you goin' at a time like this!"

"I'm goin' to get the key from the super. Knock on that other door and see if that lady we met when Viv moved down here is home. Maybe she keeps a key for her." His words echoed up the stairwell as the foyer door banged shut.

Fortified by the notion that they were doing something that would help them get to the other side, she wiped her face and tapped number 5508.

Mrs. Pretchet answered her door. She was a white-haired widow of many years. She wore a black dress with small white polka-dots, cream colored stockings, and, unlike Jessie Rose, she appeared the full extent of the seven decades she had spent on the "Lord's earth, by God's grace."

Mrs. Pretchet had looked through the peep hole of her apartment door when she had heard all the commotion in the hallway. When she saw Jessie Rose and her husband, whom she had met and identified with as people from the South and old times, she immediately began to fumble with the many locks on her door.

Jessie had only knocked one time before the door swung open. "Hello, Mrs. Pretchet, you remember…"

"Yes certainly. You're Mrs. Bowman, Vivian's mother," she said speaking calmly and in low soothing tones.

"Somethin' is wrong with Vivian and we can't get her to open the door. Did she leave a key with you?"

"Yes she did at one point, but one day the oldest boy locked himself out and I gave it to him and never got it back."

Jessie clenched her eyes and bit her lip to hold the tears back and returned to the green door.

"Mrs. Bowman, I don't mean to upset you, but there was quite a gathering of people there last night."

"Vivian, open this door!" Jessie Rose banged the metal door with a closed fist. "Little Von, this is Grandma. Are you in there? Come and open the door, baby."

Little Von awoke before his mother, rubbed his eyes and looked around the room. Thick black clouds took the place of the sun that usually showed through the window and he felt cool in his underwear. He missed the sun's warming rays on his skin. He wondered if it was still night. First he heard only rain against the window, but then another, but more distant sound.

"Vivian, can you hear me? Are you all right in there?" Jessie stopped and listened to the silence and the storm gathering force outside. Mrs. Pretchet could feel the pain that Jessie Rose was living. Her first husband had died from mustard gas poisoning during World War One. In 1930, her son had been lynched by an unreasoning Alabama mob. Mrs. Pretchet's sorrow was long felt. She relived it now watching Jessie Rose trying to reach her daughter.

A flash of light lit the gray and dank hallway as Jessie pounded with red hands. "Vivian, please open this door. Little Von, this is Grand…"

Little Von recognized his grandmother's voice and began shaking his mother. "Momma, it's Grandma Jessie. She at the door." He moved toward the edge of the bed, but Vivian, still drunk and very close to being sick, reached out and grabbed him. She pulled him close and slid her hand over his mouth. Tears filled her eyes. She wanted to hold her ears to block out the sound, but she dared not free her hand. "Go away, Momma." she cried in a whimper. "I don't want you to see me like this." Little Von squirmed to get away but Vivian held him still.

"Vivian, please open this door right now or I'm gonna get somebody to open it." Jessie said, in a voice approaching panic.

Mrs. Pretchet grabbed Jessie by the shoulders to calm her, slowly pulling her back from the door. "Mrs. Bowman, let me try."

She spoke precisely and rapped the door vigorously with the back of her knuckles. "Vivy? Viv, this is Mrs. Pretchet next door. Are you in there, honey?" Her own eyes glazed over as the memory of her own son, neck broken, head cocked to the side, his body swinging limply, bore down upon her. One mother's child was not different from another's. It was her pain as well as Jessie Rose Bowman's.

Tears ran from Little Von's eyes over his mother's hands as her grip grew tighter. He began to writhe frantically. Thunder punctuated the pounding noise that came from the other end of the hall.

"Mrs. Bowman, I think I heard something like crying." Both ladies stood absolutely quiet listening, and then each began to pick up the sporadic child-like sounds. Jessie hammered the door with new zeal. *"Vivian, come and open this door! Right now—you hear me!"*

Little Von, struggling to breathe, began screaming on the inside of his mother's hand. He kicked away the cover and tried to force the lower half of his body over the side of the bed. His mother pulled him back. His breath came only in small hissing wisps between the fingers. Vivian, still drunk from the night before, held him tighter. Little Von continued to struggle. He had to get away, he thought, had to get to Grandma Jessie for both of them.

Gerry Sanitoni ran up the stairs with Elderiah close behind. Both men were rain soaked by the time they reached the building, and out of breath when they reached 5509.

"Viv, this is Gerry," he said, sedately. "Can you open the door for me, babe? Listen Viv, your mother is here and she is very upset. Why don't you open the door and let her know that you're all right?"

As he talked, he jiggled keys around a large ring, trying one and then the other in the lock. After trying each key, he swiped long strands of dark wet hair back across his bald spot.

Vivian tightened her grip over the small child's face. Crying loudly, she was no longer conscious of what she was doing. She didn't realize that her hand sealed the air from her son's nose.

Little Von kicked wildly as her grip grew tighter. Frantic and unable to breathe, the child began to urinate. The wetness pooled around the outline of Vivian's body shocking and sobering her. She looked down at her struggling son. Horrified, she released him and wept.

Little Von moved from the bed as lightning flashed throughout the small room. It was as if the sun itself had momentarily come into the tiny cubicle. He began to walk slowly toward the door at the end of the hall.

"Little Von, come open the door. This is Grandpa. Come on now you can do it."

Gerry Sanitoni slid another of the master keys into the lock and held his breath. The lock gave way with a pop. "This is it' folks." Gerry pulled the key away and pushed the door open. It came to a sudden stop as it reached the end of the chain. Little Von shrieked in the dark hallway as he heard the door bang against the chain.

"Little Von, this is Grandpa. I'm gonna shut the door and you take the chain down."

The sound of his grandfather's voice was calming and reassuring. In a burst of confidence, he ran through the darkness into the kitchen to drag one of the chairs from the table to the door. Lightning lit the room again. He froze for a second waiting for the rumble of the thunder to pass. At the other end of the hall his mother's sobbing reached him like endless waves rushing to the shore. With only a glance toward her bedroom, he returned to his work.

"Come on boy!" Elderiah said, trying to visualize the small child's hands working the catch. "Show your grandpa how you can work that chain."

The chain fell free.

Elderiah was the first through the door. He grabbed the wet-bottomed child with one hand, reaching for the wall light switch at the same time. "There now, little man, Grandma and Grandpa here now," he said, slowly patting the boy's back to calm him. "You don't have to..." Elderiah stopped in the middle of his sentence, deciding that it might be best to let the child cry as long as he needed to. He pulled Little Von's head close up under his chin. Little Von cried. The song of his gasping and crying was unbroken. He was released by the smell of his Grandfather, a scent of shaving lather mixed with the starch that Jessie Rose ironed into his shirt collars. It was a small part of the panorama of smells that came with the security of the big white house on Wooden Street.

Jessie Rose looked around. The air was stale with liquor and cigarette smoke. Bottles and overflowing ash trays lay everywhere. With a pained look, Jessie made her way to her daughter's room at the end of the hall.

She saw Vivian crumpled into a sobbing ball on the bed. Her body trembled as Jessie pulled her close.

"Oh Momma," she cried making no attempt to hold back the tears. "I was doing so well...so well. I don't want you to think of me this way."

"Honey, don't worry about that. You all right now. I'm here wit you."

Sitting on the edge of the bed, Jessie held her daughter for a long time. There was no need for any words. Beyond all else they were mother and daughter.

8

Robin walked down Speedwell Avenue. He followed the Reed Street hill down to Fredrick Douglass Drive and the Building Authority that doubled as a daycare center, down to Building Six where he waited every day for Little Von. As he waited, Art Taggart showed up.

Art Taggart had always been the smartest black student in every school he had attended. Perhaps the smartest student black or white, but comparisons were avoided. Even with great intelligence, Art Taggart had a yoke to bear. He had been declared legally blind in the fourth grade. His vision was corrected by wearing triple-thick glasses which made his eyes large and disproportionate to the rest of his face. Nothing corrected the constant teasing by the other kids who called him "goggle face", "telescopic man", and "nigga in a fish bowl." Robin never teased him. Art Taggart had been Robin's best friend even before elementary school.

"Eh Rob, you skip today?" Art laughed, seeing that Robin was dressed for school, but hadn't been seen all day.

"Hey man, I went, but I just couldn't make it to any of my classes. I tried, but..." Robin shrugged his shoulders.

"Yeah man, I heard you had a big night with Scootch and everybody Friday night. And then there was a party at your place that ended pretty heavy with your Grandmother showin' up or somethin'."

"No man it wasn't quite like that. Is that what you heard?"

"Something like that. It ain't all over school or nothing, but Benny was telling me all this stuff in the hall between classes. I was trying to get to class so I didn't get it straight. You know I don't like Scab anyway."

"Yeah, but..." Robin looked up the hill to the Housing Authority where he saw Gerry Sanitoni, who had asked him earlier how his mom was getting on. Arthur looked back over his shoulder to see what Robin was looking at.

Robin wondered how it had gotten to Benny, and then he remembered Benny and Charlene together in the hall. The party was probably going full tilt when Charlene came home. "...Yeah ..." Robin continued, "but they came the next day when they couldn't get my mother on the phone. I wasn't even there. I had gone to work already." Art laughed. "You went to work? Wasn't there a lot of thunder and lightning and shit on Saturday?"

"Yeah, lots of 'and shit' like lightning, and me running around with those metal carts. Tell ya man, my boss up there is an ass. If I didn't need the money to help out, I'd quit."

"Was your mom…" Arthur paused. "Was she drinking?"

"No man, she was just sick from the night before."

"I didn't mean to say that your mom was a alcoholic or nothing like that."

"I know man. I don't think she is. She doesn't seem to drink any more than the rest of her friends. It just seems to affect her more. I mean she's not like Cootie or Sara Leaman." Arthur laughed. "Yeah, Sara gettin' like Cootie."

"Robin sighed. "I don't know man, I just couldn't handle school today."

"Oh," Art said, looking at the Housing Authority building. "You here to pick up your brother, huh?" Robin nodded. Arthur laughed. "Don't give me that bull, Thompson. I didn't come down with yesterday's rain."

"Yeah." Robin said, in a matter-of-fact tone. "I always pick him up after school. Why you laughin'?"

Arthur searched his face. "Oh, I thought you were here hawkin' on Joleena."

Robin looked hard at his friend trying to understand how Joleena, of all people, had come into the conversation. Did everybody know about that too? "Whattya talkin' about?"

Arthur smirked. "Get off it, man. Everybody knows Joleena and her mother works there." Arthur punched Robin in the arm. "See you later, Slick. I'm late for my eye appointment." Arthur left Robin staring up the hill with his mouth open, trying to finish his sentence. Robin had always half paid attention to Little Von and his jabbering about what he had done everyday—what games they played, who cried etc. Somehow he had missed this subtle thread woven in the fabric of his little brother's meandering stories.

For the first time since he had arrived in the projects and had been picking up his brother after school, Robin walked up the steep stairs leading to the Housing Authority with curiosity and a bouncy step.

Little Von's face lit up into a big smile when he saw his brother's unexpected shape towering across the floor. "Rob!" he said, racing across the toy scattered room. "What you doin' here? How come you not waitin' down the hill like you always do?"

Robin scanned the room from wall to wall while he talked. "Oh, I just thought I'd come up and see if you needed any help carrying your stuff," he said putting his hand on his little brother's head without looking down at him. "So...a...how was school today?" He took a couple of steps backward and looked around, but there was still no sight of any Clearys, Miss or Mrs.

Little Von had been trying to explain exactly what he had been doing when he was abruptly cut off.

"Von, where's Miss Cleary?" He said, gazing down the hall.

"...What?" Little Von said, startled.

"Where's your teacher? You know what's her name a...a...a Miss...what's her name?"

"Who? My teacher?" Little Von, asked puzzled.

"Yeah."

"Oh there she is."

Robin's head snapped down a long hall to a small closet off to one side.

From an open door, Robin saw someone bending over tugging away at some item buried in the closet's bottom. He ran down to offer his assistance.

"Can I help you?"

The beautiful, but middle-age face of Mrs. Anna Cleary sprang from the closet with a small scream. "Oh, please forgive me squeaking like a little church mouse, but I didn't know anyone was standing there."

Robin marveled at the mature likeness of Joleena. "I'm sorry, Mrs. Cleary. I didn't mean to scare you. My little brother said you needed some help."

Little Von looked up puzzled. "No I...ouch!" he was silenced before he was finished.

"Oh, thank you. That's so nice of you to offer. You're Von's older brother, Robin. Von talks so much about you, but we haven't seen you since he started here."

"Yes ma'am, I know. He asked me to wait for him at the bottom of the hill so his friends wouldn't tease him about being picked up."

Little Von, who could care less about what his friends thought, wrinkled his nose and eyebrows. "No I ...ouch." He pushed his brother's hand off the crest of his shoulder.

Robin pulled the old Packwood typewriter from the bottom of the closet trying to make its awesome weight seem like no problem.

"If you could just bring that to the front for me, I would really appreciate it."

The machine was incredibly old and heavy. Robin lugged it to the front desk and set it down as gently as possible.

"Thank you so much. As you can imagine, I hate pulling that beast out, but we can't wait till the Housing Authority fixes the other one so..."

Robin, exhausted and red-faced, smiled and backed away. He took a deep breath and pulled Little Von by the arm through the door.

Outside, Little Von looked up grimacing again. "Robin, how come you told Mrs. Cleary that I told you..."

"Von! You almost blew it man."

"Blew what, Robin?"

Wiping the sweat from his forehead with a handkerchief, Robin looked away from his little brother laughing. "Never mind."

"Tell me, Robin, what did I almost blew?"

"Naa."

"Aw Robin."

"Never mind pea-nut head, bul-let nose, almost-died-when I smelled-your-toes."

They ran the rest of the way down the hill to Building Five, Robin making it a game by staying just within an arm's distance. Robin pulled the heavy foyer door and Little Von ran past to the stairs pulling himself along the rail, and dragging his feet to make them hiss on each step in rhythm as he tried to repeat the new rhyme, "Bul-let head pea-nut..."

At the top of the stairs, squirming from one foot to the other, Little Von waited for his brother to open the apartment door. "Hurry up, Rob. You a teenager and can't open a door yet."

Robin stopped jiggling the lock just long enough to look menacingly at Little Von who stood with his legs crossed. As the latch slapped back, Little Von bolted down the hall to the small bathroom without waiting.

Robin looked at the key sternly. He pulled it hard to the left until he felt the metal begin to give and fold to one side. He carefully bent it back into form. He waited and grabbed it again. Quickly and without warning it slipped free. Robin frowned at the key for having come free without having given him a clue as to what he had done to make it happen.

In the kitchen, he opened the refrigerator door and stared at the barren shelves. He took out the carton of milk and carefully shook it to feel its weight. He drank what was left. He grabbed a jar of peanut butter with its sides nearly scraped clean, the jelly, and a bag of bread with one regular slice and two heels. This was how it was when his mother drank. He wondered when she'd shop again. He wondered when she would be able to shop again.

Since he lived in the projects, he had learned to adjust to his mother's drinking and non-drinking periods. When she was sober, he thought about things like Joleena or what it would be like when he got his first car, or when he would get anything more than a kiss. When she was drinking, he thought about getting Little Von breakfast, lunch, and dinner, getting his teeth brushed, getting him in and out of baths, what time he should be getting him in bed, and the drudgery of getting clean clothes for the both of them.

Then there were other, more pressing responsibilities, like the bills. Should he wait on the new ones, or pay the long overdue ones now with his own money from his job at the supermarket? There were always some of both. Should he shop? Then there was the awkwardness of the phone. What should he tell callers? When should he tell them to call back? What time he had to himself, he spent wondering—worrying if he'd done it all right.

He stood motionless in front of the open refrigerator. His heart quickened its pace as he began to mentally count the other warning signals besides the empty refrigerator. The dishes were piled from one end of the sink to the other. His mother had taken the savings book from its secret hiding place before pay day. He tried to remember if there had been verbal signs he had missed like: "Wait in the car, I'll be right back." Robin thought about the many times he had waited. He wondered what was the longest period of time kids waited in cars while their parents drank in bars. Robin looked at the bread lying on the counter. One of the edges had turned green. He pinched it off and threw it into the trash.

He thought about how much he hated it when his mother left the apartment saying, "Rob, watch Little Von. I'll be back in awhile." *Awhile.* It gave him a chill. How long is awhile? Is it the time it takes to go to the cleaners and back? Or is it the time it takes to cruise the Bahamas? He wondered where the Bahamas were and thought he'd like to be there now. Sometimes things would be completely normal for weeks, and then, without warning, she simply didn't come home.

Robin never waited for a full binge. When he saw the signs he began to gear up, like a runner in a relay race who begins to jog with his hand outstretched behind him waiting to take the responsibility of the baton. He looked about one last time hoping to find a full jar of peanut butter that he had perhaps overlooked. He gave up. When he couldn't find a clean knife in the drawer, it made him think about Lillian.

At times she had been more a mother than a sister. Two years older than he, she fought his fights on the playgrounds at school, cooked, kept the house immaculately clean, and still managed to bring home A's on her report card. How could she have done all of it just like it was the normal thing to do? That had been before they had to move in with Jessie Rose.

"Hey Von!" he yelled to the back of the apartment. "You want half a peanut butter and jelly sandwich?" No sound came from the bedroom. Robin laughed as the threw the knife into the sink. Normally the silence meant the beginning of a "come and find me" game. He grabbed the sandwich and started down the hall.

In the closet of the bedroom, Little Von sat on a pile of dirty sheets striking matches one-by-one excitedly watching the flame burn down toward his finger. When he felt the heat, he shook the burning matches hard three times and threw them, more concerned about his nearly-singed finger than where the smoking matches had landed.

Robin crept down the long hall slowly, purposely stepping heavily on the squeakiest floorboards to build anxiety and excitement. "I am a tiger..." he said, slowly and deliberately growling each word from the narrow of his throat, "...and I like to eat little boys for my dinner."

Little Von squealed as Robin ripped back the curtain that substituted for the closet door. "Don't eat me, Mr. Tiger!" he cried, kicking wildly with his eyes closed. Robin pulled the curtain back and immediately smelled sulphur and burning cloth.

"Von! What the hell are you doin' in there playin' with matches, man?"

He grabbed Little Von by the arms, jerking him out of the closet. Robin was petrified that he might be sitting on a pile of sheets and clothing ready to burst into flame. Little brown spots were visible all over the crumpled sheets. "Damn, Von, look at this!" He was on his knees shaking out each sheet separately sending spent matches flying in every direction. Satisfied that the smoldering areas were no longer alive, he turned to his brother. Little Von huddled, unmoving, on the bed.

"Jesus Christ, Von! Do you know what could have happened? You could have burned the whole place down." He turned one last corner before flopping down on the bed, elbows on his knees, head in his hands. He could feel his heart pounding in his chest. Prickly heat rose along his spine and over his face. He took a deep breath and then another. "Von, never play with matches, man! Never, never, never!" As he finished the sentence he looked around and saw Little Von still in the exact position he had landed when he had flung him from the closet. He looked scared and pathetic and for a moment Robin thought he saw himself as a child.

"Come here, Von. It's okay. The sheets are okay now." Taking him by the shoulders, Robin pulled Little Von close and wrapped his arms around his small frame. He listened to the broken rhythm of his breathing. "Where's Lillian now?" he thought to himself. Robin was sure she would know the perfect thing to say at a time like this.

Little Von sobbed. "I'm sorry, Robin, I didn't mean to set the sheets on fire."

"It's okay, Von. I know you didn't mean to do it."

"I didn't know," he sobbed.

"Listen, man. Would you sit in front of Kresge's uptown and play with matches in front of God and everybody?"

Little Von wiped his eyes with the sleeve of his shirt and looked back at his brother, puzzled. "Huh?"

"Never mind," Robin smiled. He hugged him again to reassure him that all was well. Suddenly his own eyes began to mist over. Robin had not cried very often since his mother and father had separated, but now he wanted to. He wanted someone to put their arms around him and tell him that all would be well.

Robin sat with Little Von on the edge of the bed, sharing the peanut butter and jelly sandwich and telling stories.

"Yeah man. One time before we all lived with Grandma, when we used to live at the deadend of Wooden Street, Dad told me to go down and burn a pile of old rags that had been lying around the basement for a long time. I was about ten and you was just about one, I think. Things were really hard then. Mom was workin', Dad was workin', and although everybody was always workin', seems like there was never any money. I kept forgetting to burn the rags and one day Dad went down into the basement and saw 'em still there. Man he got so mad." Robin began to shake his head slowly from side to side as the memory returned. For a moment he wished he had left the memory dormant.

"Did you get a beatin' man?" Little Von was engrossed, forgetting about the sheets in the closet.

"No..." Robin said, ending his voice on an upswing. "At that house the washing machine was in the basement and Mommy had thrown all the sheets next to the pile of rags."

"Ooooh nooo. you didn't, did you?"

"Well, Mommy had left them all balled up in a pile and it looked just like the other pile; I thought they were just two piles of rags—so..." Robin raised his eye brows and nodded. "I open the furnace door and threw them in."

"Oooh mannnnn, you didn't!"

"Yup. Then I went over to Lafayette to play until dinner. When I got back, I knew something was wrong, I mean real wrong. When I came in the door nobody said anything to me. Mom and Lillian just looked at me like I had polio in the face or something."

"You get a beatin' then?"

"Worse."

Little Von's mind went into light speed trying to find some action that would actually be worse, but his curiosity was too great. "What?"

"Man, Dad was so mad that he just screamed at me for about twenty minutes before I finally figured out what I had done.

Then he just walked away."

"You get a beatin' later."

"Nope. He didn't hit me, ground me, or anything. Actually I wished he had, because I figured he was just too mad to do it then, but I was sure he would get around to it sooner or later. He never did." Little Von looked surprised as Robin continued laughing. "Man I was afraid to even look at Dad for about a year after that." They laughed until tears ran down the side of their cheeks. Robin hit him in the face with a pillow and started a pillow fight.

When exhaustion brought an end to the romping, Robin lay back on his bed with his feet draped over the side and his head against the wall. Little Von pulled an old broken steam engine from under the bed and began to push it across the bedspread making chugging sounds.

Robin's thoughts ran back and forth over the resemblance of Joleena and her mother, and what had occurred at the daycare center. Suddenly he sat up straight and smiled.

"Von. Guess what?"

"Ch ch ch…What?… ch chc…"

"Naa. I better not tell you."

"What? Tell me." Little Von was excited, and let the train fall over on its side. He crawled across the top of the bed and sat next to his brother. "What?"

"Naa, I better not tell you, man, cause it's a secret." Robin drew the trap tighter. He looked away, staring up at the ceiling and beyond.

"A secret? What kind of secret?"

"Well, it's… naa, I better not," he said, still looking up. "This is big kid stuff, man, and you might spill it."

"Uh uh man! I won't tell Mom or anybody. Promise!"

"You promise?" Robin's face became serious. "Promise promise?"

"Promise promise. If I do, you can have my ice cream the next time we have it."

"Well, I don't know."

"The next two times we have it?" he said painfully, pleading.

"Hmm, well, okay. Wait a minute." Robin got up and closed the door. On the way back to the bed, he kicked the dirty and newly-spotted sheets beneath the closet drape and smiled at his little brother. Little Von looked like a cork about to explode out of a champagne bottle. Robin sat on the bed and rolled over on his side. "Von, this is a secret plan," he said in a lowered voice. "You better not tell anybody or else you'll mess up everything."

"Promise prom…"

"Yeah yeah, okay okay. Look. Friday, when it's time to come home, ask Joleena…"

"You mean Leeny?"

Robin paused, realizing that his baby brother had been far more intimate with Joleena than he. "Yeah, Leeny. Ask her to walk you home because your brother is going to be late."

"Late? How come? Where you gonna be?"

"I'm gonna be right here."

"What? How come you can't pick me up then? Why should I ask Leeny to…"

"Von! Forget it man. I ain't telling you cause you gonna blow the whole thing. Just forget it."

"Okay okay okay, I'll ask her."

"Good."

"But…"

"Von!"

"Okay, okay."

"All right. Then you bring her up here."

"How am I gonna do that? How we gonna get in?"

"I'll leave the key under Mrs. Pretchet's mat next door."

"How come you don't leave it under our mat?"

"Cause we don't have a mat, dummy!"

"Oh. Well, what about the other two locks on the inside of the door?"

"Don't worry about that. I'll leave them off."

"Ain't it gonna look funny when I open the door and you standin' in here?"

"No man. I'll just say I got back early and I was just on the way to pick you up."

"Will that be like tellin' a lie?"

"Naa. Two out of three of us will know the truth so that makes it all right."

"Rob, I better ask Mom first."

"VON! THIS IS A SECRET PLAN!" Robin closed his eyes and put his hand over his forehead feeling like he had just slit his own throat. "You can't tell anybody. Remember that. Promise

promise, or I get all your ice cream till you're twenty-five."

"Oh yeah, I forgot."

Suddenly the expression on Little Von's face became pained. He spoke just above a whisper. "Robin. What if Mommy starts, you know what, again?

A horrible scene flashed in Robin's mind: It's three-thirty, and he hears two sets of footsteps stop outside the door. Just as he's about to open it, he hears another set stop as well. Finally, he decides to open the door. All three of them are standing there looking at him. There's Joleena, tight sweater accentuating her curves, her knees showing beneath the edge of her dress. Little Von is on his hands and knees unable to find the key under Mrs. Pretchet's mat shouting "Here, Rob? Here, Rob?" And his mother, swaying slightly, her hair tied down with a scarf, her breath heavy with the smell of whiskey. She looks at him and mumbles something, but Robin can't understand. He comes closer to hear better and it sounds something like "Cre..Cr...Cress... Kresge's..".

"Robin!" Little Von said, interrupting the flow of nightmarish images, repeating himself. "What if Mommy...?"

Robin placed his hand on his brother's head and looked at him for a long moment, straight in the eyes, with all the strength he could muster. Just as he was about to speak, they heard the horn on the old Chevy and recognized his mother's voice, two stories below.

"Robin. Von. Come down and help me with the groceries."

"Von..." he started with a dry laugh. "Don't worry about it. She's gonna be all right. She has groceries."

Little Von's face went from concern into a huge smile. He held his hand out to his older brother, friend, and spoke with confidence: "The plan." Robin slapped his hand. "Promise promise."

9

A<small>T DINNER, THE TWO BOYS KEPT</small> a suspicious silence. Vivian looked at one, and then the other. Robin had been sitting at the table eating with his mouth closed, chewing slowly and soundlessly. She hadn't once had to tell him to keep his elbows off the table, or to sit up straight. Also, Little Von attacked his dinner with vigor, not talking more than drinking, not drinking more than eating, and, oddly, not complaining about the long green spears of asparagus lying on the side of his plate. Normally he called them slimy.

"Robin! What's going on between you two?"

"Nothin', Mom. Just hungry." He had been expecting something and tried to appear startled. "Yeah, just hungry, Mom." Little Von repeated stirring the small pool of butter in the mashed potatoes. Robin looked at Little Von and winked.

A<small>rthur</small> Taggart was cleaning his glasses with the bottom of his shirt when Robin appeared and dropped a pile of books on the floor in front of his locker.

"A.T., how you doin' man?" Robin asked, trying to pry his door open.

"Real good." Arthur carefully fitted his glasses around the backs of his ears as if they were made of gold.

Robin threw his books inside his locker. "All right man," he slammed his locker twice in a row, but each time it opened quickly as soon as he removed his hand from the handle. "Hey, your eyes getting any better?" He slammed it hard again. It clicked and swung obstinately open.

"No," Arthur said, brushing little bits of notebook paper from the bottom of his locker into his hand.

Robin stopped fiddling with the door. "Then why you say you're doin' real good?"

Arthur slowly straightened up, his eyes looking three times their normal size behind the glasses, and smiled. "They ain't getting any worse." He reached in front of Robin and closed his locker, holding it firmly until it clicked. "I'm always scared they'll get worse. They didn't." Both boys stood still, staring at the door, Robin with expectation, Arthur with confidence. When the locker remained closed, Robin opened and closed it for himself using Arthur's technique. "Hmm. Hey man, thanks a lot."

"Well, today is Friday. The big day." Arthur said without enthusiasm.

"Yup. Hopefully my little brother won't blow it."

Arthur took a small brown paper bag and the books he needed for the weekend from the perfectly organized shelf of his own locker. "Rob, you sure Joleena is worth all this? I'm not puttin' Joleena down or anything, but..."

"A.T..." Robin paused as Sherl Tubbs walked by. She exaggerated her walk when she noticed Robin and Art watching. After Joleena, Sherl would be everyone's next choice. In fact, she had been chosen by many guys. Unfortunately few of them kept their promise to keep it secret.

Robin turned back to Art. Robin gave a little smile and raised the corner of his eye. "You ain't that blind are you? She's worth it."

Art didn't try to hide his disappointment. "And if that doesn't work out, I guess Sherl Tubbs is next, huh?"

"It's a thought."

"Even though she has the I.Q of a Belgian waffle?"

"Who?" Robin frowned. "Joleena?"

"No. Sherl."

Robin looked confused. "What?"

"Forget it." Frustrated, Art looked down the hall. It was jammed with kids going to classes. "Rob, even if this does work out, which I doubt, how long do think it will last with everybody constantly hitting on Joleena?"

"A-looong-tiiiiime. Look Arthur. It'll work out. I got it all planned. When Little Von brings her up, I just happen to be standing there with a glass of milk, a fresh pack of Fig Newtons, her favorites, Johnny Mathis is on the box, and I invite her in..." Robin smiled and shrugged his shoulders.

Arthur shrugged his in return. "Voila."

"Yeah. No sweat. I'll call you and fill you in on all the gory details. Hey man, did you bring that cologne?"

Arthur handed him the brown paper bag and Robin stuck it in his locker.

On the way home Robin was going over his plan when the brand new Chevy Impala came to a stop beside him. Benny sat behind the wheel looking comfortable.

"Ey, Thompson! What's happenin', man?"

Robin leaned down and looked into the vehicle. Benny was rocking the wheel back and forth with one finger. "Oh man, power steering and everything."

"Hey man, can you dig this. Come on get in, man. I'll buzz you home."

Robin got in and carefully placed the bag so the cologne would stay right side up. "This is razor sharp, man. It even smells new."

Benny was purposely silent, giving Robin time to look over the color, chrome, and the space-age instrument panel. Robin couldn't help but admire the way Benny drove with one hand and tapped the bottom of a cigarette package on the dash with the other. Several ends lifted to the opening. He took one of the cigarettes from the package with his lips, lit it with the lighter and took a long slow draw. The car filled with smoke.

"Where you going, Thompson? You gotta catch your little brother, man?" Benny tapped the pack again and held it out to Robin.

"Yeah," Robin said, dragging the word out to make it sound like a burden. Robin hated cigarettes and the smell of smoke. Worse he didn't want to appear uncool. He took one of the cigarettes from the pack and began to search the panel for the lighter. "Say, man, who's ride is this?"

"It's my old man's. He's...a...in town from L.A. for a couple a days on vacation."

"He must have some kind of heavy job to handle this. I thought you said he lived in Baltimore or some place like that."

"A...well he moved when he got a...hot job offer out in L.A. about six months ago." Benny stumbled to cover the previous lie with a new one. "He's the manager of some big plant out there." Benny whipped the wheel and stepped on the gas, using speed and the sway to bring Robin's attention back to the car.

"Ey!" Robin said as the car lurched forward and forced him back into the seat. He pulled out the lighter and held it to the end of his cigarette. He took a long draw, as Benny had done, hoping he wouldn't choke when the smoke filled his lungs, but there was no smoke, only tobacco flavored air and little bits of tobacco on the end of his tongue.

"Ey man, is it red?"

"Huh?" Robin said, trying to spit the raw tobacco out of his mouth.

"Look on the end of the lighter, man. If it ain't red, it ain't hot."

"Oh yeah, right." Robin pushed the lighter back into the dash and wondered if it would click, or something similar, when he noticed Benny pulling over to the curve across from the Housing Authority. "Hey man, not here, Building Five! I got to stop home first."

Benny swerved back into the lane and in less than a minute was in front of the brick facade of Building Five. The lighter clicked as they came to a stop.

"Well, hey man, I think I'll save this for later when I can enjoy it." Robin was grateful for the excuse. "Eh, man, thanks for the ride."

"It's cool, man. I'll check you later."

Robin climbed out of the car, holding the cologne, and positioned himself carefully to watch and listen to the shiny new Chevy as it pulled away from the curb. He had a funny feeling. He'd always gotten it when something didn't fit or jive just right. Now was no exception. He tried to remember a past coversation he had had with Benny as he watched the car speed around the corner. Had he said L.A. or Baltimore? Thoughts of his own plan made it difficult to concentrate. He tossed the cigarette into a nearby garbage can and began to smile.

Upstairs, Robin stood back from the door in total disbelief. He had placed the key in the door, turned it, and the lock had opened without a moment's hesitation. Still expecting trouble getting the key from the door, he looked at his watch and saw that he had twenty minutes before Little Von and Joleena arrived—he hoped. He took a deep breath and pulled slowly. It came out smoothly. Astonished, he placed the key under Mrs. Pretchet's mat as he had said he would.

Once inside, he plugged in the iron to save waiting for it to heat up later, made up a plate of sandwiches with a fresh jar of peanut butter, and spread some Fig Newtons domino style around the outside of the plate. He looked at his watch, fifteen minutes to go.

On the way down the hall, he stopped in his mother's room

took a clean shirt from the clothes basket. He took it to the bathroom where he dampened it, rolled it into a ball and set it on the corner of the tub. After washing, he smeared the pasty deodorant from the jar under his arms. He looked at his watch—ten minutes.

In the kitchen Robin finished ironing the shirt with a grin. His father had always stressed that he should be able to care for himself if the woman of the house went on strike. Of all the survival skills, Robin had mastered one with unlimited confidence: ironing. He glanced at his watch more relaxed when he saw that he was nearly done with a cushion of five minutes. Then he heard Little Von's voice outside the door.

Panicking, Robin grabbed the ironing board under one arm, without collapsing the legs, the shirt still stretched over its back. With his free hand he jerked the iron cord from the wall, snatched the iron and the bag with the cologne. With a crash, he rammed the sink, table, and several chairs with the ironing board legs before successfully getting it out of the kitchen. Robin could hear Little Von pounding on the door and calling his name.

In the back room he hastily pushed the board with its legs outstretched, between the two beds. Next, he shook out a handful of cologne knowing it was too much as it ran through his fingers, and splashed it on. Robin buttoned and re-buttoned his shirt twice before he got the buttons lined up with the right holes. Finally he lifted the lid of the record player and turned it on. The needle slid across seven selections of the Johnny Mathis record. On the second try it settled in the first grooves and made its way toward "Misty". There was a sudden burst of noise and Robin froze. He rolled his eyes toward the ceiling as he heard Little Von dragging Joleena down the hall.

Joleena hadn't minded walking Little Von home. She had seen Robin at school and hoped he would come into the daycare center but he never did. Many of the girls at school liked him. Joleena liked his quiet manner and thought him more polite and well-mannered than the other boys.

Little Von had pointed out their apartment to her numerous times. Today the boy's ambition equalled that of three his age. When they had reached the building he had grabbed her by the hand and excitedly began to tow her up the steps puffing and yelling, "Come on Leeny! We almost there."

In front of the door of 5509, he had immediately dropped to his knees and lifted the neighbor's mat to find the key. In his excitment he missed it. He stood with a frown slapping fine powdered dirt from beneath the mat off his hands. At that point, he had said curiously, "He messed up!" and began pounding on the door and yelling his brother's name.

Joleena began to get the picture. It angered her and amused her at the same time.

"Robin!" Little Von banged on the door. "She's here, she's here!" he said, forgetting himself.

Joleena noticed that the door moved slightly every time Little Von hit it. Reaching in front of him, she pushed it gently and stood back as it swung open. Doing what she could to slow his progress, they had passed the kitchen and the living room before Robin appeared around the corner at the end of the hall, tucking in the end of his shirt tails.

"Rob, she's here! I did it and I didn't tell nobody either!" Little Von was feeling very proud of himself. Joleena watched the two of them. It seemed they were acting out a comedy and a tragedy all at once. She even managed to feel some sympathy for Robin, whose performance, because of the tremble in his voice, was less than convincing.

"Ey a..a..a Von. What you doin' home so early? Hi Joleena. What you doin' here? Did he get you to walk him down here?"

"Mmm hmm," Joleena said smiling, watching Little Von still bursting at the seams over his accomplishment.

"Rob! What you doin'? What you mean what she doin' here? The plan!" Robin had never said that Joleena wasn't suppose to know. Little Von pointed back over his shoulder and flashed his eyebrows up and down.

As the redness rose, Robin's freckles began to disappear. "Plan? Von! What plan are you talking about?" He tried to signal his brother to shut up with his eyes and smile at Joleena at the same time. "Didn't I tell you I'd be there a few minutes late?"

Little Von turned to Joleena and smiled. "Ahhh, now he remembers."

"Von!" Robin cried sternly, helplessly. "What are you talking about!"

Frustrated, but still sure he had done his part right, Little

Von fought to get his brother back on track. "Robin! The Plan! You know, two out of three big-kid stuff, member?" He leaned closer to his brother and sniffed the air around him. "What smells?" Crinkling his nose, he sniffed in several directions to be sure the heavy scent wasn't coming from somewhere else. Then he leaned back to Robin.

"Von!" Robin said through his teeth, pushing Little Von away from him.

Joleena started laughing. She had noticed the Johnny Mathis record playing in the background and she thought it made a strange contrast to the scene she was watching. The record skipped and Johnny sang; *"Looook aaaaaaaat meloooook aaaaaaat meloooook...*

"Robin had Little Von by the shoulders when Joleena interrupted. "Excuse me," she said to the two brothers, who had almost seemed to forget she was there. "I think Johnny's stuck."

Both Robin and Little Von stopped and looked at Joleena, trying to figure out who Johnny was. She pointed down the hall and both boys pivoted slowly, wondering if it was possible that someone else had been in the apartment, watching from behind.

"Damn." Robin mumbled under his breath, wondering what else could possibly go wrong. Exasperated, Robin smiled at Joleena. "Excuse me for a minute." He took several steps down the hall and turned back to Little Von and rolled his finger up and down. The two vanished around the corner.

Robin grabbed Little Von by the shirt collar as he came into the bedroom. "Von..."

Little Von was puzzled by the look on Robin's face. He smiled. "I did good, huh, Rob!"

"Von! You blowin' it, man. It ain't over yet!"

"I got her up here just like you..."

Still holding Little Von by the collar, Robin pulled open the closet drapes where the burned sheets were. "Von, you ain't gonna get ice cream until you're twenty-five unless you walk down that hall and right out of the door."

Little Von looked at the sheets and wrinkled his face. "How long is that, Rob?"

"Von! It's almost forever!"

"Okay! Will I get my ice cream if I just go outside?" Robin's heart was pounding so hard he couldn't speak. Little Von knew it was best to leave. "Okay! Let me go."

"Bye, Leeny." Little Von said, leaving the apartment without looking left or right.

"Bye, Von," Joleena wondered what Robin's next move would be.

Robin stood waiting in the thick of a very uncomfortable silence waiting for his little brother to clear the door. He glanced at Joleena and their eyes met. They were the most beautiful eyes he had ever seen. They were wide and brown like a baby kitten's. His mouth was dry. He needed a strategy, but none came to him.

"Well, now that you're here, I guess I'll be going. I was afraid Von might be alone, but…" she smiled forcing Robin to speak before he really had anything to say.

"Well hey-a-listen…he probably just got a little confused— you know, something different from the regular routine. But normally he's pretty tough for a little kid. He'll be seven soon, you know?" Robin was glad to come to the end of his opening statement. It was impossible to talk and plan all at the same time.

Joleena just smiled and nodded. It was a knowing nod, well-calculated to put the ball back in Robin's court quickly. She opened her purse and unzipped one of several zippered compartments, and retrieved a pack of Juicy Fruit gum. She took her time opening the package, giving herself something to do and Robin plenty of time to speak. When he didn't, she gave him an extension by holding out a stick of gum to him. Finally, mercifully, she let him off the hook. "I like Johnny Mathis. This is a new one. May I see the cover?"

Stunned by her sudden interest, Robin stammered. "Huh? This one playing now? Yeah, 'Misty'—everybody's always singing it." Robin turned and coolly walked along the hall to the back bedroom. There, he turned up the stereo with one hand, and with the other wiped the moisture from his forehead with a handkerchief. When he returned to the hall, Joleena was no longer standing there. A tremendous wave of disappointment and embarrassment came over him as he realized that she had probably used the opportunity to slip out of the apartment. By Monday it would be all over school. Robin exhaled deeply and trudged the hall back to the living room. He slapped the wall lightly with the album cover in anger and wondered how he ever thought "a girl like Joleena, prettiest Black girl in Morristown High, would ever…"

But when he reached the end of the hall and walked into the living room, she was sitting quietly on the couch waiting for him.

"Joleena!"

"What?"

"Aaa...I...aa—here's the album cover." Two rounds down. Robin decided to take the bull by the horns for round three. "Say listen. I was just fixing some sandwiches and some Fig Newtons for a snack. There's plenty, would you like some?"

"Sure." Joleena began reading the Johnny Mathis album cover and humming along with the record.

"Whew!" Robin said as he stood in the kitchen unable to believe he had pulled it off so smoothly. He wanted to jump up and click his heels as he had seen Fred Astaire, Bo Jangles, and Hony Coles do on late-night movies. He caught himself, that wouldn't be cool. When he reentered the living room, Joleena smiled.

"I brought milk. I guessed, well I never thought to ask so if you want something else."

"No that's fine," she said.

Robin, not wanting to appear nervous, moved toward the couch in an unhurried manner. He grew more tense as he realized Joleena was sitting squarely in the middle of the couch. He would have to sit close to her no matter what side he chose. He sat to her right on the side nearest the hall.

"Oh that's nice," Joleena said looking at the tray and doubting that he fixed snacks as elaborately every day.

"I usually fix a little something for Little Von when we get home."

Still humming, Joleena took the gum from her mouth and set it on the edge of the plate. She bit one of the Fig Newtons and moved closer to Robin.

"Hmm, these are my favorite cookies. Did you just happen to have these?"

"Yup," Robin lied. Robin had a different lunch schedule than Arthur and Joleena. It had taken Robin twenty minutes to trick Arthur into divulging what Joleena liked to eat. It had been a strange conversation.

Joleena finished one Fig Newton and slid closer yet.

"You don't mind me sitting close, do you?"

"No, no it's all right." It was all Robin could do to keep from choking on his milk. "You know, before I moved down here we use to live about a block away from each other."

"Oh really." Joleena gently nudged off her penny loafers. Turning sideways on the couch, she pulled her feet up under her so that her knees rested firmly against Robin's leg. Her look was less smiling and more serious. "A block which way?"

Robin's heart picked up speed as he tried to catch up with the "plan," which seemed to have gained a pace of its own. Robin reached to the far side of the table for a napkin and a sandwich. Exaggerating his move, he partially stood and sat back down sliding a few inches further down the couch. "You know that tall white house you see in front of Lafayette? It's the tallest one."

"Oh yeah, that one. Really?" She quickly took up the slack on the couch. One of her knees settled against Robin's leg. Robin quickly bit into the sandwich. She leaned over and traced little spirals along his shoulder to his neck and onto his jaw with her finger. Robin choked.

"Joleena I...a...I..."

"Robin, what's the matter? Is there something wrong?"

"No. It's just that..."

"Robin, don't you think I'm attractive?" She reached for his face again, but Robin caught her arm in mid-air and slid the last inch to the arm of the couch.

"No. I mean yes! What I mean is...it's just that..."

Joleena pressed him tight against the arm of the sofa. "Robin? Just what? I can tell that you like me, I mean you sent Little Von, the music, my favorite cookies, you look and smell so... manly, and there's no one here but us. What can be wrong?"

With nowhere else to go he sat up on the arm of the couch. "Yes, I know, but I...I...I just didn't want it to be like this. You know, so quick."

Joleena heard the line she had been pushing for. No longer role playing, she exploded the fury that she had hidden away.

"Well how in the hell do you think I feel? Do you think I enjoy being...being..." she waved her hand back and forth in the air looking for the right word, "*lured* up here like some kind of animal to a trap!" Her anger boiled over. Furious, she grunted and slapped Robin across the jaw. Robin fell backward off the arm of the couch and thumped onto the floor. "I'm not an animal," she said, grabbing her shoes from beneath the table. "I'm a person and I want to be treated like one." Robin jumped to his feet wanting to say something, but she was on the way to the door. Her shoes hissed across the floor as she tried putting them on while she walked.

Racing behind her Robin called out, "Joleena!"

"Get away from me!" She reached for the door knob, but the odd configuration of locks stymied her.

"Open this door!" She took one step back toward the wall to avoid any accidental contact.

Robin twisted the latch and turned the knob, stopping short of letting it swing open. "Joleena..." he paused unable to look her in the eyes. "I really feel bad about this. I really am sorry. I didn't mean this to happen like it did. I wanted it to be..." he shrugged "...special."

"I know what you just wanted."

"No that's not it, I swear. I wanted to get to to know you, and I wanted you to like me." Having said it, he opened the door.

Joleena charged by into the safety of the hallway and turned again to face him still fuming. "Then next time, just ask. Just ask."

She ran down the stairs, pushing past Little Von and his mother. Little Von was talking a mile a minute. Vivian and Little Von both stopped and watched Joleena as she slammed through the door at the bottom of the stairs. Little Von continued where he left off.

"But Mom! He said two out of three! That makes it all right, doesn't it?"

10

DINNER CAME AND WENT BY IN SILENCE. Robin sat across from his mother without raising his eyes from his plate. He could feel her anger all around him. When he finished, he quietly shoved his chair back and started toward the sink with his plate.

"Sit down!" she said, hitting the bottom of her plate with her fork. He obediently did so, and waited until she had finished her dinner.

Little Von carefully avoided his brother's eyes. He hadn't realized that he was supposed to keep "The Plan" a secret after the fact. He had done his job well and, filled with pride, had explained to his mother in vivid detail his part of the plan. He didn't understand why Robin was so angry. Neither did he understand why his mother glared across the table at his older brother from time to time. But he did understand enough not to talk unless spoken to.

Little Von tilted his plate in his mother's direction. "Is that enough, Mom?" She nodded her consent and he slipped away carefully, looking straight ahead to avoid his brother's poker-hot glare.

"Mom, I got some homework to do," Robin said sighing.

"You sit down until I tell you it's all right for you to go," she said, all the words barely squeezing between her teeth. "Why are you so worried about your homework all of a sudden? You can just get Arthur Taggart to do it for you like he's been doing. Huh?"

Robin was stunned. He hadn't been prepared for this. He hadn't even suspected that this battle was even on the drawing board. "What do you mean by that?"

"Are you gonnna say Arthur hasn't been doing your work for you?" she said, wondering if Robin was going to make things worse by adding a lie.

Robin shrugged and looked down at the T-shaped lamb chop bone on his plate. "Well, no Mom. He doesn't do it for me, but he helps me a lot."

"He helps you a lot? Is that what it is?"

"Well, yeah, Mom, you know Arthur's real smart."

"Robin, I know Arthur and his whole family. I know he's smart, but Robin, you ain't no dummy either!" Vivian pushed away from the table and crossed the floor. She took an envelope from the top of the refrigerator and dropped it on the table in front of Robin. "But being smart is not the problem. I think he, or one of you, is more than smart. One of you must be a mind reader too. At least that's what I think when two people sit next to one another in a math class and hand in the exact same answers on work papers and make the exact same mistakes on tests. Now I could be wrong, so you tell me what to think."

Robin read the high school return address on the opened envelope and felt a little something die inside of him. He pulled out the two folded sets of papers. The first was a letter from his counselor addressed to his mother. The second contained two test papers stapled together, one his and the other Arthur's. A small note was attached.

Robin slowly closed the letter along its fold lines, a sinking feeling in the pit of his stomach. He had had the identical feeling each time he had decided to cut class. It was an early morning class, one that came after sleepless nights or nights he had been too exhausted to do his homework after dealing with Little Von.

He unfolded the second.

> TO: Mrs. V. Thompson Apt. 5509
> Building #5 F. Douglass Dr.
> Morristown N.J. 07960

RE: J.R. Thompson Jr.
From: Ralph Suther, Counselor
Dear Mrs. Thompson;

As your son's counselor, I find it necessary to voice some grave concerns raised from several of his teachers. I would like you to know that each of these teachers, and myself, hold your son in the highest esteem. However, as of late, his behavior, work, and class attendance have raised some serious questions which I believe should be brought to your attention.

Upon checking Robin's records, I have no doubt that he is capable of B average work, at the very minimum, but upon checking with several of his teachers in his major courses: algebra, English, history, and biology lab, which is an advanced course, but one that I believed he could handle without problem, we find his efforts below average and some near failing.

We attributed his first year in the high school, during which time he maintained a 2.5 average, as an adjustment period, but we did expect a steady progression from that point. Instead his grades have fallen, especially during this last quarter. Not surprising, this is also coupled with an attendance problem. Although he seems to make it to school, he doesn't make it to class.

One of his teachers who had him in junior high school and who now teaches here, noticed that he has changed the group of friends he began with in high school. Arthur Taggart, for whom we also have much respect, is the only one remaining from the old peer group. Again, this is often part of the adjustment that occurs during the switch from junior high school to high school. However, upon checking I found that several of the boys are known to be at least weekend drinkers and another has a police record—hardly a bunch that we would expect a student of Robin's nature and caliber to link up with.

If there are problems at home please let us know, perhaps we can be of some assistance At any rate, we would like for you or Mr. Thompson to come in at your......Sincerely......Ralph....

Robin knew how it ended.

He placed the second letter back in the envelope and wondered how this had come out in the open so quickly. Was it really that quick? Of course he knew he'd probably get caught sooner or...actually he didn't know. He had never really thought about it. It hadn't been a long range plan to skip class. It just happened day by day until, finally, there was no point in going to class at all. Each incident had been a separate reaction to some situation, or to a particular problem that had occurred. If there were any similarities, it had been the fact that all of his reactions had, indeed, become the same reaction. When Vivian drank, he couldn't cope.

"Two out of three makes a lie all right, Robin?" Vivian said pleading. "Is that what you want your brother to grow up believing? You think that's a real good example?"

"Mom I really messed up. I know. But I'm not the only one

in this family that doesn't always do what they're supposed to do." It had been his only defense, but even as he said the words, he wished he could take them back. He saw the pain widen her eyes and tighten the corners of her mouth.

"What do you mean? What did you mean by that?" Robin shrugged his shoulder and dropped his head even lower than before. Vivian rounded the table and slammed her hand down in front of her son. "I said, what did you mean by that! Answer me!"

"Mom, you had been...I mean a lot of those times..." Robin couldn't bring himself to say it. It had never really been said before. She slapped him hard across the face, and it took everything he had to hold the tears back.

"I am your mother! Don't you ever talk to me like that. Do you understand?" Robin sat still and clung to his silence. She smacked him again. This time hard across the head. "Do you hear me?" She was yelling now, not really herself. Perhaps at herself. "I am your mother!"

"Then why don't you act like it!" Robin screamed back, standing straight up, knocking the chair over behind him. She tried to hit him again, but he was standing looking down on her now. He caught her trembling hand and held it as tears fell one after the other from his own face. "Why don't you just stop, Mom? It's you too. Not just me!"

She jerked her hand away and swung again; the blow glanced off his shoulder as he turned from her.

"Mom!"

"Go to bed."

"Mom..."

"I said go to bed!" She swung a last time. The blow sounded a loud crack as it hit the hand he had raised to protect his face. He turned quickly and left the small kitchen.

Vivian shook as she stood staring at the wall. She sat down hard, but before she was settled she was back up and across the floor. She swung open a cupboard above the sink where she kept a bottle. She reached for it, but stopped her hand in mid-air. For a moment she turned her back to the open cabinet, but she couldn't gather her thoughts. She couldn't stop them from spinning, she couldn't stop them from flashing and twisting and stabbing and grinding against one another. She turned back to the cabinet and grabbed the bottle and shot glass and hugged them to her breast. Her eyes clenched so tightly she could hear the tension ring in her ears. She tried to control her shaking body but could not. Instead, she began to scream and before she could stop herself she had thrown the half-filled bottle of whiskey and the shot glass across the kitchen smashing them against the wall.

In the back room, Little Von listened to his mother and brother rage at each other. Little Von wanted to make them stop, but he was too frightened to move. He remembered the sick feeling he had had when his mother fought with Jessie Rose and how much it had hurt to listen. This was the same. When he heard Robin storming down the hall and crying himself, Little Von cried openly. Tears blinded him and dripped down his cheeks. Just as Robin slammed the door, he heard glass shatter in the kitchen. "Robin make it stop. Make it stop." He curled in Robin's lap and put his hands over his ears. "Make it stop."

"I can't, Von." Robin cried. "I can't do anything." His tears ran down his face and fell on Little Von. He could hear Vivian crying in the kitchen. They were all crying. It was so twisted and tangled that Robin couldn't grasp it, but he had to if he wanted to survive. It was never knowing what to expect. All of it digging and swirling inside of them was slowly making them all crazy.

Vivian lay across her bed in the dark. Her eyes, red and puffy, focused on the ceiling. After a time she stopped crying and her mind went blank. She clutched a pillow and listened to cars as they passed through the project. She lay alone with no one to comfort her. There was no one to tell how much she worried about Robin and Little Von. There was no one to tell how much she missed Jessie Rose and Elderiah. There was no one to tell how she had fought not to drink despite the many times drinking crossed her mind during the day. Vivian was sober. For the first time in many months she realized how afraid and alone she was.

11

JUNE, 1957

O<small>N A HOT, SUNNY DAY IN THE FIRST WEEK</small> of June, Bill Furman eased his big blue Buick into the center lane of traffic rounding the town square. He only came to the colonial-style town on the first Thursday of every month to make sure that his uncle, Clovis Lamb, got his Social Security check past the bars and liquor stores and into the bank.

Bill Furman was a big man, a gentle man. His two hundred thirty-five pounds filled more than its share of the front seat behind the steering wheel. He made a sharp turn onto Water Street. A few moments later, he descended among the dilapidated structures that lined one side of the Hollow.

He came to a stop at the bottom of the steep hill and looked across the main street into the mouth of the Hollow. There was no mistaking this side of town. Cars, many of them Cadillacs, were double-parked along the sides of the narrow street, their owners running in and out of the bars, some emerging counting money and jotting notes on small scraps of paper.

It was 10:00 a.m. Uptown businesses where just beginning to roll down their awnings and sweep their sidewalks. In the Hollow there were no awnings or business hours. Business was ever present, day and night. There were always customers, games to be played, givers, takers, those who thrived on deceit, and those who knew no other life except being deceived. This was the Hollow, and Bill Furman knew it well. He had known its ways and fueled its fires for many years. In his youth he ran numbers without need of pencil or paper. And as a young adult he had fenced stolen merchandise. Sometimes he had handled drugs when he had to, but this was not to his taste. He found his niche moving stolen goods from one set of hands to another.

In his late twenties he had begun to grow weary of the game. Carelessly he gambled on larger scores, always believing that the right one would be the last, freeing him from that kind of life. The right one that he needed to take care of his wife, Lucretia, the way she wanted to be taken care of. He gambled and lost one night in an alley while law-abiding businessmen with legal businesses slept. It was an easy deal mysteriously gone bad. It was a setup—a double cross. He was standing in an alley smoking a cigarette and waiting for a buyer when the police drove down the only exit. A young Bill Furman bathed in headlights, with a pocket full of stolen jewelry, stood unbelieving as he was handcuffed and taken away. That night had cost him five years of his life.

Bill hadn't gone into prison a bitter man. He had understood the risk involved. But as the weeks slowly became months, without a letter, call, or a visit from Lucretia, he slowly began to change. He had done it all for her. When she had finished with him, she had moved on.

It was in the third month that Lucretia finally came. Bill sat on his side of the visitor's glass dressed in a chaotic clash of denim jacket, khaki work shirt, overalls, and government-issue tennis shoes. He had had nothing to say and remained expressionless. He had not come from his cell for an explanation. He came, more than anything else, to break the monotony that had, in three months time, become terrifying. "A man never leaves prison," his cellmate had said when the guards slammed the bars behind Bill for the first time. "It's the sameness that kills little by little, hour by hour. Even when your time is up, only your shadow leaves here." It was this systematic death that he challenged by facing her.

Lucretia Furman sat down on the other side of the glass and smirked. "Well Bill, I see you're all dressed up with nowhere to go."

Bill looked straight into her eyes until he satisfied himself that everything was as it always had been, and then over her shoulder, locking eyes with the guard who was obviously checking her out. The guard grinned, looked at his watch, and took his time leaving the room.

"Friend of yours?" she said, sarcastically.

"Lucretia, you've always had two sides. The "Mrs. Charming" you and the "bitch." I never met anyone who could say the things you say in the way you say them.

"Flattery will get you nowhere. Bet?" She said, scanning the windowless room slowly, with a flat smile on her face. Bill nearly smiled. "Yeah, the charmer. You could charm the fangs off a rattler."

"You didn't seem to mind, now did you, Billy Boy."

"Hey, I would even go as far as to say that I loved it. Everybody is young and dumb at one time or another."

"Face it, Bill" she said leaning forward and losing her smile. "Stupidity has no age limitations. Age is obviously not the culprit here." She sat back, looking at her nails, indifferent again.

"Well," he continued, "There's the other side. The bitch. One charms the fangs off the rattler, the other one wears them. But this..." Bill slapped the long number stitched to one side of his jacket, the one that replaced his name and his immediate future. "If you wanted to get away from me why didn't you just go. No, you wanted to screw up my life. Why not, it never meant anything to you anyway. You could never get enough of anything."

"No Bill, I just believe in doing things the most efficient way." She snapped. "Look, let's cut the crap." She leaned close to the hole in the dividing glass. "There were other men I could've had instead of you, and there were other men I did have in spite of you. I would have dumped you years ago, but I thought you had potential. With my brains and your back we could have had a nice life. You and all your goddamn dreams. School. Huh! Dentist school, veterinarian school. What makes you think I want to spend the rest of my life with somebody who searches for ticks on a dog's ass everyday? And all them damn vines and shit all over the house. I thought I was livin' in a greenhouse half the time. I don't care if I never see another flower again as long as I live. I wanted you because I thought you were bigger and better than the rest. All you wanted was a better bag of fertilizer. Why couldn't you play golf like other men?"

"It takes time to get the things you want in life, Lucretia."

"Well I don't have any more time to give to you, Bill Furman! I've already given you some of the best years of my life. Time...I'm fresh out. But you, on the other hand, now you have all the time you need."

"I made a mistake hookin' up with you."

"No you didn't. You would have been a fool to pass me up. No, I made the mistake. But mistakes are correctable," she said, backing down from her rage. She regained her cynical smile. She pulled a fat envelope from her bag and stood it up on its end on the table of the booth. "I could have had someone else serve these, but I wanted the pleasure myself. I get everything except for the plants of course. I saved them in a box for you. In my book, you're a loser —dull as ditch water. The only thing that bothers me is that I didn't see it right off. See, I'm not perfect after all. Just thought I'd come by and let you know."

She stood up forcing him to look up to her. "Goodbye, Bill. You could have been somebody."

He watched her walk across the room, her spiked heels echoing on the little square tiles faded from years of mops and disinfectant. At the door a man dressed in a silk suit and a wide-brimmed hat waited for her. When she slipped her arm in his, he grinned revealing several gold-lined teeth. That was the last time he saw either of them. It was then that the bitterness had started.

Ten years later Bill Furman thought about his ex-wife, and prison, as he drove through the Hollow. He spotted familiar faces, faces that had belonged to young jobless men in alligator shoes, silk suits, and felt-n-feather hats. Faces that now belonged to old jobless men who looked twice their real age, men contemplating how much longer they could maintain an empty lifestyle that devoured itself. Prison had been a blessing. He had not become one of those faces. Gamblers and politicians, teachers and would-be professional athletes who became winos while telling stories of their glory days, and a variety of soulless faces who never bothered to shave or change their clothes, all stood together solving the world's problems. It was the latter that made Bill Furman remember his dirty laundry in the backseat.

He turned the big sky-blue Buick around the next series of corners, passed two of the four churches that surrounded the Hollow, wondering if it had been a conscious effort to contain the overflow that preachers called "loose-living and decadence." Bill Furman laughed to himself and parked. From there it was a short distance to Sanbini's Dry Cleaners.

Out of habit, Vivian looked up from the steamy shirt press when she heard the front door jangle the overhead bells. She had never seen the man who bent his head slightly at the neck to clear the entrance. She watched him dump an armful of laundry on the counter. The owner stood behind the counter in a sweat-stained T-shirt, swearing into the phone.

"What do you mean? It says five hundred right on the order, you dip...!" The owner, Mario, turned to face Bill while holding his forehead and then pushed back the greying hair at his temples. He looked at Bill's shirts on the counter while he listened to the voice on the other end.

"Right. What do you think it means when two zeros and a period come after a five, piss brain—wait a minute, I got a customer." Dismayed, the shop owner held the phone up in front of Bill with one hand, and pointed to it with the other. "Idiots I have to deal with. What'ya got?"

Bill put his hands on the pile of dirty shirts. "Can I get these back by five?"

The owner tapped a sign taped to the side of the cash register. "Want'em by five you got to get them in before ten." Frown lines distorted his face as he put the phone back to his ear. "Not you, pinhead. I'm talking to a customer. I did business with your father for twenty years. If he could see what you're doing to his business…"

Bill gestured with his hands, trying to catch the owner's attention. "Hey, I'm from out of town, can't you slip these in for me?"

Still listening to the phone, the owner afforded Bill no more than a glance. Tapping the sign three more times, he walked away stretching the phone cord behind him.

Bill began to gather his shirts from the counter. Vivian stepped from the back and signaled for him to wait. She pulled a ticket pad from under the counter. "It's only a little after ten." she said smiling. She began sorting the shirts. "Just these?"

"Yeah, thanks. You sure I can get these back by five?"

Vivian smiled as she handed him the ticket. She was surprised that such a gentle voice could come from such a big man. "He makes the signs, but I do the work. I don't see any problem."

"Hey, I really appreciate this. I didn't want to get hung up here another day waiting for shirts. You sure this won't get you into any kind of trouble with…" Bill nodded in the direction of the shop owner a few feet away. He was still yelling obscenities into the phone. Vivian waved the notion away with her hand.

"Okay then. Thanks again."

Midway to the door, he stopped and looked back at Vivian, to say what, he really didn't know, but she was already dropping shirts in wheeled baskets, unaware of his presence. The owner reappeared from his office with the phone still to his ear, and slicing the air with his hand. "I've been givin' business to your family since you were dropping mustard poop in your diapers. And this is the kind of service I get!" Bill smiled as he left.

Bill's mind was preoccupied as he drove to the far end of the Hollow. He had passed Jimmy Lee's Best Fill station and was partially under the train trestle before he realized it. After ten years of being alone, it was odd having a woman affect him in that certain way. The slender woman with red highlights in her brown hair that stood behind the counter of the dry cleaners had definitely had an effect on him.

He pulled up in front of Jimmy Lee's pumps, and let the engine of the Buick go dead. He shook his head. Jimmy Lee appeared from the dark cave of his service garage yelling and wiping the grease and oil from his hands. His aged and yellowed skin barely covered the bones of his face.

"Well well well. What'dya say there, Dollar Bill!" Jimmy Lee stuck the pump nozzle into the side of Bill's car and grinned, knowing full well he no longer answered to the old street name left over from his days as a numbers runner. "Well now let me see here," he said, taking off his cap and scratching what remained of the silvery rough on his head. "This is the sixth mont of nineteen fifty sebin'. So." He said, deliberating, slowly. "I believe I'll put a quarta on fo-fi-sebin' cause I likes fo' betta than six. Uh-huh that's it. Fo fifty sebin'." He shot Bill a quick glance, mockingly waiting for the runner's nod of approval.

Bill took the ceremonial dig with a smile. "Old man, if you finished fillin' the tank you better take the hose outta my tank before I drive away and take this dumpy little ass gas station down the street."

Jimmy Lee put both hands on the roof and lowered himself so he could see through the passenger window. "Now waaait just a minute here. I got good everyday customers I don't let talk to me like that. You don't think I'm gonna be takin' no stuff from no once-a-month nigga like you. Do you?"

Bill laughed. "You lucky I bring this fine car in this little grease joint at all. You outta be payin' me for comin' in here and making you look good."

Jimmy Lee took one step back and looked from one end of the car to the other. "Yeah, I suppose you right at that. How much I owe ya?" Bill and Jimmy Lee laughed and patted one another on the shoulder through the window. "How you been, boy? Dis a new car?"

"Jimmy Lee, I believe you gettin' senile. Every time I come in here you ask me if this is a new car."

"What? This the same one you had last time you come in here? I'll be damned. Maybe I am." he said rubbing his nose with a clean spot on the back of his hand.

Bill laughed. "I think you been breathin' these fumes too long."

"Well hell boy, if you come round a little more so's a body could see ya, it wouldn't be so hard to figure out who you are every time. Say boy, pull around the side and come on in for a minute. I got somethin' I want to show ya."

Bill hung a five-dollar bill out of the window for the gas, but, by that time, Jimmy Lee had cranked the pump back to zero and started walking toward the garage. It was customary. Besides Clovis, Jimmy Lee was the only one to visit him in prison. Jimmy Lee tried to talk to Bill at every opportunity about the streets and the price they would exact, but Bill, in his youth and in his love for Lucretia, hadn't heard. When Bill went to prison Jimmy Lee saw him through.

Bill entered the garage cautiously, hoping his eyes would adjust quickly to the dim light before he stepped in one of the many different colored puddles that speckled the station's floor. "Jimmy Lee, what the hell is that?" Bill squinted at the car, his memory trying to pull up the answer with no success.

"Boy don't you know a 'yella 1933 Stutz when you see one?"

Bill looked back to the car and whistled. "No."

"Well, let me introduce you proper. This here is a 1933 Stutz Victoria. You hear of the Stutz Bearcat, aint ya?"

"I heard of it. I seen pictures of it when I was little."

"That was the most well known one. It was a fancy coup, what we use to call a roadster back in them days. Last ones was built in '33 and '34. But this here is a Victoria. Baby let me tell ya somethin'. Very few white peoples could afford one of these cars. And no negroes. Well, lessn it was Jack Johnson or somebody. Ask Clo. Car was built smack in the middle of the depression. Wasn't many of 'em built either, so this is worth somethin'," Jimmy Lee said, rubbing his fingers together.

"How much, unc?"

"Hell, I don't know. But this'll give you a clue. Back in dem days a regular everday Ford was goin' for 'round five hundred. And that was a lot of money back then. This little honey right here set you back 'round three grand."

"Wow."

"Oh this was class all the way. If I fix this bucket close to what it was when it was original..." Jimmy Lee smiled.

"You think that yellow was an original color? When you see pictures everthing looks black or white."

"That's 'cause that's the only kinda pictures you had. Wasn't no color film yet, you know. Peoples wasn't shy about color back in those days. Things were hard, but I think life was more colorful in general."

"A '33, huh? Looks way too good to be that old."

"Uh-huh. Nice isn't it? Hardly any rust."

"Looks like it's in great condition except the chrome is shot, little rust and a little dirt, the back fender rail's a little bent out. But that's no big deal."

Jimmy Lee stood with his back to Bill smiling. He held a rubber mallet above his head for Bill to see. This'll take care of it." He threw it aside shrugging his shoulders.

Bill furrowed his eyebrows as his memory began to match pictures. "Say Unc. Is this old man Pelligrini's car? The old guy who used to own the old bakery up the street."

"That's right." Jimmy Lee looked at a wrench that was blackened with grease, frowned and tossed it aside.

"Wasn't there some funny business about this...oh, it's been about twenty years, hasn't it?"

"That's right." Jimmy Lee flashed a broad smile showing all his gold-lined teeth. Finding the tool he wanted, he dropped it onto another pile on the floor next to the old car.

"Didn't somebody steal it or something like that?"

"That's right." Jimmy Lee said, smiling. He rocked the small Coke machine until two bottles fell one on top of the other in the opening.

Bill's memory became clearer. "As a matter of fact, didn't they say Sticky Taylor stole it?"

"Yeah, but everybody knew that was bull 'cause nothin' ever stuck to Stick's hand that he couldn't put right into his pocket. That's how come people got to callin' him Sticky. But dis here is how it really go:

"See, old man Pelligrini knew that bread bakeries weren't gonna be around for ever. And when sliced bread in bags started catchin' on, he could hear the funeral music. But when the bread man started droppin' bread off regular at people's do' steps, well he wasn't no fool, he could see the writin' on the head stone. Back in them days everybody made their own cakes so he knew it was curtain time for the bread bakery."

Having figured out the story on his own, Jimmy Lee laughed as he handed Bill one of the sodas and pulled down one of five wooden theater seats. He sat back and put his foot up on the running board of the antique car and took a long draw from the bottle. "Yep. He knew it was all over for the bakery. That's when he hid the car."

"That's when he hid the car?" Bill repeated.

"Hell, yeah. He knew that was the first thing the bank would snatch up when he got far enough behind on the bakery," he said, laughing. "He probably figured he was killin' two birds with one stone."

"What do you mean?" Bill sat cautiously in one of the narrow seats beside him.

"You might'a been too little, but 'member all them times Sticky came down the street past here eatin' fresh rolls and braggin' bout never payin' for'em?"

Bill didn't remember, but he knew that's how Sticky was, big mouth and small brain. "Yeah' Unc, but how did they put Sticky in the slam on that one. They didn't have the car so they didn't have any proof."

"Proof! Since when the po-leece need proof to put a nigga in jail?" Jimmy Lee turned toward Bill knowing there was no answer.

"Yeah, that's true. Especially back then."

"That's right." Jimmy Lee said, easing back into the seats. "But old man Pelligrini had that one covered too. You remember how all the young boys 'round that time kept their head rags and caps hangin' out of their back pockets when they got their hair straightened?"

"Yeah, they still do. 'Cept now they call 'em do-rags."

"Well I guess one of them times when Sticky was stealin' bread, his musta fell out on the floor, cause when the old man called the cops to lie about the car being stole, he showed them

him. She looked steadily at him, without wavering, until he made his way to the seat beside her. When he tried to smile, she looked away.

12

RICK TAGLIA, AT FIRST GLANCE, seemed to be created on one of God's humorous days. He had a strong face with a big square jaw line. The bump and slope of his nose gave his face character. His smile revealed a mouth full of perfect white teeth. His shoulders were small and his crucifix rested on a well-muscled chest. It was obvious that Rick gave no thought to the clothes that hung lifelessly from his frame. He had no sense of what matched. Clothes were simply a way to cover the body, more in winter, less in spring.

As a child most of his friends were Black. The way they moved, the way they sang, and laughed, intrigued him and magnetized his curiosity. In high school, he was the only White player on the varsity basketball team. In fact, the people of the Hollow still called him "Hoops" as a testament to the place he had earned in their hearts. Nevertheless, he didn't fool himself. He was a short spunky white kid with no future, playing "hoops." The Taglias were cops, and always had been cops. It would be no different with Rick.

The academy was a choice in the absence of other choices. In a short time he made detective. It was a tradition of Taglia men—men that Rick had little respect for, men with legacies that left a bad taste in Rick's mouth. To distance himself from the shame of these traditions would have been the wiser choice, but not one that he could live with. Instead, like his grandfather whom he didn't remember, the father whom he had no respect for and his brother Bono, whom he hated, Rick became the fourth Taglia to become a cop. He was determined to be the first Taglia to wear the badge with honor despite the fact that he was Chief Bono Taglia's brother.

Rick sat at the desk in his office oblivious to the tumultuous traffic in the police station, with his shirt sleeves rolled up. He also wore an oddly-striped tie that matched nothing in the entire office. He leaned over his desk with his elbows dug in like fence posts; his head rested on closed fist. Four black-and-white photo blowups of stolen cars were carefully positioned in front of him. Contemplating, he sat back in his chair with both hands inside of a rubberband flipping them one over the other. He would stop

for a moment when an idea hit him. He would start again when
he found its flaw. His eyes shifted to the sound of the woman's
voice that crackled over the intercom.

"Rick, the Chief would like to see you in his office," she said
almost apologetically. When he came by her desk she added, "By
the way Rick, I was thinking of doing a roast tonight over at my
place." She glanced at his tie and looked away. "I was wondering
if you'd be interested. You know, there would be too much for one
person. The leftovers would just go bad anyways."

Rick's voice was uncomfortable. "Aaa...thanks Gena, but I
got..." he waved his hand toward his office, "...all this work..."

"It's okay, Rick. Maybe some other time, huh?"

"Sure. Some other time."

Rick stood outside of his brother's door. The fact that his
brother was the Chief didn't make his life better or the task of
having to talk to him more pleasant. Chief Bonaventura Taglia,
like his father Spago, was an unpleasant man. He was fifteen
years Rick's senior. They were separated by seven sisters and
a father who made no bones about his preference in sons.
Rick's father, Spago Taglia, had been gruff and unforgiving. He
didn't tolerate disloyalty, disrespect, niggers, Jew bastards,
spicks, fags, or any "womanly attributes," like gentleness, in
a man, particularly a cop. He despised Rick, saying that he
was weak, while his first son, Bonaventura, whom he called
Bono, had been his pride and joy. When Bono came home from
World War II a decorated soldier, Spago threw the biggest party
the neighborhood had never seen. He danced and drank wine
from the bottle, toasting Bono as if he had won the war
singlehandedly. When Bono became Chief, Sargent Spago
Taglia went to his grave a happy man.

To Rick, his father and brother were one and the same. The
anger and rejection he felt toward them became a regular part of
his sporadic confessional visits with Father Benaolletto. As Rick
stood before Bono's door he thought of the Father's words, "He's
your brother, your blood. You are the same." Rick shook his head
with a smirk.

Chief Bonaventura Taglia sat behind his desk reveling in the
power that came with the office. He was short, squat, and not
very intelligent. His stained tie abruptly turned over on itself as
it came to rest on his barrelled belly. He tapped a pencil on a

report folder, pretending not to notice Rick as he entered.

"You wanted to see me, Bono?"

"Well, baby brother, how we doin'?"

Rick nodded and bobbed his head, "Good."

"Good? That's good." He sized his brother up. "Rumor has it that Gena would run bare-ass naked through a convent and lay spread eagle at your feet if you just smiled at her."

"Strictly rumor," Rick said flatly, looking around the room to avoid his brother's stare.

"What's the matter? Isn't she good enough for ya? What? She's not dark enough?"

"Gena's a nice girl, Bono. She does good work."

"Hey, who's talkin' about work?" He said, taking a well-chewed cigar from an ash tray. "There's nothin' wrong with bangin' colored girls—once in a while. I do, on occasion. Even the old man did, God rest his soul. As long as you don't forget where you're from. You know what I mean baby brotha?"

"I'm not bangin' anybody. Is that all you wanted, Bono?"

Bono sat motionless looking at his brother for a moment, shrugged and sat back in his chair. "No, that's not all. Sit down, if you have a minute. How we doin' with this missin' vehicles business? They seem to be procreatin' and givin' birth to more missin' vehicles all the time."

"I'd probably use the word trashed instead of missing. But, other than that, no leads. I'll get him."

"You'll-get-him?" Bono laughed out of the side of his mouth. He took the cigar from his mouth and held it between his fingers like a cigarette and shook his head. "Four cars in four weeks and that's it? *I'll-get-him*—Jesus Christ Rick. Let me tell you something, *Detective Hoops*, that's it, isn't it? That jungle down there..." he said pointing out of the window in the direction of the Hollow, "and all the little bunnies runnin' around in it are yours by your own choice. And you, mister, are supposed to be on top of it. When they burp you tell me what they had for dinner. When they drop their little rabbit turds, you follow the trail. And I expect to have this little jungle bunny's fury foot on my key ring before he starts boostin' cars uptown from the good white citizens. And you better watch your back." He pointed to the three-inch scar below Rick's ear. "If you think they love you so much, just remember how one of them—that Scab kid, Benny—tried to cut your throat. Is that understood detective?"

"Will that be all, sir?" Rick asked.

"No that's not all! You may be my brother and some kind of big-shot star basketball player, but you still got a damn job t' do. Is that clear?"

"Will that be all sir?"

"IS THAT CLEAR?"

"Yes-sir-that's-clear."

Bono sat back again. His voice was suddenly quiet and indifferent. "Then that will be all...brother."

Rick got up and turned to leave.

"Hey baby brother, there is one more thing. Momma's gettin' a little crazy cause you haven't been over for so long. She wants us over for dinner this weekend. I'm bringin' Terese and the kids. Sunday, five o'clock. Maybe you could wear another tie if you got one. And don't be late."

Rick was about to step through the door.

"Oh and Rick? I'm sure Momma wouldn't mind if you brought a lady friend along, providing she was of the right persuasion, of course." Bono gestured out of the door and down the hall. "Maybe somebody we all know."

Rick closed Bono's door without speaking. He walked the corridor until he came to Gena who immediately stopped what she was doing and smiled, leaving him an opening for more conversation. Her hair was piled high enough to hide a small child in it. Her makeup was just as pale as her normal complexion. He hesitated for an instant. But, instead of speaking, he went into his office and closed the door. He sat for a moment thinking, unconsciously fingering the scar below his ear. It had not been a direct confrontation with the kid everyone called Scab. It was a fight between Benny and another kid. Rick struggled to remember the kid's name. Raymond Chester. It was the Chester kid who pulled the knife just about the time Rick and his partner Steve arrived to break up the fight. Rick knocked the knife from his hand and Benny picked it up. All four of them were rolling on the ground as the two cops tried to subdue the boys. Benny picked up the knife and slashed out at Raymond. Luckily, Steve was holding his arm stopping it from reaching out its full length. What turned out to be a small gash could have been a disaster.

Rick hit the button on the intercom. "Gena could you bring the juvenile file on Benny Tillerman?" It was less than a hunch, just a thought.

Robin stood beside Joleena as she pulled notebook after notebook from her locker. She shut the door and handed Robin a pile of dittoed outlines.

"Jeez, Salinger. Catcher in the Rye again."

"You already did this?"

"Yeah, last year. Some parents tried to have her fired for teaching this." Robin smirked. "She never backed off." Robin took a deep breath. "Look, um, I'm really sorry about last Friday. It was real stupid."

"I think you've already done this number too."

"Yeah, I know, but I really meant what I said before you left. I only did it because I wanted to get to know you." Joleena looked straight ahead as she walked. She was beautiful. Robin stumbled when he tried to concentrate on the detail of her face and speak at the same time.

"Well as I said before, you should have just said something."

"Joleena, every guy in school probably tries to talk to you."

For a brief second Joleena stopped and faced Robin. She snapped around and started down the hall. "Oh, is that what you think?"

Robin had to quicken his pace to keep abreast of her. "Well it's true isn't it?"

"And do you think I go out with every guy in school?"

"No. That's not what I meant. What I'm saying is that, you could have your pick of any guy you wanted. And I'm not saying that makes you a bad person or anything, cause I think you're easy..."

"Easy!"

"No! Wait a minute, let me finish." Robin took another breath and tried to get his momentum rolling again. "I was going to say...that you are easily the prettiest girl in school. So you should have your pick. But, I'm just sayin' that I didn't want to be...you know, just another guy trying out some lines he made up in front of the bathroom mirror."

Joleena stopped walking. Her face became soft and hinted at a smile for the first time since she had entered the apartment the Friday before. "Well thank you for the compliment."

Robin shrugged. His embarrassment was obvious. They started walking again, Joleena's step was more relaxed, her demeanor warm. Robin's confidence was building.

"I thought if it sorta happened naturally..." Robin heard himself and knew instantly that *naturally* was a poor choice.

Joleena stopped dead in her tracks looking at him. "Natural! Whew. That was realllllly natural." Robin cursed his light skin. He turned away, but soon his laughter joined hers.

"What kinds of other *natural* things do you have in mind?"

"Well...I do this thing where I get my whole foot in my mouth. The whole thing. You should see it some time. Really somethin' to watch."

"Yeah I can tell you'd be good at that one." She taunted, smiling with a hint of coyness.

"The best one? I'm working on this new one where I just disappear. I do something really dumb, but before anybody can actually be sure it was me—*phuff*—gone. I don't have it down right now. Wish I did though."

"Guessed you could have used that one several times this week huh?"

"Hmm," Robin said thinking how he must have looked sailing over the side of the living room sofa. He smiled as they came to the door at the end of the hall. He was overjoyed to see Joleena smiling.

Not wanting anything to happen that might ruin it, he began walking backward, the way they had come. "Well, thanks for the notes. I'll see ya in class."

Joleena looked surprised that Robin was breaking the conversation off and backing away. "Hey aren't you gonna pick up Little Von today?"

"Yeah, but I have to check in with Mr. Suther to let him know how it went in Mrs. D-K's."

"Mrs. D-K? Is that what you call her?" Joleena walked back a few steps toward him.

"Yeah. Some of us from last year."

Joleena smiled. "Well, how do you think it went?"

"Natural. Very natural,"

"Should I tell my mom that you're gonna be um...a little late?" Joleena raised her eyebrows and cocked her head slightly.

"Yeah," Robin said, smiling. "But I'll walk him home this time." Robin watched as Joleena disappeared through the doors to the street. Hardly able to contain himself, he let out a loud whoop as he threw Catcher in the Rye toward the ceiling of the hallway. When it came down Charlene and Scootch were standing right in front of him.

The love between them was no secret. She was tough and sassy, perhaps the only girl who could keep up with someone as strong and aggressive as Scootch. She leaned on him heavily in a way most would think obscene.

Charlene's eye's narrowed. "OooooOoOoo! Go head on Robin. Makin' the move on Joleena Cleary. I seen it with my own eyes too. OoooooOooOo."

Scootch lay back, broad shouldered against several lockers, his arms a harness around Charlene's neck. "Hey what I'd tell ya? I told you Rob was smooth, babe. He just don't operate like some of them other loud jive ass fools that be hittin' on you all the time."

"Oooo Robin. You was happy too! Did you see the way he was throwin' his books up in the air like that? Go 'head on. Rob!"

Lester came around the corner. "Ey. What's ha-ha-happenin' y-y-y-yall," he said, not getting the words out quickly enough.

"Oooo Lester, you should'a seen it," Charlene said, putting one arm around Lester's neck, laughing unmercifully, squealing with delight. "We came around the corner and Rob was puttin' the moves on Joleena Cleary."

"S-s-say what? Get outta here?"

"He smooth, ain't he, Les?" Scootch said, slapping hands with Lester.

"Robin? Joleena gonna g-g-g-gi—gi—gi...give you some, man?"

"No, man! I was just talkin' to her." Robin frowned at Charlene.

Scootch raised his eyebrows. "Uh-uh, Les, man. Don't be listenin' to that. Rob was smoothin' her, man. You shoulda dug it. He was talkin' about how natural everything was and disappearin' —hey, man, he was talkin' a whole gang a shit I ain't never even heard before."

"Get outta here." Robin protested to no avail. "I was just talkin' to her after class. That's all."

Charlene cut in sharply. "Then why was you throwin' your books all over the ceiling if you was just talkin'?"

Knowing that he had been trapped, Robin fought to gain control of the conversation. "Charlene, every dude in school be tryin' to talk to Joleena. I wouldn't even be talkin' to her if we weren't in the same class."

"Yeah, but I just saw one real big difference, Mr. Thompson." Charlene said grinning.

"What was that?" Robin said, afraid of any answer Charlene—big mouth Charlene—loud-mouth Charlene, might give. He wondered if she had heard about the incident at the apartment and was now about to spill it in front Scootch and Lester. That would make him the dozens target for the next...until he died.

"She was listening to you."

Lester and Scootch wolf-howled and slapped hands.

"Get outta here." Robin said, feeling tremendous relief. "She was just being nice cause DeKorio asked her to give me some notes from class."

"Robin," Charlene was a bit more serious, "You right. A lot of dudes be tryin' to talk to Joleena, but you ever hear of her going out with anybody on more than one date? You just went from one end of the hall to the other. That might be a record. Why don't you ask her to come over to the Lafayette playground Friday night to hear the Swan Tones?"

"Oh yeah, I forgot about that."

"She lives up on the hill anyway."

"As a matter of fact you can see her house right across the field from the school," Robin said, thoughtfully.

"Yeah, man, you can sing backup on some of the tunes," Scootch chimed in, plotting on Robin's behalf. "Maybe afterwards..."

Charlene frowned. "Maybe afterwards what?"

Scootch shrugged his shoulders and smiled at Robin and Lester.

"Eh Rob, man, you better p-p-po-po-you better poke her while you -c-c-can man."

"Lester!" Charlene slapped him across the shoulder. "Stop talking nasty."

Robin never thought of Joleena in that way any more. Obvious, at least to himself, he was in love. But it was a hell of a thought. Friday.

Robin had rushed through his meeting with Mr. Suther, assuring him that he had taken the conference seriously. Then he had set out for the daycare center at an unusually fast pace. Joleena had met him at the door and told him that Little Von was still on the playground with the other kids. Then she asked him if he would walk with her to the store. The walk was more than wonderful. They both remarked how they felt so at ease together and how their conversation had been so "natural." The idea of kissing Joleena had never crossed Robin's mind, but, on their return, she had paused at the door letting him know, in her own way, that it was okay if he was willing to make the first move. Finally, and with great anxiety, he began to lean toward her. As he did her eyes closed. Just as he figured out which way to turn his head to not break her nose, Mrs. Cleary appeared.

"Well I see you two have met. I figured you might sooner or later." She eyed Joleena who smiled back.

"Yeah, we met that day when I had to walk Little Von home." Joleena said raising a brow.

Little Von came running up the hall, trying to get his coat on at the same time. "Hi, Leeny. Bye, Mrs. Cleary. Hey Rob!" He rapped himself around his brother's leg in a bear hug.

"Hey, peanut head," Robin said, laughing at the jacket turned inside-out.

Of all the children in the daycare center, Joleena had chosen Little Von as her favorite. Although she tried not to show it, he always brought a smile to her face and she to his. She dropped down on one knee, the pleats of her dress cascading to the floor, and grabbed him by the waist, "Whoa, just a minute there, cowboy." Joleena pulled the small child away from his brother's leg and turned him around and spread his arms to reveal that his jacket was odd looking. "Did your mom buy you a coat all fuzzy lookin' like this? It was a lot nicer when you came this morning."

Little Von froze for a moment looking down the front of his jacket. He put his art work down and began to slide his arms out with Joleena's help.

"Well I guess we'll see you tomorrow, Mr. Thompson," Mrs. Cleary said, using her teacher voice to Little Von.

"Rob, tomorrow's not cartoon day is it?"

"Nope. Not yet."

"I'll be here then. Bye," he said starting off toward the door without picking up his work.

Mrs. Cleary smiled. "Robin we'll see you too." She said, walking off.

Joleena was still squatting gathering up the papers from the floor. She handed them to Robin as she rose. As Robin took the papers he accidentally caught one of her fingers and they stood locked for a fleeting second. "Well, I guess I'll see you in class," Robin said feeling less awkward than he ever had with her.

"It's not cartoon day is it? I couldn't let high school come between me and Howdy Doody, could I?"

"No, I guess not. Some things are important." Robin wondered if he was supposed to try and kiss her again. "Well I guess I'll see you tomorrow in class," Robin repeated.

"Bye."

Mrs. Cleary watched her daughter staring out of the tall hall window as Robin and Little Von descended the hill toward the residential brick buildings. Although her daughter was the center of attention wherever she went, she knew that Joleena was unusually quiet for a girl her age. She was an outstanding cheerleader, yet being in front of the huge Saturday night crowds had not made her more confident as she had hoped. Instead, she had grown more insecure from all the attention her mature body and beautiful face attracted. She had dreaded the coming of this time in her daughter's life. She looked on silently, vicariously, trying to recapture the romantic flourishes of her own youth.

"He's cute, huh, Mom?"

"That depends on which one you're referring to."

Joleena didn't hide her feelings. She smiled back at her mother. "The quiet one."

"Well that leaves out Little Von, doesn't it?"

"Yup. Mom, look at Little Von. Seems like he's limping or something. Did he get hurt on the playground today?"

"No, but you know, I thought I noticed it yesterday afternoon, too. Yes it looks like he's limping on his left side." They watched as Little Von stood in front of Robin and talked to him. Robin swung him up to his shoulders and immediately had to pry little fingers off his eyes. "Well if it doesn't clear up by tomorrow, I'd better let his mom know."

Joleena laughed as Robin, still unable to get Little Von's fingers off his face, came to a complete stand still.

"Mom, can I invite him to dinner Friday night?"

"I don't know, Leeny. What would your father say?"

Joleena's voice became high-pitched. "I don't know, Mom. You could say it was your idea, and that he was real nice."

Mrs. Cleary wrinkled her brow while she thought, and then smiled. "I suppose—well why not? I can still handle your father."

Joleena burst through the door and shouted down the hill as calmly as she could manage. "Robin! My mother wants to know if you would like to come to dinner Friday night?"

Mrs. Cleary protested, but Joleena shushed her.

Robin turned trying to face the sound of her voice. "Von! Let go my eyes, man. I can't see."

Little Von was laughing and clinging tightly. Their combined weight bobbled from side to side.

"What? What'd you say?" Robin said, yelling in the direction he thought was up the hill.

Joleena laughed as Robin blindly stumbled off the curb and quickly back up again. "I said, my mother..." Mrs. Cleary pinched her daughter on the arm, but Joleena pushed her back inside the door. "My mother wants to know if you would like to come to dinner Friday night?"

Robin grabbed one of Little Von's wrist, clearing the vision of one eye. He discovered he had been talking directly to a tree.He turned uphill to where Joleena stood. "Yeah...sure...a...what time?"

"Mom what time? What time?"

"Um, um, um—how about seven-thirty? Seven-thirty."

"How about seven-thir..." Mrs. Cleary suddenly grabbed Joleena's arm. "NO! NO! Seven," she said, rushing. "We don't want your father sitting around like a grumpy bear because he had to wait for his dinner."

"Seven," Joleena said, straining to hold her excitement back.

"Okay, seven." Robin waved just as Little Von slammed his hand back in place over his eye.

"Sub-mar-ine," Little Von sang sitting on Robin's shoulders.

He covered Robin's eyes so only he could see, acting as both the captain and the periscope. As they swayed and staggered, he yelled out directions to which Robin, both the submarine and the crew, had to respond, "Aye, aye, sir."

Robin made the noise of the engines and repeated orders like a sailor. Little Von purposely ran him into several objects. Laughing, he gave Robin orders to back up and torpedo them.

When they reached Building Five, Robin was exhausted. He lowered Little Von down on the stairs beneath the foyer. They sat watching people as they passed by.

"Robin, that was great, huh?"

Robin looked up the street to the project office building. The colors of the sun bathed the building in pastel shades. Little Von settled down next to him. "Yeah, it was really great." Robin chuckled and sighed at the same time. He couldn't believe that things had turned out so well after his plan to lure Joleena upstairs had turned into a disaster. He didn't think that Joleena would ever speak to him again. Instead, he had been invited to dinner. "I wish things could work out like that all the time."

Little Von smiled. "We can play submarine anytime. I like it. You wanna play some more before we go upstairs?"

"No, no, no. I'm too tired now. Tomorrow, okay?"

"Sure?"

Robin smiled. The lights of the Housing Authority blinked out one by one. Suddenly his mind jumped ahead to Friday night. Joleena's father—whom he had only heard rumors about, none of them good—sits across the table scowling. Joleena and her mother are huddled on one side of the table hoping Robin won't make any mistakes. Just as suddenly the scene switched to Joleena eating upstairs in his apartment. Vivian has cooked a good meal and has gone back to her bedroom. As Joleena talks, Robin worries that his mother will return drunk.

"Robin!" Little Von said, punching Robin's arm. "I got to pee!"

Robin's focus returned. Little Von was no longer sitting next to him, he was standing with his knees together.

Rob," Little Von looked around. "If you gonna have trouble with the key, I'll just go in the bushes around the side."

"Just go in the bushes, Von." Robin sat down again and toyed with the vision, thinking, but avoiding being pulled in. Still the thoughts gave way to a rising nervousness. He shook his head to clear away the thoughts, but the fear that had accompanied them remained.

13

Now that he had successfully caught Clovis, Bill Furman relaxed. The chase had become a monthly tradition. Usually, after the chase ended at the teller's window of the bank, Bill ferried his uncle around town for the better part of the day paying bills and picking up the necessities that Clovis needed for the month. The most dreaded of these stops included a trip to the Food Fair supermarket.

It had taken months to convince Clovis that buying all his groceries under one roof was smarter than visiting a dozen specialty shops. With that idea eventually accepted, Clovis had found a whole new world of things to argue about: which cart to take, the automatic door that would one day "...mash up an arm or leg. Where's the regla door?" the green peppers that never looked as fresh as they did at old man Ceritano's market, and on and on. The truth about the automatic door was that Clovis felt hurried as it swung away from him. The door, Bill figured, not only took away his control over the matter of coming and going, but also seemed to give him a time limit in which to make good of the opportunity.

Bill wondered if supermarkets were as disturbing to all old people from the '20s and '30s. Or was it just Clovis. It seemed that Clovis was more than a little intimidated, and even at times awestruck, by the mountains of fresh fruits and vegetables, as well as the abundantly stocked shelves that lined the long aisles of the supermarket. He maintained a look of disgust as he went from one section of the market to the other.

Following his uncle, Bill thought to himself how difficult it must be for a person like Clovis who nearly starved to death during the Great Depression of the '30s to see unlimited pounds of meat lying in open refrigerated cases. Through Clovis's eyes he saw the ice cream in many different flavors. In Clovis's time it would have only been vanilla made by his mother's hand from fresh cream and snow or ice. Fruit and vegetables were piled everywhere. Such a marvel should have been a great comfort to someone from the days of the Depression. Bill watched Clovis who seemed almost angry.

By the time they had reached the checkout counter, Clovis

would be berating Bill about waste and telling personal stories about himself and Bill's mother when she was just a baby. People always stared at Clovis when he reached an angry pitch, shouting, "...in 1932 peoples didn't eat for so long they stopped fartin'."

Once he got his uncle home and the groceries put away, Clovis would insist that his nephew stay for dinner. When he asked what Bill wanted for dinner, Bill would always carefully suggest something that they hadn't gotten at the store that day, and of course Bill would have to go back out to get it. It was Bill's way of squeezing in some free time that he needed to do his own errands. That is also how he happened to be in front of the dry cleaner's twenty minutes early.

Bill found a parking space just hidden from the slow parade of people making their way through the Hollow. As he walked, he laughed silently to himself. Nothing changed in the Hollow, not from month to month nor from year to year. Cars hurrying to no place in particular still slowed down as they passed through the Hollow to see who was standing where on the busy block. So many people in so much of a hurry doing so little. Nothing had changed. He laughed again and ducked into a doorway hoping not to be recognized by a man he had known from prison.

The man, driving a white Cadillac, pulled over to the curb alongside a young attractive girl in a tight skirt and high heels. Bill watched their exchange from the doorway. At first the young girl seemed interested. She halted her long dark-legged gait and looked at the man disdainfully. Then she stepped toward the curb without changing the expression on her face, enticed, but less than interested. The girl stepped back from the curb, yelling obscenities as the man spirited the car away on screeching tires. The girl stood in a cloud of exhaust fumes, her middle finger extended toward the car and its driver. She continued on as if the incident had never happened. Nothing had changed.

Stepping back onto the sidewalk, Bill looked across the street and tried to see through the lettering on the window of the dry cleaners. He checked his watch, crossed the street and stood before the shop door. He fought the notion that he had come early in anticipation of seeing the slender lady behind the counter—that was foolish. It was also the truth. He watched her through the window as she went from counter to counter bagging and hanging newly-cleaned clothes as if searching for clues, to what, he didn't know. Eventually, the Italian owner replaced Vivian at the counter as she went to the back room. Bill stepped away from the door and walked to the corner, not wanting to be waited on by the owner. He looked at his watch again. It was five minutes until closing. A few minutes later the Italian man came out of the door of the shop and paused to light a cigarette. He quickly turned up the street and passed Bill, trailing a light scent of body odor. Bill waited until the owner turned the far corner before starting back toward the shop.

Vivian heard the bells above the door ring and yelled from the back, "Just a minute, please!" She had hoped the bearish man with gentle, droopy eyelids would return, but she had lost the thought as she prepared the shop for closing. "I'll be there in a moment!" she yelled again.

Running shirts on the press made the backroom of the laundry fifty degrees hotter than the rest of the world, and when she came around the corner, nearly trotting, she was wiping the sweat from her forehead.

When they saw each other neither spoke. Vivian smiled politely as she came up to the counter. Bill reminded himself why he had come and began to fumble for his clothes ticket, but Vivian was already hanging several of his pieces on the rack above the counter top.

Bill pulled the crumpled ticket from his back pocket and tried to flatten it on the counter. "Do you still need this?" he queried, smiling sheepishly.

"Not really," Vivian shrugged. "He keeps the pink copy for his records." Vivian took the ticket and was about to drop it in a box when she looked at it and stopped.

"Furman?" She looked at Bill closer than she had been able to before. "You aren't from around here are you?"

"No-yes—well, I used to be years ago, but after high school I moved a cuppla times. I still try to get back once a month to see my uncle." Bill left out the unnecessary details of his years as a numbers runner and then a prisoner. With the silent admission to himself that he came for more than his laundry, he could feel his nervousness begin to compete with his confidence. "My name is Bill—Bill Furman, what's yours?"

Vivian smiled. "Bill Furman. You know, somewhere in the back of my mind I thought I knew you, but I haven't seen you for nearly twenty years. You went to Morristown, didn't you?"

"For a while I did."

"Boooy you sure...look different...I mean you were really sk...you were really tall even then, but..." Vivian stopped short realizing what she had been trying to say was that Bill Furman still looked liked Bill Furman plus about seventy-five pounds that he desperately could have used twenty years ago to balance his tall, gaunt frame—a frame that had looked so awkward and emaciated that he had kept to himself as an underclassman. That is why she didn't remember much about him in high school. And what she remembered of him marrying was hearsay. Hearsay was abundant in the Hollow. Many made a life's occupation of it. Jessie Rose had said, "A wise person picks up little of it and keeps none of it."

Bill smiled. "That's okay, you can say it. I'm fatter now." Bill patted his stomach with both hands.

"No! I wasn't going to say that!"

"Yes, you were. How come you stopped talking then?"

The truth was that she didn't want to bring up his past, but this was an easy out. "No, really. I was going to say how much better you look with a little weight, but I felt...well, you know."

"Yes. No matter what you say, I do know." Bill said patting his stomach again.

Vivian smiled and handed him his clothes and dropped his ticket onto the day's pile of pink slips. "Well, you made it in with these just in time this morning."

"I don't think your boss would have taken them if you hadn't come when you did."

"You're probably right."

"Hey! I really appreciate it. I owe you one."

"That's okay. Anytime."

Bill wanted to say more, but already he had said more than he had to any other woman in a long time. It had been years. He started to speak and realized he had lost his place. He smiled and turned toward the door.

Vivian pretended to go back to work while skillfully watching as he closed the door behind him. Out of habit she reached to shut the cash register as she did after every customer had paid when she noticed it had never been opened. She ran to the door. "Hey! you forgot..."

Bill put one hand up to his forehead and then threw the shirts across the back seat of his car. He crossed the street smiling. "I guess I got caught up in the conversation."

"Doesn't take much to get you caught up, does it?"

Embarrassed, Bill shrugged his shoulders. "Hey! You never told me your name."

"Oh, I'm sorry. I guess I got a little caught up, too. It's Vivian."

"What?"

"Vivian," she repeated, a little louder. "My name is Vivian."

"No, I mean Vivian what?"

"Oh! Thompson," she said laughing. "Vivian Thompson."

"Vivian Thompson. How come I don't remember you from school?"

"Oh, I was pretty occupied back in those days. I think I missed a few things."

Bill leaned against the corner of the building, comfortable again. You weren't one of those girls who fell in love as a freshman and stayed with the same guy all through school, were you.?"

"Well, not quite that bad," she said smiling. "I fell in love as a sophomore and stayed..." She let the sentence die.

"Yes, I see. I did something similar some years later."

"You married your first love, too."

"Yep."

"Are you still married?" she asked, somewhat hesitantly and as naturally as she could manage.

"Nope. How about you?"

"No, not really. We've been separated for a long time."

Bill let the pause hang too long. Every passing second made it harder to continue. He took a deep breath. "Well, what do you say we have dinner some time?"

"I would like that. When?"

Bill thought for a moment and decided he could eat with Clovis anytime. Actually, Clovis would be elated to know that he had regained an interest in life again. "Why not tonight?"

The smile faded from Vivian's face. "No, I can't tonight. I'm having dinner with a friend."

For a moment rejection washed over Bill like an ocean swallowing an ant. He had stuck his neck out and gotten it chopped off.

"But, " Vivian said after a moment's thought. "How about tomorrow night?"

It was a simple enough thought. And Bill wished he had thought of it. "Sure! Sounds good," he said, with a renewed smile. "I have a few things to do, but why don't you give me your number and I'll call you."

Vivian smiled, very happy that the opportunity wasn't lost. "Well, okay." She went back into the shop and returned with her number written on the back of a laundry slip. She gave it to him, and watched him drive off.

She went back inside feeling like someone other than the Vivian she had been for a long time. She was not depressed, not worried, not hiding her ever-present fears, not wanting a drink; she was happy. She felt as if, and admittedly it was silly, but, she felt as if she wanted to dance around the dry cleaners. "How long has it been since I've felt this?" she wondered. It was an excitement about life she hadn't felt since her school days. It was the feeling standing on the stairs of the high school after the conference with Mr. Suther she had tried to recapture and couldn't. "Joy!" she said out loud. "That's the only word that could describe it exactly." She pursed her lips as she realized how perfectly the word described her feelings. It frightened her briefly to think that kids—so much in a hurry to grow up—were rushing away from the joy of their youth, a joy they would only recapture in fleeting moments in their adult years.

Out of habit she reached to close the cash register that still had never been opened. She smiled as she realized she had given the pink slip to Bill with her phone number on the back of it. She punched NO SALE.

14

It was 5:30 Thursday evening. Rick Taglia fought to keep his mind on the stolen cars as he turned onto Water Street and proceeded toward the Hollow. At the light, he noted cars, drivers, and license plates. He saw Vivian Thompson from the cleaners, old man Ceritano from his market, and others as they closed for the day. He realized these were the places where he was rarely called for help. Not like the Pail and two other bars, the cafe, the magazine stand on the corner, the makeshift bar-b-q with the picnic tables set up in a lot that belonged to who-knows-who, the corners, curbs, the maze of alleys, and roof tops. It was staggering to think of so many places a man could have his throat cut. At times the Hollow could be a fortress of thieves. He smiled to himself as he sped around the corner and headed for the hospital.

Tina Phillips, dark and youthful, emerged from a side door of Memorial Hospital dressed in her nurse whites and a sweater. She began walking at a fast clip toward home. When she heard her name being called, she stopped and scanned the parking lot. Seeing that it was Rick she became subdued as she pulled her sweater around her shoulders and examined the lot again, this time to see if anyone would see them together.

Rick closed the car door and approached her slowly. He kept his hands in his pocket to avoid scaring her off. "Hi."

"Hi, Rick. I thought we said we weren't going to do this any more."

"Yeah, I know..." he said, taking a deep breath. He spoke with his eyes for a minute and shrugged.

Tina eased a bit and tried to smile. "You know, you're still having conversations without me. I can tell the way your eyes dart around."

"Yeah, I know. I still have trouble talkin' out loud sometimes. Especially around you. My thoughts just don't seem to find the way out." They both stood in silence, occasionally looking around the parking lot to see who might be watching.

"Well, I gotta be goin'. I promised Marlon I'd be home in time for dinner."

"Hey how is he?"

"He's great" Tina smiled. "He's the only thing that keeps me going."

"The only thing?"

"Yeah. That and my job, my mom and dad." After she said this, she knew that it wasn't what he wanted to hear. It hurt his feelings. "He asks about you sometimes. Wants to know when you are coming over again."

"What did you tell him?"

Tina sighed. "I told him maybe one day when things were different. I'd better go Rick. I don't want to get into this."

"Okay. I was just wondering if things would ever be different. I mean, there are always going to be people like your father and your brother. They are as bigoted as any whites. How long are we suppose to wait for somebody else's permission to be together?" Rick hesitated, speaking with his eyes. And then, "… to love each other."

"When you finally do talk you have a lot to say, Rick." She turned away and leaned on a parked car. "I don't want to hurt you. I never said anything about feeling love." Struggling with the words, she faced him again.

"You cut everything off before either one of us knew what we were feeling." Rick moved closer to her.

"Rick! I gotta go."

"All right. All right. But let's not just let things drop. Let's just talk. Forget about anything heavy. Just talk. Okay?"

Tina blew hard. She didn't know how to avoid the pain that seemed inevitable. What she felt was good. Seeing Rick was more than good. She had lied. It wasn't planned for her husband Carl to suddenly run off the way he did, he just did. Carl, Steve, and Rick had been close friends since high school. Carl and Steve had entered the academy together a year after Rick. Rick had been one of the groomsmen at their wedding. After the horrible night of the shooting, Carl had never been the same. All the time Rick had been there for both of them, especially after Carl disappeared. Rick and Tina began spending more and more time together on the phone, lunches, movies, at the park with her son Marlon. And then, love just happened. For awhile, the world around them thought it wonderful that she had someone, a close friend as well as someone from the Department, who could comfort her. Then everyone seemed to notice that it was more than comforting. Soon the hatred and the name calling made it all very dirty, like mud stirred in a clear pond. The anger had shredded Tina's family, setting one against the other in ways she never thought possible. Finally, she gave in.

Her face was twisted with frustration as she looked into his eyes. "Rick, why did you come back? We can't do this. I can't go through this again. I can't take another loss. I just can't."

"Tina, I just want to talk. Promise. I'll keep it light. I swear."

The sun felt good on her face. She let its warmth fill her. "You'll keep it light?"

"Double swear."

"Who will keep me light?" She nearly smiled

Rick, more relaxed, fought the urge to take her into his arms. Instead, he just said, "You'll do fine."

"Okay. Just talk."

"When?"

"Okay. Pick me up here. Sunday at three."

Jimmy Lee was lying under the yellow Stutz Victoria on a roller board when he heard the bells signaling that he had a customer. He loved working the little station that sat by the stone bridge. It was his life. However, the Stutz was a life's dream and he was deeply infatuated with the idea of bringing it back to life. To that end the bell was an interruption, an annoyance.

He pushed himself from under the running board and grimaced when he saw that it was one of the Taglia's. It was hard to forget the abuse that he had endured at the hands of Bono and his father, Spago. They made no attempt to hide the fact that they held stray dogs in higher esteem than "niggers". He had tried not to hold it against Rick, but it was hard. He groaned, dreading the encounter, and took his time.

"What can I do ya?"

"Fill it please, Jimmy Lee."

Jimmy Lee made his way around to the back of the car and stuck the nozzle in the tank, all the time watching and remembering. Bono's words still burned in his ears. "Nigger, do you really expect the city to protect you and pay for the gas at the same time. Jesus Chris..." he had said chewing on his cigar, "...be a good boy and clean the windshield. Protecting niggers is dirty work." When the vision was over, Jimmy Lee looked up to see

Rick standing next to him.

Rick sat on the end of the car with one foot on the bumper. He looked at the old station and then down to the ground looking for the right words. "I remember when I was kid I used to think that riding around with my father in the squad car was the greatest thing in the world. He was always a bastard at home, but when he put that uniform on, I thought that he was really someone important." Jimmy Lee listened without looking away from the pump. "I didn't think anything was more important than the way he saved people from the bad guys all day long. I used to brag about it in school to my friends." Rick paused listening to the clicking sounds that the numbers made as they spun on the pump dial. "And then one day we came here and I heard my father talking to you like...like you were some kind of trash. I couldn't believe it. The things he said were so ugly it frightened me. I didn't want him to get back in the car with me. I wanted to lock him out. I remember you pumping gas, just like right now, as if nothing were happening—just watching the pump. You know what he said when he got back in the car?" Jimmy Lee didn't speak, but his eyes flickered. "I remember. He said, *That's how you gotta treat these jigs to keep them in line.* I remember he laughed and slapped me on the leg. I remember it because I jerked my leg away from his hand and when he saw how disgusted I was, he slapped me right across the head and said I had a thing or two to learn about being a man."

The pump clicked. Jimmy Lee gave it two more short squeezes and hung it back up. When he turned to face Rick, Jimmy Lee's face was less hard than it had ever been for any other Taglia.

"I guess the part that frightened me the most was that all the time I thought everyone at home had been willing to endure his cruelty and brutality because his job was so important. I figured he was just so tired from chasing bad guys that when he got home, he was a little crazy. Truth is my father was a bully. He bullied everyone, me, Bono, my mother, the dogs..." Rick smiled sarcastically and shook his head. "When we pulled out of the station that day I wasn't sure who the bad guys were anymore. Now, I always feel like I have to apologize for being a Taglia when I come in here. Maybe I do. But, I'm not like my father or Bono, Jimmy Lee. I want you to know that."

Jimmy stood for a moment knowing it must have taken a lot

for the young cop to say what he had. He turned and screwed the gas cap back on. "How old are you, Hoops?"

"Twenty-seven."

"Your brother know you been seein' Tina Phillips?"

"Yes, but we're really not seein' each other anymore. So..." Rick shrugged.

Jimmy Lee smirked and glanced at the pump. "Twelve fo' the gas," he said, getting the business out of the way. "Why? Cause'a her brother?"

"Probably. She didn't say as much. But that's probably it. He's just as bad as Bono." Rick gave Jimmy Lee a twenty and walked around the side of the car and got in. Jimmy Lee followed him, making change. "Keep it, Jimmy. I'm sure the city owes you at least that much."

"Hoops? You better watch your ass, son. However mean you think yo' father was, Bono is worse." Jimmy Lee's face grew more stern. "And so is that fool Tina got for a brother. He don't respect life and he don't care about dyin'."

"Thanks, Jimmy Lee, if you see anything or hear anything about..."

"The fool wreckin' every car in town?"

"Yeah, I could use the help."

Rick held his hand out to Jimmy Lee through the open window.

"You got it." Jimmy Lee gripped it firm and smiled.

Jimmy Lee walked back to the garage. Once inside he studied the Stutz. "What shall we call you?"

Jimmy Lee rubbed the Stutz's fender, gently endowing it with new life. "...Bertha, no...Bella naa, hmm. Well don't worry we gonna find you a name. Let's get yo' lights shinin' and yo' wheels spinin', then I'll come up with somethin'." He smiled as he lowered himself down to the roller board. A moment later he vanished under the car.

Little Von stood in the narrow space between the kitchen table and the sink, watching his big brother. Robin's head was bent to a mountain of books. He couldn't remember the last time he had seen his brother read a book after school. If he ever did any homework, it was done in a rush after he got dressed in the morning, just before he went out of the door. But there he was, at the kitchen table, motionless, except for his pencil rushing from one side of the page to the other.

"Bye Rob," he said. "I'm gonna watch some TV."

"Okay man. Don't turn it up too loud." Robin waved with one hand while turning a page with the other.

Little Von raised his eyebrows in bewilderment.

Vivian pulled the brown two-toned Chevy into the parking lot and blew the horn as a signal for the boys to come and help her with the groceries. Little Von ran to the window and stood on his tip-toes and yelled. "Mommy, you home?"

"Yep, I think so!" she said happy to hear the excitement in the child's voice. She pulled a grocery bag from the backseat and made her way to the door.

"Rob! Rob!" Little Von shouted as he burst into the kitchen and grabbed Robin by the hand to stop him from writing. "Mommy's home and she gots groceries!"

"Has, Von." Robin sat back in his chair and sighed with re-lief. It had been a hard week. After the meeting at school with Mr. Suther, he wasn't sure what kind of shape his mother would be in. He had wondered if they would see her at all, but she was home and she had groceries which meant, thank God, that she was sober. Joleena came into his thoughts. He wrote her name on the inside of his notebook and looked at it longingly.

Robin got up to meet his mother by the door. Little Von was already standing on a chair, working to open the locks. "Hi, Mom!"

"Hi, Von. How's my big boy?" Vivian said, smiling down, a grocery bag in each arm.

"Good. You bring me any treats?"

"Yep. Look in the bag. I got you some Vanilla Wafers. Mmmm. Sound good?"

"Yum."

Robin tensed, knowing it was his turn. "How you doin' Mom? How was work?"

"Work?" Vivian smiled, her eyes wide when she entered the small kitchen and saw books sprawled everywhere. She pushed the two grocery bags across the counter closer to the refrigerator. "I must admit, it was definitely one of my better days in that place. How is the new class working out?"

Robin felt good not having to look away from his mother. "It was all right. It's the same old stuff I did before, but DK's a good teacher."

"Robin, move your stuff around to the other side of the table. I have to get some dinner going for you and Von."

"How come? You going out?" Robin asked, his sense of well-being replaced with concern.

"Not really. Clovis got some papers from the bank that he didn't understand and he asked me to come down and read them to him. It shouldn't take long. You know how old people get nervous when they think something isn't taken care of. He sounded pretty worried."

As she finished her last words, she already had several hamburgers in the skillet hissing. In another minute she had emptied the last grocery bag and spread french fries over a flat pan.

"Listen. If I get any calls, take a message—no better yet, tell them to call back in an hour. I shouldn't be gone that long, though." And with that said, she disappeared down the hall toward her room.

Robin felt some relief. Vivian's plan didn't sound like it included drinking. He also knew that Clovis had a definite routine. With Clovis there were three important things in life. One was business, one was drinking, and one was fishing. Each was serious in its own place, but seldom did he mix them together.

A while later, Vivian took one last hurried look around her small kitchen and wiped her hands on a dish towel. "Von, you have enough french fries?" Little Von looked at his plate and then across the table to his big brother's. He nodded yes while trying to chew an over-stuffed mouthfull.

"Okay then. I'll see you guys in a little while." She pinned several loose strands of her hair with a bobby pin, waved, and was gone.

Standing in front of Clovis's door, a floor below her own, she could already hear Robin yelling at his brother to stop stealing french fries from his plate. She contemplated going back, but she had already knocked twice and could hear the locks being undone on the other side of Clovis's door.

Bill Furman had been standing over the stove carefully shifting the position of the Italian sausage in the frying pan when he heard a soft knock on the door. He listened to see if Clovis or Jimmy Lee would stir from their chairs. "Clovis! Jimmy Lee!"

The old men ignored him and continued arguing and watching Walter Cronkite delivering the evening news. Taking one last look at the spaghetti sauce bubbling on another burner, he walked to the door wiping his hands on an apron that had once belonged to Clovis's wife many years before.

Clovis leaned toward the hallway with a sly grin on his face as he strained to pick up any sounds he could as his nephew swung the door back. But there was no immediate reaction. Bill and Vivian stood there staring at each other for an eternal moment. Clovis eased himself back into the chair and smiled. The two men slapped each other's hand and returned to arguing with Walter Cronkite.

15

DARKNESS HAD FALLEN QUICKLY. Patrolman Steve Seward scribbled down the license plate number of the car turned over on its side at the bottom of the embankment. He scrambled back up the steep slope using his flashlight to help him pick his way among the rocks and soft dirt. It didn't take long for him to check the numbers against his list of stolen cars and make a positive I. D. Moments later several more patrol cars arrived. Detectives and patrolmen searched the area for clues while other uniformed officers made efforts to disperse the growing crowd, with little effect.

Rick Taglia came to a screeching stop at the edge of the throng and was out of his car before the motor died. He ran through the headlight beams knowing a fresh wreck could mean new clues. He pushed his way to the edge of the embankment and watched as firemen covered the area of the gas tank with fire extinguishers. "Hey!...." He bent his knees and began a controlled slide to the site. "Hey! Hey! Guys! You're blowing my prints. Stay away from the doors please." Annoyed, the firemen ignored him.

"Hey Taglia. There's a danger of fire here. You do your job and we'll do ours. And by the way, your brother's a prick."

Rick threw up his hands and worked his way back up the hill. Steve Seward put his two-way receiver back on its hook and walked over to Rick. "Hoops, dig this, man. The water boys were here before most of our guys. You got any new ideas?"

"Personally I think some kid enjoys picking up new cars for a couple of hours and wreckin' 'em and it's really startin' to piss me off."

"Bozo...I mean, the Chief is gettin' a little huffy. That was him on the radio. He was even squawkin' at the Fire Chief. I think he pissed him off."

Rick was brushing dirt off his pants. He laughed out loud. "Bozo? Is that what the guys call him?" He laughed again.

"Well, not me. Just some of the guys."

"Bozo. I like it. Did anybody get anything before those pinheads started hosin' down the place?"

"Not much. Just this." Steve handed him a small brown paper bag and waited, smiling. Rick pulled out a tiny envelope holding it by the edges and a large black handkerchief that had obviously been folded triangle style. "Hey Hoops. Anybody might have had a nickel bag of reefer, but how many White boys you know wear do-rags? Must've fallen out of his back pocket."

"Well, that eliminates White boys stealin' Black-owned cars in a Black neighborhood. Jesus, Steve, with a mind like that I don't know why you haven't made detective yet."

Seward switched on his flashlight and held his hand, dark-side-up, under the beam and then he held it on Rick's. "That's why and you know it. But, don't worry Hoops, my man. Our day is comin'. The first thing they gonna do is put all you whities on welfare, pull your self-esteem down a few strokes. And whatever line Bono stands in to get his check, the window is gonna close just when it's his turn. Yes sir. Our day is comin'."

Rick laughed and shined the flashlight back on Steve's hand. "The first thing 'they gonna do'? What do you mean *they*? Where you gonna be during this great erection?"

"The word is insurrection. Hawaii," Seward turned his head and spit. When he looked back, he looked Rick in the eye and was silent. It was a simple act that told Rick this was more than just a joke. It was something Steve Seward had thought out. Rick, Steve, and Tina's husband Carl had been friends since grade school. They played basketball together in high school. They were inseparable. Rick had convinced them of the importance of getting into the Academy and encouraging other Negroes. Steve Seward was Rick's true brother. Rick knew, below the humor, this was some kind of pitch.

"I ain't gonna be hangin' around forever directing traffic. Ever since we been together in grade school we've done everything about the same, runnin', basketball, books, women—everything. I was never any better than you. And you was never better than me. Think about it, man. We came on the force the same time. You been a detective for a year already. You think Bono's considering making me the first Negro detective in Morristown?" Rick started to speak without anything certain to say.

"Right. Maybe if this were Newark or Harlem. But it ain't. Let's face it. Bono hated Carl because he always spoke his mind. Bono likes me less than he likes you. And I'll tell you somethin' else that eats me. Every Negro with a gun wants to shoot a colored cop 'cause they figure he's a sellout."

"Steve. Come on man. You ain't no sellout. Neither was Carl. What's eatin' you tonight?"

"I know that and you know that. We let you talk us into being a cop so Negroes would really have someone to look out for 'em. But everybody don't see that, Rick. No. Screw this. I'm gettin' out one way or another."

"Hawaii? That's ten thousand miles away! You crazy?"

"It's only eight thousand. We been fishin' in Poke all our lives. You know what a marlin is? Now I ain't talkin' about no skinny ass sail fish like you see hangin' up on people's wall behind their desk. I'm talkin' about five hundred, seven hundred pounds or more! And mister, that's no bull!"

Rick forced a laugh. He used the evidence bag as an excuse to look away.

"There's something else you might want to think about too. All kinds of people live together on them islands, Rick—Filipinos, Portuguese, Japanese, Chinese, Negroes, and not enough whites to be concerned about. It might not be a bad place for a retired white cop and a beautiful nurse with dark skin to make a go of it. Think about it."

Just then there was an explosion. Both men threw themselves to the ground. A scream arose from the crowd as the initial fireball curled upward. The car in the gully was engulfed in flames. Rick jumped up and kicked the dirt and yelled at the firemen. "Great job, assholes."

Steve Seward's smile was serene. "Time for crowd control. Hawaii…" He smiled backing away. "Think about it."

Jimmy Lee roared up in the hook and leaned out of the window. He pointed at the burning wreck. "Well. No need 'n me hangin' around now. I'll get her when she cool off in the mornin'."

"Hey Jimmy Lee. How'd you get here so quick?"

"I was on the way home from havin' dinner with old Clovis and I saw the crowd. I figured it was another car." Jimmy Lee motioned Rick closer to the window. He held out something between his thumb and forefinger. "Hey Hoops. You know what dis is?"

Rick took the item and turned it over a couple of times in his hand trying to read the letters. "What's this? Some kind of funny harmonica or something."

"Nope. It's a pitch pipe. Singers use it when they start a song without music. I found it over in the grass when I was lookin' fo' a way to get the hook-line down to the car. Might be just some kids, but..." he shrugged.

"Thanks, Jimmy Lee. This might be something."

Earlier that night in the projects, Clovis the Lamb stood at the window of his first-floor apartment watching as Bill and Vivian strolled towards the Pocahontas dam. Dinner had been good, with Clovis telling old tales, word perfect, that he had told each of them many times before. Bill and Vivian stole glances at one another, reaching for this thing and that thing across the table. When dinner was over and dishes washed, the two left for a walk.

The full moon glistened on the rippled surface of the water as it spilled like a glass sheet over the raised edges of the dam. As they stood in the pale light listening to the water, Bill offered his outstretched hand and searched for the right words. Not wanting to seem foolish, but also unable to contain the feelings awakening within him, feelings that he had forgotten existed, he watched as Vivian opened her small delicate fingers to receive his.

"Viv, this is so awkward for me. It's been years since..."

With her free hand, Vivian placed a finger across his lips to silence him. There was no need to speak. She understood everything, the silent thoughts, the hollow thumping in the center of her chest, and the inability to capture the rush of emotions with simple words.

For the first time since they met, Bill examined her face openly, the smooth skin of her cheeks, her lips, the line of her jaw as he traced it with a finger—back to her neck and the fall of her hair with its red highlights glinting in the moonlight, and her eyes. Her eyes he had saved for last. He delighted in their electric brownness. He felt a slight tremble from her as his fingers followed the silkiness of her eyebrows. He leaned close and they kissed, cautiously at first and then passionately as they began to understand that they had found one another.

Bill smiled as they separated, "I haven't felt this way in years."

"...In years. Yeah that sounds about right," Vivian said, smirking at the moon. "I haven't felt anything in years."

"Don't you think we're too old to be fallin' in love like two school kids?"

Vivian slipped her hand under Bill's arm and they began to walk along the footpath that followed the water's edge. She looked at Bill. "Is that what we're doing?" Bill sighed. Understanding his shyness, something that attracted her, she pulled his arm in closer. "Jessie Rose, that's my mother, and my dad have been married for forty years. Sometimes they argue, but even when they do, their voices never get much louder than when they tell each other jokes. I'm not saying that she doesn't get a little crazy sometimes, they just never seem to fight about anything. Their relationship always seems so perfect that I just assumed it would be the same for me."

"Was it?"

Vivian smiled softly as her mind wandered over the years.

Bill helped her over a spot where the path became muddy. Then they were side by side again.

"No. But I don't feel bad about it or bad toward him. We were so young. I feel stupid when I think about it now. We were in love. No one could have talked us out of it."

"Is this the same relationship that kept you busy most of the way through high school?"

"Yes."

The water was quieter now, gurgling only occasionally as it found its way around rocks and other debris. Vivian took her time, listening to the change and watching the movement of fireflies. "I went to the high school the other day for a conference with my son's counselor. You really feel your age when you see what you used to look like. I saw these two kids walking through the hall all wrapped up in one another. It was like looking at myself twenty years earlier."

"How old is your son?"

"I've got two sons. Robin is fifteen and Levon, my baby, will be seven soon. My oldest is eighteen. She's off to nursing school in Orange. How about you?"

"Unfortunately, or fortunately, depending on how you want to look at it, we never had any. Perhaps that was best considering how things turned out." Bill remembered the last time he had seen his ex-wife Lucretia, but the vision faded as he looked at Vivian. "I grew flowers instead of babies. Did you and your ex have problems?"

"Worse. He was a musician."

Bill, being a practical person, laughed.

"Ah. So you think I should have seen that one coming, huh?"

"Well, come on. A musician?"

Vivian fell silent as they passed some men sitting around a fire by the river. Their voices were loud and exaggerated and it sounded as though it had been awhile since any one of them had been sober. One of the men threw a bottle that crashed on the opposite bank. It exploded with a pop. Vivian realized how secure and at ease she felt with Bill.

"I'm sorry. Maybe I shouldn't have said that."

"No, that's okay. I was just thinking how most people don't understand what it's like to be a musician, or an artist of any kind. I mean to feel what it's like to have something burning in your gut that you can't get away from. Musicians don't get much support from anyone. Instead of supporting them while they try to reach impossible dreams, people tell them they're stupid and irresponsible. People tell them to spend the rest of their life with a regular nine-to-five job that they hate, but that's okay because it lets you eat and pay the bills. Maybe you even get to catch a movie or something once a month."

"Well that's how it is for most people, isn't it?"

Vivian smiled. "But that doesn't make it right."

They came to a tree which seemed to have three trunks growing from the same base. One of the trunks looked as if it had been broken, but continued to grow only a few feet off the ground before it was able to turn skyward again. Vivian sat on the low limb and Bill sat on the dry grass facing the water. Bill enjoyed the sound of her voice. He listened intently, not missing a word.

"It would be like telling people that flowers are gray and that they shouldn't expect anything more," Vivian said, using a metaphor that she was sure would strike home with Bill. "And if they accept that, the flowers would remain gray in their minds and these people will never look for anything more. But once you see the colors for yourself and smell the different perfumes that each one has, you can never go back to what most people believe. You'd rather starve first. People—everday people—just don't understand the passion that musicians feel. Like that painter who cut his ear off. What was his name?"

"What? Over a painting?"

"No, over a woman. But it was about passion. Passion that

everyday people don't feel as they sleep-walk from day to day. Trust me. I know that walk well."

Bill suddenly remembered how Lucretia had called his prized Hawaiian orchids *hula weeds*. "Passion, huh. I tried to play the sax a little bit in junior high school, but the kids who sat next to me in the band complained so much, I gave it up."

Vivian laughed. "I used to go with him to gigs on Friday and Saturday nights. You could feel him start to come to life about two hours before it was time to play. He'd get antsy and hard to talk to. Even short, if he couldn't find something simple that was right in front of his face. It was like his energy for the night was filling him up with no way to get out. When he got up there and started to play, you could see that the stage was his real home. And it wouldn't take long before he started to lose touch with the world.

"What instrument did he play?"

"He was a string bass player. He'd get upset if you called it a fiddle. It was a bass. When it finally came time for the guys to play, I would watch the crowd. They really would get loose on the bandstand. They took their breaks in the parking lot. They shared a bottle in a brown paper bag. Some of them came back a lot looser. It wouldn't take long before the whole room got wound up. You could see them start to move in their seats. Before long the dance floor would be packed. The more the audience responded, the higher they'd go until you knew for sure they had no awareness of where they were anymore."

"Yeah, I've seen bands really burn like that. Then I'd run home and pull out my sax and toot, toot, toot, but the only thing I'd burn would be my mother's ears."

Vivian smiled. "Some have it and some don't. Don't feel bad though; it's a gift. Most people can play if they have a few lessons, but when you hear someone who was born to play...or sing...paint or even cook...when it's a gift, you know it."

Bill flashed on a memory and started to laugh. "There used to be this old Black guy with one leg that came around the shop down in Patterson. He must have been in his seventies, I guess. Played a harmonica. He had a little bench he sat on near the corner playin' for people passin' by. Every now and then when the shop got quiet, I'd come to the door and listen to him blow that thing. He had it. Probably made more on the street with his tin cup than I make in the flower shop."

"Yep," Vivian nodded. "When it's a gift, you can tell. On the real slow songs, somethin' like 'Moon Indigo' or somethin' like that, he'd lean so low and close to his bass you'd think it was talking in his ear or something. Then they would kick off something the jitter bugs could cut loose on, and his face wouldn't be big enough to hold all of his smile."

Bill tried to feel and see what Vivian was describing, but all of his memories came from the dance floor instead of the stage. He visualized small rooms with densely packed sweaty bodies whirling back and forth, over shoulders, under legs, people yelling and women with pressed hair complaining about the heat while their hair returned to natural.

"It would take hours for him to come down after it was all over."

"Like when they walk race horses around after a race?"

"It was a lot like racing. Sometimes getting paid was a gamble too."

"Did you get into it?" Bill asked.

"Sure did. Had to. We girls sat together while the guys played. It was different for us because we knew more about music than anybody else in the place, except for other musicians that showed up to check out the competition. We were there for the music almost as much as the guys. We caught every little bip and bop, every little slur, and also the mistakes that couldn't even be called jazz.

"We knew the pressure they were under when the union guys came around checking for cards. They actually brought sticks and axe handles when they heard a non-union band was playing a union hall."

"I guess you're right. When most people go to a dance, they never see or think about stuff like that. You saw a lot, didn't you?"

"Yeah, I guess. Being with the band taught me a lot about people too. It helped me to cross racial lines. They played some of the White clubs uptown and I really could see the difference in the way they had to play."

"More reserved?"

"To say the least. And it was real strange to have the crowd cheering for you one minute, and then have to eat in the kitchen the next, but you made a lot of friends you normally wouldn't have. It was pretty exciting sometimes. Yeah, I was really into it in the beginning."

"Then?"

"Then the first baby came and the money got hard, and even harder after Robin came. Everything seemed like a problem after that."

"Wanna walk?" Bill asked, sensing tension in her voice.

"Sure."

"With our first one it wasn't quite so bad. She sorta tagged along when we couldn't find or afford a babysitter. It wasn't even like anything changed much except for where the bills came from. Jessie Rose kept her across the street while we worked. We'd pick her up in her pajamas and there'd be no problem. But after Robin came, things really got desperate. With two extra mouths to feed there was no time to be out of work. Certainly no time to be waitin' for gigs. I fell in with a crowd at my job that drank pretty heavy. He was working two jobs all the time. We started to fight a lot. I ran to Jessie Rose a lot. I guess that was wrong, too, but I didn't know what else to do. It just wasn't anything like it was supposed to be."

Bill helped her over another muddy place in the path. "How long did it last?"

"Well, we never did divorce, but we separated on and off for quite awhile. After we were apart for awhile, we both would want to try again, but it just kept ending up the same way every time. Each time it got more frustrating and more vicious. One time we got back together, I was pregnant before we got in the door good. That was Little Von." She wiped her tears as they turned toward a vacant lot overgrown with grass and weeds, and the brick apartment buildings.

Bill bent over and plucked a dandelion that grew on the side of the path. He handed it to Vivian in place of the words he could not find to comfort her.

Vivian took it and laughed. "This is what I get for spilling my guts out, huh? A weed."

Bill let his eyes droop sheepishly. "Now wait just one minute. Is that how you see this? A weed? This, my love, is one of the hardiest plants in God's botanical creation," he said in a voice meant to cheer her. "It's one of the purest of all yellows, and one of the first to appear, after the crocus, in the spring, and one of the last to die when the snow comes. Actually dandelion is just a nickname. The real name is *Taraxus Officinale*. Pretty good huh?"

"Boy."

"Down South, in the country, old women herbalists and mid-wives use it to make remedies and tonics for rheumatism and urinary problems, digestive ills, liver, spleen…all kinds of stuff."

"Whatever ails ya," Vivian said, smiling.

"Well…as weird as it might sound, it was a pretty exact science. I really love 'em."

"The midwives and herbalists?"

Bill smirked. "No. The dandelions. Look at all of them over there, and there." Bill pointed to the grassy areas that ran beside the Pocahontas and at the grassy patches dotted with yellow that struggled to survive the foot traffic between the brick apartments. "Their enemies are many, but their conquerors are few. Even with only the moon to show them, they look like sun droplets before they close for the night."

Vivian stopped walking. "You see a lot in little things, don't you?"

"I see a lot in you. Wild dandelions growing in field or valley is God's way of writing *I love you*."

Vivian stopped. She ran her finger gently back and forth across the yellow velvety growth. "Like I said, once you see something for what it really is, it's hard seeing it any other way. I guess a weed is just a flower growing where it's not wanted." Bill came close to her. She reached up and pulled him down toward her and looked into his eyes. They kissed and held each other warm from the chill that had come with the night air. When they parted Vivian let her head rest on Bill's chest and held the dandelion close to her face. "I don't want to feel like a weed anymore."

16

THE FOLLOWING FRIDAY CAME QUICKLY. Robin was more jittery than a bowl of Jell-O on a freight train. Vivian stood sober and teary as she tried to shape Robin's shirt collar to hide his tie.

"Come on, Ma, that's too tight!"

"Robin!" Vivian gave him a light slap on the arm. "Do you want me to fix this or not?" Little Von came in.

"Rob, you stink with that stuff again." Robin plucked him in the head and Little Von slugged his brother on the leg.

"Von!" Vivian yelled. "Go back in the other room and watch TV!" He did so, mumbling under his breath.

Robin laughed. "Jeez Mom. You're more nervous than I am."

"You're not nervous?"

"No, I'm not nervous. I'm scared to death."

"Robin, there's nothing to be afraid of." Vivian finished his tie and stood back looking and listening.

"I'm afraid I'll get all tongue-tied and not know what to say. Plus her father...you don't know what he's like."

Vivian did know, but she said nothing. "Robin, just do the best you can. Nobody will ever ask for any more than that. Just don't do or say anything that you wouldn't do or say uptown..."

"I know, Ma, in front of Kresge's. Right?"

Vivian smiled and wiped a tear. She went to the cupboard and took down two pans and put them in a brown-paper bag. "Don't forget to stop by and give these to your Gramma."

"Okay, Ma."

"You sure you don't want a ride? I don't mind."

"No. I'll walk. I need time anyway to get myself together." Downstairs at the corner of the courtyard, Robin, wearing dress slacks, jacket, and tie, turned and waved at his mother in the apartment window. The window in the living room slid open. "Bean head!" the small voice rang out. Robin could see his mother grimace and shake her head. Then she waved again. Robin waved back, turned and started for the Hill.

As Robin came to his grandparents' driveway, Elderiah Bowman was straddling a row of petunias, pulling weeds and spent blooms. When he heard the footsteps he stood up and smiled. Tossing the weeds to the side, he began to squint. "Now hold on.

Don't tell me. I know I know you from somewhere. But can't just recollect...I know." Elderiah snapped his fingers. "You that fella down to the bank that always waits on me. That right?"

"Gramps, you act like you ain't never seen me in a jacket before."

"Gramps! Did you just call me Gramps? Well now. Let's see. I ain't got but one grand boy could be old as you. But I don't think...wait let me check." Elderiah reached behind Robin's ear and came back with a quarter. "Well I'll be! Whoo wee! Look at you boy. I didn't even recognize you in all them fancy clothes. You ain't courtin' are 'ya?"

"Gramps, you been pullin' money out of my ears since I was five."

"Well how else would I know who you was. Wait. Who was the greatest pitcher ever live?" Elderiah stood quietly, expectantly

"Gramps come on. You know I know. All right. Satchel Page. Kansas City Monarchs. Negro league." Elderiah smiled. "Well boy. You don't look none too excited for a youngin' courtin'. Looks like dinner with the parents, I'd say judgin' by the way you dressed and by the way your lips are hangin' down."

"I got some real problems."

"You nervous about what to say and how to eat right, and most of all, 'bout meeting her father, right?" Elderiah put his arm around his grandson and walked him up the driveway.

"You hit it right on the head, Gramps. This is terrible."

Elderiah smiled. "Naa. You been taught all the right things, els'in your sister or your grandmam would have killed you by now. Hey. You a good person. You look sharper'n my straight razor, and I'm your grandpa, so you got charm. I know what you need," Elderiah said putting his arm around Robin. They walked up the rest of the driveway and under a white-arched trellis clustered with big red rose blooms. Some were fully open and others were tight buds. The perfume was thick as a cloud. "Hey boy. How you like my Don Juans? Somethin', ain't they? Even the bees get drunk under here."

Robin smiled, and then an idea hit him. "Hey Gramps!"

Elderiah laughed. "I'll cut you some even better ones that will stand up straight when the door opens. Now go head in and see yo' grandmam before you really get in some trouble."

Jessie Rose was already standing on the stairs to the

backporch wiping her hands on her apron. "Sounds like to me he already got enough trouble." Elderiah and Jessie both laughed. "Who this girl you courtin'?"

"Gram, her name is Joleena. She lives over on Hilliary." Robin said, pointing toward Lafayette. "Who's her family?"

"Her last name is Cleary."

"Who you talkin' bout? Eddie Cleary—Eddie Jr.?" She said, getting her generations straight. "Married to 'er...a...what's her name, Elder?"

Elderiah placed a small bucket of water next to another stand of roses. He stood frowning, looking at nothing. He suddenly came back to life. "Jessie, he married that Robinson girl. What's her name? Anna Robinson that used to live with her aunt over on Green Street. Real nice girl. Used to attend Mt. Zion. I don't know why she married Eddie."

"Yep I think I heard somebody at school say his name was Eddie." Robin had a sick look on his face.

Jessie Rose cocked her head to one side. "Well, don't you fret none about Eddie Cleary Jr., 'cause I remember how to deal with him from when he use come round here badgering Vivian. Come on in here and let me give ya somethin' to wack 'em with."

He looked to his grandfather. "Joleena's Dad used to date Mom?"

"Tried." Elderiah winked and went back to cutting roses.

"I hope he's not holding a grudge, Gramps."

Inside, the house was filled with a familiar aroma that Robin had known all of his life. "Gram. This was a pie day? Man, I really miss pie days. You used to stay in the kitchen all day bakin' pies."

"Yep. I miss havin' one or the other of you around all day pesterin' me and playin' in my dough."

"Yeah, I miss bein' here too."

"And Little Von was the worst of the three. He eat up half of it fo' I ever get it on the pie. Now I tell you who didn't miss a pie day. He would pretend he was just stoppin' to see yo' momma, but I always knew what he really wanted."

"Who you talkin' about, Grandma. Mr. Cleary?"

"He was the worst pain you ever saw. And what made it really bad was that Vivian had no interest in him whatsoever. That girl didn't have any mo' interest in that boy than she did in makin' snowballs in July. So I ended up stuck wit'em in the kitchen while she was upstairs talkin' on the phone wit yo' daddy. That's probably why he's rough on 'ya."

"He hasn't been rough on me yet 'cause we haven't met. But all the other guys that been over there...well I can't say what they say, Gram."

Jessie Rose smiled without stopping her work. "Well, I can imagine."

Elderiah came in with a beautiful bouquet of mixed roses. He laughed as he listened to Jessie. "Well, it ain't you. It's just boys in general."

Jessie took one of the sweet potato pies off her windowsill and wrapped it in wax-paper. "Well, you just hand this to 'em and you won't have to bother with him no mo'."

"Thanks Gram. That's great. You too, Gramps. I feel a lot better now."

Elderiah gripped his shoulder and smiled. Just then a bell rang on the oven and Jessie shooed them both out of the kitchen. On the front porch Elderiah stopped Robin at the top of the stairs. "Hold on, boy. You might need just one more thing." Elderiah reached in his pocket and pulled out an old-fashioned watch and chain. It had a silver casing and was inscribed on the inside of the face cover. It read: "To my young man Elderiah" And then below that the name Elderiah Jr. was inscribed. Below that was Robin's name.

"Your uncle, Elderiah Jr., lost it for a long time. He was heart broke so bad that I went out found another one. It wasn't as nice as this one cause it wasn't as old, but he never lost it, I'll tell you that. Two years later when we was about to sell the old truck I was really gettin' under every inch of it looking for somethin' or another and there it was hung up on the springs under the seat. It won't on the floor, so you wouldn't have seen it that way. You had to get up under there to see it. So now it's yours."

Robin didn't have a free hand. All he could do was stare at the polished silver with his name etched on it in fine lines. He looked up at Elderiah with no words.

"You ain't got time for a whole lotta thank yous now. You best be gettin' ready for Eddie Jr." Elderiah stuffed the watch and chain into Robin's jacket pocket.

Robin smiled. "At least I got something to whack him with now."

Down the street and halfway down the block, Robin turned and looked at his grandparents. Jessie Rose stood on the porch, smiling and dabbing her eyes with the lace handkerchief that she kept in the pocket of her apron.

He had thought about taking the short cut through old man Bush's backyard, but he had seen the hand with six fingers waving at him from the pen where he kept his dogs. "Looking mighty good there, Mr. Thompson," Bush called out. He swore at his dogs who stood on their hind legs trying to lick his face. Robin kept to the sidewalk.

Wooden Street had always been a quiet dead-end street, its pavement growing narrow and broken until it eventually disappeared into the mouth of a drainage pipe. In the summers before he had gone to junior high, the kids of the street would dare each other to crawl through the ribbed pipe filled with rocks, broken glass, and an occasional rat or two, all the way to the railroad tracks at the bottom of the hill. That game had come to a sudden end one summer when Tobie Mitchell, who had grown considerably from a steady diet of Twinkies and cream soda, got stuck in the dark pipe. For three hours Tobie had listened to the echoes of little scurrying feet and the shrill squeal of familiar animals. Everyone on the whole street came out to watch the fire department try to get ropes around his feet to haul him out. Tobie, nearly crazy out of his mind, cried and screamed shamelessly for the entire time. Pipe-crawling came to a sudden end on Wooden Street, with only its memory to haunt Tobie till he finally moved away.

To the left of the pipe, Boogers Hill sloped and fell away sharply. To the right of the pipe was the dirt path that led to Lafayette and Joleena's house beyond that.

Halfway up the path, Robin could hear the kids cheering around the basketball court. It was a Friday night tradition, but this night the playground would be packed as the fans of the Swan Tones added their number to the regular hordes that swarmed the grounds to watch sweaty muscular bodies fight and dance in a basketball ballet.

At the end of the trail and at the beginning of the front parking lot, Robin followed the blacktop pavement around to the back of the school, circling wide to avoid being seen carrying flowers and pie.

Hundreds of kids were on the playground crowding the lines of the basketball court, yelling and screaming with the changing momentum of the game. The ends of the court were lined with parked cars. Their owners drank wine and beer while beating their horns to show their displeasure of a certain play. There were no referees. All disputes were settled loudly and quickly by the players themselves.

Doing his best to go unnoticed in the huge crowd, Robin rounded the corner of the school maintenance shed and stopped suddenly, nearly colliding with a parked car. It was a new Cadillac. Robin was instantly struck by the beauty of the car, with its fins and long flowing lines of chrome. He walked carefully, peering into the windows, awed by the elegance of the soft white leather interior. He couldn't even begin to imagine what the dash of the newest Cadillac would look like. He approached the driver's window slowly, with anticipation. As he came level with the driver-side window, two heads popped up from the front seat. It was Benny and Charlene. Neither was able to hide the shocked expressions on their faces, least of all, Charlene. She had been caught with her blouse wide open, her dress crumpled around her waist, with the worst of all people, with no possible excuse. Looking from Robin to the basketball court, she quickly buttoned her blouse and pushed her skirt down. She slid from the front seat of the car and walked sullenly away toward the game and disappeared into the cheering crowd. Robin wanted to walk away. But it was too late for that now. He heard the power window on the driver's side ease down.

Benny calmly pulled out a cigarette. "Hey man," he grinned. "What can I say? Charlene's a fine broad." He blew a wide cloud of smoke and watched the place where she had entered the cheering mob.

Robin quickly looked from one side of the playground to the other. No one seemed to pay attention to anything other than the game. "Hey man. What goes on between you and Charlene is between you and Charlene,"

Benny took another deep draw. "Yeah. I would like to keep it that way." he said, in a business-like tone. "I mean, you know how touchy Scootch gets sometimes, the way he can blow things all outta proportion." Benny looked Robin in the eyes for the first time and grinned. His face was bruised on one side. Robin re-

flected on the confrontation Benny and Scootch had the night the
Swan Tones sang beneath the street lamp in the projects. The two
had nearly come to blows. Now Robin was sure that it would happen sooner or later, and when it did, it would be vicious and violent. When it happened, he wanted to be anywhere but between
the two of them.

Robin turned to the long field separating him from Joleena's
house. Benny started the car and pulled up along side him. "Not
too cool walkin' a mile with a pie and flowers to see a classy chick
like Joleena." Benny leaned through the open window, looking
down at Robin's shoes. "Dust will kill that shine you worked so
hard on."

"Ain't you gonna sing tonight?" Robin said, looking for a way
out.

Benny looked up at the sun making its way slowly toward
the horizon. "Yeah, tonight. But that ain't now. The game ain't even
over yet. Come on, man. It ain't nothin' but a five-minute drive
and on the other hand a fifteen-minute, crowded, dusty walk. If
them fools see that pie you can forget it. I'll take you first class,"
he said, waving his hand around the interior of the car.

Robin looked at the field and thought about Joleena's last
words about making her father wait for his dinner, and the shiny
new Cadillac. "Yeah. Sure." He couldn't help smiling as he sank
into the leather seats. "Whose is it?" Robin said running his fingers over the push buttons on the armrest of the door.

"My father's," Benny said without emotion. "Smells rich,
doesn't it?"

Robin just smiled, not wanting to get too friendly. If it ever
came down to choosing sides, he didn't want Benny coming close
to thinking of him as an ally. Robin noticed that Benny's face had
a small bruise and was slightly puffy in one place. "What happened to your face?"

Benny smirked, "Just some—nothing."

They circled back around the maintenance shed, away from
the crowd, to the front of the school and down Hazel Street and
out toward Evergreen Avenue. Benny came to a stop behind several cars waiting to turn onto the main street. He looked into the
rear-view mirror and saw Rick Taglia getting out of an unmarked
police car behind him.

"Oh shit!"

"What!" Robin said startled, turning to see what had frightened him. Benny's face became palid.

"Hold on man, it's Hoops."

Benny spotted him and threw the big Caddy into reverse, slamming into Rick's car and knocking him to the ground. Without looking either way he slammed the gear shift into forward and swerved onto the main street. Several other cars coming in the opposite lane were forced onto the sidewalk honking their horns and swearing at the two as they passed.

The force of the turn slammed Robin's shoulder against the door. "Benny! What the hell is going on! You steal this car?"

"No, man. I told you it's my father's."

"Then what you runnin' for?" Robin said, holding onto the dash as he watched Benny dodge around several slower cars.

"Hey man, you think Hoops gonna believe me, man? I put that scar behind his ear. You heard about that, didn't you?"

"Just tell him!"

"Oh right!" Benny laughed. "A little chat with the Taglia brothers? Hey man, Bono don't be askin' no questions, man. He'll find a way to get me 'cause I cut his brother." Benny's eyes were wild. He swerved into the lane of on-coming cars, hit the curb and slid back into his lane. "'Sides. He don't like anything that don't look vanilla."

Robin was horrified. He jerked his head around to face the back window.

Benny laughed. "You better get your head down. He might have his gun out."

Robin could see Rick Taglia's car in the distance coming down the hill. It was frantically swerving from side to side trying to get around slower traffic. Benny sped the car down the hill toward the Hollow and familiar territory which was away from Hazel Street and Joleena's.

When the cars had collided, the pie in its heavy plate had flown from Robin's lap and cracked the windshield of the Cadillac. It dropped to the dash and slid back into Robin's lap right-side-up. The roses were strewn all about the front of the car. Halfway down the hill Benny tried to take a curve too fast. Robin screamed as the car swerved sideways directly in front of another car on the other side of the street. The other driver tried to turn sharply, but not enough to change his forward momentum. The two cars crashed broadside. Robin lowered himself in the seat, his arms crossed in front of his face as the sound of breaking glass and crunching metal permeated the air. The Cadillac left the street and crossed a lawn in front of a large Victorian house throwing grass and dirt high in the air. Benny fought to regain control by pushing the gas pedal to the floor. The car punched through a wooden fence and back onto the street, its bumper dragging, tires smoking, the rear-end fishtailing sharply. Benny squealed with delight.

Robin jumped up in the seat and turned backward in time to see Rick Taglia smash into the other car. When Benny heard the crash, he looked into his rearview mirror and laughed. "Eat that, you guinea son-of-a-bitch." He made a sharp left and roared through a neighborhood normally crowded with young children jumping rope and drawing hopscotch squares on the pavement. Benny looked ahead to a spot where there was a break in the line of parked cars. He slowed and made another left into a narrow alley lined with garbage cans. He missed some and hit others, sending them flying and spilling their contents into the air. The tires squealed as he slammed the brakes, twisting the car onto an adjoining street without losing much speed. Nervously looking from the street to his mirror several times, he let the big car fall beneath the speed limit. "Piss on you, Taglia!" he said, panting. "I win again."

Robin, flushed, panicked, and out of breath, looked at the flowers strewn about the car. "Benny! If you didn't steal the car, why you doin' all this?"

"Hey man, it's cool. I lost him, didn't I?"

"Benny..." Robin stopped short realizing that there was no point to reasoning with Benny about the rights and wrongs of the situation. Benny could care less. "Benny. I want out. Stop the damn car and let me out."

"Guess this ride ain't classy enough now to be pulling up in front of Cleary's place. Ey, Rob?" Benny had a distant look on his face. He was manic from the chase. The speed, danger and the need to escape all seemed to excite him.

"Benny, stop the car so I can get out!" Robin looked around the floor of the car till he saw the pie sticking out from under his seat. Somehow it had managed to fall right-side-up again. Still, it was ruined. The windshield, now a spider web of cracked glass, was less fortunate. He looked behind him, expecting Rick Taglia to appear suddenly, shooting. The street behind was clear, but he still envisioned himself in jail, listening to his mother and trying to explain. It was another moment in his life that wouldn't play well "...uptown, on the sidewalk of S. S. Kresge's, in front of God and everybody."

Benny slowed the Cadillac, its radiator smoking and whirring, and turned down the driveway of an abandoned house. Robin could see that the driveway was overgrown with tall grass, but through the cracks on his side of the windshield, he could see that Benny was following a pair of single tire tracks around to the side of the house. They followed the tracks to a place in the rundown fence where the post had been torn away to create an opening large enough for a car to pass. After passing through this, and crossing over a small grassy knoll, Robin saw that they had entered the back of the Paradise Lawns Cemetery, now full and no longer in use. He was relieved to know that it had been years since the last person had been buried in the "for-whites-only" cemetery. In fact, there was little evidence of any surviving relatives, as most of the graves where unkempt and overgrown. Still he felt guilty for having invaded the final resting places, as Benny, uncaringly, drove over graves and flat markers. The only thought that kept him hopeful was knowing that all of Benny's back-tracking and side-winding had brought them back in the direction they had fled. The graveyard stretched sharply up hill. The main entrance was less than a block from Joleena's street.

Benny followed the maze of the winding road through the steam of the broken radiator and the twilight until the main gates came into view. "Hey man, I gotta let you out here. Cain't take no chance going back out on the main road. You know where you at, don't you?"

"Yeah," Robin said flatly, trying to gather as many of the unbroken roses as possible. "Benny, man. What if somebody saw us?"

"Ain't nobody saw us. It all happened too fast. You was so far down in the seat, you didn't see nothin' yourself."

It was true. It had all been a blur and a flash. And if he was really lucky, God might have been busy shopping in Kresge's during the whole ordeal.

Robin got out with what was left of the pie and flowers. Benny backed up and went the way they had come. Crossing the avenue, Robin could see the flashing lights of three patrol cars parked on the side of the road where Benny had first rammed Rick's car. There was an officer questioning people on the side- walks and he could tell by the red lights flashing in the sky that there were other cars farther down the hill. Robin walked on to Joleena's.

17

THE SIGN ABOVE THE DOOR of the cottage-style house said "Home Of The Clearys." The letters had been burned into a panel of wood with jagged edges and then varnished.

Robin had been warned not to be late, but he was. His nerves were shattered. He set the pie and flowers down on a porch chair and straightened his clothes the best he could without a mirror. He could hear footsteps coming toward the door and quickly grabbed the flowers. Before he grabbed the pie, the door flung back to reveal Joleena's father.

Edward Cleary Jr. looked Robin up and down. With a disappointed sneer he looked at his watch. Before either spoke, Anna Cleary was there.

"Robin, are these for me?" She stepped in front of her husband smiling.

"Yes, m'am. They came from my grandfather's garden." Robin held out the flowers, bedraggled and dropping their petals.

"Oh Robin, that's so nice. Won't you come in?"

Robin smiled as he passed Eddie Jr. and thought the worst was over. But the evening was young. Dinner went on to reveal levels of fear yet unknown to him. At one point Robin had been concentrating so hard on eating without spilling his soup that he didn't hear Eddie Cleary ask about his future. It had left an ominous and tedious silence hanging over the table. Joleena and Mrs. Cleary glanced back and forth as the uneasiness became more and more unbearable. After several gentle kicks under the table, Robin answered with a sudden, "huh?" This was only a momentary relief, as Robin brought the conversation to a grinding halt with a series of monosyllabic darts of, "Yes," "No," and "Mmm." These were accompanied by shoulder shrugs and a painful absence of eye contact. It wasn't long before the cheerful disposition that Mr. Cleary had put on at his wife's request—or rather, insistence—abruptly fell away. It was replaced by his normal suspicious, overprotective, coarseness. "After all…" he would say later with a coy smile, "I—tried."

Everyone, especially Robin, felt relieved when dinner was over and the last plate had been taken away. Considering what he had been through, Robin marveled at the fact that he had actually survived the ordeal at all. He sat up straight and smiled confidently waiting for the next round.

Afterward, Joleena suggested that she and Robin retire to the living room. Robin sat poker-faced deep in the old living room sofa, with his eyes bolted to a tiny television set that occasionally lost its picture in a storm of sparkling static. He sat motionless, pretending to ignore Joleena as she giggled and recounted each of the evening's blunders. She slid close to him and pulled her knees up under her, mimicking what she had done in Robin's apartment. She smiled. He could feel the wind of her breath in his ear. Quickly, he slid further down the sofa and glanced at the swinging door that separated them from her father. Every time she moved closer to him, Robin moved away. He fully expected Mr. Cleary to blast through the door like a bull raging after a red cape. Each time he moved, Joleena laughed and pulled him back into the depression of the sofa caused by their combined weight.

For an hour Joleena had coaxed him with her gentle voice, always moving closer when she felt his tension relax. Her beauty was captivating and eventually he took one final look toward the kitchen and slipped his arm around her. She leaned hard against him, letting him know that she wanted to be kissed, and exactly how. He kept his eyes open to the last minute to assure that the union would be perfect. And then it happened. In a swoosh of air and in two quick strides, Mr. Cleary had crossed the room and sat on a coffee table squarely in front of them. Robin leaped straight up to a standing position. This time Joleena was knocked to the floor.

Eddie Jr. didn't look angry or disturbed. In fact he didn't seem to notice Robin and Joleena at all. Totally focused, he sat on the edge of the table with his knees tight together balancing the pie that Robin had left on the front porch. With great care he began to separate the wax paper from the dented surface of the pie. He closed his eyes and raised the pie to his nose and smiled.

"Mr. Thompson," he spoke without looking up from his task. "Is it possible that this is your pie? I just found it sitting on a chair on the porch where we met this evening."

"Damn! Damn! Damn! Damn! Damn!" Robin screamed, inside his head. "THE GODDAMN PIE!" If he had thought it any louder, everyone in the room would have heard. "Yes...sir."

"I see," he said as he pulled the last of the wax paper away. He held it up to his nose. "Although it doesn't look like a sweet potato pie from Jessie Rose's kitchen, it smells like a sweet potato pie from Jessie Rose's kitchen. Is it at all possible..." he said, letting his eyes slowly roll up to Robin's full height. "...that this sweet potato pie is from Jessie Rose's kitchen and was on its way here when some terrible mishap occurred?"

"Ah...yes sir. I dropped it. And ah...it looked kinda funny and so ah...I left it on the porch because..." Robin shrugged as the word Kresge's came to mind. "...cause it looked kinda funny...after... But my Grandmother did make it just...a.. for you." It was the truth. Robin was sure that the God of Kresge's and Jessie Rose would approve of that part.

Edward Cleary's face snapped into a surprised smile. "For me?"

"Yes sir. She said..."

"She remembered. I would never miss a pie day if I could possibly help it. Does the family still call them 'pie days'?" Robin started to nod until he saw that Mr. Cleary had no real interest in his answer. "That woman would spend all day in that kitchen baking the absolute best sweet potato pie you have ever..." Edward looked up to see if his wife was following his story when he noticed that she had indeed been following it word for word with her hands on her hips.

"...Well anyway..." he cut himself off, "...that's another story for another time." He handed the pie to Anna. "Dear, why don't we have some in here? Joleena, set up the trays while your mother cuts the pie and, in the meantime, Mr. Thompson and I will have another go at conversation."

It was well after conversation, pie, and Edward Cleary's departure that Robin began to relax. Joleena ran into the kitchen to answer the phone. While she was gone, Robin reached into his jacket pocket for the silver-cased pocket watch. He checked each pocket only to discover that the watch was missing. He looked through the pillows on the sofa as well as under every square inch of its bottom. The sofa had no visible springs to hang the watch up. It was simply missing. Satisfied that it was not in the "Home Of The Clearys" his mind roamed back over the images of Benny, the Cadillac, and the earlier events of the evening. None of them were scenes worthy of the sidewalk uptown in front of the

Kresge's five and dime store.

Robin was nervous as he crossed the dark playground. He could hear each footstep echo several times as it bounced from building to building and back to him again. It was very dark, but this was not the sole source of his uneasiness. There were police cars and milling crowds at the far end of the playground near the maintenance shed where he had seen Charlene and Benny earlier. Robin wondered if Benny had been dumb enough to come back to the playground.

He looked back and saw the Cleary's porch light fading to a small white dot as it merged with the others along the street. He tried to make a decision. Then, with a sharp intake of breath, he veered to the left of the school to avoid the crowd. He had enough of crowds and police for one day, maybe for a lifetime. At the far end of the school, he crossed the parking lot and followed the dirt path. It led to the end of Wooden Street and to Boogers Hill.

It was a moonless night and the hill was steep. He stood briefly at the top under the street light and tried to make out the curve of the slope. As a child, he had spent many winter days on an American Flyer barreling down the rutted surface over an ominous mixture of snow and ice. Many were the times he had witnessed broken arms and legs when the less cautious had slipped over the side and had ended up in the back of Jane Nool's garage at the foot of the slope.

Robin stepped over the curb and hoped for a controlled slide. As he picked up speed, he followed the hill's sloping curve until, at last, he came to a halt beneath the last street lamp on Willow Street. He was panting and covered with dust.

He walked with his head back trying to catch his breath. "Home," he thought. It offered little security. Looking across the waters of the Pocahontas, he saw the brick buildings of the Fredrick Douglass apartments. The lines of apartment windows were randomly lit. He looked for the lights of 5509 as he walked, but the view was blocked by the beginning of houses that lined Willow Street. Suddenly a voice called to him.

"Hey, Rob, that you man?"

Robin stood still, tracing the direction of the sound. "Hey, Lucky, that you? I didn't even see you sittin' up there."

"What you tryin' to say, man? You couldn't see me in the

dark? That what it is? You cold, man." They both laughed, each knowing that Lucky's inky-black complexion had never been a hindrance in any way. If anything, it highlighted his magnetic personality. Lucky looked like he was fresh off the boat from the heartland of Africa. He was black on the verge of blue. His lips were large and thick, and his hair, a short woolly skull cap. He kept it brushed and razor-lined. Lucky was smart, a charmer. He was never without a date or a girlfriend despite the fact that he was fat.

"Come on up."

"Naa. I better not. It's gettin' late," Robin said, knowing that it was not just late, but late on Friday night. He wondered if Little Von would be home alone. "I'll catch you tomorrow on the way up to my grandmother's house."

"Hey man. I didn't say stay all night. I just said come up for a minute, have some Kool-Aid or somethin'. I got some Oreos left too, I think," he said, looking around his chair at the carnage of the evening. "We used to be friends," Lucky prodded. "'Member how we use to sleigh ride down that hill you just broke your ass tryin' to get down?" The chair reared back and hit the house as Lucky loosened his laugh. It was totally inappropriate for his round fat-cheeked face, sounding more like a wounded hyena than that of a two-hundred pound Masai.

"You heard that, man?"

"Did I hear it? I thought it was the Greenman comin' after my ass or somethin'." The shrill laugh came again from Lucky. Robin laughed both at the thought and at Lucky's laugh. After a time the laughter quieted and then it exploded again.

It was the first time since they were in elementary school that Robin had even thought about that supposed creature with the facial features of a human, the body of an ape with shiny green hair and long fingernails. It was supposed to live in the woods on the side of Boogers Hill and roam along the railroad tracks for several counties. But it was thought that it particularly liked the area around Pocahontas and Boogers Hill because of the large number of young children who lived close by.

"Damn, Lucky!" Robin laughed, as he tripped through a pile of junk food trash on the porch.

"Damn what?" Lucky tried to look innocent while gulping Kool-Aid directly from a two-quart pitcher.

Robin fingered through the wrappers on the porch in search of something to munch on. "Hey man, kids believe in some stupid stuff. Now you know somebody just made that stuff up and everybody, I mean everybody, from the Holla to the end of Collinsville, including parents, believed it." There was a short silence as they relived their individual Greenman horrors when they were small against the night and alone on Boogers Hill. "Maaaan..." Robin waved his hand in the air. "...there wasn't no Greenman."

"But what about that time that Shirley Wright said it tried to grab her when she was comin' home from school on the dirt road?" Lucky said. "'Member that, man? Her clothes were ripped and everything and she was all scratched up and had bruises everywhere."

"Aw man, her boyfriend, Roger, probably did that." They both roared. Lucky laughed so hard Kool-Aid started slopping over the sides of the open pitcher.

"Yeah, 'member how crazy he got when he was in love with her?...Ouuu wee!"

"He'd try and kill you if he even thought you were gonna say somethin' bad about Shirley."

"Yeah. She hated his guts, too."

"Yup, he knew it too. He probably figured the only way he was ever gonna get anything off Shirley..." Lucky laughed. He stammered, trying to catch his breath. Tears streamed from his eyes. "...the only way...the only way he was ever gonna get anything off Shirley was to dress up in some furry green suit and try to paralyze her with fear."

Robin doubled over. His sides began to ache, the waves of laughter unrelenting. Lucky got up, still laughing, and went into the house. Robin put his feet up on the rickety banister and rocked his chair back like they had been doing for years and listened to the unseen crickets.

The screen door banged lightly as Lucky came back out and took his chair. He took out a cigarette pack and began to tap its bottom. "Hey, Rob you want one, man?"

It had been an awful day. "Yeah, why not?" Robin said. He was happy to be with a friend and in a warm familiar place. It seemed to be the right time to tackle the problem of cigarette smoking.

Lucky took a marijuana joint out of the package and handed it to Robin. He fumbled about for matches.

Robin looked on in disbelief. "Hey man, what's this? You smokin' reefer too? Where you get this from?"

"Hey man, ease up. Don't get all bent out of shape if you ain't never tried it."

"Man, we said a hundred times when we was little that we wasn't never gonna do no drugs."

"Ey man, when we was little we didn't know what drugs were. Smokin' reefer ain't like doin' drugs anyway, man. We ain't gonna turn into no junkies or nothin'. I even read in a book where jazz musicians smoked this stuff way back in 1920's. Indians been using it forever. Hey I tried it one time and I just laughed a lot and that's all there was to it. Just try it one time and check it out."

"Lucky, I don't know, man. I don't think I want to do this. Who did you get this from anyway?"

Lucky took the crudely-rolled cigarette and held it away from his face. He passed the match back and forth across its end, trying to perform the ritual with confidence, but actually very unsure about what he was doing. "I got it from a friend of yours."

"What? Friend of mine?" Robin said, surprised. "Who, Scootch?"

"You know. Your friend Benny. Scab."

Robin's face twisted in disgust. "Maaan. Benny ain't no friend of mine."

"He ain't? Then what was you doin' cruisin' the graveyard with him? Who's car was that he had? Looked like it had been in a demolition derby or somethin'. Ey man, you think Benny's the one been stealin' all them cars?"

The statement left Robin reeling. If Lucky saw them, who else might have seen him with Benny, in a car that was probably stolen, sneaking through the graveyard, and only blocks away from the scene of a crime. Robin was unable to reply.

"That's the only reason I pulled it out in the first place. I was in the graveyard tryin' to get some off of Becky's sister Erma. You know Erma?"

Robin didn't, but he nodded yes to make Lucky get on with it.

"She fine, ain't she man? I been tryin' to connect with her for....I don't know man, but for a long time."

Robin nodded again, becoming more and more uncomfortable.

"Anyway, I saw you cruisin' the graveyard with Scab, and I knew you couldn't be all that friendly with Scab, so since he's the one that always has all the reefer, I figured you musta been smokin' with him."

"Did..." Robin struggled to remember the girl's name having only heard it once. "...Erma see us?"

"Yeah, but from her position she couldn't see who was in the car and I didn't say anything. You know I didn't want her mind too far away from the subject at hand, as they say. So what was you doin' with Scab if you wasn't smokin'?"

Robin flashed through the day which had been disastrous at best. "You say it made you laugh, huh?" he questioned, looking at the joint.

Lucky shrugged. "Hey man, that's all I got out of it. It wasn't even like being drunk or nothin'. This being your first time, you probably won't feel anything. I didn't my first time."

Robin took the joint from Lucky's hand. He hesitated for a moment as he prepared to tell his trusted friend the whole of it. He began by inhaling deeply.

Lucky was mesmerized by the marijuana and by Robin's story. His mouth sagged open and his eyes drooped as he did his best to follow the details of the ordeal.

A sharp noise, like a breaking branch, and a muffled scream came from down the street and the bottom of Boogers Hill. Lucky smiled and slowly rolled his head toward Robin. "Damn. Greenman gonna have to go on a diet after tonight."

Robin laughed. To be more exact, he heard himself laughing in long, exaggerated tones. He felt like the edges of his reality had become fuzzy. Suddenly he felt like an actor delivering his lines and the audience listening at the same time. Lucky was wrong. He *was* feeling it the first time.

Sliding sounds came from the direction of Booger Hill. Both boys rocked forward in their chairs laughing and leaning over the rail to see who was falling down the hill this time. They could hear a voice, but the image was still distorted by the distance and the shadows cast between street lamps.

"...shoulda known it was too dark..."

Robin and Lucky screamed "Art!" Robin was unable to stop

laughing. Every time he even looked at Lucky he burst out all over again.

Arthur Taggart appeared under the second Willow Street lamp still brushing the dust from his clothes. He walked straight toward the sound of the laughing. He stepped up on the stairs of the porch and stood watching the two. "What's the matter, you guys drunk or something?" he said flatly.

Robin and Lucky began a new wave of hysteria. They were nearly in control when Lucky pointed to the back of Arthur's pants covered with a thick layer of brown dust from the hill.

"See man, I told you. It just makes everything funny, that's all." Lucky held his hand out and Robin slapped it, still laughing.

Arthur, unperturbed, began slapping at his pants, sending up clouds of dust. "I knew It was too dark to be coming down Boogers Hill. But I came this way to tell you what happened on the playground tonight. Rob, I was gonna call you when I got home," Arthur said very seriously. He waited for the boys to stop laughing.

Slowly, as they became more aware of Arthur's gravity, Robin and Lucky ground to a halt.

"Somethin' wrong, Art?" Lucky said pulling himself up on the chair.

"You in trouble or somethin'?" Robin followed.

Arthur took a deep breath. "No it's not me. It's Scootch. It finally went down."

"What are you talkin' about, man? What went down?"

"Benny and Scootch finally got into it on the playground tonight. Scootch got stabbed, and I guess Benny's in jail."

Shock ran through both of the boys as they turned to stare at each other. Robin struggled against the marijuana to refocus his attention. He felt trembly and out of sorts. His brain continued to keep all of his systems going, but at the same time it refused to give him one general concept of how it was going as a whole. He tried to concentrate harder.

There was silence. Arthur came onto the porch and sat on the railing closest to the post where he knew it would be strong.

Lucky dug out the last two Oreos and threw them up to Arthur and waited.

"I don't even know where to begin. Somebody saw Benny and Charlene messin' around in a car while Scootch was playing ball and told him, probably during a time-out or somethin'."

Lucky and Robin looked at each other, their eyes wide.

"Scab went back to the playground after all that?" Lucky said to Robin. "He should have been hidin' out somewhere."

Robin shrugged.

Arthur looked puzzled. "What are you guys talking about?"

"Nothing man. Go ahead. What happened?"

"Well, Scootch didn't do anything then; he just kept on playin'. The game went late because they kept getting into ties. But you could even tell that something was wrong, 'cause Scootch started playing kinda crazy, like he was the only person on the court." Arthur shrugged his shoulders. "When it was finally over everybody was going crazy and everything, you know slappin' five, but Scootch walked right over to where Charlene was."

"Umm," Lucky said. "I feel something bad gettin' ready to happen." Lucky sat straight up in his chair. Robin just groaned.

"Charlene started running toward him smiling 'cause they won the game and then...POW!"

Robin's face was distorted as he tried to imagine the impact of the blow. Lucky covered his face with his arms and moaned slow and throaty.

"No shit, man, he nailed her straight in the jaw. She stumbled back a couple of steps and then her knees just unlocked and she went down."

Robin's eyes were closed tight. Lucky squirmed sideways in his chair.

"That's not even the worst of it. Everybody just turned around from what they were doing and stood still looking stupid. When they saw Charlene going down with her eyeballs wavin' all around, girls just started screamin'."

"What'd Scootch do? Was he standin' over her waiting for her to get up?" Lucky said, anxious to get the story going.

"No, man. Charlene was out like a light. She looked like she was doin' the Hucka Buck when she went down."

"Ohhh man."

"If I'm lyin', I'm flyin'. He wacked her and watched her go down, but she didn't even hit the ground before he was walking toward Benny."

Robin whistled. "I know this is gonna be ugly. Did Benny start haulin' outta there."

"No, man. I know Benny ain't stupid, but he's just so mean, he does dumb stuff sometime. But this time he was just as shocked as everybody else. He just stood there looking at Scootch coming toward him. Finally, it seemed to dawn on him that he was in trouble. He looked like he was just getting ready to do something, but it was too late. Scootch was right on top of him—POW-POW-POW!" Arthur hit his palm with his fist as he talked. "Man, Benny looked like a helicopter the way his arms were spinning around."

"Did he go down?" Robin said.

"Almost. He was just about on his knees when Scootch came over and stood right over top of him to make sure he wasn't getting up. I don't know where he got the strength from..." Arthur said, holding both hands straight up in the air, "but Benny whirled around and hit him with a haymaker and caught him by surprise—BLAM! The whole playground just went nuts screamin' and yellin'. They made a huge circle around both of them. Everybody was pushin' and pullin' so they could see good."

"Did Scootch take it, or did he go down?" Lucky asked excitedly.

"Well, we've all seen Scootch take some punches that would have almost killed a grown man, but I guess he just wasn't expecting this one. He stumbled backwards for about twenty feet before he finally fell. The crowd just split open and he went sailin' through backwards. People started yellin', Get 'im Scootch. Get 'im Scootch!'"

"Especially Matt, I bet." Lucky threw in.

"Ey I'm not surprised, cause Matt hates Scab," Robin said.

"Actually, I don't know where Matt was," Arthur said correcting both of them. "But I'll tell you what, people were so crazy for blood, some of them started yellin' for Scab."

Lucky chuckled. "Yeah, but they probably just wanted Scab to get up so Scootch could pound the crap out of him some more."

"You probably right 'cause I don't know anybody who likes him except some of his thug buddies and some girls dumb enough to believe all that jive he talks."

Lucky whistled. "I guess Charlene's dumber than I thought she was."

Robin thought about Benny talking him into getting into the

Cadillac that evening and grew disgusted with himself.

"Well, she was definitely stupid this time," Arthur concluded. "Anyway, Benny got up first and staggered over to Scootch who was still on the ground trying to shake it off. Benny started kicking him in the ribs like a wild man. I guess he knew if Scootch got up he was dead."

"Ey, where was Matt all this time?" Lucky asked.

"I don't know, man. He was there during the..." Arthur stopped and furrowed his brow. "Ey man, I betcha Matt was the one who told Scootch in the first place 'cause every time Scootch was on a time-out, he would be talking to Matt on the side. The last time, Matt looked real crazy pointing over by the shed, you know, where they keep the plows and stuff. Then Scootch just yelled at him, 'I'll deal with it,' or somethin' like that, and pushed him away." Matt must have gotten mad after that and took off.

"Anyway Scab was kicking Scootch in the ribs and suddenly Scootch reached up and yanked his foot out from under him and Benny went down."

"Did Scootch get 'im then?" Lucky asked, getting excited.

"Dived on 'im and gave 'im three good ones. POW-POW-POW! And then Benny did something you'd expect him to."

"What?" Robin asked, not particularly enjoying the story.

"Threw dirt in his face. You know that dry powdery stuff around the back stop?"

Both boys nodded, frowning.

"Well Scootch had kicked his ass all the way over there from the basketball court. Scootch jumped up and started rubbing his eyes like he couldn't see. He staggered almost all the way back over to where he first turned Charlene's lights out. Benny jumped up and started running after him thinking that Scootch was blind. Just as he got to 'im—POW! I thought he was dead after that man. Scootch had been just waitin' for him. Just when Benny was raring back to tag him, Scootch unloaded. He hit Benny with a upper cut so hard, it raised him off his feet. When he came down he didn't move."

Both Robin and Lucky had distorted faces. Both their eyes were jammed shut. Both whistled and oooed.

"Man, you could feel it. Everybody was holding their heads and faces—you could feel the pain just watchin' it."

"How did he get stabbed then?" Robin asked.

"Shut up, man" Lucky snapped, "and let him tell it. Go 'head, Art. How did he get stabbed and shit?"

"Well, most people probably missed it 'cause it happened so fast. They were telling each other about this hit or that kick. Everybody's hands were flying around acting it out, you know how people do when they watch a fight and shit. But I saw it." Scootch stood up taking his time wiping the dirt off his face. Benny was out cold, I mean his body was twitchin'."

"Oh man, he was twitchin'," Lucky growled. "He deserved it. I knew he was gonna get it sooner or later. Then what?"

"Scootch turned around and looked at Charlene. She was standin' with some girls—well actually they were kind of holding her up 'cause she was still shakin' like a leaf. Scootch started walking toward her again and the girls that were with her started yelling, 'No Scootch, don't do it!' Most of them just left Charlene standing there, except for Mary Slatter, and she would have split too, but Charlene had a grip on her that wouldn't quit. Scootch had a real crazy look on his face, man..." Arthur twisted his face into a scowl. "...I never seen him like that before. He reached for her, and Mary and Charlene both screamed, and then Benny was up. He pulled a knife from somewhere, ran over to where Scootch was, and stuck him. And he was gonna get 'im again, but—you ain't gonna believe this—then Hoops was there! I mean he was there out of nowhere!"

Lucky and Robin froze.

"Hoops!" Lucky shrieked, jumping to his feet.

"Yup. Hoops.You know, Rick Taglia, Hoops just...appeared and shit. He was there, swear to God, man. Must have been there watching all the time. He had Benny in a choker. Scab's feet were danglin' off the ground and he was still trying to get to 'im with that weird knife he had. You could still see the blood on it."

Robin sat back in the chair stunned.

Lucky shook his head. "Wow. Greatest day the Hill has ever had and I missed the whole damn thing down here, sittin' on my ass, eatin' Oreos."

"When Benny finally figured out who had him, he really went crazy and started yellin', 'You want some more! You want some more!' I don't know why he said it, but that's what he said. He started thrashing all wild. Then Hoops gave him a really hard shot right to his kidneys and Benny just went limp. Hoops pushed his face into the ground and took the knife, whipped his hands around his back, cuffed 'im, and hauled him off to the car…" Art threw his hands up in the air. "A few minutes later an ambulance was there, and a whole bunch of cops…man oh man. There was so many lights, place looked like Christmas and shit."

"I know why he was sayin' that. He said it 'cause Scab cut him once before," Lucky said, showing both of them with his finger where the cut was. "It was sorta an accident though, 'cause Hoops was breaking up a fight between Benny and Raymond and he just sorta got cut."

"Yeah, that's right." Art said, remembering. "Man, you should have seen Charlene. She was so out of it. They took her too."

"Jesus," Lucky said, looking over his shoulder to Robin. "And you thought you had a hard night."

Robin was leaning on the arm of the chair. He rubbed his face with his hand. He was exhausted. "Too much, man. Too much to take in at one time."

Lucky sorted through the cupcake and candy wrappers on the floor until he found the joint that had fallen on the porch. He lit it again while Arthur looked on quietly, and handed it to Robin. Robin took it and inhaled deeper and less cautiously than he had the first time. He didn't choke. He didn't want to think anymore.

"Hey man," Lucky said with face suddenly contorted with worry as he took the joint from Robin. "Is Scootch gonna make it?" He took a long draw.

Arthur slid off the edge of the rail to the floor and placed his back against the post and looked up into the night. "I don't know, man. I don't know." He looked at Lucky holding the joint out to him. He took it and imitated what he had seen them do, the best he could. He took his glasses off and rested his head against the post. "I don't know man. Scootch is a good dude. Benny should have been the one. I don't know."

Robin and Arthur left Lucky's porch solemnly. They both walked quietly for a long time. Finally, Robin told Arthur about the ride with Benny.

"I can't believe he went back to the playground after all that." Robin breathed heavily having discovered it helped him maintain a little control over the marijuana.

"Actually he had to, didn't he? I mean the Swan Tones where

supposed to sing, weren't they?"

"Oh yeah, I forgot all about that," Robin said. "I just thought he was being real bold. He's so crazy, he's scary to be around."

Arthur began to laugh. It was nervous tension releasing itself, but the more he laughed the better he felt. Soon he was laughing at the top of his lungs.

"What in the hell are you laughing at? You starting to feel that reefer?"

Arthur just looked at Robin and continued to roar. They were under the train trestle. Arthur stopped walking and leaned against the stone foundation panting. "No I...I don't feel anything."

"Then what you laughing at?"

Arthur was trying to catch his breath. It took several attempts. "You handing Mrs. Cleary those roses, all bent up?" Arthur was laughing hysterically, but he couldn't get enough air to make sound. His stomach and head were bouncing up and down.

Robin leaned against the rock wall thinking over the event and laughed himself. "Geez, that must have looked dumb." He looked up and sighed. The moonlight coming through the trestle made a striped pattern across his face. "I don't know, man," he said, his laughter giving way to sullenness again. "From what I've seen, everybody got problems. My mother has enough problems for two people. I got Mr. Suther, Joleena's father; hey, even Little Von got problems. The other day he asked me how to fight. He said Jing-Wei...you know the kid downstairs...kinda funny lookin' one...was tryin' to beat him up every day."

"Oh yeah. I think he's half-Japanese or somethin' like that. So what you tell Little Von?"

"Told him to look as vicious as he could and if he even thought he was gonna get hit, bash 'im over the head with a stick or somethin'."

Arthur laughed and smashed his fist into his hand. "Yep, that's what I would have told him too. The element of surprise is a worthy defense."

"Yeah, that's what I told him. It ain't like fightin', just self-defense." Robin shook his head. "You know man, up on the hill nobody would even think about bothering you if you were smaller or something like that. Damn. You wouldn't even think like that. Down here though, anybody can't protect their ass gets it kicked.

I told him to take his best shot on the first hit—try and knock him down hard and then stand over him like you dare him to get up or somethin'."

Arthur laughed and tried to visualize Little Von standing over somebody looking vicious. He couldn't, and he knew Robin couldn't either.

They came to the stone bridge. The Best Fill sign for Jimmy Lee's was turned off, but the boys could see Jimmy Lee bent over the Stutz. Arthur went in and got two sodas and came back out. He handed Robin a vanilla cream. "Ey Rob, I want to ask you about something."

"What?"

"Listen, I know you been tryin' to get it together with Joleena and all, but I was wondering if you had something going with Patsy Clarke on the side?"

Robin looked at Arthur. "Patsy? Patsy Clarke? What makes you think that?"

"Well it may not be you so much, but I think she's got a thing for you or something."

"Patsy Clarke?"

"The other day when I was helping her with her locker, one of her books fell out and it had your name all over it like a disease or something."

"Patsy?"

"She picked it up quick. Probably thought I didn't see it. We just hung around talking until the bell rang. Ey man. I've been knowing Patsy since we was little kids, man. She used to be all giggly and fat face. I spent most of my time tryin' to keep away from her. But have you seen her lately? Man, she has boobs and everything. She has a few pimples too, but basically..." Arthur used his hands to show how each of her areas had grown.

"Well I sorta see her once and awhile, but I never really check her out or anything. I mean to me she's just sorta...Patsy...you know." Robin shrugged, uncomfortable with romantic thoughts of her.

"She's really fillin' out. You probably been too wrapped up in Joleena to notice."

"I guess so. Ey man, you sound interested."

"Yeah, maybe a little bit, but I think I'll let her cool her crush on you a little before I make a move."

"You think she's got a crush on me just 'cause she wrote my name on her book a couple of times? Girls do that kinda stuff all the time, man."

"Rob, it wasn't no couple of times, man. I told you the book looked like it had Robin Thompson disease on it or somethin'."

"No man, it's nothin' to me."

"Well, no big deal or nothing. I just wanted to make sure you didn't have nothin' goin' on the side with her."

"Nope. I don't think I could handle anything on the side. This one thing is tough enough." Robin had never heard Art sincerely express an interest in girls and could tell he was uncomfortable doing so now. "So you gonna hit on her?"

"No, not like for sex or anything. I think I kinda really like her a little bit."

Robin laughed. "Kinda, really, a little bit?"

"Yeah. What's wrong with that?"

"Eh, it's cool." Robin laughed. "I didn't know anything was going on."

"Well I was just thinking about it." Art was silent while he organized his thoughts. "Hey Rob."

"What?"

"What you gonna say if Scootch ask you about seein' Charlene and Scab?"

Robin sighed and shrugged. "I don't know, man."

They reached the front of Building Five and slapped hands. Robin waited until Arthur was further down the street before he called out. "Eh, if you hear anything about Scootch let me know."

"Yeah, you too. Ey, by the way did you feel anything?"

"No. I don't think so."

Arthur waved and merged with the night.

18

At TWO FORTY-FIVE ON SUNDAY AFTERNOON, Rick stood leaning against his car in the hospital parking lot. It was a wreck. The car's smashed right front side had been pulled out by the guys in the mechanics pool. The right tire and wheel had been replaced, along with new headlights, bumpers, and the windows on both sides. He shook his head.

Reaching into his pocket, he took out the silver pocket watch and read its inscription. He closed the face cap of the watch and glanced toward the door where he expected Tina to emerge. As he turned back, he felt a sharp pain against his side, the wind left his lungs and just as suddenly, he was on the ground. Bewildered he looked up to see Tina's brother, Sam Phillips, standing over him. Sam was over six feet tall. His scowl revealed several teeth missing. He was so angry that spit flew from his lips as he spoke. "Cracker, I don't care who you are! You keep yo' pink ofay ass away from my sister or I'll break yo' head in half. Yo' brotha's, if I have to. I mean what I say, too."

Without hesitation, Rick jumped into a crouch. Before he stood up, he let one leg sweep out in a small arc just above the ground and caught Sam at the ankles. Sam's feet went up into the air bringing his shoulders down hard on the parking lot pavement.

Rick was up standing over him fuming. "And I don't care who you are! What goes on between me and Tina is none of your goddamn business. If you want to make it some of your business —get up! Come on!" His tone was not official. It was a personal matter between him and Sam, and it was long overdue.

Sam jumped up, charging toward Rick. He collided into Tina who had come out of nowhere. She stood with her back to Rick facing her brother. For a moment, the three of them were sandwiched together. Tina pushed Sam away screaming in his face.

"Sam. Stop it! Stop it right now!" She was growling through her teeth clutching his shirt. "I am goddamned sick and tired of you and Daddy and everybody else getting into my life. I told him to come here 'cause I wanted to see him!" Sam tried to pull her hands away from his shirt, but couldn't. "Did you hear me?

'Cause I wanted to see him. Now get out of here." Tina was tenacious and vicious when angry. Her lips stretched thin, her scalding gaze held Sam in his place. She pushed her brother back.

"What kind of motha are you bringing this pink bastard around Marlon all the time!"

"I'm not like you, Sam. You're angry at the whole world. And it's none of your business what kind of mother I am or whom I choose to see. Now get out of here."

Sam scowled at Rick and then at Tina. He kicked Rick's car to release his unspent anger. He walked backward pointing a finger toward Rick's face.

"I'm sorry for this. You know Sam, he's just as bad as Bono." She took a tissue from her uniform pocket and brushed some pebbles from Rick's cheek. "You been sweeping the ground with your face?"

"Just for a second. Is it bad?"

"I'd come in and get some ice on it if I were you." Tina nodded toward the hospital. "It's gonna be red for awhile." She was close to his face. They kissed, losing awareness of the parking lot. They might have been standing in a field of wheat in the middle of Nebraska.

"Rick, I'm still gonna need some time with all of this," she whispered in the kiss. "I know what I want to do. I'm just not as brave as you. I have to get myself geared up for all the Sams and Bonos in the world."

"We'll be together. You won't be alone."

"I know that." They kissed again, vaguely aware that there were people getting off a bus nearby.

"Jump in. I'll take you home."

"I can't. One of the nurses went home sick. I'm covering part of her shift. I gotta go." She fingered one of the dents in the car. "I heard about the excitement on the hill. I'm glad you didn't end up in one of my beds looking like your car."

"Would you have taken care of me?"

"What do you think?" She smiled. Rick shrugged. "Do you know who you're chasing?"

"Yeah. I'm pretty sure. I'm real close." Rick smiled and watched her as she walked back to the hospital. He took the silver watch and chain from his pocket again and read the inscription. "To my young man Elderiah. Elderiah Jr. Robin."

Rick could hear everyone talking at once as he stood outside the door. It sounded like a brawl in a courtroom with Momma defending, Bono prosecuting, and everyone else swaying back and forth. Nothing had changed in all the years he could remember. There was one unusual sound, crying. Someone was crying. Normally that was Momma's part, but she was still yelling.

Rick looked back to his bashed car. He'd rather be with Tina or Steve, perhaps even Sam, than to walk through that door. Sam he could fight. Sam was only one emotional maniac. He used the tissue that Tina had given him to check his face one last time before he went in.

When Rick stepped in, it was as if the open door created a vacuum. Every sound went dead, sharp and sudden. Then the room cleared, except for Momma and those who had sided with her and the children who crawled and raced in and out of the room. He thought he saw Gena...Gena? She was walking toward the bathroom crying. "Gena?" The family crowded around, all talking at once before he could get an answer.

"Ricky, Ricky, Ricky. I knew you would come to you' momma. I knew you no forget." She reached up and held his face in both hands. "Bono say you no come, but I know. I know. I say my Ricky would not invite such a nice girl like this Gena," she said, as she pointed toward the bathroom. "...and no come. No!"

Rick could hear muffled crying. "Mom? That's Gena? Why she cryin'?"

Mrs. Taglia tried to speak low so only Rick could hear. "I hate to say 'cauz he'sa my son, but that Bono." A disappointed sadness contorted her face. "He say sometings about you and colored girls. I try to tell her, but she listen to Bono...you no worry. She's a girl. Girls cry." She smiled and pulled his face down to kiss it. As she came close she saw his cheek, scraped and bruised. "Ricky! What happen! Bono come quick! Ricky is hurt. Ricky you come. I take care of you." In another second, the room was filled again with the whole family, including Gena and one of the sisters. Bono stayed in the dining room with his dessert.

"Momma." Rick grabbed her by the shoulders. "It's nothing. I fell." Rick put his finger up to the scrape. "Look. No blood. I'm just hungry."

A sad look came over his mother's face. "But Ricky, we already eat. We wait but, Bono said..." She paused and frowned. "You come, Ricky, sit witha your friend and I fix you dinner." She looked around triumphant. "You see! I told you he come!"

An hour later the phone rang. Rick and Bono were arguing on the front porch. The rest of the family was happily arguing inside. Gena burst through the door out of breath.

"Rick! Rick! It was the station." She sobbed and waved her hands frantically trying to control herself. "It's Steve Seward. He's been shot."

Rick was halfway to his car with Gena following. She was still frantic. "Do you want me to come?" she shrieked. Rick looked back at Bono who obviously had no intention of leaving his second dessert.

Bono feigned concern. "Call, and let me know how he is. Call the station too." He stuffed his mouth with pastry. "I'll take Gena. No problem. My pleasure." He took another bite.

It was the next morning when Steve Seward's eyes blinked open. Rick had been there all night sleeping in a chair. Tina was near the bed. "Rick! I think he's coming to."

"I got the meanest freakin' headache..." Steve mumbled. "Where am I?"

"That ain't bad for someone shot in the head." Tina checked his IV.

"Can you dig that? You got shot in the head." There was a small hand mirror by the bedside. Rick held it up so Steve could see the huge bandage around his head. He looked at Tina.

"Damn! Is my wife here?"

Rick sat on the side of the bed. "No. You're not married."

"Oh, good."

"Did you say somebody shot me? Who?"

Rick laughed. Steve was alive and making jokes. "Some joker named Chad Wissner. He'd done a lot of stuff before, but armed robbery was out of his league. Probably thought Beeman's would be an easy first job. Of course, you just happened to wander in. I think it pissed him off."

"Dumb ass shot me?"

"Hmm."

"Did I shoot him back?"

"Collapsed his right lung, shattered a rib, and blew him backward through the potato chip carousel. One good shot. I don't think Mr. Beeman appreciated the commotion."

Steve tried a small laugh. He held up his hand. Rick touched a gentle five.

"You know I always aim for the heart." Steve's eyes closed as he tried to slow the throbbing. "He shot me in the head and I'm not dead. Hmm. What the hell did he shoot me with? A sling shot."

"Tina saved it for you."

"A twenty-two?" She held up what was left of the bullet for him to see.

Rick took the bullet and turned it over in his hand. "Stupid bastard fired four rounds. The doctors don't even think it was a direct hit. Probably a ricochet. The slug was stickin' out of your head. Actually I felt sorry for the bullet."

Tina moved around the bed quickly without wasted movements. When she finished, she came and stood by Rick's side. "The doctor said you hit the floor pretty hard. He'll be in later to check reflexes. But, overall, he thinks you'll be fine."

Steve opened his eyes and smiled. "It's good to see you guys together."

"That's the way it's gonna be from now on," Tina said putting her arm around Rick's shoulder.

Steve moved his feet, toes, and legs under the covers. Rick spoke idly while he and Tina watched with concern. Steve made a fist with his right hand and tried the same with his left. He opened and closed his left hand twice, repeated it with his right, and again with his left. "Tina, a couple of my fingers tingle on my left hand. Is that because of the IV?"

"I'm not a doctor, Steve. But if it's just a tingle, I wouldn't worry too much. You probably have some swelling from the fall as well as from the bullet."

"Jesus Christ! The man takes a head shot and he's complaining about tickling fingers," Rick joked.

"Hey man. Dig it." Steve smiled. "No complaints. I'm left-handed. I can't shoot with numb fingers. I've definitely made up my mind." Rick heard him clearly and still didn't know what to make out of it. Steve simply said, "Hawaii."

19

JULY

Jᴇꜱꜱɪᴇ Rᴏꜱᴇ ꜱᴀᴛ ǫᴜɪᴇᴛʟʏ ɪɴ ᴛʜᴇ ᴄᴀʀ as Vivian negotiated the ever-increasing traffic around the park square in the center of town. Little Von, oblivious to the fact that he was on his way to see yet another doctor, the fourth in two weeks, knelt on the floor in the back and ran the plastic bicycle across the seat. It had come from a Cracker Jack box now temporarily forgotten.

Vivian looked across at her mother. Jessie Rose sat strong-chinned and looking straight ahead.

"Momma, Dr. Wingfield, Dr. Finestein, and Dr. Brooker said there's nothing wrong with his leg."

"Vivian, I say that boy is favorin' that leg. Didn't you see him limp when he come across thet street?"

"Momma, he had been playing on the playground when Joanne Cleary called. Maybe he just bumped it or something," Vivian coaxed, hoping more than being sure.

Jessie Rose softened her tone of voice and turned toward the backseat. "Von, did you hurt yourself when you was playin' at the daycare?"

"No Grandma," he said, pushing the toy bike up one side of the seat and down the other and making engine noises.

Jessie turned back to the windshield.

"Momma…"

"Vivian, I don't want to hear it! There's something wrong with that boy's leg. I can feel it right here," she said, holding her fist over her abdomen. She had nothing more to say.

Little Von sat on his mother's lap in the the sterile examining room. He had fallen quiet, for he understood that another strange man would soon be in to see him. His eyes wandered around the room, taking in the huge frosty overhead lamp, the eye chart on the far wall, and the high couch with the crinkly paper pulled over it.

He wasn't as afraid as he had been the first two times. Those times he had thought that he might have to stay overnight by himself, or maybe get shots with long needles. Instead, the other doctors had told him to jump up on the table, jump down, walk around the room, and then they pronounced him "fit as a fiddle."

He looked at the examining table, comparing the distance from the top to the floor. "Mommy, I can jump off that couch just like I did the other ones."

"I know you can, babe.

"Shhhh!" Jessie Rose waved her hand in the air and made them both speak in a whisper. In her life, a trip to the doctor was a little less than a trip to church. And this wasn't some country doctor they came to see, no sir, this one was a specialist.

Little Von spotted something next to the examining table that brought back all his original fears. A nurse had left several long instruments that bent at odd angles. Among them was an oversized syringe with metal rings for the fingers. He stared at it for a long time, afraid to ask if it was for him.

The door opened a crack. A small windup motorcycle raced across the floor with a little man on its seat. When it crashed into the wall on the far side of the room, the little man popped up about three feet in the air and fell to the floor with the aid of a little plastic parachute.

"What in the dickens...!" Jessie Rose shrieked and squinted through her bifocals.

"Wow! Look Mom, a cycleman." Little Von jumped to the floor.

"Hey, did anybody in here see my cycleman?" Dr. Bowenstein asked, entering the room, carefully using the exact wording he'd heard through the crack in the door.

Dr. Howard Bowenstein was a bone specialist, an honor graduate of the Harvard Medical School and the president of his class twenty years before. He had made his fortune while he was still relatively young. Now he split his time between research and the children's free clinic. He was tall with an athletic appearance. The pink of his scalp showed through his thinning brown hair. His prominent nose and the rest of his face was sunburned, giving him a look of leisure, as if he had been to some foreign place where only rich white doctors could afford to go.

Little Von was torn between fear and delight. Long black hairy arms stuck out of his hospital greens. "Is that your cycleman?"

"Sure is. Want to see it?" Bowenstein offered. He sat on the floor with his back to the wall, his legs spread apart to make an arena for the scooter.

"Can I, Mom?"

Vivian smiled. Jessie was still trying to grasp what was going on.

Little Von ran across the room and sat beside the doctor's knees.

"Here, sit like this so you can do it better." Bowenstein picked the child up and made him sit the same way as he, working the toy with his arms around Little Von. He watched Little Von's flexibility.

"You sure got some hairy arms, mister."

"Little Von! HUSH YO' MOUTH BOY!" Jessie Rose yelled. "...a...we...we brought him to see Dr. Bowenston about his leg," she said trying to cover for what she thought to be a lack of manners.

"Bowenstein," Vivian corrected.

The doctor smiled at Jessie and Vivian and put the cycle in Little Von's hand, showing him which wall to send it to. "Bowenstein, huh." he said, without breaking his concentration on Little Von's leg. "Well I guess you came to the right place."

"You the doctor!" Jessie said, unbelieving.

"Yes, ma'am. And this must be Levon Thompson," he said patting the boy on the head. Little Von was totally oblivious to what was happening around him.

"Here goes!" Little Von erupted, releasing the cycle. It took a turn of its own and crashed a few feet from Jessie Rose's feet. "Whooop!" she yelled as the little man and the parachute nearly landed in her lap.

"Catch it, Grandma!" he shouted.

Bowenstein laughed. His voice was deep and resonant. "Levon—is that what people call you?"

"Nope. They just call me Little Von."

"Okay then, you can call me Doctor B. That's what people call me. Other things too, sometimes," he said, smiling at Vivian. "Why don't you walk over there and get the cycleman and bring it back over here, but don't run because these hospital floors are veeeery slippery."

"Okay."

Bowenstein watched carefully as Little Von stood up and crossed the floor. His eyes darted in different directions, following the transfer of weight that accompanied each step. When Little Von was on his way back he stopped him. "I'll bet you can walk in a real straight line. Can you do that?"

"Sure, wanna see?"

"Yep."

Little Von made believe he was walking on a tightrope, his arms stretched out. When he got back he sat down quickly, trying to get the little man back on the cycle.

Bowenstein came over and sat next to Vivian on a rotating stool with rollers on the bottom. "How long do you think he's had the limp?"

Jessie Rose sat back, assured the fighting to get there had been worthwhile and that Bowenstein, or whoever he said he was, was indeed the doctor even if he didn't act like one.

Vivian took a deep breath. "Well, his teacher at the daycare center called about a month ago, but..."

"Yes I know. It's hard when they are so young. Injuries come and go everyday." Bowenstein bit his lip on the inside. His mind raced through the possibilities and the questions that he needed to narrow them down. "Is he particularly prone to accidents? Does he seem to be more clumsy than other kids?"

"No. Hardly ever falls or anything."

"Good. Does he complain about the leg? Looks like his left hip is being compensated for by the way he rotates it when he gets up and down."

Jessie Rose began to smile. She knew the exam was nearly over before she had known it started. She felt sure they would find the problem she knew existed. "Doctor Bowenstein," Jessie said with authority, "that boy never complain about anything. You can hardly make him sit still to eat a meal."

Bowenstein smiled and waited for Little Von to move naturally.

The cycleman ripped across the floor again just in time to escape through the door opened by a nurse entering the room with a chart.

"OH-OH!" Little Von yelled, as the toy raced out.

"That's okay. Better go get it before one of the orderlies thinks it's a bug and steps on it. Don't run, okay?"

"Okay."

The nurse gave Bowenstein the medical history chart that Vivian had filled out in the lobby. She stood in the doorway, watching the boy retrieve the toy from under the receptionist's desk. The doctor took took the chart and rolled his stool close to the door. He watched Little Von get up from the floor again. Then he was quiet for a moment as he looked over the chart.

"Well, I don't want to get ahead of myself, but I think I have a hunch about what's going on."

Jessie Rose braced herself for the worse. "What is it, Doctor?"

"I'll tell you what. Before I go guessing all over the place, why don't I get him up on the table and take a closer look. Then I'll decide whether or not we should go for X-rays."

Jessie sat back, her face still reflecting her fear. He had tried not to say anything unnecessary, but he had made no attempt to allay her fears.

She had a bad feeling. She reached over and held Vivian's hand.

Little Von came back with the cycle and the little man who had apparently parachuted safely to the receptionist desk. He also had a lollipop. "Hey Mom, look what the lady in the hall gave me."

Vivian smiled, although she'd become worried. Her heart beat a little quicker than it had before. "What flavor?"

Little Von took it out and looked at it closely. "Red."

"Hey Champ, come here for a minute." Bowenstein picked him off the floor and sat him on the examining table. "You wanna see something neat?"

"Okay."

"Tell you what. Let Grandma hold the cycleman so she can get a better look at it and take a look at this."

The doctor went to a metal closet behind the table and sorted through several boxes before returning with a set of bone joints. "You know what these are?"

Little Von looked hard. "Look like bones."

"That's right, but not real ones. These are plastic models. Do you know which ones they are?" Little Von looked harder as the doctor brought the models closer. He shook his head slowly.

"Well, that's okay. I'll tell you. Let me see you bend your arm."

He did. "See this one helps you so you can do that," he continued indicating the elbow model. He put it aside. "Okay, now, lay back on here and let me see you raise your leg up." He did. "Good. This one," he held up another model, "lets your leg move around so you can walk." He moved the femur back and forth, showing how the ball rotated in the socket. "This is what your hip joint looks like. Here, you try it."

Little Von moved the leg bone back and forth and soon discovered that it would move in other directions as well. "Look Doctor B."

"Yep. Yours can do that too. Now, I think if we can fix your hip joint a little bit, you could walk better and run faster. How does that sound?"

"Really?"

"I think so. You wanna try?"

"Okay."

"And then we'll have some real fun. Do you know what an X-ray is?"

"Nope. I heard people talk about them though."

"It's a picture that we can take. It shows us what your body looks like on the inside."

Little Von was silent. He couldn't imagine what it would look like. "You mean guts and everything? Will it hurt?"

"Well, for me, bones. I don't fix guts. Used to, but they were too hard to see on the X-ray pictures. But bones really stick out so you can see them. Don't worry. It will be fun. Maybe a little cold, but fun."

As Bowenstein worked on the table with Little Von, rotating his upper leg from side to side and back and forth, Vivian took out a tissue and wiped a tear from the corner of her eye. She could see that Bowenstein was quickly eliminating possibilities and would soon have a name for the problem. A name other than "bump" from the playground. Jessie Rose, feeling the foreboding pressure in her chest as well, squeezed her hand.

After the X-rays were developed, Dr. Bowenstein took them into a room that had large lighted panels on the wall. Little Von sat up on a high stool near one of the panels.

"Well. Here's what you have." Dr. Bowenstein shoved one of the X-rays under a clip on the panel. "It's a funny looking picture, isn't it?"

"Yup. But I can see them bones," Little Von said, smiling.

Dr. Bowenstein pointed around with a pencil. "These are guts, but you wouldn't know if somebody didn't tell you, huh?"

Little Von made a face and shook his head.

"Do you remember when I showed you how this bone moved and how it fit right here?" He tapped Little Von's hip.

"Yup."

"Well, look up here. Do you see this dark shadow?"

Little Von said yes slowly, but Dr. Bowenstein could tell he wasn't sure. "Well, look at this." He put his fist in the palm of his other hand and shaped his fingers around it. Then he moved it around. "See? This is what we were doing to your leg." He looked over to Vivian and Jessie to make sure they were following his explanation. Jessie was still frowning and looking at the X-rays.

Bowenstein continued imitating a hip joint with his hands. "If these were just bones they would be grinding together. And that wouldn't work, so the body has cartilage..." Three blank faces stared back at him. "...like gristle..." They came to life, nodding and relieved.

"You mean like when you eat chicken and there's that rubber stuff on the knuckles. It's like white..."

"Right, right. That's it. That's cartilage. That knuckle is really the chicken's joints. It looks like knuckles because a chicken's bones are so much smaller."

Vivian came to her own conclusions. "Doctor? Is there something wrong with his?"

"Yes. The bone and cartilage work together. His cartilage isn't well-developed and it's affecting the bone. It's called Perthese disease. At this time there is only one other kid in the state that has it. A little girl his age down in Trenton." Jessie Rose sat back in the chair. She put her hand to her chest. "It's correctable," Bowenstein said, smiling. "That's the good thing about catching things when people are young and growing. We can do something about it."

Little Von looked back to the X-ray. He couldn't see the cartilage, but he knew approximately where it should be and he knew that something was wrong with it.

"How would you like to have that cycleman?" Dr. Bowenstein put his arm around Little Von and gave him a hug.

Vivian took out a tissue and wiped a tear from the corner of her eye. "Perthese? Is that right, Doctor?"

Bowenstein nodded. "There were three doctors who worked it out, so actually it's called Leggs-Calve-Perthese. Perthese, will do, I'm sure."

Vivian sat at the kitchen table. Little Von stood before her leaning on a new pair of crutches and moping while she tightened the straps that held his left heel near his buttocks.

It had been a week since Dr. Bowenstein had found the imperfection in his hip on the X-ray and three days since the clinic had fitted him with crutches, hip harness, and a sling that held his left heel near his buttocks. Little Von had looked at himself in his mother's full-length mirror and refused to go outside of the apartment. Today, Vivian had decided, one way or another, he had to face the world. "You can't stay up here for twelve months you know," she had said. He had responded he could, but after having stood in the middle of the floor crying for nearly fifteen minutes, he had agreed. And then, surprisingly, he insisted that he do it alone.

He took his ball and let it roll down the stairs in front of him. When it got stuck in the corner, he used his crutch to bat it away. Downstairs in front of the foyer, he held the ball tight against the door with his good foot and pushed the heavy door by leaning forward. When the door opened, the ball rolled out. After he played in the courtyard and explained to several familiar faces who passed what Dr. B had told him about his hip, he hid the ball in the bushes and made his way, three-legged, as Clovis Lamb called it, upstairs to the apartment.

On the second day he found that he could get the ball back to the apartment by tucking it in between the straps that held his heel up in the air. On the third day the other kids who played in the fenced-in courtyard decided he could still play kickball by simply leaning forward on his crutches and swinging quickly with his good foot. The team who picked Little Von got an extra player to make up for the handicap. On the fourth day there was nearly a fight over the extra player because Little Von could run and kick nearly as well as the rest of the players, but the extra player was still used because he hadn't figured out how to catch the ball and hold the crutches at the same time. On the fifth day the teams were even again. When the ball passed the point that was iden-

tified as the infield on the blacktop court, Little Von was allowed
to kick it back into the infield with his good leg. When the ball was
in the air he knocked it down with his crutches and batted it toward the infield players.

With a week off from work at the cleaners to help him make
the transition, Vivian sat at the kitchen table and said a small
prayer of thanks that the child had nearly resumed a normal life.
She had feared that the hard people of the projects would look
down on him and treat him as if he were a reject, or damaged.
Instead she saw that they responded to him as he responded to
himself. In Little Von's mind, he had not lost the use of a leg; he
had gained two more.

Bill Furman pulled the big Buick into a space in front of the
fenced playground. Little Von ran up to him with his good leg and
crutches hitting the ground unevenly spaced, one behind the
other. Bill picked up the child high over his head, crutches and
all. "Hey there, boy. How you doing with all those legs you got?"

"Good! You want to see my new trick?"

"What kind of trick?"

"Okay, watch. " Little Von ran to the other side of the courtyard and propelled himself forward, hopping and pushing
smoothly until he reached the back fence. When he turned, he
glanced quickly to see if Bill was still watching. Then he lifted and
bent his right leg back until it mirrored his braced leg. For a time
he balanced perfectly still. Then, by leaning from side to side, and
moving each crutch as soon as the weight was transferred to the
other, he walked the length of the court without using a leg.

"Ey boy! That's really something." Bill looked up at the apartment window where Vivian was smiling. "They can't slow you
down at all, can they?"

"Naa. It's not so bad. Mommy said in two more weeks it'll be
one month and then I'll only have eleven to go."

"So the doctor said a year?"

"Yup, if I don't walk on it. He said if I walk on it, it will make
it worse. Then I have to stay on crutches longer."

"Heck, that ain't so bad for a guy who can walk without using his feet."

"Bill, you gonna stay for dinner?"

"Yep."

"Good. Can we go for a ride after dinner?"

"I don't see why not."

"Mommy!" He yelled to the upstairs window. "Bill said we could go for a ride after dinner!"

"I heard him. You better come up in a little while and wash your hands."

"Okay."

"I'll see you in a little bit, Spiderman."

"Okay. Don't forget you said we could go for a ride."

"Promise, promise," Bill yelled back from the foyer door. Bill's mind bounced from his flower shop to Vivian to Little Von's leg, in a rapid blur. As he rounded the second flight of stairs, a sharp pain stabbed his chest. Falling to the side, he leaned heavily on the wall. His eyes darted back and forth looking for a possible reason for the pain. This was more than heartburn. He thought about his weight and his heart, knowing that this was on the right track. The pain subsided. His weight had been on the increase for years. Now that he was in love and happier with his life, he had eaten more carelessly and his weight had increased even more. Bill considered seeing a doctor, along with eating less. He decided to diet.

Alone again, Little Von continued to work on his three leg skills. After falling several times, he finally began to get the basics of twirling on one crutch. He stood on the grassy area beneath the apartment windows trying to visualize what he might do next, when he suddenly hit the ground and tumbled over the slight slope. At the bottom he looked up and saw Jing-Wei, who was standing with the missing crutch held above his head. Jing-Wei gave an exaggerated and mocking laugh.

Little Von looked up to the apartment window, but no one was there to intervene.

"Oh, my poor wittle leg. Oh my poor wittle leg," Jing-Wei taunted. "I'm hurt. Everybody look at me. Look at me."

Jing-Wei forced a laugh and ran around the side of the building toward the laundry, pretending to use the crutch as he ran.

Little Von got up and hopped behind him. When he came to the corner of the building, two hands came out and pushed him over and down the slope again. Again Jing-Wei stood at the top laughing. He ran to the front of the building.

Mad and determined not to be bullied, Little Von pulled his leg out of the sling and walked two steps before he heard the words of Doctor Bowenstein in his head. "Now you must not walk on that leg no matter what or it might be a lot longer than a year! Remember. No matter what." He slipped the leg back into the sling and hopped with one crutch to find Jing-Wei.

The laughter stopped. As Little Von hobbled around the corner, he saw why. Jing-Wei's mother stood in front of her son. In her hand was a wide black strap.

"Mommy, Mommy don't!" Jing Wei begged. He stood looking at his mother horrified. "Little Von and I were just playing a game. We were just playing. Ask him. Huh, Little Von...We were just playing ...right!"

Jing-Wei's mother looked at Little Von. He was breathing hard, his clothes disheveled and dirty from the fall. She turned back to her son without speaking and tightened the grip on her strap.

Seeing the look on her face, Jing-Wei threw the crutch down and tried to run, but his mother was right behind him, screaming at him and flailing as she ran. "You lie me, Jing! You lie lie all time!"

Jing-Wei ran to the fence and tried to clamber over, but his mother was right behind him. She caught him by the shoulder and strapped him quickly and repeatedly. She bared her teeth and made a high-pitched straining sound each time she hit him. Finally Jing-Wei stopped fighting back and fell to the ground and tucked himself into a ball to protect his head and face. She reached down and pulled him up without compassion. Then, with another loud wack to get him started, she pushed him toward the crutch lying on the ground.

Jing-Wei picked up the crutch and stood motionless with his head down.

"Gib it to eeem, terl eeem you sarry!" she slapped the strap on her side, Jing jumped. Some of Jing-Wei's friends had gathered at the far side of the playground and were holding their hands over their mouths to hide their laughter, but it could easily be heard.

Jing Wei scowled, his eyes and face hot with anger.

"TERL EEEM!" She screamed again.

"Sorry!" Jing said letting the crutch fall against Little Von. Then he mumbled so only Little Von could hear. "I'm kickin' your ass for this. You know I will too." Jing-Wei walked slowly toward the door.

He tried to make a wide arc around his mother when he came to her, but she let one end of the strap go, doubling its length. "Whack!" it sounded, catching him partly across the shoulders.

"Neba do that gin!"

After Jing-Wei and his mother disappeared through the foyer door, the boys watching laughed out loud and retold the beating blow by blow. When they saw Little Von making his way toward the door, they began to tease.

"OOO man, Jing's gonna get you for that. You wait and see. What you gonna do?" They all OOOed and laughed together.

Little Von stopped in front of the door. "I didn't do nothin' to him."

"Yes you did! You made him get a beatin'."

Little Von pulled the door back and started up the steps. "I didn't do nothin' to him." His words barely echoed off the dirty cement floor, but the fear grew as he heard Jing Wei crying behind his green apartment door.

Bill cruised the narrow historical roads of Jockey Park that wound their way through the woods, now dense with greenery and wild flowers, until they came to the clear water spring on the far side of the grassy meadow.

Little Von sat in the back, high on his brother's knees, his arm over the front seat and around his mother's shoulders. Through the window he watched the white shafts of sunlight play through the trees and dance across the tops of wild ferns on the forest floor. Then he saw the spring where his mother washed her car on hot days. It was a welcomed get-away from the asphalt of the projects and the thick New Jersey humidity. "Hey Bill! We gonna wash your car?"

Bill Looked at Vivian. "Hey, that would have been a good idea since we got all this help. Shoulda thought of it before we left."

Clovis Lamb gave Joleena, who sat between him and Robin in the back seat, a gentle poke in the side. "See I knowed there was some reason why they ask us to come." Joleena had fallen in love with Clovis as soon as she had met him. She looked at Robin and laughed after giving him a not-so-gentle poke.

"Next time, Von. We didn't bring any soap or anything."

Clovis wrinkled his lips. "Hmp," he said toward Robin in a low voice. "If you prays reglar it pays off once in a while." Clovis unconsciously tapped his jacket checking the contents of the inside pocket.

"Clovis!" Liberty said, squeezed between Vivian and Bill in the front seat. "What the hell you mumblin' about back there?"

"Prayin'," Clovis said looking straight ahead. "I don't have time to explain it to ya." Liberty held out her middle finger.

After Bill found a parking place, the group found an empty picnic table on the edge of the grass and woods and began spreading the contents of two large coolers. Soon everyone was busy eating potato salad, fried chicken, boiled eggs and pickles. They told stories of the past and exchanged recent gossip. Also on the table was an array of cups, soda bottles, large bags of Wise potato chips, pretzels, and two small pint bottles, one of Seagram' Whiskey, and another of Gordon's Gin.

After the meal Little Von found a playmate in the field who took delight in watching him play ball with his crutches and no feet. Robin and Joleena went off on their own. Joleena locked her arm under his while they walked and talked slowly, with thoughtful pauses and long smiles.

Clovis ignored the conversation at the table and watched the kids. First he watched Little Von and tried to remember what it was like to run through a field behind a ball without a care in the world, having never paid a bill, or even been to more than kindergarten, or even thought about a woman—just free, totally free, stark-naked free to the world, bursting with curiosity. He tried to imagine what it would be like to go to sleep without a hindering thought of any kind, without memories of anything beyond what he had done that day, forgetting all the moments before and planning nothing for the moments to come.

Liberty, Bill, and Vivian laughed, but only the eyes moved through the wrinkles of Clovis's face as he switched his attention from Little Von and his new-found friend, to Robin and Joleena midway across the emerald grasses of the park. Clovis sat still against the backdrop of voices at the table like a star sits silently against the night. He watched and strained to imagine what they would talk about. His heart pounded slowly and hard as he realized their new love in all its intensity. He watched. Only for a brief second did he unfold his hands in his lap to take the paper cup with whiskey and ice, but he didn't take the time to drink it; instead he continued to watch as he saw them sneak a kiss they probably hoped no one had seen. But Clovis did.

They sat in the grass. The sun was at Joleena's back, highlighting the red in her hair, her breast a silhouette as she leaned over languidly looking for four-leaf clovers. Clovis's hand tightened around the paper cup. He closed his eyes and remembered his wife.

Liberty's speech had already become more dramatic. She drained her cup and filled it once again. "...oooh baby, that woman was a witch, Bill. I don't mean to talk about your wife..."

"Ex," Bill corrected.

"Well, whatever. She still a witch. Somebody nice like you...how you ever get wit somebody like that?"

"Well..." Bill trailed off. He smiled and topped the remainder of his gin and ice with tonic, and then he refilled a ginger ale for Vivian.

"Well? Is that all you can say?" Liberty laughed, nearly choking on her drink. "I 'member one time about seven years ago around Christmas time, you was still in the joint, a bunch of us was down the Pail gettin' juiced. She was sittin' with that ugly shiny-tooth fool from down South somewhere. They was sittin' a few tables behind us when she caught him looking at Dora Betts. Dora's tits and b'hind use to be so big I don't know how she ever got 'im in a dress. And Dora was a real nice girl, real nice, but she was always big—you know," Liberty said, taking another swig. "Clovis, you 'member Dora...Look at him. How long he been 'sleep?"

Bill and Vivian looked at Clovis. His head was bent over, his lips open, and his fingers still around the cup.

"I don't know," Bill said laughing. "You get old, you come and go."

"What you mean 'get old'. I take little naps all the time," Liberty said, raising her hand as if she were going to slap Bill for implying her age. "Anyway, that was before she got sick."

"God, wasn't that awful?" Vivian said, remembering how Dora Betts had died from cancer.

"Yeah baby. That cancer ate that girl up till she was pitiful. So sad. Anyway, that witch Lucretia walked right over to her table. And the next time Dora turned around to sneak a look at that ugly man, Lucretia was right there. Dora looked up and Lucretia snatched her wig off and threw it over on the bar. That woman was somethin'. Bill, where she at now?"

"Don't know. Don't care."

Little Von ran up to the table with his little friend, who was blond and about the same age. "Mommy, can we have some ginger ale?"

"Yeah. What's your friend's name?"

"I don't know. Can we have some chips too?"

"My name is Tommy," his friend said, watching Vivian with big eyes as she poured the soda.

Little Von and his new friend compared the color of their cups and joked about the red cup making cherry ginger ale and the yellow one making banana ginger ale. They laughed silly laughs and drained their cups and asked for more.

"Mommy, what's wrong with Clovis?" Little Von asked.

"Nothing baby. He just asleep. Go 'head and play now. We gonna have to go in a little while."

Little Von hurriedly put down his cup on the edge of the table and started off toward the ball lying in the grass. His friend, anxious to catch up, barely got his cup on the table's edge before he ran off. Vivian reached to catch the cup before it fell, but in the process she knocked Clovis's cup into his lap. He didn't respond.

Vivian jumped up and began to wipe him off vigorously with a napkin while holding him by the shoulder. She talked to him but there was no reply.

Bill laughed at the large wet spot on the front of Clovis's pants. "Hey Unc, you too old to be doing something like that, ain't you?"

Clovis didn't open his eyes, neither did he make any effort to move.

Bill stopped smiling. "Oh my God, Viv, is he all right?"

Vivian called his name loud and sharp while Liberty looked on frightened. "Clovis! Clovis! Wake up Clovis, we got a little mess here." Vivian shook him and watched his hand fall from the table to the wooden seat. "

Oh God!" Liberty said, coming alive. "Clovis! What's wrong? What's wrong! Bill, we better call an ambulance!"

Bill looked around for a phone booth and saw one on the far side of the field. The distance alone reminded him how far from the town they were. "Too far, Lib. He'll be dead before they ever get here. Liberty help me get him to the car. Viv, you get the kids."

"Mommy you want to play with us?" Little Von said, as Vivian ran up to him.

"No, baby. Clovis is sick and we gotta go, so say goodbye to your friend." Vivian continued to run. Little Von stood still in the field. Tommy came and stood at his side.

Vivian was trying to keep herself from crying, but she knew her eyes were filling as she approached Robin who was fighting to keep Joleena from putting dandelions in his hair. "Hey listen, you two," Vivian said, kneeling on the ground beside them.

"What's the matter, Mom?"

"Something is really wrong with Clovis. We can't get him to wake up. We gotta go right now and get him to the hospital." Vivian's mind thought of Clovis, lying down in the crowded car. "Rob, can you call somebody to come and get you guys?"

Robin's eyes wandered for a second.

Joleena spoke up. "I can call my mother. She's home. She can come."

Vivian looked distressed at the idea.

"Mom, I can probably get a hold of Lester or Lucky. Lucky's always home around dinner time." Little Von and his friend came running up, side by side. Tommy was carrying his crutches and Little Von's sling was dangling from his waist.

"Good. Joleena, I really don't want to bother your folks. Robin, there's a phone booth over there. Robin, try your grandfather if you can't get them." She turned to Little Von. "You stay with Robin and Leeny and get your leg back in that sling." She gave him a kiss on the forehead. "I'll meet you back home," she said already running back across the field to the car. Bill had pulled the car right up on the grass. Vivian jumped in and they sped away.

"Robin, we goin' now?" Little Von asked. He was puzzled.

Robin ran his hand over his head stretching on his new responsibility slowly and deliberately. "A...no Von. You...a...you can play with your friend for a little while longer. Me and Joleena are going over there to the phone to call somebody."

"Robin, is Clovis gonna die?"

Robin thought about his sister, Lillian, who would know what to say. Joleena looked to him for an answer as well. "No,

Von. He probably just had too much to drink. Go play now. I'll call you when it's time to go."

Little Von slowly put his leg back in the sling. He thought about his mother's "Other Self" which he hadn't seen since Bill had started coming around, and he didn't want to see it ever again. But he had never seen an "Other Self" in Clovis. He had seen Clovis drunk, but he had never thought of it as an "Other Self." Maybe, he thought, Clovis's didn't come out very much, but when it did it would make him so sick he had to go to the hospital. He wondered if his mother's "Other Self" could make her go to the hospital.

"People shouldn't drink," he said to his friend. Tommy didn't answer.

Joleena leaned against the corner of the phone booth and watched as Robin ran through his pockets looking for change. When his hand came out of his pocket a marijuana joint, twisted at both ends, fell to the bottom of the booth and rolled toward her.

Robin watched the look on her face as she grappled to understand what it was. She bent down and slowly picked it up and looked at Robin. Disbelief was all over her face. Joleena knew that it wasn't tobacco, both by the smell and the rough way that it was rolled. None of her friends had tried it, but still there was nothing new about reefer. People always talked about it along with gambling and making their own still whiskey. Of those she knew who did smoke it, many were also using other drugs and frequenting jail cells for one reason or another. She turned with it and walked away to the trash can near the table where the others had sat.

Robin, still holding the phone off the receiver, waited for her to come back. She didn't. Instead she looked at him across the distance, a cold distance he could feel in the pit of his stomach. She dropped the joint in the trash and sat at the picnic table, her head down.

Robin put the dime in the slot and dialed. After fifteen minutes he hung the phone back in place and sat across from her. Neither could speak. Robin attributed the silence to Joleena's anger and was about to tell her that his grandfather was on the way to pick them up. When he saw tears run down both her cheeks, he felt a sinking feeling in his stomach.

Her hurt had gone deep, and he had been the cause of it. Joleena put her head up and tried to cover her face with her arm. She looked around the table and found a napkin. Breathing heavily to calm herself, she blew her nose and wiped her eyes. Finally, she looked at him without speaking, giving him no choice but to wait.

She caught her breath. "I don't...I don't want to...a...be around you if you're gonna do this. I can't even believe you would try it, let alone carry your own." Joleena began to sob again.

"Joleena," Robin began with a sigh. "Really. It's not that much of a big deal. It just makes you..."

"Robin!" she screamed. "If the police had come here to take Clovis and that...garbage...had of fallen out of your pocket, what were you gonna tell them? That it really was no big deal. That all it made you do is...what were you gonna tell me, relax or something. Then what were they gonna say? 'Okay, Mr. Thompson, as long as you're just relaxing,' Robin, how could you be so stupid?"

"Joleena." Robin reached across the table and tried to take her hand. She jerked it away. "Joleena. Everybody makes a big deal about it. It doesn't even do anything but make you laugh. Really that's..."

Joleena swung her feet from under the table and moved away from the table. "God, I don't believe it. My father was right."

"Hey! What do you mean your father was right?" Robin said, coming around the side of the table, standing in front of her.

She didn't speak. She went back to the table and sat down, no longer crying but still fighting to regain control. Her eyes followed Robin as he came back to the table and sat across from her. She interlaced her fingers on the table and looked straight into his eyes.

"Over there in the field I handed you a daisy and told you I loved you. I never told any other boy that. I always thought that it was silly for kids in high school to act like they were seriously in love. I guess that was because I had never loved anyone before. Now I know how it hurts to want somebody so much you can't stand to be away from them." Joleena checked Robin's face to see how he was taking it.

"We spend most of our time together when we're not working, sometimes whole afternoons, and when I get home I start praying that you call. When I can't stand it anymore, I call you. I know you feel the same way. I know it.

"I never even told you how furious my father was when I started eating at your house every other day. My mother always took our side, telling him what a gentleman you were, and how nice you were. Especially since your mom has been spending a lot of time with my mom at the daycare with Little Von and his crutches and all, they really got close. My mother doesn't even worry about me when I'm with you any more. It feels like one big family, like we were married or something." She noticed when she used the word *married*, it was the first time Robin seemed moved.

"Go 'head, I'm listening." Robin said, feeling the fear and anger in her stare.

"Robin I can't hardly bring myself to say what I have to say right now."

"It's all right. Go ahead."

"Robin, no, it's not all right!" She yelled across the table. "I shouldn't even have to be talking like this. Why did you have to go and mess everything up? It was going so good." She started to cry again.

"Hey...don't cry."

"I'm not," she said, grabbing for another napkin. "I'm just gonna say it and whatever happens... happens."

Robin sat back, not knowing what to expect.

"I like most of your friends except for one or two like Scab..."

"Benny isn't my friend," Robin said, quickly.

"Well at least he's gonna be away for awhile. Anyway, I would never tell you how to pick your friends. But drugs...I don't want to be with you if you're gonna get into drugs. I don't care how long it takes me to get over you. I don't care how much it will hurt. I won't be with you."

There was a long silence. "Joleena, smokin' a little reefer ain't doin' drugs. I told you..."

"I don't care—no, I do care. I feel like I'm going crazy already inside, just thinking of not being with you. But you have to decide," she said, her voice becoming more and more quiet. Then she looked him in the eye and added:

"Now."

Tommy McPherson's parents were at a table behind a small stand of maples. The smoke from their firepit carried the smell of hamburgers and hot dogs across the field to where the children played.

"I smell hammmburrrrgerrrs," Tommy sang, his eyes wide.

"Mmmm," Little Von said, running his tongue over his lips.

They ran into the woods and up the path to the table. "Hey Tommy, ready for a burger?" His mother smiled at the two boys, but mostly at Little Von with his crutches and brace.

"Yep. We're hungry."

Jill McPherson eyed Little Von as he maneuvered around the picnic table. "Is it okay with your mom if you have a burger with us?"

"She had to leave," Little Von said. "My brother Robin's the boss of me now, and he don't care about stuff like this."

"Ohhh," Tommy's mother said, turning to her husband. "Just like guys."

Tommy and Little Von got to their places at the table. Little Von stuck his crutches between the bench and table top. Tommy's mother instinctively wanted to help, but it was obvious help wasn't necessary.

At the grill, the parents stood talking, their backs to the kids, speaking low.

"What do you think he has, Jill?"

"God, I don't know, but it just scares the hell out me to think that something like that might happen to Tommy." It was a warm summer evening, but the thought had given her a chill. She ran her palms up and down the sides of her arm as she looked over her shoulder at Little Von and Tommy playing at the table.

"Well, it looks like he does all right with it, whatever it is."

"Yeah, I guess. Kids don't even bother to slow down." She went to the table smiling. "Tommy, what's your friend's name?"

"I don't know. What's your name?" he said, turning to Little Von. Both boys were drinking Kool-Aid and had red mustaches.

"Levon Thompson…"

"Levon Thompson," Tommy repeated to his mother.

"But everybody just calls me Little Von."

"But everybody just calls…"

"Ah…I heard him, Tommy. Thank you."

"Little Von, is that right?"

"Yes."

"My name is Jill McPherson and this is my husband, Jim."

"Hi Jim," Little Von said. Unlike Elderiah and Jessie Rose who still called their close friends by their last names, he was used to calling adults by their first names like everyone did in the projects.

Jill and Jim looked at each other.

"Well what do you huuungry guys want on your burgers?" Jim held the ketchup over their buns.

"Lots of ketchup!" they said in unison.

Jim watched Little Von close his bun and wrestle the burger up to his mouth. "Say, that's some outfit you got around your waist there. What did you do to your leg?"

Little Von washed the bite down with some Kool-Aid. "I didn't do nothin' to it. It just got that way."

"Oh, I see. Is it some kind of polio or something?"

Jill frowned. "Jim, he's probably too little to understand what he has. He's only about five or six."

"No, I'm six and a half," Little Von said, pausing between bites. "It's some kind of Perthese disease. It's in my hip. The ball don't rotate smooth," he said, repeating the phrase exactly the way he had heard his mother say it many times. He made a C with one hand and placed his other fist in it and moved it around as if it were broken. Then he bit his burger.

A truck horn sounded in the distance and Little Von froze, waiting to see if he would hear it again. It sounded, and this time he could hear the engine in the distance as well.

Little Von jumped up from the table, grabbed his crutches and looked through the woods. "That's my Grandpa's truck! He comed to get us!" Little Von was down the trail before anyone could say much, yelling back over his shoulder. "Bye, Tommy! Bye, Jill! Bye, Jim!"

20

THE WILLIAMSES LIVED in the single-story style brick apartments that stood near the Pocahontas dam. Home alone, Matt Williams opened a large book, allowing the pages to separate themselves, revealing a sheet of typing paper with a pencil sketch of Patsy Clarke. It was an amazing likeness of the girl, just like Joleena's had been. But for Patsy he had made improvements. There were fewer pimples and he had erased some of the chubbiness. The picture lay between the same pages where Joleena Cleary's portrait had rested two months before. He rubbed with his bare finger to shade in the space of her eyebrows until it was nearly too dark, but more mature and appealing.

A noise at the front door jerked him out of his daze. Someone was knocking. As quickly as he had gotten it out, the atlas was closed and back on the shelf. The knocking was steady and impatient. He snatched the inner door open and saw the neighbor's dog sitting with its back to the screen door. The young pup was watching a group of small children playing with a ball. Every time the ball went into the air, his tail wagged hard against the door. Matt banged the noisy aluminum bottom into the dog's hind end, scaring more than hurting it, sending the pup off the porch, yelping with its tail between its legs. He slammed the inner door and marched to the phone.

"Hello, is Patsy home?"

He was greeted by a motherly voice on the other end. "Yes she is...but I don't know if she can come to the phone...wait a minute, let me see If I can find her. Who's calling please?"

Matt hesitated. It was no secret that mothers who lived up on the hill were leery of boys from the projects. "It's...um...Matt." he said, hoping that it would end there.

"Matt?" her mother repeated inquisitively.

"Yes, Matt Williams."

"Oh yes...well...well hold on. I'll see if I can find her."

Matt wasn't sure if he was hearing or feeling his heart pound in his chest. Giving his whole name was definitely not part of the plan, especially since the fight and the stabbing on the playground.

"Oh that's really great," he said out loud. He continued thinking to himself and listening to see if she really intended to look for her daughter. "Everybody knows the Williamses," he thought. Then he corrected himself and the anger returned. "Everybody knows Scootch."

"Who did you say it was?" a voice said somewhere in the background. "Who?...Matt?"

After footsteps and what seemed like an eternity of bobbling and knocking the receiver around, Patsy answered. "Hello."

"Hi, Pats. This is Matt. What's up?"

"Oh hi, Matt. I thought my mother had said Matt, but you had never called before and I couldn't figure out who she was talking about."

"Well...a...I did call before,...but you were out. Didn't you get my message?"

"Nope, never did. Did you give it to my mom or my little sister?"

"Oh it was...a...your sister. Yeah, it was your sister I talked to."

"Well then, I'm not surprised. Hope it wasn't anything important."

Matt had been trying to get his nerve up to call for three weeks. That in itself made the call important.

"No, not really. Look I was just wondering if you wanted to go and maybe get a soda or something later?"

"Gee I don't know Matt...wait a minute, let me ask."

Patsy covered the phone, allowing only mumbling to be heard through her fingers. Matt tried to swallow, but his mouth was too dry. She uncovered the phone.

"Hey, Matt?"

"Yeah."

"I guess I could, but it would have to be quick though, 'cause I have to go with my mom until about four and we eat around five so that wouldn't leave a lotta time. I don't know if it would be worth walking all the way up here for that, would it?"

Matt was elated. It was a definite yes, no matter the duration. "No, that's okay. It's not that far if I just take the tracks and cut up Booger's Hill."

"Hey Matt, wait a minute. I have an idea." Patsy covered the phone for a moment, but then she laid it down. Matt could hear her walking away. When the footsteps stopped, he heard her yelling. "Hey, Art. What if I meet you at the movie?" There was silence. The other voice was off in the distance. Partially covering the phone, she said: "Matt's on the phone. He wants to get a soda later. Sounds like he needs someone to talk to. Maybe he needs to talk about Scootch or something—I don't know. But it shouldn't take that long. I'll meet him down at Mr. Beeman's. After dinner you could meet us there or I could just meet you at the theater." The footsteps began to return.

Matt took the phone away from his ear and held it and his other fist up in the air above his head. "ART? Damn!"

"Hey Matt? Yeah, I think I can…"

"A…Patsy…um….my mom just came in and said she wants me to help her with some stuff tonight. Maybe we…a…some other time huh?"

"Yeah, Matt, sure. Anytime. Just call. Say, how's Scootch?"

Matt groaned. "He's fine. Gettin' better all the time. Hey I gotta go now."

"Okay. Well just call if you want to get…"

Matt was furious. He held the phone away from his head, barely able to contain himself. He was waiting for her voice to stop so he could hang up. "Okay—bye."

Slamming the phone in its cradle, he ran to the bookshelf and grabbed the atlas by its spine and shook it violently. When it released the attractive smiling sketch of Patsy Clarke from between the pages, he tossed the book away and caught the floating paper before it hit the ground. He tore it into smaller and smaller pieces, then flung them in the air. They fluttered to the ground like ashes.

Matt crashed through the door, hitting the dog who had returned. The pup rolled down the steps squealing and squirming onto its back, its paws bent fearfully over its belly. It looked up with wide eyes as Matt stepped over it and raced between the buildings.

In a rage, he tore through bed sheets and small children's clothes that hung on the clothes lines without looking back to see if any had fallen. As adrenaline and anger entwined, he effortlessly scaled the hurricane fence and jumped to the narrow dirt fishing path running along the side of Pocahontas. Dirt flew in every direction as his heels pounded hard with each step. Matt leaped onto the top of the concrete retainer wall of the dam and walked dangerously close to the edge through the rising mist of the waters crashing below.

Jumping to the bottom, he saw a turtle out in the water, sleeping on a log. Angrily, he picked up a large rock nearly too big to be held in one hand, and heaved it in the direction of the turtle. Three more followed in the same fashion. Unaware of the falling rocks, the turtle slept on until finally one of the rocks bounced off the end of the log. It struggled to get its feet under as Matt hurled larger and larger rocks. Finally Matt had a rock so big he looked like a shot-putter in a track meet. The turtle slipped below the surface, leaving Matt straining to hold the miniature boulder in both hands. Using his whole body he did his best to heave it to the spot where he had last seen the turtle. It crashed only a few feet away from him. The back wash soaked his feet and the ground around him. The one-sided war ended, leaving Matt more angry and frustrated than before.

He ran the length of the path, slipping and sliding in and out of the water. His only stops were at the small cove where the rope hung from the tree, and again when the path came to an end at the bottom of the stone bridge. With his senses more intact and his breathing calmer, he scrambled up the side of the bridge and sat, dejected, muddy and wet on the slate that crowned the bridge wall. "Ho," he said as a picture of Patsy, pimples and all, flashed through his head. Then he thought of Joleena and Robin, and his anger doubled.

Like angry bees stinging him one after another, Matt's thoughts swarmed each with their own pain: his father who thought of him as the weaker son, his brother whom everyone knew, Joleena who loved Robin, and now Patsy, with her pudgyness and pimples, who should have fallen to her knees to be with a Swan Tone, loved Art. Matt never heard the people who spoke to him as they passed. His expression was blank, his handle on the real world broken as the increasing mass of his anger, like lava, rose to the surface and boiled over.

Then he heard the sound. It was a grinding sort of chattering mechanical noise punctuated by what sounded like a shotgun blast every now and then. Other people noticed too. People who had first noticed him sitting on the bridge with his feet wet and muddied, now stood looking toward the trestle in the direction of the noise. Then it appeared.

Jimmy Lee had pulled out all the stops for the maiden voyage of the Stutz. Armed with goggles and a racing scarf flapping in the wind, he sat behind the wheel of the Stutz Victoria. It was shiny with a new coat of canary-yellow paint. The newly-chromed rails, which had served as bumpers in earlier days, flashed momentarily as the train trestle blocked the fading evening light. Cars honked excitedly as they passed in the opposite direction and Jimmy Lee waved proudly, his chest stuck out with all of his gold-lined teeth showing.

Matt's eyes were transfixed by the spokes of the wheels that glistened brilliantly like perfectly straight silver rays as they spun. The white-walls of the new tires were flawless and striking. The top was neatly folded down and appeared like a white shawl around the Stutz's backseat. On top of it all sat Jimmy Lee prouder than the Egyptian hood ornament, waving at the cheering crowd that grew by the moment.

Jimmy Lee turned from the street and glided past the pumps and into the shadow of the garage. With his heart racing, Matt slid off the wall and followed. His once-wide smile thinned as he was jostled by the crowd. He stopped by the pumps satisfied to watch from there as a gathering of old men slapped Jimmy Lee on the back congratulating him. Matt stood and stared until the car backed away from the garage, this time filled with old men.

The Stutz took to the street, chugging and clanging. It backfired and stopped dead. Jimmy Lee hit the floor starter and the Stutz sprang to life and died again. "Come on, June Bug!" Old man Tully Willis yelled.

The Stutz fired up with two more loud shots and they were off again in a cloud of smoke with Jimmy Lee sounding the horn, *Aaaaauuuuuuugga! Aaaauuuuggggga!* The Stutz Victoria roared through the Hollow with its back to Mathew Williams. The car turned left at the corner into the sun. The light reflected off the smooth curve of the trunk and sides, creating the illusion of a corona around the name "June Bug" written in flaring script across the cover of the spare tire.

"So, Jimmy Lee found a name, " Matt mumbled. He watched for a moment more and then turned toward home visualizing himself behind the wheel of the Stutz. No one noticed him as he picked his way through the crowd.

It was evening and Bill Furman, in dress pants, shirt, and pullover sweater, was down on the floor with Little Von on his back.

"Are you ready?"

"No! No! Not yet!" The small boy said, frantically searching for a way to hold onto Bill's big body.

He grabbed two handfuls of Bill's sweater.

"No, don't hold onto my sweater. You'll stretch it out of shape."

He grabbed Bill's shirt collar.

"Ey—I can't breathe." Bill coughed and laughed. "You wanna sew my buttons back on?"

"Aw!" Little Von complained, afraid Bill would start bucking before he figured out a way to brace himself. He pushed his legs down as far as he could and tried to cross them at the ankles under Bill's stomach, but they were too short.

"Von, real bronco riders pinch their knees in tight."

"Yeah, but they got..."

"Have!" Vivian yelled from the kitchen. "They *have* Von. Come on now. You can remember that. We tell you every day."

"They have ropes that go into the horse's mouth," Von said, frowning toward the kitchen, wondering what difference it made which word he used.

Bill's eyes flashed around the room. Finding nothing, he grabbed his tie, bit it in the middle, and gave the ends to him. "Better be ready now cause here-we-go!"

Little Von gripped his knees and held on to the ends of the tie. He shrieked and squealed each time Bill bucked, twisted, and turned. Finally Bill arched his back higher and higher until he began to feel Little Von losing his grip. And then with one big buck threw him onto the cushions of the couch.

"ONE MORE TIME! ONE MORE TIME!" Little Von screamed, scrambling off the couch and onto Bill's back.

Vivian came out of the kitchen with her camera. "Smile."

After several bucks, Bill sent him flying again. Bill sat against the back of the couch and rubbed his chest and tried to smile. "No more for me."

"Hold on, Bronco Billy," Vivian said entering the room again. She had three matching bowls of ice cream. She handed Bill and

Little Von theirs, and settled herself into her favorite spot on the couch. "Do you think they'll let Clovis out tomorrow?"

Hot from the workout, Bill had pulled off his sweater and sat up on the couch. The pressure in his chest was subsiding. "Hell, they would have let him out today if he hadn't been so ornery and stubborn. The doctor took me out in the hall and said, 'We want to keep him another day or so because we don't think his mental state is stable.' I said, 'Well Doc, he must be okay then, 'cause Clovis's mental state ain't been stable since 1925.'" Vivian started laughing. She had to hold her mouth to keep her ice cream from falling out.

Little Von had been eating quietly and quickly. His eyes darted back and forth with the flow of the conversation, but he understood only parts of it. "Bill? What's wrong with Clovis? Nobody splain that to me yet."

"Remember the other day in the park when we thought Clovis had fallen asleep?"

"Yeah."

"Well Clovis was sick and we didn't know it. He had what they call a mild stroke. Just a little one."

Little Von held his bowl up to his face and licked the bottom, then sat looking at Bill, waiting for him to say something he could understand.

"Von, Clovis had a little problem with the connections in his brain. You know how sometimes when you're playing with your trains on the floor and having a good time and everything, and all of a sudden…" he said, adding excitement to his voice, "…somebody comes along and kicks out the plug?"

"Yup, that's Robin. He do that all the time 'cause he HAVES…" he smiled at his mother, "big feet."

Vivian closed her eyes and shook her head slowly. "Hopeless."

Bill laughed. "Well, when that happens, everything stops. Right?"

"Yup."

"Well Clovis's plug didn't completely come out. It just got wobbly for a little while."

Little Von looked as if he were on the verge of understanding.

Bill smiled, knowing that he had come close. He looked

around the room, searching for a simpler way to explain the last of what he had said. "Okay Von, look at this." He went over to a lamp that sat on a small table at the end of the couch. It was a short table lamp with two bulbs. Bill took out his handkerchief and loosened one of the bulbs until it went out. Then he slowly turned it back until it began to blink on its own from the imperceptible vibration of the apartment building. "See. Most of Clovis's brain was all right," he said, pointing to the one bulb tight in its socket. "...but a small part of it went on the blink for a little while."

Little Von smiled, understanding. "Is he gonna be all right now?"

"Yeah, he's fine. But when he woke up, he was so grouchy that they thought there was something else wrong with him."

"Naa, Clovis's always like that!"

"I know," Bill said, laughing and looking at Vivian. "That's what I tried to tell them."

At that moment, the sound of four voices rose to the third floor apartment. Bill stopped laughing and pointed to the window.

Little Von, satisfied that there was no trace of ice cream left in his bowl, ran into the kitchen. Bill and Vivian stood next to the open window looking down into the fenced-off playing court. Vivian slid the window back on its track as far as it could go. Down below, Scootch, still needing a little support, leaned against the fence snapping his fingers. Matt and Robin were harmonizing behind Lester's clear and faultless lead. Bill stood behind Vivian, looking over her shoulder. She leaned back against his strength listening.

"Look at him," she said with a sigh. Her eyes were glazed over. "He's happy."

Bill focused on Robin. "He looks like a teenager again."

"Yes. He looks like a happy teenager. I always want him to look that way." A spoon bounced off the floor of the kitchen. Little feet jumped off a chair and scuffled back up again.

Bill started toward the kitchen. "He's into the ice cream. I'll go help him."

"No," she said, grabbing Bill's hand. "Let him try it by himself." She pulled his hand until his arm was around her middle and they stood close and continued to listen to the boys singing below.

"You letting him walk around without his crutches?"

"Well the doctor said it would be good to let him have some time before bed without his brace on. He mostly sits and watches TV then. He said that would keep him from going totally crazy and it would be good for the muscles in his leg to get a little exercise."

"Hmm," Bill said. "I never thought about that."

"Are you going back tonight or are you gonna stay on the couch again?"

Bill still felt a mild pain in his chest and thought it better to stay. It was time to speak to a doctor, there was no denying that. He would do it when he picked up Clovis from the hospital.

"I'll stay. They'll probably let the Lamb out tomorrow and I better be around to keep him from tearing up the place and terrorizing the nurses."

"What about the flower shop?"

"You know the shop is really getting to be a problem. I was thinking maybe you should think about moving to Patterson to help me. Or…" Bill took a deep breath knowing the next statement was the same as a proposal, "Or maybe I should move the shop up here so you can get there easier. Of course, if you would be with me to do it. Even those old unwanted dandelion weeds must be more interesting than pressing shirts in a sweat shop."

"They aren't weeds. They just sometimes grow where people don't want them," Vivian said wiping one cheek and then the other. "And I think I would like that fine."

From below a perfect blend of four voices rose to them.

Good night sweet-heart.
 It's time to-go
Good night sweet-heart

Little Von kicked his covers back. He tried his best to be careful not to startle Robin, who hated to be awakened on the Saturday mornings when he didn't have to work. Moving slowly, he bent over to the level of his brother's ear and whispered, "Rob." He waited. "Rob." He waited again, but there was still no response. "Robin." He tapped him with two fingers ever so gently and made his whisper more intense. "Robin! Wake up or I'm gonna miss cartoons." Robin rolled over, still asleep. Little Von climbed up on the bed. "Robiiiinn. You making me miss cartOOOoooonnss."

"What…what…Von! What you want, man?" It wasn't really a question. It was more like a warning. In a moment Robin would realize that he had been wakened on a Saturday morning when he didn't have to work. If left alone now, he would be asleep again in a matter of seconds.

"Come on, Rob. I need you to get the cartoons clear so they won't be all snowy."

"OOhh, Von. Geez man. Look, Bill's in there…" Robin rolled over and pulled the sheet over his head. "…he'll do it."

"That's right!" Little Von said. Forgetting to be quiet, he stood straight up and excitedly bounced to the end of the bed and jumped off. He ran down the hall and sure enough, Bill had stayed over. He was wrapped in a big shiny quilt on the floor.

"Bill!" he called, less cautious than he had been with his brother. "Bill!"

Vivian awoke in the next room and heard the commotion. "Von, don't wake up Bill if you don't have to. Turn the TV on and see if it's clear first. If it's not, I'll do it."

He hadn't thought of that. Little Von watched anxiously as the small white dot became a grey cloud on the picture tube. Finally, after a little more than a minute, he could see the grey begin to separate to reveal four men dressed in suits sitting around a table talking about adult stuff, stiff and lifeless. He scrambled into the kitchen, knowing that any minute now the adult show would be off the air and Uncle Bob, Howdy Doody, and Clarabell would be on with cartoons.

"Bill," he whispered. "Could you fix me some cereal?" He waited, but Bill didn't budge. "That's all right. I can do it, but I make a mess sometime." In the kitchen he carefully stood on the chair and cradled the milk carton in the bend of his arm over the bowl of corn flakes. He poured until he could just see the milk rise above the flakes. He sifted through the drawer until he found the spoon with the extra long handle for iced tea and put it into the bowl. As he returned to the room, the Howdy Doody theme began to play. Turning the sound up, he sat on the floor next to Bill.

"Von! Turn that down so you don't wake Bill up." Vivian

yelled groggily.

Little Von looked at Bill, who hadn't moved. "Ok Mom."

Two hours passed. Little Von had curled himself in the blanket with Bill, whom he loved and trusted like his Grandpa. He watched Howdy Doody, Raja the Elephant Boy, Heckle and Jeckle, and finally Tom and Jerry. From time to time he glanced at Bill whose face seemed strange because his eyes were slightly open.

Vivian came down the hall in her housecoat, yawning. Little Von was rocking to the music of the television program.

"Von get off Bill like that. You're gonna wake him up."

"I'm not gonna wake him up, Mom. He's really sleep. I already tried, but I couldn't." Little Von attempted to roll off Bill's side gently but he fell off in the process. Vivian looked annoyed as she waited for Bill to start or snort. She waited for his eyes to flutter. They didn't.

"Mommy, I never seen anybody sleep with their eyes open before." Little Von said, lying next to Bill's side.

"Von! Shh!" Vivian couldn't see Bill's eyes because they were blocked by the quilt. She stood absolutely still watching the covers as they formed themselves to the contours of Bill's body. She watched the place where the quilt covered Bills abdomen, it didn't move. She walked slowly toward him. At the edge of the blanket, she knelt down. Her lips began to quiver as she reached for the portion of the quilt blocking his face.

"Mommy you gonna watch cartoons for a little while with us?"

Her voice was barely a whisper when she answered "No." She stopped her hand before it actually reached the quilt, but knowing it was inevitable that she must, she let her fingers turn under the edge of the old satin quilt given to her by Jessie Rose. Already she could feel the coldness of his skin against her trembling hands. She took a breath.

His eyes were staring straight at her. They were soft and sad, unlike his mouth which was slightly turned down at the corners as if he had fought a moment of pain. She stroked his hair and the sides of his cheeks.

Something happened on TV and Little Von laughed and said, "Watch him fall now, Mommy." When the character did, Little Von laughed and turned to her and quickly back to the TV.

Vivian smiled at him. Why she felt so calm and peaceful inside, she didn't know. She reached under the cover and brought Bill's hand out and held it in both of hers to warm it. She sat with him for a time, tracing the details of his face, and when she thought she had permanently captured the essence of his being, she stroked his face once more, and gently closed his eyes and smoothed the corners of his mouth until they no longer turned down.

Another cartoon show came and went. Little Von instinctively turned up the TV, judging the time of day by the intensity of the sunlight now shining in the room. The noise woke Robin. He ambled down the hall rubbing his eyes. Little Von said, "Hi, bean head."

Robin looked at Bill and Little Von, side by side on the floor with their feet in opposite directions, and then he noticed the eerie stillness.

"Mom?"

Robin spoke without looking away from Bill.

"Mom?" he said again, stepping closer to where Bill lay on the floor. "Is he still sleeping?" It wasn't really a question. He saw the blank look on his mother's face. She sat in the chair with the scratchy cover with her legs tucked under her, staring at Bill. She began quietly sobbing. Robin looked back to Bill. "Oh, no," he said, "Von, move." He pushed the covers back from Bill and felt for a pulse.

A commercial came on and Little Von, dressed only in a T-shirt, underwear, and his socks, jumped up. He stepped over Bill. "Rob, Bill's gonna get cold with no covers." Turning toward his mother, he noticed that she was crying. "Mommy, what's wrong? Why you cryin'?"

Robin spoke sternly. "Von. You eat yet?"

"Yup, but I'm still hungry."

"Go fix yourself some more cereal and eat it in the kitchen." Robin blurted. "Now!" Little Von left, only glancing back at his mother.

Robin quickly looked at Vivian and spoke in a hushed tone. "Is he sick, Mom?" Vivian sat with her hands covering her face. Robin grabbed Bill's hand. It was cold. Then he looked for a pulse. There was no pulse. Bill's hand and arm hung limp and heavy, his skin was pallid. Robin got up from the floor and sat on the arm of the chair. Robin whispered excitedly, "Mom, Jesus, he's dead. Bill's dead." Robin's face contorted. "How did he...what happened?" He moved closer to Vivian. "Jesus..." he said, unable to look away from Bill's body wrapped in the quilt.

"He's gone, honey." Her voice was barely audible. "He's...I don't know. His heart, a stroke...but he's gone."

"Mom, I'm gonna call Liberty." Little Von was standing in the hall quietly watching. "Von, you need to get dressed real quick."

"But Rob, I don't get dressed until after the cartoons are off," he yelled back.

"Von, you got to get dressed now because in a few minutes a whole lotta people gonna be here."

"How come a whole lotta people gonna be here?"

Robin felt himself losing control. He stopped and rubbed his hand over his face, fighting to keep his words at a low pitch. "Look Von. I know you don't know what's goin' on, but if you don't do what I asked you to do...just go do it."

Little Von felt overpowered and frustrated. "Mom?"

"Go ahead, honey. Right now."

Little Von slowly started for his room. There was something going on and he had missed it. He looked around the room taking in as much information as possible. Something was strange. Robin was yelling at him for no reason and he also understood without being told that cartoons were over, whether they actually were or not. He continued looking for things out of place.

"Von!" The urgency in Robin's voice sent Little Von halfway down the hall. "Just get dressed right now."

When Liberty arrived, Robin was still on the phone. He had called the police, Jimmy Lee's station, and his sister Lillian, who was home from nursing school for the weekend. There was another call that he wanted to make. It was a need more than a want. He needed her now next to him. It seemed the natural thing to do, but his head throbbed and he couldn't think or catch his breath. His heart felt like someone hammering on the inside of his chest. He closed his eyes and talked to himself saying, "Come on now. Steady. Steady. You don't need her. Deal with it. Deal with it."

With a deep cleansing breath, Robin opened his eyes and hung up the phone. In less than twenty minutes, all, except for Joleena, were there.

21

After the ambulance had left with Bill's body and the police had questioned everyone, Robin and Little Von were on the way up the hill to Wooden street and Grandma Jessie's in Lillian's black Ford.

Robin had started crying almost as soon as Lillian walked in the door. She came in, told Robin to re-dress Little Von and put some of his things in a bag, consoled her mother, and cleaned the kitchen. On the way up the hill, Robin was still sobbing and fiddling with the wingnut screws on Little Von's crutches. He thought of how horrible it would have been if Lillian hadn't been home.

Lillian's strength was always visible. Although she looked very much like her mother, she emanated the orderliness and reasoning power of Jessie Rose Bowman. She was gentle when the world around her allowed her to be so, and now, with great love and sincerity, she became the comforter. They rode silently until they passed Pinucci's ice cream store. Little Von broke the silence.

"Lil, can we stop and get some ice cream?" His request lacked enthusiasm. It had already been a long day, filled with things he didn't understand, things that concerned Bill.

"Not right now, Von. I'm pretty sure Grandma Jessie has got some in the freezer though, okay?"

"Oookay," he said looking around to see how much further they had to go. He watched Robin crying quietly.

"Robin, has anybody explained to Von what's going on?"

Robin sniffed and tried to clear his throat. "No," he said, mostly shaking his head to get the point across. "We just got him outta there."

"I know what's going on." Little Von said, still straining to see over the dash.

"You do?"

"Yep."

"Well let's hear it. We're talking about Bill, right?"

"Yup," he said with a trace of sadness in his voice. Bill got sick while he was sleeping last night, right?"

"Well yes…"

"The plug in his brain got wobbly like Clovis's. Clovis's plug is okay now and he's comin' home today from the hospital."

"Who, Von?"

"Clovis the Lamb. His plug got wobbly too, and he fell asleep in the park. Then Mommy and Bill had to take him to the hospital."

"Oh yeah, that's right. Grampa said he had to come and pick you guys up from Jockey Park."

"Yup, he comed in the truck."

"Came, Von. He came in the truck."

"Yup."

Lillian sighed deeply.

Robin, still trying to shore himself up, was looking at her to see if she was going to tell him all of it. He was stunned to see that she was starting to cry. He could count the number of times in their lives he had seen Lillian cry, but there she was, sniffing and wiping her eyes just like he was.

"Von," she said, clearing her throat. "It's different with Bill though. He's not coming back from the hospital. He's gone to heaven."

Little Von frowned as his mind went over what she had said. Robin and Lillian were crying. "You mean his plug came all the way out and he died?"

Lillian turned the corner onto Wooden Street, shook her head and wiped her eyes. "Yes."

"We won't see him any more?"

"No, Von. He's gone to heaven."

Little Von looked sad. The heaviness pushed him back into the seat. He looked at Robin who was leaning against the window staring blankly at the floor and understood why he was crying. "Geez," he said, wiping a tear from his eye. "He sure did get to heaven fast. We was watchin' TV and he didn't even get a chance to say goodbye."

On Wooden Street, Little Von sat on the kitchen counter without noticing Savannah the cat on the floor beneath him. The cat slapped at the boy's dangling leg brace. Jessie Rose stood in front of him, telling him how great heaven was and how lucky Bill was to be there, but she knew in her heart that the final understanding of Bill's death had shaken the boy. With an untouched bowl of ice cream melting on his lap, he stared through Jessie

Rose with fire in his eyes; unbelieving, not trusting.

"Well, why did Bill go to heaven like that, Grandma? There wasn't nothin' wrong with him."

"Well, it was just his time. God said he had to go and he had a heart attack."

"Grandma," he said, impatiently and defiantly. "Bill was good, so how come God attacked his heart. God shoulda left him alone. He shoulda took Benny 'cause he a scab anyway, huh Rob?"

Robin and Lillian stood silently at the other end of the kitchen. Little Von had done the unthinkable. Never in all their years had either of them dreamed of talking back, challenging, or defying Jessie Rose in any way, but especially when it concerned God or church.

Jessie Rose turned to the two on the opposite side of the kitchen.

Rob tried to explain. "A...Grandma, Scab is this guy who lives in the projects. He gets into trouble a lot."

"He in jail now, Grandma," Little Von said, abruptly pulling her attention back. "You always say God is good and he loves us all the time, but sometime he don't listen 'cause when I say my prayers, like you tell me to, I ask him not to let Jing-Wei kick my ass and..."

Jessie Rose's face showed her shock. "Boy, I'll spank your bottom for talkin' like that."

"Yeah, Grandma, that's what happens up here, but down in the projects it's different. When kids beat you up and the other kids laugh at you that's called kickin' your ass. Huh Rob?" He motioned toward his brother for confirmation. Jessie Rose turned to Robin and Lillian, horrified at the language, but her fear for his well-being was obviously the priority. She held her temper.

Robin took a deep breath. "Grandma, things are a lot different down there. Everybody's got to deal with it," he said, not sure if he was defending Little Von or helping Jessie to deal with Little Von's loss of innocence.

"Grandma, I ask God to help, but Jing-Wei kicks my ass anyway." Little Von stopped to think, and then continued, saying, "God must be having a real bad week 'cause first he wobbled Clovis's plug and then he took Bill's all the way out! Gramma you sure you know God real good?"

Jessie Rose looked back to Lillian and Robin, more confused than ever.

"Well, if your Momma would make you go to church and Sunday school, you would understand."

"No, Gramma. I been down by the water and Clovis said God was easier to find down by the water than in a big o' empty church. But I still don't get it."

Jessie Rose was silent. Little Von was no longer Little Von. Despite the words she had spoken in anger, she had never truly wanted them to move. Now, she knew she had been right.

Elderiah had been standing at the door, watching his grandson come of age. "Jessie, you give me this boy." Elderiah grabbed the bowl from his lap. "Boy, looks like you finished with that ice cream. And I know you done wore yo' gram'mam out. Come on out in the yard and let me teach you something about roses." Elderiah picked up his grandson in one arm, his crutches in the other, and disappeared through the pantry door into the backyard.

Jessie turned to Robin. "Robin, what's goin' on down there?"

"It's rough, Gram. It makes you change. Even Little Von. But he's doin' all right. He's just growin', that's all."

Jessie Rose retired to her chair near the window. She had hoped that Vivian being on her own would help. Jessie had always been taught to pray, pray, and pray some more and she had done that. Jessie believed with all her heart that "Salvation was to be found in the house of the Lord," and she still believed that. How had she and all the Mrs. Pritchets in the world survived the cruelties of the South at the turn of the century? God was everywhere and knew all. Jessie looked around the room until she saw a picture of Vivian in a small gold frame. She closed her eyes and squeezed the small gold crucifix around her neck. "Dear God. Help this child or she ain't gonna make it. Please Lord."

Savannah leaped into her lap and they both fell silent.

Robin and Lillian left the tall house on Wooden Street and walked solemnly up the path to Lafayette, through the stifling New Jersey humidity. Robin had finished his crying, but he was deeply somber. It was hot, and sweat shone through his shirt.

"How's being away from home?" he asked.

"Good, most of the time." Lillian wiped her forehead with a

tissue. "It's not so bad. South Orange is nice. Great shopping, not that I ever have any extra money, but window shopping is fun. We have great parties in the dorm."

"How's school?"

"Awful. You wouldn't believe it if I told you how much work we have every night. Nobody makes you do it either. Either you do it or they kick you out."

Robin listened, and dreaded the fact that one day he would be faced with having to do something with his life. It was a painful thought. High school was hard enough. "What do you think happened to Bill? Was Grandma just guessing when she said it was a heart attack?"

"I asked the ambulance guy and he said it was a heart attack. When I told him I was a first-year nursing student, he showed me that his ankles were swollen cause the blood couldn't make it back up. He was a big man. I guess his heart was weak."

Robin smiled. "Mommy said that when he was in high school, none of the girls would go out with him because he was so skinny."

"Well, I guess that changes with age. Black people eat too much fat and fried foods. So we have strokes and heart attacks easy, you know."

"You sound like Dr. Wingfield or something."

"Naa, that's simple stuff. White parents know more about it because they've always been lucky enough to be able to be choosey about what they eat. Poor eating has become a part of our culture. Old black people that came from the South never had that luxury, so they just ate whatever they could. When they cooked greens that were bitter they always threw in a piece of salt pork to make it taste better. All that stuff, just turns into lard inside your veins. But they never knew that stuff so they taught us to eat the same way." Lillian frowned and grinned. "Where did Von get that stuff about Bill's plug coming out and his brain getting wobbly?"

"I don't know," Robin said, laughing for the first time since he'd left the house. "He really comes up with some crazy stuff sometimes."

"But he's smart though. I don't think either of us are as smart as you, but he's gonna be hard to keep up with."

"Well he's definitely braver than I am, talking to Jessie Rose like that."

They came around the backside of the Lafayette playground and came to the swings and sat down. Lillian grew nostalgic. "Can you believe how small this school looks now? It used to seem huge. Remember all the times you used to get into fights on the playground and I'd have to come to the rescue? I used to save your ass every other day."

Robin smiled, knowing it was true. "You did not."

"I didn't, huh?"

"Well, maybe once or twice."

Lillian laughed. "Yeah, maybe twenty or thirty."

"You should have seen how crazy this place was the other day. Huge fight. I didn't see it, but I came by earlier and there were at least five hundred kids here."

"They all go wild as usual?"

"Yep. Kids from everywhere: Collinsville, the Projects, the Hill, and there's always some you never seen before comin' up from the South somewhere. But they all went crazy from what everybody said."

"Who was it?"

"Scootch and Scab."

"Scootch Williams?"

"Yep."

"Who's Scab? Is that who Von was talking about?"

"Yeah, but I don't think you know Benny. His brother used to sing in the first Swan Tones. Anyway, Scootch caught Benny screwin' around with Charlene and they got into it after the game. Scootch got stabbed."

"Things are getting worse. I'm glad I graduated when I did."

Robin looked across the field toward Joleena's house. For a minute he thought he saw her standing at the door.

Lillian followed his gaze. "Is that where she lives?"

"Who?"

"Robin, don't give me that *who* stuff. The girl you were so crazy about the last time I was home."

"Yup."

"Yup? Is that all? 'Yup'. If she so cute, then what she doin' with you?" Lillian joked.

Robin wanted to do his part, but the fact was, he had been wondering himself how something as great as Joleena had happened to him. Now he wondered how it happened to be on the verge of ending. He just shrugged. "I don't know."

In that instant Lillian saw it, the pain, the grief, the insecurity, the feelings of worthlessness. She knew it all. And although she didn't know it until that moment, it was what she had been running from. It was all there in his eyes. Lillian placed her palm on her brother's cheek. "Hey," she whispered with her eyes shiny with tears. "You're not a bad catch. I'm proud of you."

Robin remembered Lillian crying and was grateful for a way to change the subject. "Speaking of saving my ass, I don't think I ever seen you cry. Not even when we was real little. I think today was the first time I ever really saw you cry."

Lillian stood up and sat back down, straddling the swing seat. She reached over and took Robin's hand. "When we were little and Mom and Dad were working all the time, I never had time to cry. You don't remember, I guess, but when you were only ten and Von was just born, I did the looking after you. Not just on the playground, but at home too."

"Well, I guess I do remember."

"It was kind of hard for me and I guess I was really angry after Von came home because first of all I already had enough to do with the cooking and the wash, on top of my own school work and fighting your battles. On top of everything else, I really had it in my little girly mind that I wanted a baby sister and not another one like you!"

Robin smiled. "You don't know how much I miss you being around. When something happens and I can't figure out what to do, I always think that if you were here you'd know the best thing to do. I really miss you a lot."

Lillian hugged Robin with the swing chains between them. "I miss you too, brother."

22

BILL FURMAN'S BLUE BUICK sat unnoticed on the side of Jimmy Lee's gas station as the small and informal procession of two cars and a hearse went by. In the last half of his life, Bill Furman had gone out of his way to be forgotten by his ex-wife, Lucretia, his prison mates, and old friends. He had been successful. To those of that time who had known him as "Dollar Bill" the tall skinny numbers runner, Bill Furman had been dead a long time.

Jimmy Lee leaned against the back window of the limo. His hands were rough and seemed permanently discolored from years of reaching into tight, greasy places. He rubbed them dryly, one over the other. His voice was gruff and barely audible. "These streets were mean to Nephew." His eyes teared in the interim of a long pause. "There is somethin' about these curbs and alleyways that destroys peoples. Didn't used to be that way. But it's gettin' worser all the time. Jesus." His thoughts went unanswered.

Elderiah followed the limousine from the funeral parlor in Vivian's Chevy with Jessie Rose, Little Von, Robin, and Joleena, who had shown up at the church and sat with the family. Clovis sat in the front of the black limo with Vivian. He replayed the service in his thoughts. It had been delivered to the front two pews of the church. The pews had held the mourners in an airtight vacuum. The minister, who hadn't known Bill or his family, said everything he dare say about a stranger. When the organist and vocalist, neither of whom remembered Bill, finished their performance as professionally and reverently as possible, silence enveloped the small church, making it feel like a tomb. One by one, Clovis, Jimmy Lee, Robin, Joleena, and Liberty, and the round pudgy girl who helped Bill with his florist shop, had gone forward and taken a carnation from the flower spray at the foot of the casket. Little Von, who sat with his crutches on the floor in front of him and his leg slipped out of his sling, reached in his pocket and pulled out a picture of himself riding on Bill's back. The black-and-white Polaroid showed him laughing at the top of his lungs and Bill on his hands and knees, his smiling eyes half closed. He had shown the picture to Vivian saying, "Mommy, can I? Bill didn't even have a chance to say goodbye, and I don't want him to forget me." Vivian signaled to Joleena to help Little Von to stand on the prayer bench in front of the coffin. He slipped the picture under Bill's folded hands, cold and heavy. The sensation held him in place until Joleena took him by the shoulders and helped him down. Vivian never took a flower from the spray. Instead, when they were leaving the church, she stepped from the sidewalk and wandered slowly through the grass until she came upon two large and fully-opened dandelions. Now, in the front seat with Clovis, she stroked their velvet crowns.

At the gravesite in the Heavenly Rest Cemetery, the wind blew gently through the trees and about the edges of black dresses and veils. It was a small reprieve from the sticky New Jersey heat. All wept quietly. They placed the carnations on the top of the casket. Vivian stepped forward and placed one of her dandelion above the spot where she imagined Bill's heart to be, and watched as the hoist lowered Bill and her love to its final place of rest.

Later, in Clovis's apartment, they all sat crowded together around the small kitchen table. It was pulled out from the wall and now was covered with plates of half-eaten food and desserts, most of which had been prepared by Jessie Rose. The kitchen counter served as a bar, and the adults stood or sat with their glasses half filled, drinking and talking quietly, trying to find a way to cope with their sudden loss. Clovis repeated what the minister had said during the service. "Death comes, as it sometime do, without warning, without explanation or apologies, and snatches life."

Vivian sat at the table still holding one of the dandelions. Before her was an untouched glass of whiskey. She sat, slowly twirling a dandelion in her fingers.

"Damn, Vivy," Clovis sobbed, "He was all I had left in the world." Clovis covered his face with his hands that seemed stiffer and older than usual.

Liberty turned from the counter and put her arm around him. "Clovis! Clovis you take it easy now. You just got out of the hospital yo'self. We don't want to be burying you now." Tears dripped from her own cheeks. She took his handkerchief from his wide-lapeled coat pocket and wiped his face. Then she held his head close to her abdomen until his breathing was calm.

"Clovis, you still got us. We still together. We always be together. Just like Little Von got dem crutches and that brace, you got all of us to lean on." With his eyesight blurred, Clovis reached up and patted Liberty's hand. He dropped his hand and reached for his shot glass, draining it quickly. Jimmy Lee, standing near the kitchen window, did the same before pulling Bill's car keys from his pocket. "Viv, I'm gonna bring the Buick up to my house for now. When Robby gets his license, it's his. Bill would have wanted that."

Vivian lay the dandelion on the table and turned her glass in a circle. The look in her eye was distant; she seemed removed from the moment, experiencing the event as an observer and not as a participant. "I wonder why it is that only the good die young. That's true you know," she said, looking at Clovis. "Like there's nothing else for them here."

Robin, Little Von, and Joleena appeared at the kitchen door.

"Mom," Robin said, quickly surveying the scene in the kitchen and the whiskey in his mother's glass. "We're gonna walk Joleena home, then we're going to Grandma's." It had been Vivian's idea that the boys stay at Jessie's, but Robin repeated the plan to her, hoping it would give her another moment to think before she drank from the glass. But Vivian continued to finger the glass as she cleared her throat. "Von. Are you sure you can make it all the way up the hill with your crutches?" Little Von, fearful of the number of brown bottles strewn on the counter and the glass before his mother, just nodded. Vivian stopped turning the glass and held her arms out to him. When he had maneuvered into place she hugged him and smiled.

Robin, Joleena, and Little Von walked for the first fifteen minutes in silence. Robin had taken every shortcut to make the trip as painless as possible. Joleena, realizing that Little Von's silence was for a different reason, finally spoke. "Von, can you make it all the way up Boogers Hill with your crutches?"

"Yeah. I just walk at the top part when it gets real steep, then I put my brace back on."

"Oh, I'm really gonna miss Bill," she said, fishing for the child's feelings.

"I already do, 'cause he left so fast. I don't think I like God. Gramma Jessie said that's silly, but I don't think I do."

"Von, God loves us, even Bill. But God is so smart that it's hard to understand why things happen the way they do sometimes."

Joleena looked to Robin. It was a natural place for a brother to enter the conversation, but Robin pulled himself up the hill as if he were alone and had not heard one word. Joleena, feeling his resentment like a low current of electricity, took several large steps to reach his side. "I didn't come on my own, you know." Robin shrugged. "Your mother called to tell me what time the funeral would be and asked me to come."

At hearing that Joleena had talked to Vivian, Robin looked at her for the first time since they had left 5509.

"Oh, don't worry. I didn't tell her that her reefer smoking son would prefer I not be around. I figured she had enough to deal with."

Robin returned to his silence. When he reached the top of the hill he stood waiting for Little Von, who had stopped and slipped his leg out of the brace.

Joleena stood near him, still waiting and hoping for an answer. Robin didn't take his eyes off Little Von. Joleena nodded slowly. "You bastard." She turned to the path that led from the end of Wooden Street toward Lafayette and walked alone.

Little Von reached the top, struggling with his crutches. "Rob, where's Leeny goin'?"

"Home. Come on, Von. Gramma's waiting."

Vivian had resisted the drink that the funeral seemed to make inevitable. Instead she chose to clutch the dandelion. She sat through the night, crying and remembering. When Robin and Little Von returned from Jessie Rose's they found her with a muted smile, cleaning. The sight of her, neatly dressed and rested, gave them comfort and tremendous relief. That evening, Vivian made a great dinner. "Bill loved to eat," was all she had said until the meal was on the table. They all said prayers for him and held hands. Vivian looked tired as she prayed. "Dear Lord. Help me to understand why only the good die young."

After dinner they made plans for Little Von's birthday the coming Sunday. After dessert they watched TV, laughing during the comedy, and guessing during the mysteries. They had sur-

vived a terrible and unexpected tragedy, and they were still together. Before bed, they hugged and said goodnight. The following day Vivian vanished and wasn't seen for two days.

23

WHEN VIVIAN RETURNED, she was more sick than Robin or Little Von had ever seen her and she had been injured. Liberty and Charlene sat on the end of her bed arranging a pillow under Vivian's hand, which was wrapped in a neat white bandage.

Robin felt sick. "Libby, she been with you?"

"No, child. I think she was with Sarah Leamens. Henrietta's sister." Robin remembered Henrietta Leamans from the first night that he sang under the street lamp with the Swan Tones. "Tina Phillips from across the street, she a nurse...you know her? ...skinny, dark-skin girl...pretty? Her husband, Carl, the cop, run off about a year ago..." Robin nodded yes and no. He shrugged. "Anyway, she called me and said that Vivy wanted me to pick her up from the hospital. The doctor wanted her to stay, but I guess she wouldn't. I was gonna call your grandma, but..."

"What happened to her hand?"

"Charlene. Go put some extra vegetables in that pot. Robin and Little Von can eat with us."

"No, that's all right, Lib," Robin said, looking at Little Von. "We ate over at Art's house."

"Honey, you sure? Ain't no trouble, you know. Charlene you need to go check on that pot anyway." Charlene hadn't taken her eyes from Robin since the two had entered the room. As she walked by, she used the opportunity to look long and hard. When Robin heard the door close, his gaze returned to Libby who, herself, had begun to look worn and older.

"When I picked her up at the hospital, she wasn't quite sober, but they let her go anyway. So, honey, I'll just tell you what Vivy told me. She said she had been out drinkin' late, but she went to work anyway. What time did she come in here?"

Robin shrugged. "I never saw her or heard anything. I don't think she meant she came from here." Robin looked back to the bed where his mother lay in a deep sleep. "Maybe Sarah's."

Liberty looked at Little Von. "Honey, ain't you got something to do?"

"Libby..." Robin interrupted, looking at Von who sat motionless with no expression. "We can't hide everything from him. He has to deal with it, like everyone else. This is becoming more normal than not."

Liberty sighed. "Well, you know she work on that steam press, and somehow she hit the release pedal and it came down on her hand." Liberty put her hands up in frustration. "That's the best that I can make of it."

Robin walked to his mother's side. The bandage was thick like a mitten and taped around her wrist. It was so neat and cleanly done that it reminded him of Mrs. DeKorio.

"How long you boys been down here by yourself?"

"Couple of days."

"How come you didn't come up and eat or tell me she been gone like this?"

"It wasn't the first time, Lib. We dealt with it before." Robin wanted to remind Liberty that other times when Vivian had disappeared, she had been with her. They hadn't had that option then. They had learned to survive on their own.

"She got to go back every couple of days and have the bandage changed. That's all I know. Maybe you better call your Grandma. Y'all come on up if you need anything."

Just as Liberty started to leave, Robin looked out of the window. "Lib. where's her car?"

Liberty shrugged. "You'll have to ask her when she wakes up."

The door shut again and they were alone.

"What we gonna eat, Rob?"

"I don't know. We got some food in there 'cause Mom went shoppin' the other day." Robin searched Little Von's face. He was getting older too. Maybe not older, but different somehow. "Von, I know you hungry. How come you didn't say anything when I said we already ate."

"I didn't want to go up there."

"Libby cooks good. How come?"

Little Von looked annoyed. With his brace dangling at his side, he got up and dragged his crutches through the door. "I didn't want to be around anybody, that's all." A moment later Robin heard him settle on his bed. He listened for crying, but there was none.

This time they were lucky, the fridge was nearly full. That presented another problem. Some of the food required preparation that exceeded Robin's ability. Fortunately the lamb chops didn't. Robin put the meat in the skillet and bent down to check the level of the blue flame. For a moment he thought he heard music coming from the back room. He put some water on for the frozen mixed vegetables, and again he thought he heard a thin line of music above the frying. "Upstairs," he thought, moving on to the next task. And then it was louder and unmistakably coming from the back bedroom. Little Von was playing with Robin's record player.

Although he was angry, he was put off by the fact that his brother was playing jazz. They had listened to Johnny Mathis many times together, but Little Von had merely been in the room. Robin couldn't remember him having any real interest in the music. Robin had only been listening to jazz a short time himself. Be-bop had become popular with Scootch and some of the others in the Swan Tones. Then, a little further out, where musicians transcended form, was Space Jazz. It was a different music, different from the acappella Doo Wop the Tones sang, and different from his father's big band music. He had managed to like some of it, despite the fact it had no words. Some of it was beyond any and all understanding, having no words, melody, or even harmonies that sounded like they were played on purpose. At times it lacked evidence that the musicians knew each other or were playing the same song. When Robin had replied that it was definitely out there, Lester laughed and struggled to say that they called it space music because the spaces between the notes were just as important as the notes themselves. The only time Robin didn't find it annoying was when he smoked reefer. After rehearsals, with him filling in for Benny, they sat around for long hours smoking and losing themselves in the smooth and sometime chaotic patterns the music wove. It was one of these pieces that Little Von had chosen.

Little Von sat on the end of the bed facing the record player. He held the album jacket like it was the record itself keeping his fingers on the very edge. Robin stood at the door and watched his brother concentrating on the album jacket. Little Von made no excuse for playing the record without permission. He simply looked up with no expression on his face and said, "I like this one."

"Do you know who that is?"

Little Von shook his head no. "I can't read yet, bean head."

"That's Miles Davis. We should practice your ABC's. You gonna be in the first grade in the fall."

For a while Little Von continued to stare. "Is he making all that music by himself?"

Robin smiled and sat down next to him. "No, he's just the leader of the band. See here, it says 'Miles Davis Quintet.'"

"What does quintet means?"

"What does quintet *mean*. Don't say means, Von. You sound like you come from somewhere where they didn't let you go to school or something. It tells you how many people are playing in the band."

"How many in this one?"

"Five. Quintet means five. Quartet means four. Trio means three. Duo means two. And solo means somebody by himself."

Little Von thought for a moment about the new words and about all the times his brother had just used the word *means*. Then he pointed to another part of the album. "What does that...mean, Rob?"

"That's the name of this album. You probably heard us talkin' about it before. It's called *In Your Own Sweet Way*. How come you like this Von?"

"I like the way the drums sound. Is that Miles Davis?"

"No. Miles plays the trumpet. Listen. The trumpet is that sound right there." Robin's finger danced in the air following the trumpet sound.

Little Von forced his ears to identify the brass. He followed it for awhile, and then took a deep breath when the trumpet solo finished. Robin smiled. If his brother could follow lines like that, then there would be another musician in the family like their father, and like he would have wanted.

"You like the trumpet?"

Little Von nodded yes. His emotions were still flat. "But I really like the drums best." Robin watched him search for the percussion, which had taken a backseat temporarily, but then it entered again strong and loud. Little Von smiled. "Hear that, Rob? That's the drum. Who plays that?"

Robin pointed on the album cover to the place where the players' names were listed. "Philly Jo Jones."

Little Von looked up smiling. "He plays on some of Daddy's

records too, 'cause Daddy always yells when he does something good."

"Yup. Dad likes him a lot. What does Dad say?"

"'Do it Philly! Nigga play some drums! Play that shit!" Little Von laughed. "That's what he say," he said shrugging.

Robin laughed "Yup. That's Dad."

The smell of lamb chops weaved its own thread into the room. Robin got up and flicked his brother on the head. "Next time ask first, bean head, and don't scratch up my record. And don't be cussin'." Robin smiled.

"I know how 'cause I watch how you put it on. Rob, is Mommy gonna be all right this time?"

After a pause Robin said. "I don't know, Von. I'm not gonna lie. Don't worry though, we'll be all right."

Little Von started to cry. He had held up through rough times, but now Robin could see that he was overwhelmed. "Why don't she stop Rob? Why don't she stop before somethin' really bad happens?"

"I don't know, Von." Robin walked over to the bed again and held his brother's head against his leg. "You'll have to ask her sometime. Just ask her like you ask Grandma Jessie all that stuff the other day. Maybe it will help."

24

AUGUST

Despite the scorching heat, the Swan Tones congregated in the laundry room beneath Building Five. The echo of the laundry, with its hard walls and floors, made it a perfect place to practice. The earth kept the walls cool and the room comfortable except when someone started one of the dryers.

Robin sat with his back to one of the dryers, his shirt open to absorb the coolness of its metal sides as he downed his third beer. Scootch sat against the block wall on an old five-gallon paint can, long since dried out. As always, he took in everything around him —watching—listening. "Hey Thompson, you better slow down man," he said laughing. "What's the matter, Joleena finally wearing you out?" The others oooed and laughed. "You lookin' real worn down lately. Hey man, I told you if she ever got to be too much, I'd fill in for you." The room erupted as Lester and Matt voiced their willingness as well.

Robin only smiled, and the smile was accommodating at best. He drained the rest of his beer and reached for the bag with the wine. The bag was curled down an inch from the top. He wiped the top with his hand and drank deeply, letting the liquid wash over his tongue and cheek. Scootch watched. Matt and Lester resumed talking and telling stories, both talking at once.

Robin wiped his mouth. "Man, I haven't talked to Joleena in almost two weeks."

"How come?"

Robin held up the wine. "She doesn't approve."

Scootch pulled his milk crate closer to Robin and leaned back on the same dryer, waiting for his turn at the wine. He spoke beneath the din of the other conversations. "Freakin' hot, ain't it?"

Robin wiped his forehead. "No kiddin'. The damn humidity feels like a wet bear is leaning on me all the time."

"Hey man, your Mom sick again?"

Robin sighed and swallowed another gulp of wine. He sucked the burning taste from his mouth and passed the bottle. "Yeah. She started drinkin' bad after Bill died. She took off for awhile and when she came back, it was from the hospital."

Scootch held the wine bottle up and took a long draw, waiting for Robin to continue. When he didn't, he pushed. "Really? What happened?"

"She had been drinkin' down at the cleaners while she was workin'," Robin said, taking the bottle from Scootch and looking at him directly for the first time. "Somehow or another, she got her hand stuck in the steam press." He drank again.

Scootch nodded emphatically. "She drinkin' bad again?"

"She's an alcoholic, man."

"Man, your Mom ain't no alcoholic. Cootie is an alcoholic. He die without his juice. He be drunk every day."

"She's gettin' there. She been drunk almost every day since Bill died. She doesn't sleep outside or in hallways like Cootie, but she or hardly any of her friends go a day without booze. Maybe you don't have to be like Cootie to be an alcoholic. Maybe Cootie is what it looks like when it's finally obvious. Maybe Sara Leamen is in the middle somewhere."

Scootch thought about that for a moment and nodded. Then he noticed that Matt and Lester's banter was slowing down. "Ey, Lester. Don't be believin' everything you hear, man. Lucky's old man ain't even got a car. How he gonna get Lucky one?" Scootch said, handing the wine to Lester who had stuck out his hand again.

Robin stood up and pulled the string to the fan. He took his time wrapping the string back around its holding place to avoid talking about his mother. "Hey, I can't believe all them cars that Scab had were really his father's. I could have swore he was lyin'."

"Well, I knew the deal all the time," Scootch said, wincing and holding the place where his stitches had been. "They really weren't his old man's. They belonged to the company he worked for in Newark. He always told everybody that his old man was a big-shot manager out on the coast somewhere because he wanted everybody to think his old man was important with a lot of money and fancy cars. The truth was that his father doesn't do anything but deliver special-order cars. See, he always came through the Hollow with the cars tryin' to impress people, and then he let Benny drive it around for awhile so he could do the same thing."

"Y-y-yep. Benny j-j-j-j-us-jus-just like his old m-m-man."

Matt took the wine from Lester, drinking and holding his silence.

"As a matter of fact…" Scootch continued. "…Scab's old man never really lived in the same house with him or his mother. I don't even think they really ever got married. Whenever he comes around he steals from Scab's mother and beats her up. That's one of the reasons I never wanted to fight with him, but he took it to mean that I was afraid of him or something. Rob, man, he been getting crazier every year—he wasn't always like that. I remember when we used to be best friends when we was little. We was best friends in Lafayette when we started the Junior Swan Tones. Then he just started going off," Scootch said pointing at his head and then to the ceiling.

Robin sat back down, reaching for the wine from Matt. "So that Cadillac was a special his old man was delivering?"

"No, that was his old man's. I betcha Scab stole it on purpose. His old man was selling reefer on the side. You know what I mean. He wasn't just delivering no cars, but it all seems to go together, 'cause Scab always had plenty reefer to smoke and sell."

"You th-th-think his old man was-was givin' it to 'im?" Lester stammered.

"Heck no," Scootch said, smirking. "Benny's old man probably ain't never gave nobody nothin' in his whole life, less it was the clap or somethin'. Scab was probably sellin' it for his old man but something must have gone wrong, or something, 'cause Scab had bruises on his face before I hit 'im."

"Yeah, he did, because I saw him…" Robin stopped, realizing that he had admitted that he had seen Benny earlier, before the fight.

Scootch turned quickly. "Did you see Scab before we got into it on the playground?"

Robin's mind twisted in a lightning blur. Art looked at Robin anxiously. "Yeah, I saw him on the way over to Joleena's. He stopped and gave me a ride." Robin turned the wine bottle up not giving Scootch the chance to examine his face. He lowered the bottle and passed it to him.

"Hmm. Except for me getting stabbed, you missed a good fight then." He reached for the bottle but stopped short of grasping it, enough to let Robin release it. For a split second they both sat with their arms stretched out with only the bottle between them, as Scootch searched Robin's eyes. Knowing that Robin had left something out, he smiled again, "I made a mistake and turned my back on him. Never turn your back on a dead snake unless you cut his head off first. I learned. Everybody learns... right, Rob?"

"They better," Robin said, feeling that Scootch had finally gripped the bottle enough for him to let go. Robin felt his pulse pick up.

Art jumped in. "What about Charlene, Scootch?"

"She still my woman. She calls everyday. I had to smack the taste out of her mouth on the playground, but she know she deserved it. "

"I heard it was more than a smack." Robin looked around the room at the others. They hummed and nodded in agreement.

Scootch turned up the bottle. "She deserved more than a smack."

Art smiled. "I told you, man. She did the Hucka Buck when she went down. I ain't lyin'"

"But somebody is still stealin' cars, and since Scab's doin' some time, it can't be him," Robin said, changing the subject.

There was a hard, loud kick against the door before it swung open. The boys sat frozen as the humid dank air and outside light filled the room. It was Lucky and Little Von. Lucky jumped into the middle of the floor. "CRIPPLED KID DELIVERY."

Little Von came up behind him and wacked him with one of his crutches. "I ain't no crippled kid. You wanna race me?"

Everybody yelled at Lucky. "Ey m-m-m-m-m-m-m-man, what you tryin' to d-d-d-d-do, give every-every-every-everybody a-a-a-a heart afreakin'tack!".

Lucky laughed, which made everybody laugh. "Hey Les. Calm down, man, before you swallow your tongue or somethin'."

Art stood up laughing and unscrewed a bottle of eye drops. Lucky pulled open both dryer doors looking for beer. "Couldn't be in here—could it, guys? It'd get all shook up like that."

"Ey midnight..." Matt said, "Were you here when everybody was making contributions?" His words were beginning to slur as the wine and beer began to make their presence felt.

After putting in his eye drops, Arthur tripped over the edge of Lester's box seat and fell to the floor, taking Lester and Lucky with him.

"Jesus, ART!" Lester yelled as he tried to get out from beneath him.

Lucky laughed and held his hands up. "Sorry guys, I thought it best to leave his guide dog in the car, but I see now that was a mistake." Everybody laughed except Arthur, blind from the eyedrops. He rolled over onto his back and started cleaning his glasses with his shirttail. Robin grabbed him by the arm, pulling him toward a seat. Scootch reached around the paint can and took one of his beers and tossed it to Lucky.

Robin was still laughing. He took a big swig of his beer. "Thanks for bringin' Von down."

"I had to go up there anyway. No big deal. We're even."

Little Von began to notice the litter of cans around the small space. "Rob, you drinkin'?"

"No, man. We just havin' some beers. That's all."

Lucky smiled at Little Von and then back at Robin, showing nearly all of his perfect teeth. "Say, look here, this is getting contagious. I hear Joleena doesn't approve of fraternizing with the use of spirits either. So this must be a final toasting."

Robin raised an eyebrow and spoke without hesitation. "Ey man, piss on that. Joleena doesn't dictate what I do."

Little Von disapproved of the way Robin spoke about Joleena. He glared at his brother, but held his silence.

Lucky scratched his head. "I don't know, Rob. I might reconsider If I were you."

"Why?" Robin said in a flat tone.

Lucky shrugged and raised his beer, looking at Robin out of the corner of his eyes. "Rob, we are talking Joleena here, arent' we?" Mock moaning filled the room, followed by more laughter.

Matt verbally struck out at Arthur. "What you laughin' at, Binocular Man? Steppin' Fetchet'll get some off Marilyn Monroe before you ever have sex with Patsy." Matt remembered his phone call to Patsy and the date that never was. He hid his anger in his laughter.

"Is that so?" Art said raising an eyebrow.

"That's right. And if she do give you some, how you gonna find it with them blind ass eyes of yours?" The laughter had a barroom looseness to it. Arthur, his eyes now clear and a beer erasing his self-consciousness, slowly looked in Matt's direction, waiting for the laughter to abate.

"Matt, speaking of sex, your hand pregnant yet?" The room exploded. Scootch's laughter could be heard above the rest. He was leaning against a dryer with hands over the place where he had been stabbed. "It's gonna be twins for sure."

Everyone laughed except Matt, who began to lose control. Lucky doubled up on his side. Arthur fell against Robin and slapped his hand, making Robin spill beer on his pants. Lester lay on his back, laughing and kicking one of the dryers. Little Von, tightening a screw on his crutch, seemed oblivious to the whole matter.

Matt stood up over his brother, scowling. "Screw you, Scootch," he said, almost spitting the words out. He slammed through the door.

With everybody struggling to catch their breath, Lucky pulled himself into a sitting position and looked at Scootch. "You know, if I were asked, I'd say your brother doesn't like you very much."

"Well, nobody asked you, Midnight."

"No, seriously, anybody else notice Matt's been more strange than usual?"

Little Von finished with his crutch and started for the door. "Rob, I'm goin' outside to play."

"No, Von. Why don't you stay in here 'cause it's gettin' dark out."

Little Von frowned. "Piss on that. I want to go outside."

"Von!" Robin yelled, but the laughter and yelping were so loud from that he was barely heard. Lester, noticeably drunk, crawled over to Little Von and held out his hand. Lucky did the same. Little Von slapped five on Lester and unexpectedly swiped at Lucky with his crutch. "I ain't no crippled kid," he said, glaring at Lucky. Laughter erupted again as Lucky used his arms without grace to protect his head from the swinging crutch.

"Deal with 'im, Little Von," Scootch yelled, clapping and spurring him on. "Slap that purple-skinned son of a bitch in the head with one of them crutches."

"All right, Von. Go 'head out." Robin interrupted. "But don't go too far. And don't be cussin'."

Lucky jumped up and held the door open. "Please accept my apologies," he said, smiling.

When Little Von maneuvered himself out of the door, Lucky

sat down again and pulled out a crumpled cigarette pack.

"Hey man, you got an extra one?" Scootch said, feeling for his own pack.

"No. But I got one we all can share." Lucky pulled the joint from the pack, lit it and took the first toke. "Here Rob, you look like you need a good laugh."

Robin took the joint and inhaled until he could hold no more. After a few seconds he let the smoke stream out slowly. "Hey. It don't make me laugh no more like it used to."

"Yeah, me either." Art said. He unbuttoned his shirt and leaned back on the cool wall. "Now, when I smoke reefer, I just start thinkin' and shit."

Outside, Little Von walked without feet, balanced without feet, twirled on one crutch, and finally began a game of counting how many crutch steps he could take without putting his foot down. Each time he had to put his foot down, he went back to the starting point in front of the stairs leading to the foyer door.

In his first attempts, he was unable to go farther than fifteen steps, but as time passed, he quickly added distance with every effort. First he made it the whole length of Building Five. Soon he made it out to the street. After an hour had passed, he was able to turn the corner of Building Five, follow the sidewalk back along the front of the fenced courtyard, and make it to Building Four. When his foot came down he was startled to find himself in front of his mother's Chevy. Someone had brought it home. For a moment his eyes started to get wet. Instead of crying, he raced back along the side of the fence in his fastest three-legged mode until he came to the foyer steps. In all his mastery, he still had not found a way to ascend stairs any other way but one-by-one. At the top of the stairs, he let his weight down heavy on the tops of his crutches to keep them in place, and reached for the door. Before he could touch it, it opened.

Jing-Wei raced past him snatching a crutch as he went by. Little Von fell on his side and rolled backward down the two cement steps to the place where he had started his game. Jing-Wei walked away, laughing, pretending to limp while holding onto the crutch with both hands.

Biting back the tears, Little Von scrambled to his feet with the new agility that he had accumulated over the summer months and was on Jing-Wei before Jing realized he was coming. He snatched his crutch back, leaving Jing-Wei stumbling headlong into the fence that surrounded the play yard.

The Swan Tones plus Robin, Lucky, and Arthur Taggart emerged from the laundry, preceded by a cloud of marijuana smoke. They stood on the slight hill where Building Five was perched, watching the standoff.

Jing-Wei's mother did the same from her downstairs apartment window. Kids who had been playing on the other side of the street stopped their games and stood close to the curb to watch. Jing-Wei halted his fall by catching onto the hurricane fence. He jumped up, his almond eyes burning with anger. When he turned he found that Little Von had not run, but had come up directly behind him, foot and crutches firmly planted, and was staring back with an equal blaze.

Robin started down the small hill, but Scootch caught him by the shoulder. "Rob, everybody has to learn...right?" Robin didn't speak. He quickly looked back to his brother standing alongside the fence.

Little Von took two slow steps to his left. Jing-Wei moved slowly until his back was against the fence. Little Von no longer looked like the victim, but an equal opponent. The challenge incensed Jing-Wei. He reached out and grabbed the crutch again in an attempt to pull Little Von to the ground, but Little Von held strong. When Jing-Wei felt the resistance, his anger exploded. He pulled his other fist back, but before he could unleash its fury, Little Von gripped the cross handle of his other crutch and swung up from the ground with an adrenaline quickness. The heavy wooden crutch landed a bone-crushing blow on the side of Jing-Wei's head. It caught him with his fist still high in the air. Little Von came back quickly and brought the crutch down hard on Jing-Wei's head. Jing-Wei almost avoided the blow, but the fence stopped his backward movement. The crutch slammed into the bridge of his nose. Blood poured down the front of Jing's face as his head snapped first left and then right in an attempt to stop the intense pain. But it was useless. Jing-Wei fell to his hands and knees as Little Von stood firm, balancing on one foot, his lips quivering, his two crutches thrust outward, poised to strike again.

The children playing on the opposite side of the street

cheered and ran wildly to get closer. Robin turned to Scootch, who was still holding his arm, his face a combination of surprise and glee. "Jesus, you see that?" The marijuana tainted the reality of the scene. Robin looked from side to side. The kids screamed as they crowded closer. No doubt some had suffered Jing-Wei's brutality. Lester, Matt, Arthur, and Lucky smacked hands and howled in the exhilaration of the moment.

When it was obvious that Jing-Wei was unable to get up, Little Von lowered his crutches and began to back slowly away, all the time watching Jing-Wei.

"See, everybody learns." Scootch said, slowly, in a drug-induced calmness. He let go of Robin's arm and slapped him on the back. "He didn't turn his back either, but it doesn't look like the snake has any teeth left."

Robin resisted his desire to run and lift his little brother into the air. He walked to the bottom of the foyer stairs and stood by Little Von's side with his arm around him. He could feel the occasional tremors that ran through his younger brother's shoulders. "Hey man, you did it. You did it all by yourself. You was dealing with it."

"Did I whip his butt?"

"No man, that was definitely an ass kicking."

Little Von smiled. He stood leaning heavily on his crutches, breathing fast, and looking up at his brother. The kids were screaming and re-enacting the fight. Liberty clapped from an upstairs window. The foyer door opened and Jing-Wei's mother appeared, walking slowly with a wet towel. At the bottom of the stairs, she stopped. "Lit Von. You do good. Jing-Wei booley. Get wat he diserb." She walked down the sidewalk to her son and waited quietly for him to get up. When he did, he cried loudly at the sight of his mother. She wiped his face and held the wet towel to his nose as she walked him inside, winking at Little Von as she passed.

Robin and Little Von tramped up the stairs toward apartment 5509, Robin stamping in half time so his brother could keep up, singing:

Pea-nut head,
bul-let nose,
almost died when I smelled your toes.

At the top of the stairs, Robin stood, as usual, fumbling with the key in the lock. Little Von waited quietly as he had ever since the incident with the "The Plan." Taking a deep breath, he said "No hurry. Take your time."

Robin looked down, smiled, and then returned his attention to the lock.

"Hey Rob?"

"What?"

"Remember how you said you was gonna get all my ice cream because I messed up on the plan?"

"Yup."

"Well, you never took any. When does that have to start?" Little Von wrinkled his nose and waited for the answer, sure to be painful.

Robin looked at the unyielding lock and swore to himself that he would never have one like it if he ever owned a house. "Well, seeing how you did so good today, I guess we can forget about it."

"All right!" Little Von said, smiling.

The lock popped open for no apparent reason. The key slid out effortlessly.

"Robin, what's for dinner?"

"I don't know," Robin said, pushing the door open. "We'll have to see what we got left."

"You go see. I have to go to the bathroom."

Little Von quickly made his way down the hall. Robin turned into the small kitchen and stopped. The cupboard door where the glasses were kept was open. Robin's heart quickened as he stepped back into the hall and walked toward his mother's room. Little Von stood in the doorway of the bedroom, motionless, his face blank. Robin slowly walked the length of the hall until he came to Little Von. They stood side by side.

Vivian lay asleep in her bathrobe, propped up against the headboard of the bed with pillows. A quiet snore escaped her open mouth. Her burned hand was wrapped and resting on two pillows at her side. Her other hand held a glass half-filled with whiskey. A bottle of Seagrams lay empty on its side where it had rolled halfway between the bed and wall.

Robin felt a hollowness in the pit of his stomach. He felt the teenager slip away and the weight of total responsibility take its place. He had always understood what Little Von had meant when he spoke of the "Other Self." Seeing Vivian propped against the headboard, drunk, burned and exhausted, made him understand like never before. He walked through the room, the air thickened by the smell of whiskey-laden breath and body odor saturated with alcohol. He took the glass from her hand and placed it on the headboard. The marijuana made him stare when he wanted to look away. He could feel his paranoia building, trying to take him over. It was making him crazy. Little Von had been right. This was not their mother. He couldn't visualize it all uptown in front of Kresge's. He backed up to the door, not wanting to turn his back on the "Other Self," trying to think of something to say to Little Von. But there was nothing to say. Little Von had seen it for what it was long before he had. "Come on, Von," Robin said. He pulled the door closed.

25

Joleena stood at the door with a parent of one of the students. Today, like the last half hour of everyday, she carried a small stapler and combined the day's work of each student before he or she disappeared through the door. After saying her goodbyes, she took a seat on the edge of a cluttered desk listening to her mother speak on the phone in a polite, but anxious, tone. Joleena quickly scribbled a note. She shoved it in front of her mother to read. Mrs. Cleary covered the mouthpiece and whispered. "You're leaving now?"

"Yes. I have something I have to do."

Oblivious to the voice on the other end, she looked into Joleena's troubled eyes. The dark circles betrayed the smile her daughter offered.

Joleena strode across the room to Little Von's table.

"Von, how would you like me to walk you home?"

"Can't."

"Why not?"

"You know. Robin's coming."

"But it's still early. If we leave right now, we'll catch him before he gets out of the door and surprise him. It will be our 'Plan.'"

"Okay," Little Von said. He reached under the table for his crutches.

"Robin, are you smoking in there? Robin. Robin, do you hear me? I told you, you weren't allowed to smoke." Vivian's outburst was halted by her coughing.

Expressionless, Robin held his head with the same two fingers that held the cigarette. He placed the cigarette in the groove of the ashtray and walked to Vivian's door. "How can you possibly be drunk, Ma? You haven't been out of the house. Your hand is burned up, you're too sick to walk. How did you get another bottle?"

"What do you mean too sick to walk? Who are you to be asking me questions? You're not suppose to be askin' the questions around here—I am. You're not the mother—I…" Vivian gripped the side of the bed as the phlegm and stomach bile choked her. She wiped her mouth with a washcloth and pulled herself higher onto her pillows "I told you that you weren't allowed to smoke. What are you doing smoking in there?"

"Ma..." Robin said, angrily. "You got another bottle in here somewhere, don't you?" Robin stepped inside the door and began pulling out the drawers of the dresser, something he never would have done a year ago, something he would never do now if Vivian were sober, but she wasn't, and he was no longer the Robin that he had been.

Vivian eased herself to a sitting position on the side of the bed holding her hand to keep it from throbbing. "What's wrong with you? Get out," she said, breathless. "I don't have no bottle in there. Get out of here!"

With little more concern than he would have had if he had been looking for a tie, Robin quietly closed the drawer and returned to his room and lit another cigarette. Knowing she would call after him, he turned up the record player and tried concentrating on the words, hoping they would offer some relief. The Platters' music gave love the smooth velvet-like meaning he thought it should have. But love, whatever that was, seemed more of a mystery with each passing day.

The muffled sounds of kids playing in the fenced court reminded him it was time to pick up Little Von. He had opted for the daycare as opposed to hanging around the house while Vivian was sick. With new purpose and a reason to get out of the house, Robin grabbed his jacket and stood by the window. Suddenly he saw Arthur Taggart walk by. Sure that Arthur would look up to his room, he pulled back quickly not to be seen and then, suddenly, heard a voice behind him. Vivian was standing at his door.

"Turn that damn thing down. There's somebody at the door."

Sweat beaded Vivian's forehead. She looked exhausted and whipped as she held the walls for support. When she reached the bathroom, she closed the door behind her and sat on the edge of the bathtub with her head over the toilet, holding her bathrobe with one hand the bowl with the other. She wiped her face with a towel and felt behind the water tank for the pint-size bottle of bourbon.

Robin took another drag and clenched his teeth. He listened to his mother gagging in the bathroom at one end of the hallway and Little Von pounding on the door at the other.

Robin twisted the knob with one hand and slapped angrily

at the chain lock twice before it fell away. He was more than a little surprised when he jerked the door open and saw Joleena. Her beauty was as unsettling as it had always been.

Little Von frowned. "OOh, Rob,. you smokin' in the house again. Mom gonna get you if she find out. It stinks too, don't it, Leeny?"

"Can I come in for a minute?" Joleena asked realizing that her words did not sound as confident as they did in her mind. "I want to talk."

Robin's thoughts flashed to his mother hanging over the toilet in the bathroom. "This really isn't…"

"Sure, you can come in, Leeny. You don't have to ask him, 'cause my Mom said anytime, remember?" Little Von swung his crutches through the door, reached back, and pulled Joleena through and headed down the hall dramatically holding his face away from the cigarette as he passed his brother.

Robin didn't move, making it impossible for Joleena to come in any further. "Von," he said, trying to cut him off, "come in the kitchen. I left a sandwich for you."

"I don't wanna eat. I'm gonna change so I can go play."

"Von, just stay here."

"Robin," Joleena said, pulling his attention back. "I need to talk."

Frustrated, Robin sank back against the wall and silently watched Little Von approach the bathroom at the end of the hall.

Joleena fought back a tear. "How's Clovis?"

Robin nodded without speaking, leaving an awkward silence.

"Good. I'm glad to hear it," she said looking away to gather her strength. "So..It's been two weeks and you haven't said one word to me."

"I haven't had anything to say." His voice was small and trailing off as he looked down the end of the hall. "I've been…"

"…busy?" Joleena smirked. "God Rob, don't I even deserve something more original?"

Robin shrugged as he watched Little Von at the end of the hall.

"I know we had love, Rob. How could we have so much one day and nothing at all the next? I really thought you loved me. I know you did."

The warmth of his cigarette was nearing his fingers. He tried to move past Joleena to the sink in the kitchen, but she put her hand on his chest and stopped him while he was close. "Was I wrong, Robin? Who was it standing right by this door who said they wanted things between us to be different—special?"

Robin looked into her eyes for a brief moment and then again down the hall. The bathroom door opened. Vivian didn't notice Robin and Joleena. Her vision was focused on Little Von who she heard in the adjacent room. With her hair and robe in disarray, she entered his room. "Hi, baby." Her voice sounded like a cartoon.

Little Von jumped. He had been caught off guard, but in a glance he knew that she was drunk. Grabbing his crutches, he pushed by her, walking in quick steps, his crutches held one in each hand, his brace swinging freely at his side. Joleena watched as Robin scowled at his mother. Vivan went back into the bathroom and closed the door.

Joleena was shocked. She had stumbled onto Robin's and Little Von's secret. Joleena pushed past Robin and followed Little Von into the kitchen where he sat bawling. "Hey, hey. She's gonna be all right, Von."

Little Von snapped, "No she's not! She's sick. And she smell like she just been drinkin' and she's gonna leave soon." The words were wet and garbled. Joleena knelt down in front of his chair and pulled him in close. "No, no she won't. She's gonna be right here." And then she turned to Robin. He flicked the butt into the sink and sat down on the other side of the table with no expression on his face. "Rob, she wouldn't try and leave the house, would she?"

Robin, cigarette pack in hand, half-attempted a smile, but it came out more a sigh. "No. She's too sick." He held a new cigarette in his lips. "Too drunk. I don't know." His voice had grown calm and distant.

"What happened to her hand?"

"She burnt it on the job."

"You gonna call your grandmother or somebody?"

"I don't know, I don't know!" Robin ran his hand over his face and visually anchored himself to the ceiling. "No, she gets like this sometime. She'll be all right in a couple a days."

Joleena held on to Little Von, astounded. "A couple of days.

What are you guys gonna do for a 'couple a days'?"

Robin threw a spent match toward the sink and blew a short burst of smoke across the room. "Joleena, look. Just stay out of it. It's no big deal. She'll be all right."

"What!" Joleena's face contorted. She could hear the toilet flushing for the second time in as many minutes and then the sound of glass breaking on the floor. Little Von flinched in Joleena's arms. She felt the terror running through his body.

"No big deal? Robin, are you crazy or something? What's wrong with you? Your mother is really sick in there. Little Von is scared to death."

"Joleena, he's just a little kid and doesn't understand. She'll be all right. In a couple of days this will be over."

"How can you be so cold?" she said through clenched teeth. "I'm scared too! There's nothing normal about this. Rob, he's six. He's in kindergarten for most of the day and spends the rest in daycare playing with blocks and crayons. He doesn't understand and he shouldn't have to!"

"Joleena he'll be all right."

Without thinking, she reached across the table and punched Robin's arm as hard as she could. "Robin, wake up! Not if this keeps up he won't, and neither will she. Look what it's doing to you. This isn't all right. Not for Little Von, you, or anybody else. Christ!"

Robin jumped up. His chair slammed against the wall. "Hey, maybe you still live up on the hill all sweet and comfortable with everybody sitting around the table talking about how their day went, like Ozzie and Harriet or something, but it's different here! I live here and I'm taking care of things, and if you don't like it, get out! You gave me a choice two weeks ago. I didn't call. You should have gotten the message by now."

"Robin, this doesn't have anything to do with where I live." Little Von looked up, still crying. "Rob, stop yelling at Leeny. She didn't do nothin'." He swung at his brother, and knocked the cigarette from his hand.

"Von!" Robin swung at his brother only missing because Joleena pulled him out of the way. "Look, Joleena. Just because you have the nicest boobs in Mo-town High doesn't give you the right to come in here and take over."

"What! What did you say to me?" Joleena moved Little Von

to the side and slapped Robin in the face. He was just sitting up from picking up his cigarette, and it flew out of his hand again.

Filled with rage, Robin found himself towering over Joleena, his hand raised, trembling. Then he saw Little Von, his brace gently swinging at his side, his nose running, and holding his breath. He was clutching the chair wild-eyed, as if he had seen a ghost. Little Von was looking at him as if he, and not Vivian, had been taken over by the "Other Self." Robin lowered his hand.

Joleena had held onto Little Von and turned her body and face to prepare for the blow. After an agonizing wait, she slowly uncoiled and simultaneously moved Little Von to another chair.

"Joleena, I didn't ask you..." Robin said, in a pleading voice. "I didn't ask you to come here. I didn't ask you for your help or your opinions. I didn't ask you to worry about any of this. It's none of your goddamn business."

Without fear, Joleena raised her finger to Robin's face. "If you want to think this is normal, go ahead. If you want to drink and smoke reefer with the rest of those lazy bastards, you can do that too. But this is not right. How can you let Little Von go through this every day?"

"It's not every day."

Joleena turned to Little Von. "Von, how long has your mom been sick?

"I don't know."

Robin looked tense and Joleena saw it. "Where had she been?"

"Sarah Leamens," Robin added.

Joleena moved closer to Little Von to comfort him. She didn't know Sarah Leamens, but she knew her reputation. Sara Leamens could out-drink the best of them. After seeing her drunk in the middle of the day on a Sunday, Joleena's mother had used the word "pitiful" to describe her. "Robin, you know Sara Leamens as well as I do. Maybe better. She wasn't working, Rob? How long?"

Robin threw up his hands. "All right, Joleena. She'd been gone for a couple of days and when she came back she was hurt."

"Well, how long ago has that been?"

"I don't know! Maybe a week. You happy? You satisfied? So what? Will you leave now please?"

Joleena turned to Robin. "A week! No, I'm not satisfied.

Vivian's slurry voice echoed down the hall. "Robin! Robin! What's going on in there? Who you talking to?"

"Rob, she's real sick. And if she's not taking care of that hand, something awful could happen." Robin turned his back to Joleena and held onto the refrigerator with both hands. Robin fell silent. Joleena knew the silence would offer no more answers, no matter how long she waited. She moved toward the door.

Little Von reached over and grabbed her dress, "Are you coming back, Leeny?"

Joleena looked back at Robin. "No Von. I'll see you at the daycare though. Don't worry. If you get scared, you can come up there." She looked at Robin. "You're not different from anybody else, whether you show it or not. You have feelings and you're scared and I know it. Why do you think you have to do this alone?"

Robin just looked at her.

After a moment, Joleena sighed. Resigned, she nodded. "Yeah. I'm gone."

26

THE HEAT WAS ALREADY THREATENING when the truck with Bowman Disposal printed on its side found its place in front of Building Five. After staying up most of the night to bring Vivian aspirin and listening to her groan, Robin finally called Jessie Rose. Joleena was right. She had been right about many things. Robin had sat in the dark, alone, deep in the scratchy chair, and cried. He couldn't hold it together anymore. He was at his end.

When Jessie and Elderiah arrived at seven o'clock, he cried. Jessie called Dr. Wingfield who promised to come as soon as he could. After fixing them a breakfast of pancakes, eggs, sausage, milk and coffee, Jessie sent her husband off to work and Robin and Little Von outside.

Downstairs, Elderiah started the big truck with Robin and Little Von hanging on the door.

"Grandpa, can I honk the horn?"

"Well sure, but not now 'cause it's so early. You don't want Sanitoni to call the cops on us?"

"Naa, I guess not. When can I come up to the house?"

"Anytime. We'll go for a ride."

"Okay, Grandpa."

Robin helped his brother off the door step and faced his grandfather.

Elderiah put his hand on Robin's. "Rob, you been handlin' this like a man. Don't feel bad 'cause you called. You did the right thing."

"How come it feels so bad then, Gramps?"

"What's there to feel good about?" This powerful thought brought relief. It brought a sense of peace that was overwhelming and painful all at once. He had heard it before, and rejected it and the one who had brought it to him.

"Yeah, I never thought about it that way. It must be just as bad for you. She's your daughter."

"No. She my little girl. That's how I keep tryin' to make it in my mind. Every time I look though, I see something else. It hurts awful." Elderiah sniffed. "We'll all get through, boy." Elderiah patted Robin's hand and gunned the engine of the truck. Robin jumped down and looked up the street. "It's all clear, Gramps."

Robin smiled. "It's a lot clearer than it was. It was hard, but I'm glad I called now."

Elderiah started to roll backwards. "Yeah. I'm just glad you called first or Grandma would be wearin' out yo' backside."

Robin frowned. "First! Did Liberty or Charlene call?"

Elderiah smiled and shook his head no.

Robin thought about Joleena.

Elderiah smiled again. "Not more than ten minutes after you hung up. She apologized for callin' so early, then said she couldn't wait any longer. You say it's clear now."

Robin laughed and nodded. "Okay, Gramps. All clear now."

Elderiah backed the truck into the street and smiled at his grandsons. When the truck had rumbled through the streets of the Fredrick Douglas Projects and out of sight, Robin led Little Von across the street and through a hole in the fence that lined the upper part of Pocahontas.

"Where we goin', Rob?"

"Let's get on the other side of Poke and sit on the dam head."

"How we gonna get over there without walkin' all the way around?"

"I know a place where the river is narrow. There's a big 'ol tree that fell across from one side to the other and we can walk across."

"Can I just take off my brace to get across?" Little Von asked smiling.

"No Von! How many times we gotta tell you, man? You don't walk on that leg until Doctor Bow tells you to. Doctor Bow said if you stay off your leg and give your hip a chance to heal, you can throw your crutches away in about nine months."

"I know. In nine months."

"Nine months ain't that long. If you keep walkin' on it though, you might really mess it up and you might never get off."

"Then how am I gonna get across the tree?"

"Von man, I told you it's a real fat one."

Little Von was relieved, until they reached the root stump of the overturned tree. "Rob, this tree ain't as fat as you said it was."

"Just go ahead, bean head." Robin said, picking up his brother. "I'll be right behind you."

Little Von inched out a short way and turned around. No

way, man. It's your tree, you go first!"

"No. No. You stay there. I'm comin' right behind you."

"Forget it! Get me down."

"No, man. I gotta go behind you so I can hold you by the back of your pants while you go across."

"Rob! Get me down. I'm not doin' it."

"How come?"

"It's your idea and you won't even go first!"

"Von, I can't hold onto you if I go first. Look, man, you just have to deal with this."

Little Von looked down at the green waters of Poke as it came around a bend and swirled quickly under the tree with its fallen branches. Without speaking, he inched forward. When he got to the middle he turned to make sure his brother was there. "I thought you was gonna be holdin' on to me."

"It wasn't time yet, but it's time now." Robin came up close behind, stuck one finger in his belt loop, smiled and flung his brother, crutches and all, into the air. Little Von screamed. With nothing solid beneath him, and his crutches flapping back and forth, he looked as if he was trying to fly. He was still screaming when he hit the water. His crutches were immediately swept away. The bottom of his brace bobbed up and down with the swift current. Little Von wrenched himself around to see where he was headed. Another huge splash and Robin was right beside him. Robin turned over on his back and rushed right by his brother. Little Von screamed at him.

As suddenly as the river had swept them away from the fallen tree, it had deposited them on a sand bar. Robin was laughing as he sat on the bottom and watched Little Von doing a vicious dog paddle. "Hey! Hey! Slow down. You can't swim on sand."

Little Von, unsure, slapped the water a few more times before he opened his eyes to notice that his crutches had washed up on the sand before him.

"Robin you crazy or somethin'! What you throw me in for?"

Robin lay on his side laughing. Once in a while he would pick up his hands and imitate Von's frantic doggy paddle and then lapse into another laughing fit. Little Von looked around himself once again, making sure he was completely secure.

"Hey, man. That was the meanest doggy paddle in the whole world."

"Geez, Rob. You been drinkin' or somethin'? It stinks in here."

Robin started laughing again. "Hey man, you got some green shit hangin' off your head."

Little Von picked the green lettuce-like seaweed from his head and threw it at his brother. "Shit."

"Von! Stop cussin'."

"Well, how come you can cuss?"

"Von, I'm a teenager now. I can cuss and smoke too if I want to."

"But Rob you stink when you smoke."

"Von, that's what they have cologne for."

"Rob, you stink when you wear cologne too."

Robin made a face at his brother and imitated his doggy paddle again.

"Come on, Von. Let's do it again."

"What? Rob, I almost drowneded."

"Drowneded? No you didn't, dummy. You could have walked all the way down here."

Von looked at his brother unbelieving. Robin stood up dripping, his shirt sticking to his back, the current swirling around the bottom of his legs no higher than his knees. "See. Come on. One more time."

Leaving his crutches on the sandbar, Von stood up to fight the current. On his first two attempts he was swept back to the sand bar. That in itself was fun. He was free of his brace, wet, and muddy. No other thoughts crowded him as he splashed and played. They jumped from the tree together as the hot sun beat down, holding hands several times until Little Von, now fearless, raced back and leaped on his own.

After an hour they headed for the dam. A quarter mile away, the water fell over the dam in a muted roar. Soon the two brothers reached the top of the dam head and lay down to bake in the sun.

Little Von sat quietly for a long time until, one by one, thoughts of his mother emerged from the background. Without realizing it, he began to cry. One of his tears fell and surrounded an ant and lifted it off the concrete. Little Von picked it up with a stick and dropped it into the slow-moving water making its way toward the waterfall. When the stick of the ant came abreast with

Robin, he scooped it up and put it back on the dam head. "Von, you shouldn't kill things unnecessarily. That's what Grandpa always says."

"Robin. She's not gonna be all right this time."

Robin poked at his clothes with his finger. The sun was strong and had dried them quickly. "Von, Mommy has a lot of problems. Not just her burned hand. Grandma and Grampa are probably taking her back to the hospital." Robin pulled him close. "Grandma said it's probably her liver."

"What's that do?" he asked between tears.

"Your liver is right about here." Robin put his hand over Little Von's abdomen. "When you drink, it's your liver that gets that junk out of your body. Mommy's liver ain't doin' too good. It's failin' cause she drink so much." The truth had more to do with scar tissue, but rotting was quick and simple.

"Can they fix it in the hospital?"

"Well Von, I ain't even totally sure that's what it is. That's what Grandma thinks and that's why she has to go in. It might not be the only thing."

"Rob, how long we gonna be here by ourselves?"

Robin had been trying to avoid this question, but the time had come. He took a deep breath. "Von, we can't stay down here no more."

"Where we gonna go? Back to Grandma's?"

"You are. I'm going to Dad's. It will be easier on Grandma and Grampa that way."

Little Von let his head fall against his brother's chest and wailed openly. His shrieks came one after another. Robin looked up into the sky and fought the pain. "Von, they won't let us stay down here just the two of us 'cause I'm only fifteen and I really can't take care of everything."

"Why not? You cook a little." The words were whiny.

"There's a lot more to it. Like the bills and stuff like that. I had to quit my job 'cause Mommy was sick so much. And we have to go to school and I didn't do that good last year either. Everything will be much better. It'll just be like before we came down here, except I'll be over Dad's."

"But I don't want you to live somewhere else. I want you to be where I am, like we always been." Little Von's sentence trailed off into tears as he realized that, once again, he had no say or control over the matter.

"Yeah, I don't want us to be separated either, but it won't be bad. You'll see. Dad's is right next to Layfayette. You can see my room from your bedroom window. You won't have to worry about anything." Little Von hugged his brother. What was left of the Pocahontas on their clothes and their tears mingled together. Robin held him close. His heart ached. "You know how close Dad's is to Grandma's. You can look right out of Grandma's window and see Lafayette and Dad's at the same time."

"But I hardly ever saw you before we came down here, and we lived in the same house."

"That's because you were so little then. You didn't know how to deal with anything like Jing-Wei and stuff like Mommy being sick all the time."

Little Von sat up and looked at his brother. "Now I can."

Robin looked into his brother's eyes smiling. "Now, you hardly ever cry when Mommy starts drinkin' and..." Robin looked for the words. "...and starts gettin' into her "Other Self.""

Little Von looked up. "No Rob, the "Other Self" gets into her. That's why she's not like Mom when she be drinkin'." Robin nodded pensively. It was definitely a child's view. Yet, perhaps it was the truth. "Well, anyway, you ain't so little any more and I'll come and get you and we'll do a lot of stuff together."

"You promise?"

"Yep."

"Rob, I don't want you to call me Little Von any more. I'm bigger now. Just call me Von."

Robin smiled. "Okay, Von."

A pebble bounced off the dam head and into the water before either of the boys could see what it was. Then another hit Robin square in the back. He looked up to see Charlene jumping up and down on the dam head on the other side of the waterfall. She was yelling and couldn't be heard over the crashing waters. She wore a faded maroon Morristown High sweatshirt and cut-offs that revealed her strong thighs and flat stomach. Robin watched the action of her breast bobbling up and down before he waved back. Putting his hand over his ear and shaking, he signaled her to come around. Just as quickly, Charlene signaled him to come around. Robin pointed to Little Von and held up his crutch and signaled for her to come around again.

Charlene gave Robin the finger and made her way down the dam head.

In ten minutes Charlene's head slipped above a line of bushes and vanished again as the rough terrain rose and dipped. Finally, she walked down the center of the dam head sure-footed and unconcerned about falling. She plopped down, straddling Little Von from behind and hugged him. "Hey Von, how's my little man?"

Little Von looked at Robin.

"How she know already?"

"How did I know what?" Charlene said.

"How did you know you suppose to call me Von instead of Little Von?"

"Von, I always call you Von, and my Mom always calls you Little Man."

"Oh yeah. That's right."

"Charlene, ain't you 'fraid of fallin' off the dam?"

"Nope. I come out here all the time when I want to get away from people buggin' me."

"Charlene, how come you ain't scared?"

"Von, I used to be, the first coupla times I came out here, but I got tired of everybody laughin' at me. Von, you got to deal with it. You can't be scared of every little thing that happens. If you don't want to fall in the lake, don't look at the lake. If you don't want to fall on the rocks, don't look at the rocks...see?" she said, pointing over the side. "Don't look down there. You got to deal with it."

"Well," Von thought, it must be true. Robin, Scootch, and even Charlene—a girl—knew that you had to deal with stuff that scared you. "Piss on it. I ain't scared."

"Von!" Robin said scowling.

"That's what you and Art always say." Little Von ignored him and quickly wiped his eyes so Charlene couldn't see that he had been crying. Slipping his ankle back into his brace, he got up with his crutches. Without hesitation, he started down the slope.

Charlene smiled and moved next to Robin so she could see better. "Do it, Von. You can do it."

When he went down and back he turned again, this time doubling his speed. When he came back he slipped his brace off and sat dangling his feet over the side of the dam head. Charlene clapped and put her arm around his shoulders. "See, I told you you wouldn't get wet or fall." Charlene felt along the bottom of Von's shirt. Then she noticed the green tint around the sheepskin lining of the waist band of his brace. "But you feel damp like you been wet." She leaned close. "You know I thought you smelled like Poke. You guys been swimmin' with your clothes on? I was wonderin' why you guys was sittin' out here fryin' in the sun. You was tryin to get dry, huh?"

"Yup. Me and Rob was jumpin' off that big tree down there."

"Was it fun?"

"Yup, wasn't it, Rob? First I was scared, then bean head pushed me in."

Charlene looked at Robin. He was smiling, warm in the sun. His pale feet stuck out from under his pants.

"Yeah, I really needed to do somethin'. Everything was gettin' pretty crazy with my Mom and..."

"Joleena."

"Yeah, that too." Robin sighed. "I just felt like doin' somethin' crazy."

"I figured that's what was goin' on when I saw you over here. We came down to see how Vivy was doin', and your Grandmother was there. She was waitin' for the doctor."

"Yeah. I know she gonna end up in the hospital 'cause she can't hardly eat nothin' without throwin' up. Plus her hand and shit...piss on it."

Von smirked. "See, you said it again—two words."

"Robin you gonna get in trouble for gettin' Von's brace all messed up?"

"In trouble from who? It's been wet before when he fell in the pool down the playground. I'll just throw it in the washer."

"I didn't fall in," Von interrupted. "Jing-Wei pushed me. That was before I kicked his ass."

Charlene laughed. "Yeah, I heard about that. I'm sorry I missed it. I heard you kicked it good too. Last time anybody got a good ass kickin' around here was me up at Lafayette."

"Yup," Von said, matter of factly. "I heard about that too."

"Speakin' about Lafayette, how's Scootch?" Robin asked.

Charlene overdramatized a frown. "What you askin' me for? You seen him since I have. You be singin' with him all the time. What you askin' me for?"

"Well, guys talk different to each other than they do to women. I just thought you might know more about his condition than he told us."

"Robin, it's obvious we don't go together anymore. The man kicked my ass in front of God and everybody."

Von started laughing. "Yup, That's what I heard." Charlene playfully punched him.

"Why don't you ask his brother Matt?"

"No. I don't ask Mat nothin.' He was strange when I first met him. And I think he's gettin' stranger all the time."

"Well, don't be askin' me 'cause I don't know or care."

Robin flashed back over the conversation from the laundry and wondered why Charlene had lied. Scootch said she had called every day—as if it had become tiresome. What did she have to lose? What did she have to gain?

"Heard anything about Benny?"

"Robin." Charlene turned to face him. "Listen, let's get this straight. There wasn't nothin' between me and Scab. What you saw up at the shed at Lafayette was just somethin' stupid I let Scab talk me into."

Robin smiled. Charlene hadn't known that he was beneath the stairwell when she leaped into his arms. She had lied again.

"By the way, was you the one who told Scootch?" she asked, not really thinking that he had.

"You know I didn't, 'cause I left with Scab. I didn't know anything about it until way later that night when Art came by Lucky's. Sounded bad though."

"Must have been that retarded Matt."

Charlene looked at Robin again. "Believe me it was as bad as bad gets. I was so embarrassed." She looked soft again.

Robin looked up at the sun. It was starting down toward the horizon. "Von, you about dry?"

"Yup, but I stink."

"We better start back and see what happened with the doctor."

"Oh, I forgot to tell you." Charlene said. "The doctor was leaving when we came. He said he was gonna check her into Memorial."

Robin hugged Von. "Is my grandmother still there?"

"No. She went to get some things so she could stay down

here tonight. Your grandfather came and picked her up. My mom is with her now and you guys are gonna eat at our house tonight."

"Your mom is with our mom?" Von said, with wide eyes.

Charlene put her arm back around him. "Don't worry, Von. They won't be doin' no drinkin' with Jessie Rose comin' back down."

Robin had been thinking the same thing.

"I'm cookin', so what do you want?"

"Spaghetti," Von said, with excitement back in his voice, "Cause you cook even better than Mommy."

"Okay then. Spaghetti. And for sayin' that, you might even get some ice cream."

27

H<small>E WANTED SOMETHING DIFFERENT</small> this time, something more than a stolen car. The night swirled around him, empowering and releasing the last of the inhibitions that had held him inferior. Tonight he needed a climax. Something more than he had ever attempted. A final proving.

When he sped away in the first stolen car, the rush had been incredible. When he looked into his rearview mirror and found no police lights or sirens, he had screamed out loud. Three cars later, bored with his new adventure, his life returned to the depths of his brother's shadow. As he sat in the stolen car at the red light, he saw a police cruiser three cars back in a secession of lights. In his excitement he stalled the car, panicked, jumped out and ran to hide in the darkness. He was there, flattened against an alley wall behind a dumpster, sweating profusely, when he saw the stolen car drift forward through the light, heading downhill on its own.

Three blocks below, he heard the crash. An instant later, a blackout spread for a half mile in every direction. His pulse hammered, and still there were no lights or sirens. And then, suddenly, the night was shredded with flashing lights and the sirens of engine companies from all over the county. Soon people spilled into the streets and were pushed back again by bull horns and barricades. Candles flickered from apartments. Emergency generators kicked on in stores. And still the thrill had only fulfilled him for a short time. After he had sent several more cars hurling through empty streets in the chilled hours of early morning, the thrill had dissipated. Tonight Matt knew he needed something more. He craved the rush like any junky and scanned the night for new opportunities.

R<small>obin</small> was sitting on the stairs in front of Building Five looking up at the stars. He was amazed how seldom he noticed the spectacle of the universe, and how thoroughly his small world had dominated his attention. He had not thought about his future, only the small isolated incidents that connected one minute to the next. This moment, free from everyone and everything, was a brief interlude between the last and the next. And then it passed.

The foyer door gave its usual whine and Charlene popped through. She sat on the stairs next to Robin. "Robin, was my mother still up?"

"Naa. When I put Von down she was in a chair sleeping next to the TV. My grandmother was lying on the bed with my mother."

"Did Von wake up on the way down? I can't believe he went to sleep without his ice cream."

"He had a long..." Robin tried to remember when the present crisis had started; he couldn't separate one from the other. "He's had a rough time. Some of it is catchin' up to him now. He was out like a light. I took a bath and then I got him in and he started slowing down as soon as he got in the warm water." The conversation died while Robin gazed at the night sky again. Charlene tried to see what he was looking at, and seeing nothing out of the ordinary, gave up. Robin finally thought of something to say.

"Thanks for dinner. It was great."

"Robin. You always so goddamn quiet sometimes, it drives me crazy. You're welcome," she added without pausing. "You know, I used to not like you 'cause you was so quiet. Scootch always said that was your way. He thought you was being cool. I just thought you didn't know what was going on."

Robin leaned back against the cool cement stairs, making room between them. The feelings of dislike had been more than mutual for the opposite reason. He smiled.

Charlene's eyes narrowed as she talked. She actually resembled Liberty's "crack-lid" glare as Jessie Rose had called it. "You didn't like me either, did you Robin? Did you?" She pressed.

Robin shrugged. "Charlene, I never said nothin' like that."

"You don't have to. I know. Don't be tryin' to cover with me. I know what all you yellow niggas up on the hill think. You think everybody lives in Fred Douglass is hoods or sluts. Like you better or somethin' cause you live in houses."

"Charlene, where you comin' from? All the guys that I ever hung tight with, except Art, live down here. So that ain't true." Robin felt some enjoyment. Charlene had broken the rules by showing her feelings. Robin was eager to hear how she'd recover.

Charlene leaned back on the stairs and moved closer. "I'm sorry. Maybe not you, but you know I'm right. I'm right about you, too. And you know it. Everybody thinks you so cool, and you are in your own way, but not like they think though. Tell the truth. When you first came down here, you were scared to death."

Robin smiled. "Go ahead, Char. You seem to have all the answers tonight."

Charlene laughed. "Robin Thompson, don't try to pull that bull on me. You cute, but just because you swim in Poke with all your clothes on don't make you tough." They both remembered the sight and the smell, and laughed. Charlene closed the gap even more. When she could look him in the eye, she lowered her voice. "But that's why I like you." Then she kissed him.

Watching Jimmy Lee work on the old Stutz through the dirty windowpane was like watching a silent movie. Matt could hear the music in the background and Jimmy Lee would move his mouth from time to time and dive back into the innards of the Stutz. It went on for an hour. Matt sat on the bumper of Jimmy Lee's tow truck. The truck had been a thought, but it was the Stutz that started his nerves tingling and broke a light sweat on Matt's forehead. The Stutz, with its shinny chrome and old-time flare, created the exhilaration that made his eyes wide and his breath come in short strokes. Matt had even thought about Bill Furman's Buick. The life in the Buick had died with Bill. The Stutz was alive with Jimmy Lee's excitement. It had to be the Stutz.

Matt leaned forward and stuck his knife under the edge of the window frame, easing it up till a slender thread of light appeared. Grinning, he let it down with a small thump.

Jimmy Lee looked up from the hood not knowing if the sound had come from the radio or if someone had entered the shop. He looked around. The door was locked. The window showed only the reflection of the inside of the shop with himself as the center piece. He returned to the engine.

Matt made no attempt to hide. He stood boldly, looking back.

Jimmy Lee leaned over the engine, a rag in one hand and a wrench in the other, shaking his head. He flung the wrench over his shoulder. It landed on a pile of tools on the workbench behind him. Jimmy Lee took a swig from a Coke bottle and looked around the room feeling something he couldn't see. Placing the empty bottle in the crate next to the machine, he headed for the bathroom. The feeling of a presence was still with him and growing stronger. "I'm getting old," he thought. He pushed the feelings away and concentrated on keeping his flow in the center of the toilet. Just as he reached to flush, he heard laughter. The lights went out and the door slammed behind him.

It was only a kiss on the cheek and still Robin fumbled for a correct response. Charlene spoke before he could finish examining the list of possibilities.

"Listen, Rob, my mother told me you guys weren't gonna be down here much longer. I didn't believe her and she didn't know for sure, but now I'd say she was right." Charlene waited.

Robin thought about it. The summer was nearly over. "If my mom goes into the hospital, I'd say we'd be gone in a couple of days."

"That fast, huh? I was hoping there would be more time. God, what a crazy summer."

"Hmm."

"Well, Joleena will be happy. I mean you'll only be a block away. You movin' in with your Dad next to Lafayette, right? You guys can walk to school together."

"Well, Joleena doesn't have anything to do with it one way or the other. You know we split up."

"That's what she gets for tryin' to control people and tell them what to do. She lucky you didn't tag her like Scootch did me. You don't miss her, do you?"

Robin was surprised by his anger. He was angry that Charlene had somehow made the break-up Joleena's fault. "It wasn't Joleena's fault at all. It was mine. Then things got so crazy with my mom and everything…" Robin shrugged.

Charlene let the silence ease things for a moment. Then she smiled. "Robin, I have something I want to give you. A going-away present."

"Really?" It was another Charlene right-turn, but one he felt he could roll with.

Without another word, Charlene rose and slipped through the foyer door. Robin followed her up four flights. Upstairs, in front of her green door, Charlene slipped a string with a key from around her neck. Putting it into the lock, she jiggled it several times, swore, took it out, jiggled it again, and the lock popped open.

Robin smiled. "You too, huh?"

"I hate these damn locks. Nobody can get them open without a fight."

"Hmm. I thought I was the only one."

"No. I'm cussin Spumoni Sanitoni out if he don't come and start fixin' this one real soon."

They went inside. Charlene's and Liberty's apartment was identical to every other. "Char, I need to use your bathroom."

"Mmm. I like it when you call me that. You know where it is. When you come out, keep your eyes closed."

"You didn't have to go out and buy nothin'."

Charlene smiled. She hadn't.

Robin flushed the toilet and turned on the water in the sink. "You should have gave it to us before Little Von fell asleep."

"He's too young for this one," she said smiling.

"What?" Robin said, unable to hear over the toilet flushing. He came out. "Okay, my eyes are closed."

Charlene took him by the arm and gently pulled him down the hall and around the corner. "It's in here." She led him to the couch in the living room.

Robin opened his eyes to a candle-lit room. Charlene turned him and sat him down. Her eyes glistened in the candle-light. She moved close and kissed him long and hard. When they parted lips, Robin was speechless. She waited for a short moment, and when there were no words or effort to refuse her, she kissed him again. Without any reason, except that he had no power to do otherwise, Robin began to kiss her back. The candle had been burning for an hour when Robin left the apartment. Its wax was pooled at the base of the holder, its cooled drippings cascading on its side.

Robin pushed through the foyer door and resumed his position under the stars. They were brighter and held more fascination than before. Arthur Taggart walked under the street lamp and up to Building Five. He drank from a brown paper bag with its top rolled down the neck of a bottle.

"Hey Art, what you doin' down here this late?"

"Just on my way home from Pat's. Thought I'd walk by and see if your light was on." Art held the bottle out to Robin.

Robin smiled. "It's a good night for it."

Arthur smirked. "No kiddin'."

Robin took a long draw from the wine bottle and handed it back to Art. He went back to looking at the stars. Art looked up to see what he was looking at. Robin sighed. "It's unreal isn't it?"

Art nodded casually. "It's up there all the time and nobody even notices it. Ey, do you ever think about other beings on those planets?"

"Art, man. There ain't no way we the only living things in the whole universe."

"Maybe God made us first and when he saw how screwed up we turned out he said forget it. Maybe he chalked us up to a bad experiment." Art reached over and smacked Robin's shirt pocket. "Rob, you out of cigs?"

"I dropped them in Poke today and I haven't had a chance to get any more."

"Okay." Art pulled out his and gave one to Robin.

"Art, you dog. You was gonna smoke mine first, huh?"

"Hey. Didn't I share my wine with you?"

"Art what you doin' with a whole bottle of wine this time of night anyway?"

Art smirked. "What you doin' with that funny grin on your face talking about the wonders of the universe. Something is goin' on and you holdin' back."

Robin started smiling. "Well, there's good news...and bad news."

"You too, huh. Well, damn, give me the good news 'cause I don't need no more bad tonight."

Robin looked around to see if any extra ears were waiting for his short-kept secret. He was smiling so hard all of his teeth were showing.

"Well?" Art was impatient.

"I was upstairs, man, and she was all over me."

"What!"

"I ain't kiddin'," Robin nodded. "Candles and everything."

"Joleena? I thought you guys split."

"No, are you kidding? We did."

"Who then?"

Robin looked up to the top floor.

"Charlene!"

Robin nodded again.

"Well, I already know the bad news," Art said, thinking about Benny and Scootch.

Robin put his hand on Art's shoulder. "Hey man, you can't tell nobody. I mean nobody."

"Ey," Art said frowning and laughing at the same time, "It ain't me. You better hope Charlene don't tell none of her big-mouth friends."

They were just above a whisper now. Art slapped Robin's hand. Robin was noticeably more enthusiastic. Art, realizing the importance of the occasion, allowed him the moment. "Charlene. Wow. How was it?"

Robin rolled his head back and forth. "Hey man, I know why Scab risked his life now. She's sweet. Very...very...very sweet." Robin started laughing when he noticed that Arthur actually looked like he was in pain. "Art, somethin's wrong. Spill it."

Arthur took a long swallow from the bottle, capped it and put his head in his hands. Robin didn't push. He waited.

Art reached into his back pocket and pulled out a long envelope and handed it to Robin. "There's good news and bad news." Robin looked at the return address.

"Stanford? We ain't even juniors yet; they writin' you already?"

"Read it."

Robin scanned the letter. "Whoa, man! They want you to come second semester next year. When the hell is that?"

"Second semester is after Christmas. I'll have enough credits to graduate anyway."

"I can't believe this. How they know about you? They got some kind of secret service keepin' track of 'smart niggas, potential trouble makers'?"

"You ain't gonna believe this. Mr. Suther. He called them and told them I was interested in law a year ago."

"Damn! And I thought messin' with Charlene was excitin'."

"Well, as a matter of fact, that brings us around to the bad news."

Robin stopped with the bottle halfway up to his mouth.

"Patsy's pregnant."

Robin sat the bottle down on his leg and leaned forward. "What? How did that happen?" Art just looked at Robin silently.

"Yup. She told me tonight." Art took the bottle and turned it up.

"What she gonna do, man?"

"She wants to get married and shit. You believe that?"

"Man-o-man. She tell her parents yet?"

"No, but she said she missed her period. When she miss one or two more, everybody's gonna know whether she tells or not."

"Hey, man. How come you didn't tell me you and Patsy been doin' it?"

"I don't know, man. I just didn't want anybody to know."

"Here, man. You better have another drink," Robin said, handing the bottle back to Art.

And then there was a huge explosion. In the direction of the stone bridge, the sky turned orange.

Jimmy Lee hit the door with his fist. "Hey! Who's that? Open this son-a-va-bitchin' door right now!"

Matt laughed again climbing behind the big wheel of the Stutz. "Hey, hold your horses, old man. I've been waitin' for you to finish this for a long time." Matt ran his hands over the tan leather seats, the last thing Bill Furman had helped Jimmy Lee to find.

"Finish what? Open this goddamn door!"

"Finish what?" Matt laughed. "What do mean 'finish what?'" Matt tapped the horn twice quickly, allowing its raspy bark to answer the question.

"Get the hell outta my car else I'm comin' through this door and kick your little bony ass into the middle of next January."

Matt's laugh was sinister and taunting. "Yeah, old man, that's a pretty flimsy door. I'll bet on it against your old ass though." Matt looked for a key.

Jimmy Lee frowned in the darkness. The light switch was on the outside leaving him with only the light from the shop coming under the door. He turned around in an angry circle. It was impossible to keep up with all the generations of the Hollow's children, but sooner or later they all made their way into the old Best Fill station to turn the crank on the soda machine.

"Goddamnit I know who you are. You one of them Williams boys."

Matt was engrossed in his search, barely paying attention to Jimmy Lee. "Yup. That's right."

"I knew it. You Scotty. The one they calls Scootch. Hell, you just got stabbed, what you doin' breakin' into my shop? Open this goddamn door!"

Matt was furious. He leaped off the seat of the Stutz and ran right up to the surface of the grimey door and pounded it. "No, wrong! Wrong! Wrong!"

The reverberation inside the small bathroom was like a small explosion. Jimmy Lee stumbled backward, nearly falling into the toilet. "Oh you the weird one...Matthew."

Matt kicked the door.

"You always been a little strange, but you ain't never been in no trouble with the po-leece. Don't do nothin' stupid now, son. Just come over here and open the door, let me out, get yo'self a Coke and we'll forget about it." Jimmy Lee was disgusted. With all the thousands of metal tools laying around the floor of his shop, the only thing he could find to protect himself was a toilet brush and a can of Comet.

Matt jumped back into the Stutz. His frustration increased. Not only was there not a key, there was no place to insert one. He slammed his hands down on the wheel. Gauges, buttons, and knobs was all there was to be seen. With both hands, he returned to the assault on the dashboard. The noise of Jimmy Lee's shoulder ramming the door beat a steady tattoo along with the single windshield wiper as it spun halfway around and back again.

Matt pulled another knob and the lights came on. Matt's anxiety reached a peak. He slammed the dash and bared his teeth. A small compartment popped open, but that was all. "Jimmy Lee! Where's the goddamn starter? Is this one of dem crankers?" Matt jumped out, looked around the front, and jumped back in. "You might as well tell me."

"Oh I'm gonna show ya. Wait till I get ahold your skinny little ass."

Matt started the dashboard sequence again, but more feverishly. Still nothing. He slammed his knee against the door and jerked the gear lever that stood tall from the floor. In the process he stepped on a button on the floor that he had assumed was for the high beams. The engine rolled over with a backfire and the car lurched into Jimmy Lee's tool bench. Matt shot forward like a rocket. Both headlights, sticking up like eyes on the end of a lobster's antenna, burst in puffs of shattered glass.

Jimmy Lee's heart sank. He had depended on Matt not knowing about the old floor button ignition. The pain of his shoulder was sharp. But not three feet away Matthew Williams was stealing June Bug, his pride and joy, his dream.

The freshly-tuned engine purred along with the blood rushing through Matt's head. He grabbed the claw top gear shifter and slammed it backwards unprepared for the quickness with which the car hurled itself.

With a final agonizing grunt, the bathroom door shattered and Jimmy Lee spilled out onto the shop floor, toilet brush in hand, just in time to see the Stutz crash rear first through the garage door. Jimmy Lee was up on his feet running. Hopping through the debris and out into the service yard, he saw Matt stall and crank the engine again. He had come to a stop not more than a few feet from the gas pumps. Jimmy Lee's fervor was building. He would pull him out of the seat and beat his brains to mush. He looked at the toilet brush. Disgusted he threw it to the ground just as the Stutz fired up. He picked up a long wrench. Matt fired the engine and started forward, right for Jimmy Lee. Jimmy Lee tried to stop, but slid on the oil-speckled sand. He went down to one knee, twisted around and got up running. He shot back through the splintered opening of the garage.

Matt turned the yellow car just in time to avoid re-entering the garage door himself. The wheel was stiff and took all of his muscles to hold the turn. He smashed through a rack of oil cans and toppled the large drum of dirty oil. It splashed and coated the bright yellow Stutz, the ground, the windshield and Matt's face in a black slimy muck. In his panic he held the accelerator to the floor as he fought the wheel, but the tires, now slick and spinning, gave no response.

Jimmy Lee came through the ruins of the garage door holding the long wrench swearing and hollering. He watched as Matt and the Stutz Le Baron went into a spin. The tailend of the car ripped one of the pump machines off its foundation. It was Jimmy Lee's worst nightmare. A fountain of gasoline shot into the air toward the stone bridge. When it came down it coursed through the bridge's gutter and sped past the Pail of Ale and to-

ward the condemned wooden shanties. Jimmy Lee ran back inside to the phone, but the lines had been ripped out during Matt's
first pass. He ran to the service yard. Matt flew by with the look
of a frightened child, his oil-stained face in sharp contrast to the
whites of his eyes. The car fishtailed toward the stone bridge, the
tires smoking and whirling without purpose. Jimmy Lee watched
helplessly as Matthew Williams slid into the bridge and crashed
headlong into its short stone wall. The night momentarily hid the
details of the crash until the metal and gnarled chrome ground
against the stone and cement. A single spark sent a river of fire
in both directions over the bridge. The spare tire with "June Bug"
written across its cover was a brilliant blazing top as it came back
past the station. The wind licked the tire like a torch as it shot
under the trestle and started up the hill. It slowed and came to
a spiraling stop in the middle of the street near the doorway of
the Italian bakery where the car's original owner, Antonio
Pelligrini, had keeled over from a heart attack some twenty years
before.

There were no shadows as the trail of fire found its way back
across the stone bridge to the station and ignited the station's un-
derground tanks.

Jimmy Lee had seen a filling station go up in flames as a
small child and, without hesitation, had followed the burning
spare tire to higher ground. He scrambled up the rocky sides of
the trestle and threw himself down behind the girder that crossed
over the street, hugging his knees. A blinding fireball lit up the
night. The windows of the station exploded in unison, and in
another second the station was simply gone. Jimmy Lee covered
his head with his hands as indistinguishable pieces of his station
rained all around him.

On the other side of the bridge, the stilted ruins were little
more than tinder for the raging blaze. One by one, the shanties
crashed to the ground. Jimmy Lee watched from his railroad
perch and hoped none of the local winos were in there too drunk
to run. The stone bridge was a passage between two blazing
bookends, and at its center, the mangled wreck of his Stutz hung
like a see-saw over the waters of the Pocahontas. A rushing circle
of fire engulfed the sides of a customer's car. Seconds later the
gas tank exploded. Black smoked filled the air. Jimmy Lee tried
to spot his hook truck. But the brilliant flames against the night

sky made it impossible. There was another explosion. When he ventured to look over the scene again, the Stutz, Matt Williams, and all of Jimmy Lee's Best Fill had vanished.

28

SEPTEMBER

Robin stood with his back to the hallway wall, his Sears Monotone at his feet. It was the last item to be moved. Otherwise, apartment 5509 was empty. The smallest sound echoed through the deserted living room. The lamp, the scratchy chair, the wobbly three-legged table, all had found their ways to other apartments, Jessie Rose's, or the dump. Robin stared. It was as if the apartment had been a stage and "The Thompsons" one of its plays. Now the apartment was empty and the stage was ready for the next set of characters to move in and play out their roles. The only thing that remained was the vine, long since browned and died. It sat in the window. Robin picked up his record player and locked the green metallic door for the last time.

Lillian watched her brother hand Jerry Sanitoni the keys. They shook hands afterwards. After several steps, Robin turned around and looked up at the third-floor row of windows. Lillian wondered what her brothers felt. She had missed this episode and didn't quite know how to comfort them.

She looked in the back seat. "Von, you excited about going back to Grandma's?" Von leaned over the back seat and shrugged. Lillian was further puzzled. "You're not sad to be leaving, are you?"

"Sorta'," he said, leaning on his elbow.

"You want to stay here?"

"Yeah. I have friends here now."

"Yeah, but you have lots of friends at Grandma's too."

It was a long thoughtful pause. His eyes flickered back and forth.

"They're different though." His eye contact was brief. "Not like down here."

Lillian listened. "How, Von? What do you mean?"

"Just different. Up there they don't know too much."

"Are you excited about school? It starts in about a week, you know."

Little Von had no conception of time. That's what adults

were for. He had looked forward to school starting again for what seemed like forever. In the wake of all that had happened, school had never been mentioned. Now his mother was sick—very sick. She was sick in a way that was frightening for him to think about. In the face of being forced to leave a place that had finally become home, school seemed unimportant.

Robin got in the front seat and pulled the door closed. He pulled out a cigarette and tapped it on the dash. Von fell back in the seat, moaning and struggling to get his window down before his brother could light up. Lillian looked at Robin, sure he would make some statement. Instead, he turned to his sister and said, "Well?" Lillian continued trying to start conversation. She made comments and asked questions, but their answers were flat and without emotion. She gave up.

Lillian looked up at Building Five one last time and wondered how they had survived. Little Von sat in the backseat, looking down, fiddling with his brace. Robin sat blowing smoke out the window and looking up the street and then up toward Charlene's and Liberty's apartment. It was that sinking feeling in his stomach again. It had been with him for so long it was almost normal. A beer sounded really good, no, a joint. Both. It would take both today. He glanced at 5509.

Lillian backed the car from the stall and followed the street past the playgrounds, and made a left turn over what was left of the stone bridge. Large trucks were blocking the street as they worked to carry away the burned wreckage of the stilt apartments and Jimmy Lee's.

"I can't believe he didn't get killed." Lillian frowned as she was forced to follow the detour around Center Street to avoid the trucks.

Robin came out of his daze. "Who's that—Matt?"

"Yes!" Lillian said, angry at the indifference. "The fool that had nothing better to do but blow up a gas station and drive that old car through the side of the bridge? He burned down half the Hollow."

Robin smiled, unmoved by his sister's emotion. He glanced at the charred remains of the station and returned to his cigarette, "Matt's crazy."

"Crazy? He's real lucky to be alive."

"Well, he lucked out," Robin said, raising his cigarette.

Von pulled himself up to the seat back. "Rob? You think Matt would have drowned if Cootie hadn't been there? You think he woulda made it?"

"Nope, 'cause Matt can't swim," Robin laughed dryly.

"Yup, he lucked out then," Von echoed.

Lillian turned up Spring Street towards town. "Who's Cootie?"

"Well, that's what makes it so funny," Rob explained. "See Cootie is this wino, half out of his mind all the time. He been drunk for so long that I doubt he got any mind left. He never bothers anybody though. Matt teased him every chance he got. I don't think Matt had anything against him. Cootie was about the only person Matt could jump on without gettin' his ass kicked.

"One time Cootie came staggerin' through the playground in these old baggy pants he probably picked out of the garbage somewhere. We had just got finished singin' and was sittin' around. When Matt saw Cootie he jumped up and started callin' 'im. Cootie came over 'cause he probably thought Matt wanted him to buy some wine for him, but when he got over to where Matt was, Matt started making fun of him. Cootie's too far gone to care about stuff like that, but then people started gettin' in on it and Matt got carried away with himself. He grabbed Cootie by the belt loops when he tried to walk away."

Little Von came to life. "Rob, you mean that time when Cootie's pants fell down?"

"Yeah. His pants were just barely hangin' off his butt in the first place, and his button popped when Matt grabbed 'im. His pants fell around his ankles and you know everybody went nuts. Especially Matt." Robin let his mind drift. He tried to visualize what had happened at the stone bridge. "Wish I could have been there when Cootie pulled him out of Poke. Must have been funny."

Lillian's face twisted in worry. Robin had told the story with little more than amusement. A year ago Lillian knew her brother would have been horrified by such a scene.

"Shoulda just left him in there."

"Yeah, but you know what? It's like I said. Cootie doesn't care about anything like that. He like—you ever read about Buddhism or Zen?"

"No. And what do you know about it?" she asked sarcastically.

"Art," Robin said, with a laugh, thinking how well reefer and discussions about Zen went together. "Art reads anything he gets his hands on, a dictionary, the stuff people staple to telephone poles—anything. Then we end up talkin' about it. Zen is really interesting though. Cootie is like a monk. When he be drinkin', he's not thinkin' about how he shouldn't be drinkin', or what he gonna do when he's finished drinkin'. When he's drinkin', he's drinkin', when he's hungry he looks for food, when he's tired he lays down and sleeps—wherever he is." Robin shrugged. "When he saw Matt in the water strugglin', he just pulled him out. He wasn't thinkin' about bein' no hero or revenge. That's just the way Cootie is," Robin shrugged. "It was just the next thing to do." He shrugged again.

Robin took the last drag off of his cigarette and exhaled. "I wish I could be like that." He looked at Lillian. "You know, simple. I can't do anything without thinkin' I probably shouldn't be doin' it or I'm doin' it wrong or ten thousand other things. Too much goin' on in my head all the time. Too much to do. Too much to think about. Cootie just does the next thing."

"Is Matt in jail now?"

"No. He's here, up on the psych ward," Robin said, pointing through the windshield in the direction of the hospital.

Lillian guided the Ford around several medians and into the Patient Visitor Parking Lot. "Robin, I don't think we should be doing this. What if we get caught?"

"Come on, Lillian. Von hasn't seen Mom in almost a week. We won't get caught if we do it like we said. Von, make your brace loose so you can get your foot out fast if you have to."

"I already did."

Robin looked over the seat. "Von, you remember the plan this time, right?"

"Yup. The whole thing. I just act like I'm comin' for a checkup for my leg." Robin reached over the seat and they slapped hands.

Von walked awkwardly like it was his first day on crutches. Robin, who pretended to help him, walked up the front stairs of the hospital and right past the nurse's information table with its sign: "No Children on Adult Floors." The nurse, who was busy shuffling papers and answering the phone at the same time, watched over the rim of her glasses as they headed for the elevator doors. She covered the phone and yelled out. "Boys, do you know how to get to pediatrics?" Robin looked over his shoulders and smiled as Lillian stepped in front of the nurse asking information. The boys slipped into the elevator and Von held his crutch in the opening, giving Lillian time to reach them. She stepped in and the doors closed behind her. Immediately Von kicked his leg out of his brace and with Robin's help they wrestled his pants, shoes, and socks off. Lillian took a paper examination smock and a pair of slippers out of paper bag, replacing them with Little Von's clothes.

"Well, no one should question you now, man."

"It's cold with this thing on."

"Yeah, but it's the only way you gonna get to see Mommy."

They held their breath. When the doors opened, the floor was practically empty except for an old man shuffling down the hall. He was pulling a pole on wheels with a bag hanging from it. A hose ran from his arm to the bag. Von stared until Lillian tapped him on the shoulder.

They entered the room. The first two beds had their curtains drawn. A light snore came from the second. Vivian lay asleep in the far bed near a window sill lined with cards and flowers. Her face was thin and her color that had once been rich now looked yellow. Von was immediately frightened and began to breathe fast and shallow. Over and over he thought, "Deal with it. Deal with it." But the sight of his mother, the smell of disinfectant, and the bleakness of the room was all too much. His lip began to tremble. Vivian had more tubes than the man in the hallway and it was obvious, even to Von, that she was in far worse shape. Besides the one that hung from the pole with clear fluid, there was a clear tube taped to his mother's nose and another that came from under the covers and ran to a bag attached to the rail along the side of her bed. Her burned hand had been freshly bandaged. Her lunch, which sat on the adjustable server, was untouched. Lillian pulled the curtain around the bed and sat so she could see the door. "Von, you go on the other side of the bed. If you hear the door open, you know what to do." Robin took the crutches and slid them under the end of the bed. Von sat in the chair near his mother's head and slipped his hand through the rail and placed it on his mother's arm.

Vivian opened her eyes and saw both of her sons at one time. She felt a hand on her leg and looked to the other side to see her daughter. She tried to smile. Von wiped his nose with the sleeve of his gown.

"Hi, Mommy. You all right?"

Vivian tried to talk and coughed. She had been sleeping with her mouth open to breathe. Her lips were chapped and cracked on one side. Like a professional, Lillian moved to her side and took a glass of water with a straw and a napkin from the tray and held it to Vivian's lips. Vivian's weakness showed as she struggled to pull the liquid through the straw. When she finished, Lillian took a jar of vaseline from the brown bag and massaged a finger full across her lips. Vivian smiled. Robin watched his sister's movements. Without thinking, she did what had to be done. Her response was automatic.

The door opened. Lillian shot a glance at Von. He slithered to the floor and under the bed. One of the floor nurses came in and smiled at Lillian and Robin.

The nurse checked the woman in the first bed and then made her way to Vivian. "Hello, Mrs. Thompson. How are we doing today?" The nurse quickly and professionally checked the chart that hung at the foot of the bed. She felt Vivian's pulse and forehead. "Has the doctor been in to see you today?" Vivian nodded again. "Did he schedule you for surgery?"

Vivian glanced at Lillian and Robin. Robin's eyes were noticeably wide. Lillian looked expectant. "Two days," Vivian managed dryly. "If things don't get better."

"Okay then. We'll come back and see ya in a while." The nurse smiled at Lillian and Robin and was gone.

Von listened for the door and returned to his chair with a question on his mind.

Vivian smiled. "That was pretty good," she said, trying to sound better. "Whose idea was this?"

"Rob's. It was a good plan, huh Mom?"

Vivian eyed her older son. "You plannin' again huh?"

Robin smiled.

"Mom. What's surgery?" Von asked.

"Well, they want to operate."

"Mom, you ain't gonna let them do that, are ya?"

Vivian looked at Lillian who was reading her chart. Their eyes met. Lillian put the chart down.

"Maybe they can take some of the bad stuff out."

"But Mom…"

"Hey you. Don't worry about this. The doctors know what they're doing. How about you? You been good for Leeny and Mrs. Cleary?"

"Yup."

"Robin, did you go by and tell them Von was going back to Wooden Street?"

"Yeah."

Von frowned. "No you didn't, Rob. You told me to do it." Von smiled at his mother. "But I told 'em and Leeny said she would come by and see you soon."

Vivian looked at Robin and sighed. "Von, you see that pretty card right there? Get it." Little Von took the card from the window ledge and handed it to his mother. "No, give it to Robin." Robin took the card and opened it and began reading silently.

Lillian watched. "Well, what does it say?"

"Yeah. What does it say, bean head?"

Robin handed the card to Lillian and shrugged. Lillian read it out loud.

Dear Viv,

I really miss you. I wanted to come to see you right away. Mother thought it would be a better idea to wait until you got settled in. It's hard.

I feel like I lost a family. Especially now that Von— that's what he insisted I call him now—isn't at the daycare. At least he'll only be on the other side of Lafayette.

Don't worry, I'll stop in and check on him. I love you very much and I'll be there soon.

Love
Joleena

Lillian looked at Robin. "I think she wrote that to you."

Vivian tried to shift her weight. "Lil, raise my head please." When Lillian turned the crank at the bottom of the bed, Vivian winced and put her hand over her abdomen. Lillian slowed down. When her position was comfortable, Vivian looked at Robin in a way that made him think she was Liberty. Her eyes narrowed. "Robin, when you're fishing down at Pocahontas it's not a big deal when you throw back a catfish or a carp. But this is real good catch and you better think twice before you throw back something you might want later."

Robin's pain was consuming him. He only lacked the tubes and hospital bed, but the pain was there. "Mom, I don't know what to do. I don't know what I want."

"Robin!" Vivian barked. "How would you feel uptown with Joleena in front of Kresge's in front of God and everybody?"

Robin shrugged.

"Robin, don't be stupid." Lillian looked disgusted. "Grow up. What is it you guys are always saying?"

Von said, "Deal with it. You gotta learn how to deal with it."

"Yeah. Now it's your turn to deal with it."

The overwhelming pain came from his gut. It came slowly at first and then quicker and bigger and bigger, making a knot so big in his throat that Robin thought he would explode. He buried his head in his hands and cried. "Mom," he said, trying to catch his breath. "All this is too much. It don't seem fair."

Vivian didn't let up. "Nobody said life was easy or fair, Robin. Do you think Bill's dying was fair? Fair is where farmers take pigs in the fall. Love is no different, and it doesn't get any easier to understand. So don't think you can run from it for the rest of your life." Vivian started coughing, and Lillian helped her with another drink.

"Mom," Von said, cocking his head to one side. "How come you always talk about doin' stuff uptown in front of Kresge's and God?"

Lillian, wanting her mother to rest, spoke up. "Von, sometimes it's hard to know if you're doing the right thing, so you have to ask yourself if you would do—whatever it is—uptown in front of Kresge's with God and everybody watching."

Little Von seemed to get it, but Lillian could tell that the real meaning had fallen short. "Von, a better one for you might be, don't do it if you wouldn't do it with Grandma standing right next to you." The look on his face was crystal clear.

"Like playin' with matches and stealin' cookies?"

"Yeah. Would you do that in front of Grandma or up in front of Kresge's with God watching?"

Little Von looked at Lillian wondering if she was stupid. Then hesitated, wondering if Robin had told anyone about the sheets. "No."

"Well, if you wouldn't do it up there, you shouldn't do it any-where." Lillian let her youngest brother think about it for a few seconds. "Remember that fight you got into down in the projects with that kid who kept taking your crutches?"

"Jing-Wei."

"Right. Now, would you have done that uptown."

"Yeah, 'cause that's different. Everybody knows that Jing-Wei is crazier than Matt Williams, huh, Rob? God probably knows by now too." Robin and Lillian started laughing. Vivian shook her head and said he was hopeless and then they all noticed that Dr. Wingfield was standing there smiling.

Von started sliding off the chair. The doctor smiled and held up his hand and said, "Don't bother. It's a stupid rule anyway, and I had nothing to do with it." Vivian tried to smile at him. He studied her. "So how you doing Viv?"

"It hurts," she said indicating her abdomen.

"That's what the test says too."

"What else did the test say, Doctor?" Lillian asked in a pro-fessional tone.

"Well, not much that a first-year nursing student would un-derstand or me either if someone didn't explain some of it, but...it basically adds up to—*we shouldn't wait.* Viv, I'm gonna schedule you for tomorrow night with Dr. Eppleburg. He's real good."

Von looked up with a bright glow. "How come we don't get Dr. B to do it, he's real good."

"Well, different doctors do different kinds of work," Dr. Wingfield said smiling. "Now Dr. Bowenstein is one of the best when it comes to bones, but we need somebody good with other parts."

"You mean guts?"

Dr. Wingfield looked at the child. "Yes, I suppose that says it close enough." He leaned over Vivian and pressed his hands along her sides. Vivian bit her lip. When he pressed on her abdo-men she cried out. "Yeah, Viv. I think the sooner the better." When Wingfield sat down, Vivian let out her breath. He scribbled on the chart and rubbed his face. "Kids, why don't you give your mom a big kiss for now and tell your grandmother I'll give her a call to-morrow. I have to do some more poking around on my old friend here."

One by one, and being careful of her tubes, they each kissed their mother. She, in turn, squeezed each of their hands, holding them long and looking into their eyes before she would let them go. Dr. Wingfield kept silent respectfully as they bonded each to the other.

"Mom, I'll get in tomorrow before they prep you," Lillian said.

"See ya, Mom," Von said, secure in the fact that many good doctors were watching out for his mother.

Robin tried to speak, but couldn't.

"Von."

"Huh?"

"Don't forget. Uptown in front of Kresge's."

"I know. In front of God and everybody."

"I love you.

"I love you too. See ya when we come up with another plan." Von smiled. Vivian looked at the three of them standing together. She mouthed the words again.

When the door closed, Wingfield turned to Viv. He eased his hand under her bandaged hand. "Viv, I've known you and your family most of your life, so I'm not gonna lie. Things don't look good."

Vivian raised her hand two inches off the bed. "Burned it up pretty good, didn't I?"

"Yes. But it's not your hand I'm worried about. I think your liver is shot. On top of that…" Wingfield puffed out one cheek and tapped on the chart without looking at Vivian. "We haven't had much luck with the infections. I don't know what else to say until we go in and take a look-see. If there's anything I can do to help you get things in order, you let me know." There was a moment while he let Vivian adjust. "I really wish you hadn't left the hospital."

29

WHEN LILLIAN PULLED UP in front of the sign that said "Home of the Clearys" Robin moaned. "I'm not sure I want to do this."

"You want to do it. The problem is that you don't know how to undo what's been done."

Robin thought. "Yeah. That's what it is. I need Art here to give me some advice. Now that I think about it, though, Art's got enough problems of his own."

"So who am I? The leper of Wooden Street?"

"Naa, but you're my sister. That's different. Y'know what I mean?"

"Try me."

Robin looked at the front door. "Well, I just cut her off."

Lillian furrowed her brow. "Brother, what do you mean by 'cut her off'?"

Facing the conversation was like going to the dentist and facing the drill. "Well, things were going along great. She didn't like some of the things the guys were doin'..."

"Like what?"

"You know. Just regular things that guys do. She said I had to make some choices, and I cut her off." Robin left the marijuana out of the story and allowed Lillian to assume he was talking about drinking.

Lillian turned in her seat to face him. "Are you hanging out and drinking all the time? How can you do that with Mommy in the hospital dying from drinking?"

"No! We just have a couple of beers sometimes after we sing. That's all. No big deal." For the first time, Robin recognized that he was hiding the truth about his drinking. It was a big deal. He was doing the very thing that he hated in his mother. His drinking had started with a casual few beers. Now he was no longer particular about what he drank or who he drank with. If Cootie had offered him a beer, he would sit down and drink with Cootie, especially now. Drinking and smoking had become much more than a way of quenching his thirst and passing the time. It had slowly become the core of his social life. It had been, he realized, the key to his acceptance among his friends. It was when he felt best. When he wasn't drinking, smoking, or just hanging out, he was worried and depressed.

"Well?"

"Well what?"

"You know, you always do this. If we talk about nothing important, you joke around great. But the moment we talk about something really serious you get quiet and go away somewhere. Sometimes I think if I didn't say something, you wouldn't come back."

"Well, what do you say?"

Lillian took a deep breath. She was insisting on direct talk and that was something the family rarely did. "Robin, Mommy's in the hospital without a liver because she drinks so much. Are you gonna start drinking too?"

"Naa. I have a beer once in a while, but that's it. I ain't like Mom. I can deal with it."

"You can deal with it."

"Yes, I can handle it. Listen, I don't want to talk about this now. What am I gonna say to Joleena?" Robin wished he had a beer.

"What do you feel?"

Robin shook his head. "I'm all confused."

"You know she loves you. Do you love her?"

The perspiration beaded up on his forehead. He wanted to run away screaming. Not love. Not love. His mouth was dry.

"Well, do you love her? Look. You're sweating. That means yes, I think."

He had panicked and changed the subject. "Lil, do you think Mommy is gonna die?" Lillian answered without emotion. "Probably. I didn't understand everything on the chart, but her systems are failing. She doesn't have much to fight with."

Robin looked at Lillian unbelieving. How had she said it in one mouthful—no tears, no grief, no worry, no anger? His thoughts switched to Little Von. "Oh man. How is Von gonna deal with this?"

"I'm more worried about you. I think Von knows somewhere inside himself. He saw how sick she was, and he didn't ask to go to Grandma's. He wanted to go see Clovis."

"Yeah, I thought it was strange when he asked if he could go see him for awhile. First I thought he wasn't ready to leave the projects. Then I knew it was for some reason I didn't understand. What do you think?"

"I think it was scary for him to see how sick Mommy really is, all the tubes and machines attached to her. She is so weak she couldn't drink from a straw. I think he wanted to talk to someone who would give him some straight answers." As she finished her sentence, Lillian could see that Robin had checked out again and was grappling with the reality of it for himself.

"You and Mommy are so much alike! " Lillian tapped his arm. "Robin, someone is waiting for you on the porch."

"What?"

"Look."

Joleena had come out and was leaning on the post. It was her generosity to spare him having to knock on the door.

Robin said, "What now?" Lillian was quick with her words. "You'll think of something. Just be real. Deal with it, bean head."

A breeze gently pushed Robin from behind. It stirred his thoughts until one phrase was clear. "Deal with it." Joleena was radiant in the fading afternoon sun. To see her was rejuvenation. She ran from the porch and flung her arms around his neck and kissed him. "Damn it, Robin Thompson, you better be coming here to tell me that what you did was stupid and that you'll never do it again. At least you'll do the best you can do for now, but certainly..." she said, gently rubbing his lips with her finger. "...that you won't stop talking. You have to let me know what you're feeling. Especially with your mom and everything. And one more thing, that you love me. And you have to say it."

Robin was overwhelmed. "Yep. All of it. Honest."

"Not good enough, Mr. Thompson! Say it, if it's true. Don't, if it's not."

Robin smiled. "I love you, Joleena. More than anything."

Joleena kissed him. "Robin! Wait."

"What?" Robin said, but Joleena was already up the stairs and through the door. She came back holding the silver pocket watch.

"Wow! It was here all the time."

Joleena looked puzzled. "You know that cop called Hoops?"

"Sure. What about him?" Robin felt his muscles tense.

"I was walking home from uptown the other day and I passed the Best Fill. Well, what used to be the Best Fill. Jimmy

Lee was standing there talking to him. I used to get sodas there like everybody else, so I stopped to say I was sorry about what happened. When I got ready to walk off, Hoops asked me to wait a minute. He went to his car and came back with this. He said he was pretty sure it belonged to you."

"Did he say anything else?"

"He said that you should take better care of the important things in your life." Robin sighed and smiled. "Robin, I really agree with him too." Joleena hugged him again.

Anna Cleary came out on the porch. "Robin, you're just in time for sweet potato pie. You'll have to come in and try some, and tell me if it comes close to Jessie Rose's. Joleena's father has already eaten half of it and says he still can't say."

Robin grunted through his smile. "Man. How am I gonna get out of this one?"

"Guess you'll just have to deal with it!"

30

VON HAD STOOD FEARLESSLY in front of Building Five and waved to his brother and sister as they drove away. He had agreed to call either from Clovis's or Liberty's when he was ready to come home. He made his way through the foyer door and stood in front of Clovis Lamb's apartment.

He made a fist and knocked as hard as he could.

"I be dare in minute." Clovis yelled. He pushed himself from the deep chair and shuffled stiffly to the door. "Well, well, well. Look who we got here. How you doin', great fisherman?"

"Okay." Von walked in with his eyes focused on the floor. He kicked his leg out of his brace as he fell into the couch next to Clovis's chair. "Clo, was you sleep?"

"No. What makes you think I was sleep in the middle of the day?" Clovis said, falling back into his chair.

"Clo, you sleeps anytime. And you don't have your teeth in. You always take your teeth out when you sleep."

"Well, I wasn't 'sleep," Clovis said, the bottom part of his mouth more animated than the top. He took his teeth off the coffee table and put them in his mouth. "How's yo' Momma, boy?"

"They gonna operate and look around."

Clovis nodded. He'd seen it come to this many times. In the old days there were no Black doctors or Black hospitals. *Coloreds* died quietly, or not so quietly, at home in their own beds.

"Clovis, let's go fishin'."

"Can't."

"How come?"

"Doc said I had to stay in awhile longer."

"Sure is a lot of doctors around. Everybody got one, even me. Your plug still wobbly?"

Clovis had heard the story of Bill's explanation. He grunted. "Naw, my plug is where it's suppose to be."

"Then how come we can't go fishin?"

"I done told you, boy. The doctor."

"Clovis. Who knows more, the doctor or God?"

"Most of these here doctors don't know nothin'."

"Well didn't you say God was easier to find fishin'?"

Clovis stared at the television despite the fact that it wasn't on. He thought about Vivian and his own life and the happy years he spent fishing on the Mississippi river during his Missouri childhood. He thought about his nephew and how little happiness he managed to find in his short time on the earth. He thought about his own wife.

The apartment suddenly felt like a tomb with its pictures in dusty frames and glass knick-knacks that hadn't been moved in years. So much in his life had become quiet and lifeless, and now the doctors had demanded the same of him if he wanted to live. He rearranged the wrinkles of his face. After several attempts, he got up without speaking and left the room. When he returned he was sporting his straw fishing hat. "Come on boy, let's go catch that sonavabitch while I can still see and walk to the river."

The sun had long since started its descent to the horizon, but there was still an hour or two of smooth fall sunlight. The trees surrounding the river were a blazing autumn spectacle. Clovis stood, pole in hand, meditating on the water's edge. He had always wanted a perfect fishing partner, one who didn't try to tell him how to fish, and Von had always wanted someone to teach him how. Now they were together.

"Here boy, let me see you make a cast."

On the first try, Little Von sent the hook, worm, and sinker sailing over the Pocahontas's murkiness and into a spot just before the current quickened at its center. They sat side by side on a log. In the first hour the pole had come to life twice. With no more than a glance at the rod tip, Clovis knew it wasn't Kitty. "Crank that sonbitch in, boy!" Clovis yelled. And Von did.

The tranquilizing gurgle of the Pocahontas brought calm like an old friend.

"Clo, is my Mom gonna die?"

Both sat without taking their eyes from the spot where the line entered the water. Clovis, ever chewing on his gums, reached over and put one finger on the line. "Boy, the onlyest thing between us and that ugly ass catfish is this thin line. And the onlyest thing between us and God is the thin breath we breathe. You ever hear people say, 'Only the good die young'?"

"Yeah. My Mom says that all the time."

"Well, she the one that said it to me when Bill left us. And he sure was good. Your momma is a wondaful lady, boy. Wondaful.

I been knowin' her for some long time. You shoulda knowed her before she started…well you know." He pointed at the crutches. "Everybody got their crutch, boy. I got mine like you got yours. Sometime they help. Sometime we don't want to give them up." Your momma was lonely and had a lot of heartache. She had a bad crutch with that bottle. When Bill came along he was much better to lean on. And that's the way it otta be. Like I see Robby lean on Joleena. She a good one to lean on, like Bill. Dependable. But when Bill left us…well, I guess that was awful hard."

Clovis's mouth was dry and his heart ached. "Vivian always been good to me. She good to everybody she meet. Nothin' you ask her she won't do for ya. Maybe she didn't do everything like she shoulda, but she's kind. That's what really matters. She the one that taught me not to be afraid of dyin'. She said that dyin' was easy. She say livin' is what people do poorly. Yes sir. Do seem like only the good die young."

Little Von thought about Clovis's words and began to weep. Emptiness.

Vivian was going to leave him forever. He had only had her when the "Other Self" and the tall bottles had allowed it. They had won and would allow no more. The "Other Self" had taken her and left him empty. He wept, clutching his sleeves. He had been swallowed by the shadow of his greatest fear. He sobbed and quivered, weeping from an open mouth. Clovis pulled him close and began to rock slowly, his dry wrinkled hands against the smooth caramel skin of Von's face. He turned and watched the river race into the distance. A tear fell from the tip of his nose. Clovis puzzled the tragedy of life and the promise of joy that would weave themselves throughout this child's life. He had so far to go. It was too much to ponder. He shook his head at no one. "Come on boy, let's get on back."

The waters of Pocahontas seemed calmed by the orange pinks of the fading evening sky. In the distance a star could be seen.

Von looked at Clovis. "What about Kitty?"

Clovis gave a dry chuckle, baring all his gums. "Well, let's leave that sonnavabitch in that stinkin' river! That's where she belongs."

ORDER FORM

I WOULD LIKE A COPY OF *CRUTCHES*

PRICE PER COPY **$14.95**

allow 3 days FIRST CLASS MAIL **$3.00**

allow 14 days BOOK RATE MAIL **$1.75**

TOTAL _____

Check, Money Orders or Credit Cards Accepted

VISA/Master Card Number: _____

Mail To:

Dandelion Press
P O Box 11633
Olympia, WA 98508
1-800-525-1990

_____
Name

_____
Address

_____
City

_____
State   **Zip Code**